Chaos Calling

Book 1 of The Xenthian Cycle

E. M. Williams

Happy Reading!

To request authorization or to make other queries, please contact E. M. Williams and Circle Star Publishing at inquiries@emwilliams.ca.

For more information, visit emwilliams.ca.

Stock photo by Brxxto via Unsplash

Cover design by Wesley Lyn

for A, J, and J,
with all my love

Author's Note

Chaos Calling is a fictional work drawn from my imagination, and is set in twenty-first-century Toronto. Early on, I decided that my worldbuilding would include a diverse cast that reflects the city's complexity.

This novel includes both Chinese Canadian and Anishinaabe characters, among many others. I have not attempted to depict their respective spiritual beliefs, teachings, or cultural practices from an insider's perspective—there are many talented writers from both communities undertaking that important work.

It's also important that you know that Miinikaa First Nation is a fictitious place. In the world of the novel, however, its placement north of Sudbury would situate it within the very real Robinson Huron Treaty, which was signed in 1850 between the Government of Canada and First Nations people and includes modern-day Sudbury and a great deal of Ontario. There are thirty-nine First Nations that collectively make up the Anishinabek Nation in Canada. Visit www.anishinabek.ca for more information.

I also wish to note that Chinese Canadians, as one of Canada's largest cultural groups, continue to make valuable contributions to this country on innumerable fronts. As a starting point, readers eager to learn more could visit the Chinese Canadian Museum in Vancouver (https://www.chinesecanadianmuseum.ca/) or the Chinese Cultural Centre of Greater Toronto (https://www.cccgt.org/), either in person or online.

For more context concerning my creative process, please see the acknowledgements section, located in this book's appendix. Additional resources are available on my website: emwilliams.ca.

Content advisory: This novel includes significant monster violence. It touches on mental health (including depression, anxiety, grief, sudden loss, and suicide), elder care, breast cancer, police and military violence (particularly against Indigenous people), and Canada's living legacy as a colonial state, including the Sixties Scoop and residential schools, and the ongoing impact of both of these government policies on Indigenous people.

Prologue: The Queen

Stars wheel above our nest as the veil between worlds thins. We fix our gaze upon it, waiting for the merest flicker of a vulnerability.

Soon, whisper our departed mother-sisters from their sacred places within the nest memory. ***Soon, your turn comes***.

The swarm pushes against our scales. We resettle our coils, forcing them to make space. They are restless to hunt. Each day, sea ice gathers on the horizon, and the greyfish schools retreat farther beneath it. Our hunters roam in ever-widening arcs to catch the stragglers. Without fresh skal to strengthen their attacks so that they might puncture the ice, the nest will starve.

But our skal, like our nest's ascendancy, has dwindled across the generations. Our best hope is to pierce the waning veil and hunt for more precious skal in the worlds beyond.

Soon, our mother-sisters whisper. We draw their long-dead presences closer, some strong, some now faint with age. ***The moons are close. The veil thins. And this time, its glimmer will pulse above* your *nest***.

The swarm squirms against us, twitching in anticipation as we sift through the nest memories of previous hunts. Which shore shall we find? For there are as many worlds as there are stars, and not all prey carries skal of equal might.

At last, the veil thins to the barest sliver. We tap the skal reservoir within our scales until we pulse with its power. The veil echoes this rhythm, beating in time to us. The swarm bunches closer, augmenting our will as our skal blasts into the sky. The veil quivers a final time and yields.

Rise, we command.

Braying with excitement, the scouts launch themselves into the air to cluster at the edges of the torn veil. For all our might, we have made the tiniest of holes, so narrow that only four of our smallest scouts may squirm through. Our skal rushes ahead of them, blazing a tunnel through the veil's twisting folds until its terminus in the alien world is secure, anchored by our power.

At the edges of our awareness, we perceive their orange bodies as they slither out beneath strange stars. Their scales flex as they skim over the waters of this new world. Lights burn on the far shore in configurations unlike anything contained in the memories of our mother-sisters. But the night air is thick with the intoxicating scent of alien skal.

Pleasure spreads across our scales as they disappear through the dark.

Part One

Toronto

Chapter 1

Anna – Raccoons

Toronto, ON: Sunday, August 17

"I already told you, Anna. I don't want the china or any of Mom's other stuff. Stop making this complicated."

Anna Lin counts to ten as she paces her galley kitchen, the cordless handset pressed tightly against her ear. Keys jingle on Jason's end of the line. It's 9:45 p.m. in Toronto, which means it's 6:45 p.m. in Vancouver. In fifteen minutes, her twin brother's night shift starts at St. Paul's Hospital. *Too bad. For once, he can make time.*

"Before she died, I would have taken you at your word," Anna says, struggling to stay composed as remembered shame bakes her cheeks. "Remember the hospital? Literally the first thing you did was yell at me for throwing out that half-frayed lap quilt she used all the time."

After the funeral parlour's staff had removed her mother's body, packing up Chun-Mei's room had kept Anna's hands busy while she waited for Jason. Until her brother had appeared in the corridor of the palliative ward, flustered from his rush from the airport, Anna hadn't realized how much she'd clung to the idea of his arrival, to them being a team again. Their shouting match had erupted right in front of the nursing station.

"I'm almost finished with the house. I've only got her study left." She takes a steadying breath. "Forgive me for wanting to be sure."

Through the phone, a door squeaks and closes. *I should have done this by email,* she thinks. *Too late now.* The microphone is strong; she clearly hears the tumble of a lock and the sound of his footsteps moving down the hallway of his condo. "Still holding onto that, huh?" he mutters at last. "I said I was sorry."

"That's not why I called." Anna stops pacing and tucks the phone between her shoulder and ear, freeing her hands to grab the rounded quartz edge of her kitchen counter. She imagines pushing her frustration through the stone, not through the telephone line. *Just make this easy,* she wants to say. As children, she and Jason had been so close. With him by her side, she had never found herself the only mixed-race kid in a classroom or on a sports team. They had stayed a package deal, until . . . Her mind instinctively veers from their last year of high school. *Everything would be so much easier if you'd just help me.*

Taking another deep breath, Anna tries again. "Dad's practically living in his research lab at SickKids. I saw him for like fifteen seconds last week." Unable to sleep one morning, she'd gone over to her parents' house to get an early start on her house-staging checklist. Dr. Erik Lin had barely said hello before leaving for work, his thin face haggard above his scrubs. "He wants to put the house on the market and buy a condo closer to the hospital. And he's no more interested in dealing with her things than you are."

She resumes pacing, aware of her mounting frustration. *Jason isn't the person you unload to,* she chides herself. *Not anymore.* She takes a breath, but the words keep coming. "Taking care of the house is eating up all my time. Between Mom's decline, acting as her executor, and emptying that house, I haven't sold a single property this year." Her voice edges up and up, like a train whistling along a familiar track, shrill and unstoppable. "I don't think it's too much to ask for you to answer a few simple questions every now and—"

"Fine." The word ricochets down the line, sharp as a gunshot. Something pings in the background, and she hears the whoosh of sliding doors. "I may lose you in the elevator," Jason says in a softer voice, but his words are layered with a weariness that matches hers. "Look, do what you want, okay? This stuff is your wheelhouse."

"But—" she begins.

Jason sighs. "Dad gave me the ruby pendant for Margo. I took Mom's fountain pen and one of her framed photos of the old rose garden. That's all I want. If you need more help, call one of those junk services. There must be one you use with clients."

"Yeah," Anna says, mentally calculating the cost of outsourcing the work. Her discount is good but it's going to be tight. "Tracking Dad down for cash is tough right now. Could you—"

"Talk later, okay? I've got to go." The line goes dead.

Anna slides the phone back into its cradle, feeling more disheartened than when she picked it up. *What were you expecting?* she asks herself, staring at the red charging light. In answer, one of her last memories with her mother surfaces.

You demand too much from Jason, Chun-Mei Lin had told Anna the week before she died. *Be gentle with him after I'm gone.*

What about me? she fumes. *Doesn't he have to be gentle, too?*

Turning from the sting of that memory, Anna picks up her yellow notepad and pencil from the counter. In the two months since their mother's passing, she's been mired in endless to-do lists. This sheet reads:

CHINA DISHES (12 SETTINGS/5 SERVING PIECES)

MOM'S CLOTHES

FAMILY PHOTO ALBUMS (9)

A dozen other remnants of Chun-Mei's once vibrant life follow. She taps the pencil's eraser against the scrawled words, picturing the china. An heirloom from Erik's side of the family, the set is old-fashioned but pretty: white with delicate red and gold roses. Thinking of the dishes brings back the last time Anna saw them carefully arranged on her parents' dining room table: *Erin's fifth birthday dinner, right before Mom went into palliative care.*

Tears pool in Anna's eyes. Swiftly, she tilts her head up to trace the spidery cracks in the ceiling's plaster. *I'm so tired of crying.* She's done it twice today, first, when confronted by the fine black hair caught in her mother's antique silver hairbrush. The second time, she'd opened a drawer, found the matching pair of jade dragons that she and Jason had played with as children, and sobbed.

My wheelhouse, she thinks, swallowing hard. In the beginning, she'd hoped her professional training as a commercial Realtor would help her to deal with the house. Knowing which decisions to make is easy. Making them is another thing altogether. Her eyes have been puffy for weeks. Disrupting her mother's thoughtful cultivation of her home by packing up all her treasures is just one more desecration wrought by stage-four breast cancer. Anna is beyond sick of the rooms where her mother's perfume still lingers in the closets like a spirit, ready to ambush her with longing. *And it's me, not Jason, who has to come back there tomorrow afternoon, and the next day, and the next, until the house is listed.*

In one fluid move, Anna picks up the notepad and hurls it at the kitchen wall. Its pages fan as it flies. The faint smacking noise it makes is completely unsatisfying.

"That bad, eh?" Malcolm's voice asks. Anna spins to find her husband in the doorway, dressed in his police uniform. "Sorry, sweetheart."

He lifts the notepad off the floor and hands it to her before taking his keys out of his pocket. They drop with a clatter in the red glass dish, which sat on Chun-Mei's dressing table for years. A month before she died, her mother gave it to Malcolm, informing him exactly how it should be placed on the narrow shelf beside the sink.

Whenever the red glass catches Anna's eye, she's surprised to find her mother's dainty thing in her kitchen. But Malcolm has stopped misplacing his keys.

"I didn't mean to startle you," he says.

"Well, calling Jason was a waste of time," Anna says, tossing her notepad back on the counter. "He doesn't want anything." Her husband makes his *I'm trying not to say I told you so but I told you so* face. She sighs and brushes away a stray hair. "If I hadn't asked, he would have come back at me later, I know he would have."

"Jay doesn't care about stuff." Malcolm picks up the kettle and fills it with water. A staunch herbal tea drinker, he's ritualistic about having a cup when he comes home. "Want some?"

Anna shakes her head, rubbing the tension knot forming across her forehead. *What I need is sleep. A really great night's sleep.*

"Margo isn't sentimental either," Malcolm continues, yawning. "And they haven't got much room in that condo."

"No," Anna agrees. "He told me to call a junk service."

Malcolm brightens as he flicks the kettle's switch. "That's a great idea." He turns to lean back against the counter, grinning at her despite the circles under his eyes.

As an investigator with Toronto Police's Financial Crimes Unit, he doesn't wear a uniform very often. The exceptions usually happen on summer nights like this one, when he picks up an extra shift through the force's lottery system to work security for the sports stadiums downtown. He still looks good in it, all long legs and wide shoulders. Stepping closer, Anna runs admiring fingers through his brown hair, which is flecked with grey at his temples.

Malcolm smiles. "Didn't I have the same thought, oh, a month ago?"

"You did." Despite her irritation with Jason, Anna finds herself grinning back at Malcolm.

His eyes sparkle as he holds her gaze. "And is Jay going to help us cover the cost?"

Anna's grin slides clean off her face. "He hung up when we got to that. So, no."

Malcolm grimaces.

"I know, I know." She throws up her hands. "I'll call him back."

"It's a reasonable expectation," Malcolm says as Anna's composure starts to crumble. "Hey, I'm not blaming you." He pulls her close. "You put your career on hold to support your mom when she got sick. You're still helping your dad, and God knows, getting answers out of Erik is a pain in the ass."

"I don't blame him." Anna's eyes burn again. "That whole house brims with Mom," she murmurs into Malcolm's shoulder, blinking furiously. "I want to be done with it, too."

"Soon." Malcolm kisses the side of her head. "Call a junk service if it gets you one step closer."

"I don't think that's realistic." Anna gestures to a stack of opened envelopes beside the phone. "I don't know if you've checked, but the joint savings account is almost empty." Thinking about the state of their finances worsens the pinched feeling in her forehead. "Plus, the hydro bill came today. And the gas bill. And I haven't paid the property taxes this month."

Malcolm's lips thin as he scans the sheet. "Shit. I didn't realize we ran the air-conditioning so much." The kettle starts to whistle. He drops the bill on the counter and gets a mug out of the cupboard. "We're running out of options, baby. If Jason's not going to pony up, you've got to talk to Erik. I know he promised you the commission, but you can't carry the costs until the house is sold."

Anna grunts.

Malcolm gives her a sidelong glance. "Come on, you wouldn't do that for any other client. He can recoup it after the sale, same as they would. Or you stop working on the house, close another deal, and circle back when we've got a cushion."

"Yes, from my legions of clients," Anna grumbles, crossing her arms.

"You'll fill your roster in no time." Malcolm tosses a tea bag into his mug. He pours, filling the kitchen with the scent of mint. "Don't make this a big deal."

"It shouldn't be," she says, thinking of her taciturn father. Born in Cork, Ireland, Erik Lynn had been finishing his studies at McGill University in Montreal when he met Chun-Mei Lin at a shoe dance. When she'd approached him holding the single brown loafer he'd contributed to the pile, correctly identifying it as the match to the one he still wore, they'd introduced themselves and shared a chuckle over their similar surnames. By her mother's telling, Chun-Mei had so thoroughly swept the young doctor off his feet that he never blinked when she later asked him to change his name's spelling to match hers. "Dad's parents thought talking about money was tacky. So with Mom gone, we—"

"Don't talk about anything," Malcolm interjects.

"Especially now." Anna crosses the narrow kitchen to stand behind her husband. She slides her arms around his waist, leaning her head against his back. They stay that way for a minute. Then Malcolm turns. He still looks tired, but the longer they stand together, the wider his smile grows. Anna can't help but answer it.

Optimism flickers through her, welcome as sunshine, and she abruptly remembers a new addition to her to-do list. "Oh, I forgot to tell you my one piece of good news: Dave introduced me to a new client." Dave Montcalm had lived in the house across the street from the Lins in Dovercourt Park all through Anna's and Jason's childhood. His mother, Sarita, had also been a stay-at-home parent when they were small and formed a close friendship with Chun-Mei. The three children had grown up inseparable. In Anna's book, Dave is as much her brother as Jason. *More, in some ways,* she thinks. "Thanks to him, I'm meeting Walter Delal for dinner tomorrow."

"Who?"

"The venture capitalist?" She waits for a flicker of recognition.

Malcolm shrugs.

"He led the first financing round for Rune Software when Dave was launching his company," Anna continues.

Her husband makes a noncommittal sound.

"Anyway, Walter's venture firm needs a new downtown office. Dave put him in touch." She pulls back, starting to bounce on her toes. Becoming a Realtor was never her dream, but she's good at it. And there's nothing like the chase of closing a sale. "If I can get a sense of what he needs and close a quick deal on top of Dad's house—"

Malcolm kisses her. As his hands slide down her back to her waist and then to her butt, Anna accepts his tacit invitation to forget about their family, the bills, and everything else.

* * *

Anna collapses against Malcolm's chest. Her hands slide between his shoulders and the mattress as his go around her waist. Beneath her cheek, his chest hair is sweaty. She doesn't care. Blood thunders in her ears, tingling up her spine. She holds him tightly, not wanting to step out of the sensation that they're one person.

"Goddamn, baby," Malcolm breathes. "My life for yours." His love seems to surround her in a palpable haze as they kiss, his five-o'clock shadow scraping her cheek. He exhales noisily. "Sex isn't supposed to be this good after kids. You know that, right?"

She smiles and sits up, looping their fingers together. His pulse beats against hers. "Missed that memo."

He kisses her again, his lips curved in bemused wonder. "I swear I felt your joy when you came."

"Sure you did," she teases. "Want to feel it again?"

He kisses her a third time, but his eyes flick past her shoulder to their bedroom clock's green LED lights, which shine like cat eyes in the darkness. She doesn't have a fixed schedule anymore, but he does.

"It's late," she says.

"And I had the craziest shift. The Blue Jays won, and we had a hell of a time getting their fans to go home. You'd think it was a playoff game the way they hung around the SkyDome."

"You mean the Rogers—"

"It's called the SkyDome," Malcolm says firmly through a yawn. His eyes begin to drift closed. "Sorry," he murmurs. "I'm beat."

"Sleep. You were up with the kids this morning." Anna grabs her black-and-white-polka-dot pyjamas from the floor and takes them with her to the bathroom. By the time she's dressed, Malcolm is snoring, one hairy leg spread across the summer-weight duvet that covers their bed. *Nothing like sex to soothe a weary mind*, she thinks a little jealously.

Her own mind resumes its familiar track as Anna lies down. *Tomorrow's Monday. And Mom's gone. God, she's really gone.* She closes her eyes. *You've got dinner downtown with Walter. In the morning, you'll email Dad and then call a junk service. And send Jason the bill. Breathe. You have permission to sleep. I should have dealt with her study first. Why did I leave it for last? Everything will wait for morning. Breathe. Sleep.*

A tremendous crash sounds below their open bay window, which overlooks the house's miniscule backyard. The noise startles Anna upright, banishing her relaxed mood. "Goddamn raccoons," she mutters.

The detached garage at the back of their small garden is nearly as old as the century house. While the previous owner had the home beautifully renovated to sell in their quiet Junction neighbourhood, the garage's walls and sagging roof desperately need a face-lift. Mourning doves have roosted in the eaves. Vines have pulled the drainpipes away from the roof. Last spring, Malcolm fought a one-man war against a mama raccoon who had decided the back corner behind the Halloween decorations was the perfect place for her kits. They'd planned to renovate it top to bottom this summer, but that was before Chun-Mei's health declined and Anna stopped working.

I don't know where we'll find the money to fix it now.

Another crash sounds, louder this time.

Not on my watch. Anna gets out of bed. She gropes around the floor beside her night table for her heavy black Maglite, feeling almost sorry for the raccoon and its babies. *I'm going to scare the shit out of you.*

Closing the bedroom door, Anna points the flashlight at the hardwood floor and clicks it on, quietly walks past Tim's and Erin's open doors. The hall echoes with the sound of their heavy breathing. She resists the urge to check on them as she goes downstairs. *The faster I get rid of the raccoons, the faster I get back to bed.*

Following the main hall brings her into the kitchen. She walks through it into the sunroom-turned-playroom at the back of the house. With the flashlight, she avoids the blocks and action figures sprinkled liberally across the floor.

Outside, the light over the back door is off. The raccoons haven't tripped the motion sensor. Anna flicks it off as she steps up to the door and peers through the windowpane. *Nothing in the garden.* The white plastic table and chairs sit in their usual places. The kids' toys stand sentry in the flowerbeds ringing the patio. Directly across from her are the two steps that lead up to the garage's brown wooden door, which is closed. *Everything looks normal.*

CRASH.

Orange light lines the edges of the door, so quickly there and gone that she wonders if she imagined it. The sudden adrenaline thundering in her ears says otherwise. Anna tries to remember what they keep out there, but there's no telltale flicker of fire. *Maybe I should get Malcolm.* She half turns before she stops, remembering his exhaustion. *I'm already up.*

Anna unlocks the back door and steps into the warm summer night. A light breeze lifts the ends of her dark hair, blowing it over her shoulders. Around her, ivy rustles as it clings to the side of the garage and the garden's tall wooden fence. Between the fence, the garage's dark red bricks, and the vines, their backyard has always felt more like a secret country garden than a city yard. Yet she shivers as she crosses the deck and patio stones to climb the steps to the garage door, which they never lock. The handle turns smoothly under her palm.

Inside, cracks in the brick and a dent in the car-sized door let in streetlight from the alley, brightening the interior enough that she doesn't really need the flashlight. Malcolm's silver SUV takes up most of the space. The stuffy air smells heavily of cedar, thanks to the rotting shingles on the garage's roof and walls. But the back of her throat tastes of sulphur, too. *There's no gas line in here.*

Something rustles in the dark. Every hair on Anna's neck lifts. *That's no raccoon.*

Abruptly, the small of her back flares right above her kidneys, fierce and hot. A wild, aching sensation floods her body, bearing a tide of overwhelming memories. Her muscles spasm in remembered readiness as her breath catches in her throat. It's like she's a teenager again, sneaking out to hunt for Kalos with Jason and Dave. How many times did they chase through Toronto's dark alleys and side streets, brimming with joy and adrenaline? Her tally is beyond count. On their last run, she distinctly remembers Jason breaking the window of an abandoned warehouse with his sweatshirt-covered elbow. He'd been grinning as he led them inside. She can't imagine her sensible twin doing that now. *But he did.*

Anna makes a sound halfway between a giggle and a gasp. Instinctively, she lifts her free hand to muffle the noise. More rustling comes from the far side of Malcolm's SUV. Clutching the Maglite like a club, Anna silently steps forward. Their aluminum stepladder has fallen from its hooks on the garage's wall. Carefully, she edges around it until she spots the empty propane can that she keeps forgetting to get refilled at the hardware store.

It's completely obliterated, the metal shredded into long, thin shards of shrapnel. Several pieces are buried in the SUV's side. The closest tire is punctured flat.

Fear surges in her belly as the burning in her lower back intensifies. *Oh, shit!* Anna bites back a shout as sixteen years of coping mechanisms scream every reason why this can't be happening. *Xhen is gone. Kalos is gone. Jason's working in an emergency room in Vancouver. Dave's an entrepreneur who made a fortune in software.*

And you're a married mother of two with a faltering realty practice, not some foolish girl chasing a dream.

It's just a raccoon.

Her aching back violently disagrees. *If xhen has returned, I have to know.*

Torn between fear and longing, Anna stares into the garage's dim shadows for a long moment. Then she clicks on the Maglite.

Chapter 2

Anna – Ambush

Toronto, ON: Monday, August 18

A high-pitched sound pierces Anna's ears. She whirls. The beam of her flashlight bounces off the SUV's metallic doors, momentarily blinding her, as something serpentine —two metres long, orange, its scales shining with their own sickly light—launches itself over the vehicle and crashes down on top of her.

Adrenaline surges through her body as she thrusts her elbows back to break her fall, barely stopping her head from hitting the garage's concrete floor. Where the creature's body touches hers, Anna's skin stings. Jerking back, she glimpses a mouth filled with razor-sharp teeth beneath three split-pupiled eyes. Two are bright as candle flames. The third, above and between them, blazes dark violet. A veined orange crest, thick as a dinner plate, encircles the top and sides of the creature's head as it lunges toward her, still screeching. Half a dozen serpentine tentacles, dark as plums and each as long as her arm, lash out from either side of its head, straining for her like eager fingers as its bruised gums spread wide in a rictus grin.

The ear-splitting sound brings tears to Anna's eyes. Pain envelops her head. From between its spreading jagged teeth, a skinnier tentacle—pale yellow like the petals of a crocus—darts for her chest.

The tentacles must not touch you.

Conditioned long ago to obey that soundless voice without question, Anna grasps the Maglite and bashes it into the creature's head. It reels, shifting slightly off her body. She reverses her grip. Clutching the flashlight by the bulb, she slams the long handle into the creature's three eyes before kicking its bulk, which is far lighter than she expects given its size, toward the garage wall.

The creature crashes to the floor, writhing, perhaps stunned. Anna scrambles to her knees. It rises as she does, coiling up on itself in sinuous loops like a cobra until it looms over her. It blinks, its triplicate eyes seemingly undamaged, and bellows. Orange light flares through its scales, blinding Anna as hunger—not hers—slams through her mind in a wave, carrying the full, deadly promise of that terrible sound.

Run! part of her screams. *RUN!* Yet, pinned by the creature's glaring eyes, that command does not translate into action.

It lunges.

Frantic for a better weapon, Anna drops the Maglite and reaches for her only other conceivable line of defense, long dormant inside her. *Please,* she begs. *Please work.*

Xhen energy floods her mind in answer, as familiar and comforting as a childhood blanket. But this time, it also rises through her skin to surround her body. Anna gasps as the oceanic light fills the garage, spilling from her outstretched hands to coil around the snapping creature. Instinct prompts her to shape the pulsing energy into cords, which she wraps around the creature's neck. Pleasure bubbles in her head, combating the painful force hammering at her mind. An incredulous smile breaks over her frightened face. *Yes!*

The creature struggles, its body flashing with a harsher brightness. Pain flares in her forehead, down her back, and into the soles of her feet. Anna wills her cords to tighten as she forces the creature back. With every inch it concedes, frantic hope fills her. She pins it against the garage's wall, squeezing with her ropes of shining blue. The creature flails. She bashes it against the cedar planks, simultaneously tightening the cord. Again. And again. And again. With each blow, the garage shakes.

Then the monster roars, the skinny tentacle inside its mouth burning bright, bright white. Pain spreads across Anna's temples, quelling the more familiar tingle of xhen in her forehead. For a moment, her concentration wavers. Still roaring, the creature slips free and strikes in a rush of orange light and sound. Shrieking like a child, Anna jumps back, one hand rising to protect her face.

***Palm fount*.**

Muscle memory raises the long-buried exercise. She pools xhen in her hands. To her shock, the energy forms a short bolt of brilliant blue. It arcs from her palm and burns a streaking hole straight through the creature's mouth and out the back of its head. Its roar is cut off with a strangled, liquid sound as it collapses to the garage floor, convulsing. She tastes the peculiar tang of sulphur a second before a rancid smell clogs her nostrils.

Anna slumps against the SUV and slides down its side to the garage floor. The corded blue xhen connecting her to the monster's corpse loosens to puddle around her body in a glimmering pool. As she lets her head fall back against the car door, panting and sheathed in sweat, the ache in her back dies along with the creature at her feet.

With the immediate danger now past, raw panic seizes Anna for the first time. *Oh my fucking god.* She takes frantic gulps of air, listening to her heart thudding in her ears. Her muscles twitch almost as violently as the monster's corpse as xhen recedes into her body in a waning tide. In moments, the blue light is gone. Yet its presence remains in her mind, the door ajar after sixteen years of being bolted shut. Joy spikes within the maelstrom of confused feelings that swirl in Anna's chest. *Xhen is back. And Kalos spoke to me.*

Awe sweeps through her, making her skin tingle with pure, unmitigated delight. *Jason,* comes her next coherent thought, followed by a desperate longing to hear her twin brother's voice. *He has to know. And Dave, too. I've got to tell them.*

"Anna?" calls an uncertain voice, edged in panic.

Oh no. Swaying on unsteady feet, Anna lurches out of the garage. The porch light is on. Malcolm is standing on the back deck, their other Maglite clutched in his hand. His panicked gaze finds her with visible relief.

"It's okay," she calls softly, struggling not to pant. "It's gone."

"Huh?" He blinks, looking and sounding groggy. "I heard noises."

"The raccoons came back," she lies, forcing her voice to sound casual. After years of shared secrecy, telling anyone what's happened before she tells her twin is unthinkable. *Even Dave.* Silently, she pleads for Malcolm to ignore her filthy pyjamas, messy hair, and trembling hands. "I chased them off. Go back to bed."

Malcolm sniffs the night air, frowning. "It smells weird out here."

"Skunk," Anna says, fighting the urge to physically shoo him inside. "I'll be up in a minute."

"You said raccoons." He tilts his head. Suddenly it's the trained investigator squinting at her across the garden.

Her gut freezes. *Busted*, she thinks.

But Malcolm merely shrugs. "It's late," he says, yawning. "Hurry up."

"I will."

With a last confused glance, her husband retreats inside. *You won't sleep a wink if you see that thing*, Anna thinks as the screen door closes behind him. *I'll tell you everything in the morning.*

She slips back into the garage but doesn't turn on the overhead light. Instead, she bends down, searching the floor with her fingers until her hand closes on the Maglite's handle. She flicks its switch, fearing it broken. Brightness slices through the stinking gloom. Relieved, she trains the beam on the creature's corpse.

It's at least half a metre longer than she is tall, and twice as wide. Diamond-shaped orange scales cover its body like a shiny, lustrous snakeskin. Shuffling forward, she extends a careful hand. The supple, overlapping scales sting her skin. Anna jerks her fingertips away, rubbing them against her pyjama shorts in a vain attempt to ease the burning feeling. The creature has no legs, arms, wings, or feet, but her memory of it moving up and over the car is clear. *It either jumped or flew.*

Wary of the slack purple tentacles on the sides of its head and the severed end of the paler one sticking out of its ruined mouth, she uses the Maglite's handle to prod at it until its empty eyes tilt toward her. *What the hell are you?* she wonders, feeling sick as she stares into the glassy abyss of the creature's gaze. *Kalos never said anything about you. What were you doing in my garage? And what do I do now?*

Mom would know. An overwhelming, childish urge to drop this entire mess into Chun-Mei Lin's brisk, capable hands sweeps through Anna. *She could cope with anything.* Tears prick her eyes.

"Pull it together, Anna." Her voice is too loud in the stillness, making her flinch. Dashing away her tears with the back of her hand, she stands. "Clean up this mess."

Anna rummages for a solution, unsure what she needs until her flashlight falls on a camping tarp. Grabbing it, she spreads it between the car and the garage wall. Pulling on a thick pair of gardening gloves, she pushes the creature into the centre. Anna stands over it, breathing through her mouth as she studies its unearthly strangeness. With its body slack against the blue plastic, it looks fake, like a monster prop from one of the Valoi Knights movies that Dave loves so much. The sulphur-like reek from its crisped flesh tickles the back of her throat. She gags on a fresh wave of nausea. *Keep moving. Freak out later.*

Anna props the flashlight up to illuminate her work. *I need to make it smaller.* Quickly, she pulls the tarp over the creature's body to protect her bare feet and forces herself to jump up and down on its back. Every time her feet strike the plastic, her weight forces clear fluid to seep out of its ruined mouth until the stink makes her gag. She makes two trips up its length before tucking the tarp more tightly around the creature's body, folding it from the base of the tail toward its head until it's compacted into the smallest possible shape. There's nothing she can do about the skull, which is still huge, but her efforts seem to have deflated its bulk. She finds two bungee cords and twists them into place around the package, but the smell emanating from it is nauseating.

I need a seal. Her eyes flick again over the garage's walls, landing on an extra-large plastic bin they use to store outdoor toys. She opens it, redistributes the toys among the garage's shelves, and hefts her package inside with a liquid thud. The crest plate at the back of its skull doesn't quite fit. With a grimace, Anna contorts the wrapped shape, jiggling it until something snaps inside the package. A long tooth pokes through the plastic, glinting in the light. Shuddering, she smushes it in and jams the lid on before sliding the bin back into place.

Now for the smell. Anna opens the big garage door, wincing as it squeaks on its antiquated hinges. The alley between their garage and those belonging to their neighbours is silent except for the hum of air conditioners and the more distant buzz of traffic on Keele Street. She gets the garden hose, turning the flow on as high as she can to wash away the wet stain. The scent of sulphur, however, lingers.

A raindrop lands on her nose. *That might help*, she thinks as she gives the garage's outer wall a quick scan. There's no fresh damage, just the old raccoon-inflicted holes and the dent around the door. She can't tell if the creature crawled in that way or not. On the threshold, her gaze falls on the propane canister's remains. The metal fragments aren't marked with tooth marks as she expects.

It's like it burst apart from the inside out. Could it have done that to me? Swallowing hard, Anna grabs a pair of plyers and pulls out the pieces, kicking them beneath a nearby storage shelf. She considers changing the SUV's flat tire but decides against it. *Malcolm carpools to work anyway.* She pulls the garage door down, picks up her flashlight, and returns to the garden.

Aside from the rain now pattering on the deck and patio stones, it's completely silent. Their neighbours' houses are also dark. Only

Malcolm noticed her violent scuffle in this sleepy pocket of Toronto, and he arrived too late to help.

What would have happened if I hadn't killed it? Would it have left anything for him to find? She shivers, gooseflesh rising on her skin as she pictures herself pierced by teeth and tentacles. Nausea roils again in her belly. She grips the flashlight tightly and realizes her hands are still trembling. *I'm going into shock.*

Jason. His name is a glass of cold water in her face. When he led, she'd never worried where the chase would bring them. *He'll be so amazed,* she thinks, her giddiness returning as she hurries into the house to pick up the kitchen phone. It rings twice.

"I'm at work."

"I—" Anna's knees start to shake. "You have to come home." Her voice is too high, and as she clutches the phone to her ear, her head begins to pound. "As soon as you can. Tonight. Tomorrow. I don't care, just come."

His sigh is pure exasperation. "Look, I answered your questions about Mom's stuff. I've done everything I can to help with the house. I can't take any more time—"

"It's not that." Anna's throat is impossibly dry as she tries to swallow. "It's . . . I don't want to talk about it over the phone. Believe me, it's urgent. I need you here. You. And Dave."

"Dave?" he echoes, sounding confused. There's a long pause. When he speaks again, the contempt in his voice is audible. "We are not having this conversation now."

A fresh pit opens in her stomach. "I'm not making things up." Old anger hardens her voice, blinding in its fierceness. She had always known Jason blamed her when xhen vanished along with their teacher. Part of her even understood his reasons. "Come home. Please, I need you."

Jason's voice is matter-of-fact. "I've got night shifts tomorrow, Thursday, and next weekend. We're half staffed with so many people away for summer holidays. Margo's got rehearsals for her new play. I can't just up and leave—"

"He spoke to me in the garage. Kalos. I heard his voice." She strains to hear Jason say something, anything. "Are you there?" she whispers into the silence. "There's more. Something terrible attacked me." Her arms break out in fresh goosebumps. "I killed it." She waits, pressing the phone against her head so hard that her ears hurt. "Say something."

His swallow is audible. There's another long pause before he says, "That's impossible."

Her vision tunnels. "What part of this are you not hearing? I was *attacked* in my own house." Remembered terror courses through her body. Her voice cracks. "Xhen is back, only it's so different. We've finally got a chance to understand what happened and—"

"You said you were in the garage," he says in his doctor voice. She bites back a scream. "Anna, it hasn't been my place to comment, but this is getting out of hand. Have you talked to someone about Mom?"

"You mean someone like you?" She doesn't know whether to laugh or cry. "Jay, I could have died tonight."

"No, you couldn't," he says, sounding more impatient. "God, you were always so eager to—"

"To what?" She's shaking with fury. "To lie?"

"Xhen is gone!" His angry words hiss through the receiver. "Whatever happened, whatever you told yourself was happening, it's done. I moved on, Dave moved on, but you didn't." There's another voice in the background. Muffled noise echoes along the line as Jason covers the phone, murmuring indistinct words. "I have to go. Good night." For the second time, the line goes dead.

He doesn't believe me. Anna's eyes drop to her hands, no longer edged in blue. *But it was real. I saw it,* she thinks as the vestiges of her euphoria vanish, leaving her body heavy and numb.

Her stomach roils a second time. Anna braces her hands on the countertop and retches into the sink. Once. Twice. Shuddering, she washes the sick down the drain, wipes her mouth, and pours a glass of water. As she drinks, her eye falls on the children's tablet charging by the phone.

Two can play at this game, she thinks, sweeping it up as she storms back to the garage. *Here comes your proof, Dr. Lin.*

It's the work of minutes to pull the bin out and unwrap the creature's head. Propping up the flashlight, Anna lifts the tablet and opens the camera app. And stops, her mouth falling open.

There's no corpse in the frame, just pixelated visual noise. *What the hell?*

Frantically, she checks the light and the tablet's settings. They look normal. She takes a few photos, but the images contain only the edges of the bin and the tarp, folded around pixelated space. *Is he right? Am I losing my mind?*

Gingerly, she touches the creature's slack scales and half laughs, half sobs as the strange sting jolts through her flesh. *It attacked me. I killed it*, she tells herself, repacking her handiwork. *There's a lot here that I don't understand. But there's one more person who must know.*

Back in the house, she dials Dave's cell phone. At the height of the years that he spent running Rune Software, the man she thinks of as her second brother picked up calls at every hour. Tonight, she goes straight to voicemail. She hangs up before the beep, unable to think of a way to explain the evening in thirty seconds or less. *I'll call him tomorrow.*

As she puts the phone back in its cradle, her gaze lands on the refrigerator. Her belly grumbles a third time, now in hunger. Pulling open the door, she takes out a carton of ice cream and gets a spoon, struggling to reconcile Jason's accusing words with her battle in the garage. *He can think what he wants*, she decides as she gets into bed ten minutes later with a full belly. *No weird photograph changes the truth: That creature is real, and xhen has returned. And we have to know why.*

For a long time, Anna listens to sounds of the rain and her husband's gentle snoring, feeling alive for the first time in years.

Chapter 3

Jason – Night Shift

Vancouver, BC: Sunday, August 17

Three hours, Dr. Jason Lin thinks. He considers the time stamps beside his sister's name in his phone's call log with the intensity he once applied to deciphering anatomical drawings. *Somehow, in three hours, Anna lost her mind.*

But what if she didn't? whispers a small voice. *What if she's right?*

Before he can quash that thought, the first-floor break room seems to shrink against his skin. He starts to sweat as a memory rises, swallowing him in a visceral, long-forgotten flash:

"What happened?" Dave asks quietly as Jason opens his eyes. They're sitting cross-legged on the dusty ground in the alley behind his family's garage. "Did you find him?"

The hope in his best friend's voice makes Jason want to shrivel into a ball. Reluctantly, he shakes his head, the last traces of the energy he once commanded fading from his grasp.

In the alley's dim light, he watches as the answer they've both feared shadows Dave's face. Jason's certainty deepens as they sit, not speaking, brothers in loss as they have been in training. After a moment, Dave grimaces. "Kalos is gone. Holy shit."

Failure grips Jason's heart like a vise, and he begins to cry.

Blinking, Jason raises the sleeve of his scrubs to wipe his clammy forehead. His heart races in his ears. It feels like an invisible hand is twisting his chest into a knot. *You're experiencing the onset of a panic attack*, the doctor in him notes dispassionately. *Find a private space, quickly.*

He strides out of the break room, ignoring the curious eyes of nurses, orderlies, and residents. As the attending physician, he's supposed to keep everyone focused on their patients. Yet, as his breathing becomes increasingly shallow, he can think of nothing but his urgent need to feel night air against his face.

"Oh, Dr. Lin," Clarissa Andrews, the team's nurse practitioner calls from the nursing station. She was the one who stuck her head into the breakroom when he was on the phone with Anna. "Mrs. Harrington in Room 109 is experiencing more chest—"

"Five minutes," he says, not stopping or making eye contact, though it makes him squirm to do it. Mrs. Harrington is being treated for heart failure. Clarissa knows as well as he does how quickly people with that condition can deteriorate. When a life can pivot in seconds, forming an accurate timeline for intervention is his most critical responsibility. He's written formal reprimands to residents for leaving a bedside without properly assessing a patient's condition. He knows exactly what his mentors would say about his choice, but Clarissa doesn't call out.

No one else stops him. When he reaches the stairwell, Jason permits himself to run. Instead of heading for the street, he climbs swiftly up to the roof. Nothing relaxes him like seeing the skyline. Accessing the roof directly conflicts with the safety policies of St. Paul's Hospital, of course. During his first year on staff, a bottle of Lagavulin persuaded the security supervisor to key his card for roof access.

The fire door clangs open as he steps out into cool darkness. This close to the ocean, there's usually a breeze, and this evening is no exception; the fresh air is tangy with moisture and salt. Jason steps to one side of the door, propping it open with the loose brick left nearby for this purpose. He slides down the wall to sit on his heels, puts his head between his knees, and breathes.

When his pulse has slowed and it no longer feels like his heart is a galloping horse, Jason lifts his eyes to stare at the city. Instead, he sees himself running with Anna and Dave through Toronto's backstreets, their pimpled, youthful faces glowing beneath the streetlamps. Wild laughter echoes on the night breeze, and he feels the phantom itch of xhen in his palms.

No, he thinks irritably, rubbing his hand as he recites the litany. *Xhen was a strange little fantasy you dreamed when you were too young to know any better.*

He runs a hand through his damp hair, longer now than he wore it in high school. Changing his perception of what happened to them during those years had been much harder. When he moved to Vancouver, he had weekly panic attacks. He worked with a therapist to cope with his symptoms, claiming stress over his school workload. Privately, he used the tools from their sessions to sift through his recollections, assessing what he knew objectively to be true. It took years, but he persisted. Slowly, he put the whole embarrassing story to rest.

How long has it been since I thought about Kalos? A decade? He sighs. *Anna's so stubborn.*

Continuing to breathe slowly and deeply, Jason lets his gaze trace the roof's familiar edges. Unlike most of Vancouver's downtown core, St. Paul's dates from the 1890s. He's fond of its brown and yellow bricks and fussy, gingerbread-like wooden trim. The hospital is seven stories tall, but it's high enough to give him a view of the office and condo towers stretching up into the never fully dark sky. He's always been a night owl, like his father. They're suited to the night shift's unusual rhythms.

This city is real, he tells himself as he surveys the familiar buildings. *My work here is real. It's not Anna's fault. She's been under so much stress.*

Their mother's cancer diagnosis had been a massive blow to the family. Chun-Mei had discovered the tumour in her left breast during a self-exam. She'd been sixty-one at the time and in excellent health. Jason had flown home to Toronto three times in those early months, when it seemed surgery and radiation would obliterate her cancer. From the start, however, he'd worried about her rapid weight loss, poor blood counts, and pervasive exhaustion.

Anna, in the same city and with an infinitely flexible schedule, had shouldered the brunt of Chun-Mei's daily needs. She'd ferried their mother back and forth to Sunnybrook Health Sciences Centre for endless appointments. Once a week, Jason had joined his sister for a phone call with their mother's specialist. There'd been great camaraderie in that initially, especially since their father had refused to participate. He had been adamant that Chun-Mei needed him as a spouse, not a doctor, and delegated the task of patient advocacy to the twins.

Anna had been surprised by that choice; Jason was not. A prominent pediatric cancer researcher, Erik had treated too many children whose lives were ultimately reduced to a data file and a slice of tumour tissue stored in a cell bank for research. Jason's cursory glance through the literature had shown him the same survival curves, yet he'd believed his mother would be fine. Breast cancer was no longer the death sentence it had been in the 1980s. Optimism was realistic.

Months had stretched to years. As caring for Chun-Mei became more intensive, the strain in his sister's voice grew during their weekly calls. When their mother entered palliative care, Anna began asking him to come home. Jason had stalled, falling on the blameless excuse of his work. Their parents accepted his choice, but Anna wasn't fooled. Neither of them wanted to sit and watch as their mother—their implacable, domineering, loving mother—was hollowed out by a secondary surgery and experimental chemotherapy to become a shade of herself.

In the end, Margo had made the decision and booked Jason's ticket home. It hadn't mattered. Thunderstorms delayed his plane. He missed Chun-Mei's death by two hours.

I should have gone earlier. It's an old refrain, as worn out as the records he remembers his parents dancing to in their Dovercourt Park living room when he was a child. *Classic filial guilt,* he tells himself. But diagnosing the problem is no help. He shares the languages of medicine and research with his father, but Chun-Mei was the parent who understood him. She'd encouraged him to dedicate his life to medicine and never questioned his decision to build his career in the west.

You have great opportunity ahead of you, she'd told him whenever he called, offering to visit. *Help your patients while you can. Anna is with me.*

Self-contained to the end, he reflects. *What might she have told me if I'd come home sooner?* He's self-aware enough to know that he envies Anna for all that time she spent with Chun-Mei, though his sister never speaks about it. *I should have stayed in Toronto longer after the funeral. The hospital would have given me more leave if I'd asked. I could have helped Anna. She's got her hands full with the children. And Dad never makes this stuff easy.*

But if he's being honest with himself, Anna's grief and stress don't explain her words tonight. *He spoke to me in the garage. Kalos. I heard his voice.*

Jason shivers. He has plenty of mental health terminology for what they experienced. Finding such answers had been part of what drove his own interest in medicine. *If she's spiraled into open delusion, she'll need a therapist. I could make some calls, help her find someone good.*

They'll be thirty-five in November. As they age, Jason finds talking to Anna to be increasingly hard. They have their family in common, of course, their careers, and Dave. Yet in recent years, Anna's real estate work has dropped from their conversations, leaving nothing but Chun-Mei's decline, her worries for their father, and her obsession with selling their parents' house.

His career, in contrast, is growing. Beyond the satisfaction of serving his patients, St. Paul's busy emergency department has its own dynamic of trust. He's found pleasure in being one of the fulcrums around which its activity hums. In med school, he remembers worrying that he didn't share the innate calling to help people that his peers did. Somewhere along the line, however, medicine grew beyond a source of insight and Chun-Mei's dream for his life and became the governing structure of his days.

And he has Margo, of course, his world's undisputed sun.

On cue, his cell phone chimes. Jason takes it out of his pocket, fearing a barrage of texts from Anna or questions from Dave. Whenever they argued as teenagers, bringing Dave in as her heavy was Anna's signature move. *Just spam,* he thinks, deleting the message with a twinge of disappointment. He checks the time. It's after eleven p.m., which means it's past two a.m. in Toronto.

Dave's probably sound asleep for once in his life. If Anna's smart, she's gone to bed, too.

With no message to answer, Jason opens his photo gallery. The five most recent shots are of his wife. In the first two, Margo's laughing over dinner at Luigi's with the Wongs, their closest friends in the city. In the next two, she walks ahead of him on Kitsilano Beach, her black hair a banner in the wind, her figure slim against the backdrop of the waves. In the last, she's wrapped in a pale sheet wearing only the ruby he gave her.

This is real, Jason thinks, scrolling through the images. *We've built a beautiful life together.*

Telling Margo about his unusual teens never made sense. Raised by immigrant Chinese parents in suburban Richmond, Margo Cheung studied microbiology before switching to theatre studies during her third year at the University of British Columbia. By some stroke of fortune, Jason had sat behind her in an introductory psychology class. It took him all semester to work up the nerve to ask for her number. She'd been the one to ask him out for coffee.

From the start, their mutual interest in the intersection of science and the arts built unexpected connections between them. Optimistic and ambitious, Margo was focused on the future. She'd coaxed him through his anxieties about his undergraduate program, followed by med school and a challenging residency. He'd encouraged her decision to shift from acting to directing. There seemed to be no place in their exciting, hectic lives for his weird experiences with his twin and their best friend. And after a while, he'd stopped looking for the right moment to tell her.

Jason's beeper chimes in his other pocket. The number on the archaic screen is St. Paul's locating office. *You're like a nineties drug dealer*, Margo always jokes, but the hospital can't afford to upgrade to something more sophisticated. Not when they're underfunded. Jason clicks the pager's *received* button, ashamed of needing to be called. He stands, taking a deep breath.

He spoke to me in the garage. Kalos. I heard his voice.

Jason pockets the pager as he walks downstairs. *If Anna wants to relive that time, I can't help her. She'll have to work through it like I did.* As he reenters the emergency department to face an indignant Clarissa, Jason's concerns for his patients bury the last traces of his uncertainty.

Chapter 4

Dave – Strings

Miinikaa First Nation, ON: Monday, August 18

"Ready?" Dave LaRoque Montcalm waits for the dozen young people, all between twelve and fifteen, to nod before he turns to the classroom wall. On the ancient pull-up screen, he's projected the JavaScript block maze that they've built together over the last two weeks of their eight-week coding workshop. In the bottom corner, their blobby red avatar blinks like a recording light.

Dave hits return. The avatar slips through the blocks, following its programmed commands. As it reaches the last section, it turns left instead of right and slams into a block wall, disintegrating to a loud chorus of boos.

"Tremendous!" Dave insists over the room's outcry, lifting a child's mesh net in robin's egg blue, purchased at a dollar store for this exact purpose. "It's bug hunting time!" Flourishing the net to dispel their collective groans, he gestures to their workstations. "Let's get after it."

As their groans subside, the room buzzes with the kind of energy

Dave remembers from all-night hackathons during his undergraduate years as a computer science engineer at the University of Waterloo. *Not bad*, he thinks as the teaching assistants circulate. Carrying the net over his broad shoulder, he heads to the coat racks and shelves at the back of the room for his travel mug of green tea. Try as he might to develop a taste for the stuff, it's a poor substitute for coffee. *Especially lukewarm*, he thinks, grimacing. *Drink up, Davy. Better for your health.*

At the nearest desk, Janessa Hart pulls her chair closer to her monitor. Her dark bangs fall into her eyes as her fingers hover over the keyboard, the delicate tattoos of hummingbirds covering both her wrists giving the impression of interrupted flight. Frowning, she studies her monitor as waves of indecision pass like clouds over her expressive face. Dave takes a half step toward her, encouraging words at the ready, and feels a gentle bump against his ribs.

"You've done your part," murmurs his aunt, Leona LaRoque. "It's their turn."

Dave rubs his side with a mock pained expression but stays put. The idea to give back by teaching other Indigenous kids to code had been his, but Leona made it happen. From securing space in Miinikaa First Nation's Community Centre to getting the word out through the surrounding reserves to briefing his volunteers about the differences in teaching on the reserve compared to their usual class blocks at the university, Leona has as many fingerprints on this workshop as Dave does.

Total organizational rock star, he thinks, glancing at his aunt as he takes another tepid sip of tea. *What a chief operating officer she would have made.*

A moment later, Leona gives him a second playful jab, making her silver bangles chime. Dave looks up in time to see the red blob race across Janessa's screen. She leans back in her chair, sporting a smile full of braces as it successfully completes the maze. Dave glances around the room. She's the first to finish.

"Good hunting," Dave says, presenting Janessa with the net. She flushes as she sets it down beside her keyboard. Emma, one of the teaching assistants, ambles over to watch her demo. As she explains her steps, Janessa's face lights up. *Damn if that isn't satisfying every time.*

"Never underestimate the value in muddling through a puzzle," Leona says as though reading his mind. Her crow's feet—earned through years of fishing on the lake—deepen around her black eyes as she smiles at him. "Didn't that fancy company of yours teach you anything?"

"Plenty," Dave says, tapping his left hand against his chest. Three years after his operation, the scar from his heart surgery has healed. He points with his chin at Janessa. "She could start learning Python in the fall. She's ready."

Before Leona can comment, Dave's phone chimes. He automatically reaches into his back pocket to flick it into silent mode. Beside him, Leona nods. During the early months of his convalescence, he jumped at every chance to revert to his old life. *I'm not a CEO anymore,* he thinks, resisting the urge to check who called. *Those habits no longer serve me.*

These days, the only person who regularly texts him from down south is Anna Lin. He'd missed a call from her early that morning. *I'll set up a video chat this weekend,* he decides, remembering how down she'd sounded the last time they talked. *Annie needs to laugh more.*

His phone vibrates against his backside. Dave ignores it. Thirty seconds later, it buzzes again. Dave takes a deep breath, counts to ten, and exhales. Another buzz. At his side, Leona raises one salt-and-pepper eyebrow. Emma and Janessa also turn to look over their shoulders at him, their glances quizzical. Dave grins back, determined not to look at the screen.

There's only one person it could be. *And she doesn't dictate my calendar anymore.*

As his jeans continue to vibrate, more heads turn. Deep in his chest, the old volcano stirs, letting one jolt of molten frustration spike through his body. *Fuck off, Hal.*

"If your face freezes like that, my boy, you'll start scaring babies," Leona teases, but the hand on his elbow is gentle. "Find out what she wants. 'Look after mind and body.'"

"'And do what you know to be right,'" he finishes, echoing the teaching she'd given him during the first days of his recovery in the cardiac centre at Toronto General. He consciously forces his shoulders down into a neutral position, straightening his spine. "Excuse me, Auntie. I'll be back in two minutes."

Dave waits until he's outside the community centre in the afternoon sun to pull out his phone. The six texts and five phone calls, all placed within the last nine minutes, are indeed from Halina Mendes, co-founder and chief technology officer of Rune Software. He looks at her unfamiliar number with the 617-area code as he walks over the lawn toward the reserve's main road. *Her pressures aren't yours anymore. You had to leave Rune, but she chose to let go of you. Remember that.*

Taking a bracing breath, Dave dials.

"Dave! Finally! It's so great to hear from you. I need those papers signed, stat," Halina says in the rapid-fire voice she adopted sometime after her development team of engineers swelled to thirty-five people. They were six years into running Rune Software at that point, with two launched products and a hundred and two staff. "The patent lawyers sent you the package on Wednesday of last week. I forwarded it again on Friday. What's the holdup?"

"Hey, Hal." He grimaces, unable to deny his pleasure at hearing her voice. "Miinikaa is really beautiful in summer. You should visit sometime." He wishes they could just shoot the shit, like they did during that co-op term when they both missed out on good placements and ended up working crappy summer jobs. They used to joke it had motivated them to co-found Rune the following semester when they returned to Waterloo. "Social calls only, though."

She snorts. "Maybe when Beakhead's legal team isn't halfway up my ass."

Hearing the name of the equity firm that acquired their company tightens Dave's throat. *Keep it casual.* "What's wrong? Boston sea air isn't everything you were promised?"

Halina chuckles. "I keep meaning to get out to Gloucester for a weekend. There's a perfect bed-and-breakfast on the ocean I want to visit." Her sigh is wistful. "One day. My condo view will have to do for now."

"It's a pretty great one," Dave agrees, thinking of the party she'd thrown on her rooftop patio the same day Rune opened its Boston office. Dazzled by the sunset, he'd told himself to ignore the sick feeling in his gut.

Don't get sucked into old stories. He lifts his eyes to the birch trees along the road. Wind rustles the leaves, making them flicker green-grey-green. "What do you need, Hal?"

"The intellectual property agreement back with your signature on it."

"I read Rune-related email on Tuesdays," Dave says. "Doctor's orders. I've told you that before. So, what's so urgent that you had to text me, like, ten times in an hour?"

He hears her short, inhaled breath. *She's marshalling herself for a fight.* "We're filing a patent continuation on the Glyph algorithm," she says. "You're a co-inventor. I need your sign-off."

Dave walks a few steps before responding, scuffing the dirt shoulder beside the asphalt with his hiking boots. *It could be a new application*, he tells himself, coughing on the dust. *They could have pivoted. With Charles running the show, they're always pivoting.* "What's the use case?"

"Come on," she scoffs. "Beakhead's only got one major market. We knew that when we inked the deal."

"When you and the board forced me to sell," Dave corrects. On some level, Halina's decision to swing her allegiance to Charles Larkin and their investors, thereby shifting Rune's focus away from linguistic applications to military code cracking, still shocks him. He had believed they were a united team in full control of their capital table and, by extension, their company. "What's he using it for? Decoding insurgent transmissions in Afghanistan?"

"You know I can't talk about it," Halina says quietly. "You were never eligible for the security clearance on those contracts."

Dave's free hand clenches and unclenches. When he'd met Halina in their first-year calculus class, he'd thought nothing about her being a dual US–Canadian citizen. All he'd seen was another passionate coder who was self-taught and wanted to be self-made, just like him. Back then, he's reasonably certain that she hadn't given it a second thought, either.

But Charles Larkin and Beakhead Capital had seen long-term leverage and exploited it. By the time he'd realized that her view of Rune had splintered from his, it was too late. "No court will let you file a continuance for military use," he says. "We never hinted at anything like that in the original patent."

"The original patent was a shitshow," Halina returns. "Sandy Mercer is a sweetheart, but she didn't have a clue what she was doing. I've spent oceans of cash cleaning up that mess." She pauses, chuckling to herself. "Why am I even telling you?"

"We invented Glyph to solve translation problems and invest in Indigenous language preservation efforts," Dave spits. "Not to weaponize it."

"That's a matter of opinion," Halina says coolly. "I know Dean Ng in business development still sends you the financial statements out of loyalty. If you've opened them, you know Q3's been shit so far." She sighs. "I need a win, Dave." She pauses, giving him time to feel her words. "You may not know that Geoffrey Adams just bought a house—baby two is on the way. Or that Lucy Grady's eldest daughter starts at MIT this week. Computer science, naturally. And Parker Lesley's dad is sick again. His lung cancer's come back." Her second sigh echoes in his bones. "I could run down the whole roster for the old guard, but the takeaway here is it's just me watching their backs. And I need you to get out of our way."

Dave laughs. "Did Charles tell you to say that?"

"Charles never lied to me," Halina retorts. "He never told me 'We're in this to the end, Hal, come fortune or ruin.'"

Her mimicry is note perfect. Dave winces, remembering. "Pretty sure I'd had a few beers that night."

"You quit on us, Dave." Halina's angry words slide like a dagger into his ear. "Are you really going to be a dick now about some fucking paperwork?"

I almost died! The words quiver on his tongue as, inside him, the volcano flexes. He can practically feel his blood pressure rising. "You know what? Fuck this. I don't need your manipulation or Charles's bullshit. Find another way. You always do." He hangs up, wishing the gesture felt less anticlimactic on a smartphone.

We had an amazing business until you let that snake in the front door, Dave fumes, continuing to barrel up the road. *He fed you a lie, you got greedy, everyone drank the Kool-Aid, and you sided with Charles and forced me out.*

Says the man with nine figures in the bank, he thinks, ashamed that he's once more in the grip of his lingering rage. He stops to roll his shoulders, imagining the tension dripping away from him like raindrops after a storm.

Objectively, he's got no reason to be embarrassed. He and Halina founded Rune in 2003, just as tech companies in San Francisco were beginning to invest heavily in translation software. Their company's acquisition for $468 million USD in 2011 had been a watershed moment for Toronto's nascent artificial intelligence sector. He'd walked away with sixteen percent of the total sale.

Once he was healthy, Dave took a year off to travel, sent his parents on a whirlwind vacation, traveled to Vancouver to spend time reconnecting with Jason, met up with both the Lin twins and their families in St. Lucia the next Christmas, and took Leona and her longtime boyfriend Ryan Charron to see the Grand Canyon. Dedicating time to learning Anishinaabemowin, his birth family's language, with Leona and other elders in their community, had been the next logical step. Through that process, he'd started thinking about how best to give back on a bigger scale, which led to the workshop pilot.

Roses for everyone. All it cost me was my business partner and best friend.

"You finished sulking?" Spinning, Dave sees Leona coming up the road behind him, her hands in the pockets of her jeans. He looks around, surprised by how far he walked during the call. He can't see the break in the trees around the community centre.

"Yeah, I'm done," he says, so weary he could lie down in the dirt and close his eyes. "Sorry."

"Why?" Leona asks. "The colonized world doesn't let go of people with your gifts, David. Not until they've wrung every drop of value out of you."

"You're probably right," he agrees as they turn to walk back. Beside him, Leona's stride is a little stiff. Dave frowns. "Is your hip sore again?"

"It's fine," she says, waving off his question. "And before you ask, my cane is in the house where it belongs. I'll have a soak in that hot tub you bought me." She cackles with delight, her smile pure glee. "And I'll sleep like a baby."

He shakes his head. "Stubborn fox."

"Got me this far. Creator willing, it'll see me through."

It's hot in the dust. At the end of the road, the lake flickers in the sunlight. As they walk, Dave feels his insides loosen. Being near the water is soothing. *Hal would say you've gone full hippie,* he thinks. Annoyed, he turns to his aunt. "How do you do it? I've overheard a few of your calls. Land claim work isn't any easier than building a start-up."

"Nothing worth doing is, my boy." She gestures to the forest on either side of the road. "The land sustains me. I have you, and Ryan, and our people." Her weathered hands rise above her head, twisting her greying hair into a bun. "Like you, I listen to my body. It's much wiser than my mind."

"I guess," he says, remembering the magma flare. *Doing a great job over here.*

She gives him a sidelong look. "Setting up this workshop wasn't easy. You had to attract students and find ways to address the education gaps in their learning to do the work you envisioned. You had to convince the band council and their parents. You had to make it fun!"

His smile is sheepish. "And it would have been a mess without your help."

Leona beams. "This is only the beginning of your new purpose, David. Trust me."

Dave smiles back, but he can't shake his uneasiness. He had never counted teaching among his ambitions, although he's been pleasantly surprised by how much he's enjoyed the experience. *Is it going to sustain me over the long term?* he wonders. *Do I want to be teaching the fifth workshop, or the one hundredth?*

Talking with Halina has reminded him of one thing: how much he misses work on a grand scale, pressure and his health be damned. "I hope you're right."

Interlude: Taste

When our scouts return, they are as radiant as the stars that have blessed us.

The swarm trails us to the ocean's rim. They coil around us on the sand, quivering with excitement. Above, the first scout's purple tentacles push back through the hole in the torn veil. It pauses, searching for scouts from enemy nests, as is proper, its orange body coated in a bright sheen. The wind circling the cliffs carries the scent it bears to us—fresh, wild, and deliciously alien. The nest mind turns rapturous.

We probe the nest memories, but no hunts echo with this tang. This world is unknown to us.

As our scout circles down through the sky to our nest, we roar in welcome and excitement. Eager, so eager, the swarm clusters in tight knots around us, straining for a taste. We ignore them as the scout cowers before our coils, its tentacles lowered to the rocks. This close, the scent it carries is intoxicating. We writhe as the scout's maw opens and its mouth tentacle glides out, shining with alien skal. Half crazed, the swarm presses closer.

With a crushing flick, we slam our tail in the centre of the nest. ***Await our pleasure***.

They curl back, making space for us to harvest our prize.

Appeased, we approach the victorious scout. We open our maw and slip forward our inner tentacle, twice as wide as the scout's body. As we twine it around the scout, we taste the strange skal, its complex depths unlike any we have ever sampled. Power rushes through our body, so strong it threatens to unmake our very scales. Blazing with its strength, we share our pleasure through the nest mind, feeling the swarm's ecstasy rise to frenzied heights. Sated for the first time in many veil seasons by this rush of fresh skal, we lift our eyes to the stars in gratitude.

There, a second scout is returning through the veil. And a third.

When we have taken every glimmer of the treasure they bear, we shine with new radiance. Above, the pulsing of the veil slows and then ceases. We study the heavens, feeling a twinge of concern among our mother-sisters as the oblivious swarm rejoices. They know, as we do, that this skal harvest is too small to outweigh the loss of a scout.

The swarm does not allow us to brood for long, and we surrender to the glow of victory. After seasons of fear, one sacrifice is nothing. The scouts cavort between our tentacles, keening with their eagerness to set upon the aliens.

We send a hunting party, choosing six bigger scouts this time. As they rise, our new power easily blazes a wider path for them. They wriggle across and vanish upon the aliens' strange shores.

Chapter 5

Anna – Calling

Toronto, ON: Monday, August 18

Anna sets her fork down atop the remnants of her kale salad and drops her napkin over the plate. Her head's throbbing, her strapless bra's digging into her side, and the heels she hasn't worn in six months are killing her feet. She carefully rubs one temple, making sure not to smudge her makeup. *What I wouldn't give to call a cab.*

Around her, Montecito's dining room pulses with conversation. The Toronto International Film Festival is weeks away, but every table in the restaurant, co-founded by one of Canada's most respected Hollywood directors and tastefully decorated with his film memorabilia, is packed with glamourous-looking people. A week ago, Anna would have lapped up the atmosphere and the people-watching. Tonight, preoccupied with the creature stashed in her garage, she keeps fidgeting with the bejeweled cushion behind her back, unable to get comfortable on the dark-grey banquette seat. *It's after ten p.m. Come on, Walter. Hurry up.*

Across the room, her client, Walter Delal, Esq., sips champagne as he stands at the end of a long bench table near the closing kitchen, talking with a group of white men in navy or grey suits. *Bankers*, Anna decides. *Maybe lawyers*. Whichever they are, they hang on Walter's every word, as they have for the last thirty minutes after he "begged her pardon, he would be just a moment," but that was Morris Westin on the other side of the room, and he "must say hello."

A waiter silently materializes to take her plate. He offers her more champagne with a sympathetic smile, which Anna declines. *He probably thinks I'm the wife.*

As it has during each quiet moment today, her mind swims with her memory of xhen and the creature she killed. By comparison, everything about this evening feels surreal. The room's noise bathes her in a blur of sound as her thoughts fill with those menacing triple eyes. *What is it? Why did it attack me? What did it want? Are there more?*

She's no closer to answers now than she was the previous night. She'd lain awake a long time and slept late, waking only when Erin jumped on her feet, demanding breakfast. By that time, Malcolm had already been picked up for work. *Thank God he has a carpool*, Anna thinks. She almost dialed his cell phone a dozen times to tell him about the flat and the monster corpse stashed in the bin. Each time, she stopped herself, resolved that such news would be far easier to share in person after the dinner meeting. *If it ever ends*, Anna thinks, glancing at Walter.

After dropping the kids off at their day camp, she'd run errands, keen to stay close to her secret. Instead of heading to her parents' house, she'd puttered around, too on edge to accomplish much aside from sending one email to her father about paying for the junk service and another to book an appointment. Neither had responded, nor had Dave called her back. *I'll text him now*, she decides as her fingers squirrel through her red-sequined purse, another keepsake from her mother.

"My sincere apologies for having kept you waiting," Walter says, reclaiming his chair opposite hers just as Anna's fingers close on the phone. Releasing it, she flashes her best smile, hoping he won't sense her exhaustion. Dressed in a spotless black pinstripe suit and mauve shirt, his cufflinks dotted with diamonds the size of her pinky fingernails, Walter looks as fresh as she imagines he did twelve hours ago. His silver-streaked black hair is tied at his nape with a leather cord; not a single hair has dared to stray out of place. When Dave called to tell her about the meeting, he'd mentioned Walter will be sixty next year, but his smooth, dark complexion is so unlined that she would have guessed him forty-five at most. Over appetizers, he'd told her about moving to Toronto from Mumbai in his early twenties with a hundred dollars in his pocket and only a vague idea of starting an investment firm.

"One of the companies in my fund is making a public offering on the TSX's junior exchange next week," he offers by way of explanation. "I couldn't pass up the chance to chat with Morris and his analysts."

Unlike many of her previous clients, Walter genuinely looks chagrined for making her wait. "Not at all," Anna says. "Software again?"

"Partially," Walter answers. "A truly fascinating IOT application." Anna blinks; Walter smiles. "Internet of Things," he clarifies and launches into a long explanation that Anna, her energy flagging, only partially follows.

Come on, she chides herself. *Whatever that monster is, it's not paying any of your bills. Walter's a brand-new client with a terrific network. People like him work on referrals. Dave got you in the door, so pay attention!* Her gaze drifts to her empty flute. *The champagne was a big mistake.*

Walter, ever the perfect host, follows her eye. "More champagne?"

"A drop more and I'll be drowning," Anna says, covering the rim. Walter settles back. She picks up the narrow Moleskine beside her purse and glances at her notes. "So, for the office space: downtown locations on the subway, new buildings only, and proximity to the financial district. I'm looking for space for fifteen people, with the option to grow to thirty."

"Twenty at most," Walter corrects. "No fund investor worth their salt tolerates bloat."

"Got it," Anna says as she mentally runs through a few ideas. "I'll send some emails on my way home and see if I can set up some appointments this week." *Like, tomorrow.* She closes the notebook with a snap. Walter, however, is leaning back in his chair, the picture of ease and contentment. "You really love your work, don't you?" she says, unable to keep the envy from her voice.

"I do," Walter agrees. "Running the fund allows me to meet so many more founding teams than I did running my own companies. In cases like your friend Dave's, the interaction can be transformational for us both."

Anna grins. "Guess he made a good impression."

"Oh, yes." Walter's smile is endlessly fond. "His mother, Sarita, is an old friend. She made the introduction. I said yes out of courtesy, prepared to be very polite." He chuckles a little at the memory. "I'd still rank that first pitch he made with Halina in my top three. What a perfect partnership." He sighs. "It's so disheartening to see how their path has forked." Seeing Anna's raised eyebrows, Walter shakes out the linen napkin in his lap and presses it into careful folds. "Forgive me, Ms. Lin. I'm old enough not to tell tales out of school."

Anna leans forward, intrigued despite her tiredness. Her instinct for gossip, honed during her childhood by eavesdropping on her mother's weekly mahjong game, says Walter Delal is a man willing to spill. "Dave got sick," she says. "Wasn't some kind of falling out inevitable?"

Walter shrugs. "At the rate the company was growing, they had to raise more capital. There was no other choice. The trouble started when Charles Larkin joined the board of directors."

"Don't you mean after Halina sold the company out from under Dave?" Anna asks pointedly.

Walter eyes her crossed arms. "Is anything in this life that clear cut?" he asks. Anna, thinking of Jason and their conversation the previous night, flushes. "They faced immense pressures on many fronts. As an early advisor, I understood Dave's principal vision for Rune, of course, and the translation applications he wished to pursue with the algorithm. Platforms like Google Translate were in their infancy then, and the market was rife with opportunity. But the languages market was, and is, a pond compared to the ocean of defense. The other angel investors, who came aboard when I did, joined the Americans in pressing for the path to higher returns." He sips his champagne, studying Anna's face. "Halina was clumsy in her execution, perhaps, but I honestly believe that she saved their company. Their valuation, and Rune's ensuing acquisition price, would never have grown so high if she had done otherwise."

Anna whistles softly. "I didn't know that."

Her client gives her a droll smile. "Nor, it would seem, does Dave. Not yet. I hear from them both from time to time. From what I understand, they're embroiled in another squabble over a piece of intellectual property." He spreads his hands. "Time is a patient teacher."

A cell phone chimes. By habit, Anna glances at her purse, but it's not her notification sound. Across the table, Walter has his phone out of his jacket's breast pocket, drawing wire-framed glasses from another as he reads. Whatever he sees makes him visibly stiffen, his lips blanching as they form a grim line. He signals for the cheque, his fingers flying nimbly over the phone as he types a reply.

Anna gathers her things as the waiter processes Walter's credit card, murmuring her thanks for the meal. *I should be paying as part of my pitch,* she thinks, but Walter had reset that expectation the moment they'd sat down. *Knowing Dave, he probably told Walter I'm broke.*

"What a terrible host I've been this evening," Walter says, holding the restaurant's exterior door open as they step out into the warm summer night. Adelaide Street West is packed with taxis and ride shares ushering people out of the downtown core. "Do forgive my inattentiveness."

His manner is so changed that Anna can't stop herself from asking, "Is something wrong?"

"An awful thing," he answers slowly. "My sister's family lives in the Beaches. Three teenage boys in our community died there last night, very suddenly. Their families need help."

"I'm so sorry to hear that," Anna says as the creature looms in her thoughts. *Don't be ridiculous. If there had been more of them, it would be all over the news.* "Do you know what happened?"

Walter shakes his head, something anguished in his eyes. "I don't fully understand. I shall go there now to offer what assistance I may." He meets her eyes, extending a hand. "It was a pleasure to meet you, and I'm certain our work will be fruitful. Now, do allow me the courtesy of letting me call you a car, Ms. Lin."

"Oh, it's all—"

"I insist," Walter says. Faced with his deepening shock, Anna finds herself agreeing.

Minutes later, as she's being whisked along Dundas Street West toward home in a black SUV with tinted windows and a gloriously cushioned seat, Anna is grateful she didn't argue the point. She rattles off several emails to the managers of promising buildings, asking for appointments the next day. Then she shoots another quick email to Walter's executive assistant with her plans.

That poor man, she thinks, tucking her phone back into her purse. *If I can find him new space quickly, I can take the relocation problem off his plate.* Her thoughts leapfrog back to the garage. *How the hell am I going to explain everything to Malcolm? Do I try to walk him through it or just take him out back and open the lid? Assuming he hasn't found it already.* She checks her phone again, but there are no messages from her husband.

She texts him, just in case: **Dinner ran late. On my way.**

Stewing, she endures the rest of the ride. The house is dark as they approach, the children's shades drawn. *Good, they're asleep.*

As she steps out of the car, Anna tastes sulphur in the air. She shudders. A moment later, she spots their next-door neighbour, Nancy Coleman, on her hands and knees in the grass. Dressed in her housecoat, she's peering under her porch with a large flashlight. Anna freezes, but her back feels normal. There's not a flicker of xhen around her hands. *Relax.*

"Smell that?" Nancy calls, rising as Anna thanks the driver and closes the car door. A former nurse turned administrator for one of the hospitals downtown, Nancy is one of the Junction's accepted authorities on gardening and gossip. Hardly a scraped knee happens on their street without her knowing about it. "Rotten eggs."

Anna sniffs as she walks up the short driveway. The air is still heavy with sulphur. *Shit, it does reek. There better not be more of them.* "No," she lies. "I don't smell anything."

"I think it's a gas leak," Nancy says, her voice firm. "I'm going to call it in."

"Could be kids with a stink bomb," Anna counters, sweeping up the porch stairs. "But it never hurts to be safe." She forces herself to wave. "Good night!"

Inside, Anna kicks off her heels and follows the lights through to the playroom. Malcolm is there, asleep on the couch. The TV is still on. Relieved by the sight of him after such a deeply odd day, Anna perches on the couch's armrest, one hand dropping to stroke his hair. Her eyes skim the room and fall on a notepad lying open on the end table beside them. She glances at the penciled notes, scrawled in her husband's handwriting.

3 BOYS 14, 15, 15. COUSINS.

GREENWOOD & COXWELL.

DP PUNCTURES, TORSO, UPPER ARMS.

ANIMALS? FOUL PLAY? NO SPCTS.

ATPSY TMRW. CLOAR'S CASE.

In an instant, Anna sobers as adrenaline surges through her body, her eye riveted to the word "punctures" as the creature's tentacles stab again for her face. *Oh my god*, she thinks with crippling clarity. *Those kids, whatever happened to me. It's the same pattern.*

She glances at the television, but it's showing sports highlights. She roots around for the TV remote. Finding it, she skims channels for a news broadcast. *Jason would say that I'm overreacting*, she thinks. *I'll watch for a few minutes and then we'll head up to bed.*

Anna clicks past a lifetime movie, an American news broadcast covering a car accident in Buffalo, and a TV Ontario panel on city politics. Then, on CBC, downtown Toronto abruptly beams into the playroom as she's never seen it before. Toronto's financial towers are wreathed in thick smoke, their top thirds invisible from the ground. People clog the streets. Lights flash from ambulances and fire trucks. Condo towers sport broken windows like blackened eyes with whole floors torn apart. Two tiny people huddle forlornly on a balcony twenty stories up, waving a white bedsheet. Below, a TTC streetcar is split open like a Jiffy popcorn container, its seats on fire.

What the fuck? A shiver runs through Anna's body. Feeling the flickering burn of xhen in her kidneys, she rises to her feet. *I must have got in the car just before this happened.*

The screen cuts to a reporter doing a live report at Yonge and Dundas Square. "Toronto Police have yet to release a statement," he says in a calm voice, though his eyes look a bit frantic. Behind him, people stream up Yonge Street. Some wear club clothes, others suits or business attire. Still more are dressed in bathrobes and pyjamas. "Eyewitness reports claim—there!" the reporter cries, pointing behind the camera. The frame jumps to pan wildly across the sky, but whatever the news crew is tracking appears as pixelated noise on the screen.

Anna gasps. *There's more of them!*

"Did you get it, Maddie?" the CBC reporter's asking, his wide-eyed stare looking at someone out of view. Abruptly, he seems to refocus. He stares into the lens. "Peter," he says in a calmer voice, "I can confirm the eyewitness reports. It is a large flying, orange—"

He breaks off as a woman's hand reaches into the frame to shove him forward. "Run!" orders a female voice. The news feed becomes a blur of pavement, running feet, and screams.

No, no, no, Anna thinks, starting to tremble as the station throws the view back to the news anchor, gamely narrating the impossible scene. As the footage loops, xhen prickles in her forehead and races down her back.

My flashlight didn't hurt that thing in the garage. What are the odds guns or bullets will? She glances down at Malcolm on the couch, grateful he's asleep and not out in the streets. *If I'm right, I may have the only weapon that works against them.* Excitement surges through Anna's body. *Last night, I touched xhen for the first time in years. It must be connected. And if I figure out how, Jason will have to see I'm right.*

As determination washes through her, Anna dashes upstairs. Twisting to unzip her dress, she wrenches it off over her head. She rummages through her dresser, changing into black yoga pants, a black T-shirt, and her dark-grey hoodie. She slips on her running shoes and pauses on her way back downstairs to kiss her sleeping children.

Back in the playroom, Anna retrieves her phone and stuffs it in her sweatshirt pocket. She hovers over Malcolm, torn between waking him and letting him sleep. *He doesn't understand xhen.* When they were still dating, she'd tried a couple of times to tell him about her strange adolescence. He'd listened, but she could tell he didn't understand, not really. *There's no time to explain it now.*

Malcolm murmurs something. Anna freezes as he twists on the cushions, his eyelids flickering, but he doesn't wake. "I'll be home before you know I'm gone," she whispers, dropping the lightest of kisses on his forehead. "I love you."

Then she's out the front door, the keys to her Honda Civic tightly clutched in her hand.

Chapter 6

Jason – Spotlight

Vancouver, BC: Monday, August 18

Jason exits the boutique cradling a large bouquet of deep-pink roses, bouvardia, Italian ruscus, and myrtle against his chest. He steps into the street, only half turning to acknowledge the chirpy chorus of goodbyes behind him. *Buying flowers for your wife is not a big deal,* he thinks as he crosses the street to cut through Emery Barnes Park. Yet the clerks never fail to gush about how lucky his wife is to be married to a doctor and a romantic. Jason considered shopping online or going elsewhere, but Margo has firm opinions about which florists in town do good work. *She loves their stuff,* he thinks. *And it's practically on our doorstep.*

Access to such conveniences was a large factor in their decision to buy a condo after he finished his residency. Located on the edge of Yaletown, their building had checked every box: ocean views, walking distance to the hospital and dozens of restaurants, a cab ride away from the downtown theatres, and steps to the seawall for Margo's morning runs.

Don't forget easy access to nosy florists, he adds.

He can practically hear her retort: *You're such a bear when you don't sleep well.*

Normally, blackout blinds and a white noise machine help Jason to get a full rest when he's working the night shift, but fitful would be a generous description for his previous night's sleep. He inhales a lung-cleansing breath as he walks past the park's circular fountain surrounded by vine-covered trellises, to follow the artificial stream that flows parallel to Richards Street. He passes the usual assortment of young couples enjoying the last of the day's warmth, each accompanied by a baby in a stroller, a dog, or both. The women's heads all turn in his direction. *Checking out the flowers.* Jason stoically ignores their curious glances to consult the Bremont wristwatch Margo bought him for their anniversary last year. His next shift starts in an hour. Plenty of time to surprise her at rehearsal. And walking clears his head.

It had better, he thinks. After his panic attack, Jason's night had been subpar. Clarissa had been determined to keep him in her bad books. He appreciated her frustrations, but she hadn't listened when he'd apologized. On the plus side, Mrs. Harrington's chest pains had turned out to be acid reflux, not a recurrence of her heart failure. Confirming that had taken hours, and Clarissa had pushed to keep her another night for observation. Jason hadn't argued. The hardest aspect of his work is deciding when to discharge patients with tricky conditions. While in the hospital, there are always other actions he can take—assessments, dietary adjustments, imaging, or blood tests. Once discharged, however, their fates slide beyond his influence.

Just like Anna, he thinks as he continues up Richards Street. *Yet she still manages to complicate my life at a distance.* He shifts the flowers to look at his phone, expecting another missed call or a barrage of waiting texts. But his notifications are empty, as they have been all day. After such impassioned pleas the night before, her silence feels like a rebuke.

I only wanted that stupid blanket because I gave it to Mom. In the moment of his late arrival at his mother's deathbed, he'd been desperate for a connection to Chun-Mei, no matter how trivial. *I shouldn't have taken everything out on Anna, even if she always gives as good as she gets.* He rolls his shoulders, still ashamed that she'd goaded him into lashing out at such a stressful time. The nurses had rightly looked disgusted with them both.

His mind also keeps returning to the other part of their call. Why would anyone in their right mind want xhen back? He remembers the unholy hours they kept during those years, the school assignments they abandoned on the altar of insatiable curiosity, and the friends who were unceremoniously dropped by the wayside. *She's got Malcolm and the kids to keep her grounded. She probably slept on it and decided to leave it alone.*

Jason considers this idea for half a block and then shakes his head. *Anna's not wired that way.*

Yet he also hasn't heard from Dave. *There's no way Anna would leave him out if she believed xhen was back.*

When they'd first met in kindergarten at Dovercourt Public School, Dave had been Jason's best friend. Anna had largely ignored them, preferring the company of their female classmates until some indeterminate shift occurred in Grade 4. She'd suddenly decided Dave should be her friend, too. With both Dave's parents doing shift work—his father in policing and his mother in nursing—he'd spent most of his time outside of school at the Lin house. When the twins turned ten, Chun-Mei had bought Jason a bunk bed, reasoning that if Dave was going to be there so much, he might as well have a suitable place to sleep.

When was the last time we talked? Jason wonders as he turns right onto Robson Street. He jaywalks across the one-way street, heading for the long back alley that runs behind the Centre in Vancouver for Performing Arts, where Margo is mounting her production of Judith Thompson's *Perfect Pie*. He's lost touch with everyone else from high school, but he and Dave reconnected while his friend was recovering from his heart attack. Their calls had stopped again once Dave was well enough to travel and fixate on his new passion for teaching kids to code. *I should call anyway. Find out how that's going.*

Uneasy thoughts of his commitments to his sister and best friend percolate through Jason's mind as he edges around a couple of delivery trucks, protecting the bouquet. The theatre's back door is propped open to facilitate smoke breaks. Jason slips in, nodding to the security guard. Pausing to let his eyes adjust to the darkness, he gingerly skirts the bits of sets cluttering the shallow backstage area.

The lights nearly blind him as he edges around the dark floor-to-ceiling curtains that form the wings. On stage are the cast's four actors, all Asian women. They're ringed by the stage manager, lighting designer, and tech crew, each listening intently. Yet Jason only has eyes for the woman in the centre of the group.

Clad in hip-hugging black jeans, a metallic bronze lace tank top that shows off her perfectly toned arms, and his mother's ruby, Margo's eyes shine as she gives her notes, her hands moving in an elegant dance to emphasize each point. Not wishing to disturb her flow, Jason takes a step back into the shadows. The movement draws his wife's sharp eye.

"Jason!" she exclaims in a voice both startled and pleased.

"Sorry to interrupt." Feeling like a kid called to the principal's office, Jason lifts the flowers like a hall pass and extends them to Margo. She coos delightedly, admiring the bouquet before sweeping it into the nearest actor's hands. In the next moment, she's in his arms.

His world tunnels as Margo's perfume envelops him and their lips meet. The stage breaks into spontaneous applause that Jason barely hears. His bad sleep, even worse shift, and worries about Anna drop away. There's only his wife, her dark eyes aglow in the stage lights as she pulls back, beaming. "You spoil me," she whispers, her voice pitched for his ears alone. He holds her gaze, trusting the attraction thrumming between their bodies to answer for him.

"Oh, that's so romantic!" trills a voice behind them. As Margo steps out of his embrace, Jason turns his head to see Ivy Wong—her best friend and business partner—with her hands clasped below her chin in a pose that unknowingly echoes the clerks at the florist's shop. Sporting dark sunglasses on top of her head and a belted floral print dress, Ivy claims the bouquet as though she's just won a medal. "I'll grab a vase, Mar. There's one in the green room."

Before rushing off, Ivy throws Jason a *you've had your moment, now let the genius get back to work* look. Aware of the scrutiny surrounding them, he manages not to roll his eyes. Ivy and Margo met in a history class at UBC. Their friendship was entrenched long before Jason arrived on the scene. They'd been so attached at the hip that Jason had, at one point, considered breaking up with Margo. His mother advised him to be patient. These days, he accepts that something about Ivy will always rub him the wrong way, and that Margo adores her.

He can't deny her positive influence on Margo's career. After graduation, Ivy went into finance and helped Margo to incorporate her tiny theatre company. She continues to lead fundraising efforts each season, working her vast network to get Margo into rooms with wealthy backers. They often go on vacations together, always organized by Ivy. Last year, it had been fashion week in Paris and a week's skiing in Aspen. In November, it'll be an island-hopping vacation to the Maldives. Sometimes Jason and Louis are invited, like the summer they all went to Singapore for a few weeks. Jason had been off between his undergraduate and medical degrees and had jumped at the chance to travel. He finds Lou pleasant company, but most of the time, the women go alone.

I'd like to see the Maldives someday, Jason thinks, watching Margo settle back into her rehearsal. *But not with Ivy.*

Catching his wife's gaze, Jason waves goodbye. She smirks back, her raised eyebrow promising more effusive thanks later. Grinning as he goes back outside, Jason feels immeasurably lighter in mind and spirit. Wrapped in his contemplation of what exactly "later" might entail, his feet carry him toward the hospital on autopilot.

As he enters the retail district around Granville Street, however, a cry of alarm penetrates his mental fog. Automatically, Jason looks for someone collapsed on the ground or two cars crunched together. Instead, he spots a group of people huddled in front of an electronics store window. Curious, Jason stops and cranes his neck to get a glimpse of the TV screens inside.

It's Toronto, he realizes as the news footage flashes a glimpse of the CN Tower. His mouth drops open as he takes in the carnage of destroyed apartment buildings and panicked crowds in the streets. *Anna,* he thinks instinctively, his lower back cramping. His world seems to teeter, threatening to careen out of balance. As if on cue, his phone pings with a text. Jason checks it with shaking hands. Yet the message isn't from Anna or Dave, but his father. Panicked heat rushes up Jason's spine as he reads:

I'm @Sick Kids

They're short-handed in the ER, not going home tonight

Will call tomorrow; some interesting cases to discuss

Oh shit. Jason forces himself to keep walking, taking in deep gulps of air as he tries to regain a semblance of calm. The Hospital for Sick Children's emergency room must be nightmarishly overrun for his father, a clinical researcher known to keep eccentric hours, to have been called out of his laboratory. It's all too easy for Jason to picture hospital beds lining the corridors, full of injured children and hysterical parents.

Okay, Dad, he texts back. **Take care.**

Something attacked me in the garage, whispers his sister's voice.

No, Jason thinks. *Our training was more like a spiritual exercise. She's projecting our past onto some bigger tragedy.* He puts his phone away, dismissing his memory of Anna's frightened voice. *Whatever's happening in Toronto has nothing to do with us.*

As he enters the hospital, Jason piles that thought like another stone on the bedrock of his skepticism. He resolutely turns his attention to Mrs. Harrington and his other patients, ignoring the prickling burn in his back.

Chapter 7

Anna – SkyDome

Toronto, ON: Monday, August 18

Anna stops for a red light at Bloor Street, but her drive is an otherwise straight shot down Keele, past the dark sprawl of High Park, all the way to Lakeshore Boulevard. She tries not to think about Malcolm, about their kids, about the utter insanity of what she's doing.

What if I'm wrong? Maybe the garage isn't connected to whatever's happening downtown. The longer she drives, the more her instinct to help feels irrational. *Xhen has been gone five times as long as we trained,* she reminds herself. *You made peace with that a long time ago.*

Anna swallows as she changes lanes, aware of precisely how hard won her peace has been. And of the longing that has swept over her at odd moments over the years, its touch as familiar and haunting as an old lover's. *Xhen killed that thing.* Her fingers tighten on the wheel. *This could be my chance to understand.*

She keeps driving. Every few minutes, she pulls over as an ambulance or fire truck screeches past, lights flashing, sirens blaring. On the other side of the highway, the Gardiner Expressway West is jammed with cars heading out of the city. Toronto traffic is demented at the best of times, but she's never seen it this bad on a Monday night, not even after a playoff game. And no one's heading east like her.

Take the hint, whispers a small voice. *Go home. Malcolm will be worried if he wakes up and you're gone. Someone else will sort it out.*

But she doesn't pull over, clinging to her memory of how it felt to hold xhen again as she strains for a glimpse of the sky. Between the half dozen low-income apartment buildings clustered close to the highway and the maple trees growing along Lakeshore Boulevard, it's hard to see much until she approaches the Canadian National Exhibition's grounds. There, the horizon opens.

To her left, the CN Tower pierces the night. Normally, the tower's night lighting is enchanting, especially if the children are in the back seat. Tonight, the red and white patterns feel ominous as they slice through the dark smoke billowing up from the city below. The whole scene has a hazy, unreal feeling. *It's creepier in person than it looked on TV.* Anna forces herself to focus on the road as she replays the fight in the garage, turning it over and over in her mind.

Do I need physical danger for xhen to manifest like that? Can I touch it without something trying to eat my face? She reaches for her inner well of power; immediately, the car begins to drift to the right. There had been a time when she could drive while holding xhen, but she's rusty. Anna lets the energy go, resolutely setting her hands at ten and two o'clock on the steering wheel.

As she's passing the Princes' Gates on the eastern side of the Exhibition, the air in the car turns acrid. Coughing, Anna lowers the windows, but the smell is everywhere. *Like the whole city is on fire.* She keeps driving, searching the sky for that telltale orange flash until she notices the police car barricading the intersection of Lakeshore and Lower Spadina directly ahead.

Her chest tightens in reflexive fear. *You haven't done anything wrong. Be calm.* Then her stomach rolls. *Damnit, my license! My wallet's at home!* Her eyes dart wildly, looking for an escape, but there isn't any way to avoid this conversation. Feeling queasy, Anna slows down as the officer approaches, hoping it's someone she knows through Malcolm. *Oh shit, here we go.*

"Ma'am, Lakeshore is closed." To her dismay, she doesn't recognize the officer, a white woman stern enough to be one of her Irish aunts. What Anna glimpses of her weathered expression is exhausted but firm as she flashes her Maglite into the car. Anna flinches as the beam passes over her face, struggling to retain her composure in its glare. "Where are you headed?"

"My sister's," she lies, waiting for the demand to produce her license. "King and Yonge."

The woman winces. "Turn around and go home, ma'am. You won't be able to get anywhere near that intersection. There's a police line from University Avenue to Church Street and from Front Street to Dundas Street. It's all closed off."

"But she called me," Anna pleads. "She's got two little kids. Please, I need to find them." Putting fear into her voice isn't hard. At the same time, part of her desperately wants to confess her ludicrous plan. Then the police officer will laugh and send her home to Malcolm with firm orders to stay inside.

"Go home, ma'am." The officer sniffs sharply, her face wrinkling in suspicion. Eyes the colour of slate search hers. "Have you been drinking this evening?"

That stupid glass of champagne. "No," Anna lies. The officer's frown deepens. *I only had one!* Frantic, Anna grasps for the best excuse she can think of as she tries to breathe through her nose. "I'm nine weeks pregnant."

The officer exhales and stoops lower, her face filling the window and Anna's field of view. Crow's feet sit heavy around her eyes, and her thin lips droop with weariness. She smells like sweat and cigars. "Listen to me." The firmness remains, but it's tempered with sympathy that feels genuine. "There's nothing you can do for your sister. She and her kids are probably safe at one of the shelters. What you can do is go home and protect that baby. You're going to need a good reason for happiness, trust me."

Despite the possible champagne smell on her breath, Anna can't stop herself from leaning forward. "What happened?" she whispers, putting her hand on the woman's, half knowing the answer. "Please tell me what's going on. I . . . I'm scared."

There's a flash of something in the corner of Anna's eye and perhaps the faintest pulse of blue before the officer pulls her hand away, shaking her head. *She's going to order me out of the car. Malcolm will be livid if I get busted for drinking and driving.* But the woman says, "Look over there. The skyline, see? Look at the condo building near the Scotiabank Tower."

Anna follows her gesturing hand and gasps. The building's top floors are gone.

"And those two, there. Whole floors blown apart like they never were."

Oh no. Anna remembers the propane shard in the garage with its razor-sharp edges. At once, the immensity of the task she's set for herself rolls over her like a tsunami.

But the officer isn't finished. "The dispatchers are saying crazy things on the radio, like five hundred people dead. That it's aliens. Maybe they're right." She pauses, fidgeting with the weatherstripping at the base of the car window. Anna smells fear, sudden and spiky, and realizes the older woman craves reassurance as badly as she does.

"I saw something," the officer says, her voice quavering. "Three things, long and orange, rose from the base of those same towers. They went south across the lake ten minutes ago."

Anna shivers as the hair on the back of her neck stands up.

"They were bright, like the sun." The woman exhales a shaky breath and seems to remember Anna. "You want no part of this. Go home now. Promise me you will."

Anna tries to smile as fresh bile threatens to climb up her throat. She coughs. The officer frowns. The name tag on the woman's uniform says B. Edwards. "I will, Officer. Thank you."

The expression on Edwards's face shifts. She stares at Anna like something doesn't wash, her uneven eyebrows drawing together over her bold nose. *Dave says cops are the most skeptical people alive.* With his adoptive father on the force, he knew the truth of that long before she did. No one gives the hairy eyeball of doubt like Police Chief Henry Montcalm, but this woman could give him a run for his money. *They assume everyone's lying. And right now, you are.*

Edwards, however, doesn't stop Anna from rolling up the window. "You take care," the officer orders, stepping back. She eyes Anna as she makes an illegal left onto Spadina. Heart hammering, Anna drives up a small rise and into the heart of Toronto's condo forest.

Sporadic crowds roam the street, slowing her down. There's a heavy police presence here, too; it looks like Edwards was wrong and they're starting to push the perimeter farther west. Anna turns left on a side street and finds a parking spot to ditch the car. She'll have to go the rest of the way on foot. *What about Tim and Erin?* she thinks, unbuckling her seatbelt. *What happens to them and to Malcolm if you open this box again? Listen to Edwards. Go home.*

Oh, shut the fuck up, Anna tells herself, smothering her fear. She roots around in the back seat. One of her mother's scarves is tucked inside a box of books from their house. Anna wets it with the dregs of a water bottle and ties it around her mouth to mitigate the smoke. She locks the car and trots back to Spadina Avenue, pulling her hoodie up to cover her hair.

Smoke and sirens fill the air as Anna moves through the crowd. She's not the only person wearing a makeshift mask. *Why are so many people standing around?* She spots fussing children here and there. Other adults stand texting on their phones, occasionally lifting their devices high above the sea of heads to take a photo. Some seem excited. *Edwards said there were casualties. Why aren't people panicking?* She spots a few clusters of people heading west laden with backpacks, pushing strollers, and pulling suitcases, but they're the outliers. The rest of the crowd shifts eagerly, as though keen for answers. *They don't know they need to run.*

Ignore them. Anna walks briskly, her shoulders back and her chin up. She reaches for xhen, letting her awareness of it suffuse her posture like invisible armor. She's used this trick of presumed purpose to breeze backstage at concerts, sneak into movie theatres with no ticket and, as an adult, confidently enter tense negotiations on behalf of her clients. It works equally well now. The security contractors assembling the fence don't look at her. Neither do the three nearest police officers.

Anna makes for the SkyDome stadium's south end, moving quickly past the strip of restaurants, bars, and service shops that cater to both visiting sports fans and the local condo population. *Don't stop. There are low buildings on the other side of the SkyDome, near that train museum. I'll have a good view of the sky there.* She moves forward, certain that she'll need that advantage when the creatures return. *If they come back. And what if you're right? What then?*

An echo of joy courses through her body as she pauses across from the SkyDome's ninth gate. Despite the anxiety twisting her guts, Anna grins and stands tall. *I destroy them.*

As though in answer to her bravado, the small of her back begins to burn. The pain is so sudden that she cries out, reaching with both hands to brace against its sharpness. In unison, a pair of police officers closer to the gate turns to look at Anna. The shorter man moves toward her, a host of questions plain on his face. But as dread dries her mouth to the consistency of moldy bread, instinct makes Anna whip her head south.

Three orange shapes streak through the night, moving fast over the lake and straight toward her. Massive is the only word for them: They're ten times bigger than the thing in her garage. *Was it a baby?!* Overwhelmed, she half turns to head back to her car. *I can't do this!*

And then the creatures scream.

The sound travels all the way down to the balls of Anna's feet, making every muscle quiver. Blinding pain fills her head. Her stomach is a giant knot of fear.

How dare you be scared! You want to spend the rest of your life wondering? Her children's faces swim before her eyes. She thinks of them and of the other children in her city who must be terrified. Then she shoves those thoughts away. *It's your time. Go prove you're right.*

Light pulses around Anna's body as her invisible armor seeps up through her clothes and skin to form a shining wall. Gooseflesh ripples over her back and down her legs as adrenaline floods her limbs. The pain recedes, leaving her keenly alert and alive to her new purpose.

The creatures scream a second time. A pale, slender tentacle shoots out of each of their open mouths as orange light flashes around their bodies, brightening the sky with a rancid glow.

Behind her, the SkyDome's glass-and-metal gate explodes.

Chapter 8

Dave – Purpose

Miinikaa First Nation, ON: Tuesday, August 19

Dave bolts upright in his bed, blood pounding in his ears. He gasps, his heart thundering in his chest as though he's just run a mile, not awoken in the dead of night in a cold sweat. An artificial chill gusts down his clammy back from the air-conditioning vent in the ceiling above his bed. He falls back against the pillow, which is too soft for his liking, and waits for his brain to catch up and the panicky feeling of nightmare to subside.

Red minutes tick past on his bedside clock: 1:15. 1:18. 1:20. None of his feelings subside.

Heart attack? After his illness, it's an instinctual fear. He doesn't wear a heart monitor at night anymore. Hasn't in over a year. Dave focuses on his body. There's no telltale tightening or tingling numbness in his arms. *That's not it.* He continues to breathe hard in the darkness, sweating. Then his stomach begins to clench. *Shit, am I going to puke?* He sits up again, willing his head to stop pounding. *Did I drink too much?*

He reruns the evening. After the workshop ended and they'd

reset the classroom for the next morning, he'd walked over to Rockcliffe Bar for dinner with Leona, her boyfriend Ryan Charron, and the teaching assistants. He clearly recalls talking through the day's wins and losses, and the delight on their smiling faces as they toasted their students' progress. *I only had one beer.*

What the hell is wrong with me?

As though in answer, his back begins to burn, way down to either side of his kidneys. His next thought is instantaneous: *Anna. Jason. Something's wrong. Something's really fucking wrong.*

He's out of bed before the decision to get up fully solidifies. He struggles back into his discarded jeans and pulls a hoodie over his head. He grabs his car keys and wallet, cramming them into his pockets with his phone and charging cable. Dave scans the room, a monument to his childhood visits to see Auntie Lee. It's still decorated with posters marking each of his boyhood obsessions: Star Wars, Voltron, Akira, and the Valoi Knights. Satisfied that he's got everything essential, Dave crosses the room in two long steps. He opens the door, carefully avoiding the squeaky floorboard because even in her sixties, Leona's got the ears of a bat, and—

—he's dashing along a dirt road. Ahead, lights flash in the night. Birch and pine trees sway in the wind, their leaves rustling. Three Ontario Provincial Police cars are pulled to the side of the road. There's an ambulance, too, its red and white lights beating a steady strobe pattern against the murky green of the trees. Somewhere, a baby wails. *Oh no. Please, no.*

He runs in time to the flashing—red, white, red, white, red, white—like the world makes sense, like there's still order in it. His gloves drop from his hands—he distinctly hears the soft thud as they fall—but he doesn't stop to pick them up because he's running, running, running toward the brown Buick in the ditch on the side of the road.

"Rose!" he's screaming in a voice high and shrill. "Rose! Rose!"

Sobbing, he runs along the hard-packed dirt, his breath fiery hot in his chest. Sharp pains stab up through his legs, but it doesn't matter, none of that matters, because coming around the edge of the ambulance, he sees the front of the Buick, its hood smashed against the side of the ditch like crumpled brown paper, and the figure slumped over the steering wheel, the end of a long black braid hanging out of the open driver's door.

"ROSE!" Rage, regret, and sorrow ignite an incomprehensible pain in his chest. He drops to his knees, sobbing into his dirt-stained hands as his silver bracelets rattle. Cops cluster around him with their blankly uniform white faces, embarrassed by the rawness of his grief. The baby wails a second time as he looks up—

—and Dave blinks at the familiar cream walls and thick carpet of his aunt's upstairs hallway, dim in the glow of the nightlight she leaves on when he stays with her. *Rose*. The name ripples through his mind, spreading strange eddies that don't belong to him, of pine and gasoline and a policeman's completely unsympathetic voice demanding to see identification.

My birth mother's name was Rose. Rose LaRoque. Dave staggers to his feet in the hallway as though shifting himself free of something heavy and not fully his . . . a dream? More of a nightmare than a dream, but that's not right, either . . . a memory? *What the hell is going on?*

Fresh burning spreads up his spine as xhen's long-dormant warning system pulses back to life, as clear and insistent as the rebooting chime of his laptop. *Annie*, he thinks, as urgent fear surges through him. *Annie's in danger, not Rose. She's my sister. And she needs me. Now.*

"David?"

He freezes in the hallway. "Auntie Lee?" Without waiting for permission, Dave takes a step, pushes open the door to her bedroom, and—

—he's getting up from the dirt to take the squalling baby into his arms. The child's dark head is searing hot against his cheek, the black hair slick with something wet. For a horrible moment, he fears it's blood before realizing that the baby is sweating, the warmth nothing more dangerous than the heat of tears. No cuts or bruises mark the perfect little brown body. He takes the child into his arms and clutches his nephew, crying tears of relief and sorrow into his glossy hair as one of the cops wraps them in a blanket and he—

—meets Leona's eyes. She's sitting straight up in her bed just as he had only moments before. There's no one else in the room; Dave's allergic to Ryan's dogs, so Ryan stays at his own house when Dave's in town. In the glow of the porch light leaking in her window, Leona's eyes gleam like a cat's, bright with unshed tears.

The baby is me, he thinks numbly, staring into her strong face framed by salt-and-pepper hair, unable to speak. Warning pulses through his back a third time, accompanied by the fierce desire to go south. *The baby is me on the night my mom died. That was her body I saw in the car. And I . . . I was you. What the fuck is wrong with me?*

"Nothing's wrong with you, David." His aunt's dry voice cracks around the edges. She clicks on the bedside light, flooding the room with normalcy. "It's happening again, that's all."

What? What do you mean, it's happen—

"Your back is burning," she says, and he drops a hand to his hip, stunned. "Mine, too. Not as strongly as yours, I expect, but I remember. They're coming." She gets out of bed with surprising fluidity for a woman of sixty-five with a history of arthritis and takes his hands in hers. Her skin is warm, and the ache in Dave's back eases as she touches him. "Piiche, listen to me," she says. She'd named him in Anishinaabemowin for the robins that came and went with the seasons the first time his adoptive parents dropped him off to stay with her for the summer. He'd been eight in July 1987, and just beginning his yearly migrations from Toronto to Miinikaa. "You're speaking to me with your mind, not your lips."

Hardly daring to breathe, Dave lifts a hand, so much bigger now than hers, to take her palm. Bracing himself, he lifts it against his own cheek. Her nightmare is there: the flashing cars and the ditch and the white sheet and the wriggling, terrified baby in her arms. Only this time, the grief is washed through with love, so much love for him and his mother that his heart would drown if he were to carry it. "Auntie

Lee." He could stand there until the world ends and it wouldn't be long enough to absorb what she's only begun to explain. "How did you—"

"Later. You need to head south." She grants him a wry smile as she pulls away and puts on her housecoat. "I remember what the pull of a triad feels like. Easier to swim against a current in a thunderstorm as fight that. One of Mei's twins needs you. Anna, I expect, unless Jason's come home again."

"You know about them?" He turns to face her, stunned, as more nighttime memories flood his mind. These, however, are his own: running through the dark with the Lin twins for two and a half crazy years before their training with xhen came to a crashing end. *But I wasn't telepathic then, not by any stretch. Why can I hear thoughts now?*

"David." His aunt smiles. "Chun-Mei Lin and I knew before you were born. Why else would I have let her arrange for the Montcalms to adopt you after we lost Rose?"

A fresh wave of cold sweat breaks over Dave's skin as he gapes at his aunt, completely thunderstruck. Ignoring his shock, Leona bustles him into the hall and the washroom, telling him to pee as though he's still eight years old. By the time he's flushed, washed his hands, brushed his teeth, and gone downstairs, his shock has worn off, but not his wonder. *What else does she know? Did Rose know about me, too?*

Those questions and more simmer on his tongue as Dave enters the kitchen. There's a coffee thermos waiting for him on the counter beside a bag of trail mix. "Miigwech, Auntie," he says automatically, picking up the thermos and tucking the bag into the pocket of his hoodie. Another wave of urgent heat rolls up his back. It takes all his will to stand there instead of bolting for his truck. "But why didn't you tell me before—"

"What's coming won't wait," she says. "I'll make your excuses at the workshop. Take care not to speed. You don't want to be pulled over." Her smile turns soft. "Give Kalos my regards. Tell him it's been too long."

Dave staggers. "You know him, too?" It's too much. His heart begins to pound again.

Smiling, Leona stands on her tiptoes to kiss his cheek. "Go." With one last bear hug, Dave leaves the house. He dashes across the lawn toward his truck, which is parked on the street.

As he tears over the grass, dozens of strange images break against his mind. Compared to Leona's more potent xhen-laced memories, these are tenuous, like spiderwebs strung across a footpath. Confused, Dave instinctively glances down the street. The impressions flashing through his brain intensify without drawing him in to fully experience them: canoeing across the lake in bright sunlight, digging small feet into damp pebbled beach sand, the smell of whitefish roasting over a campfire, and driving on the highway with the windows rolled down and wind lashing hair against cheek.

Dreams, he realizes as his eyes sweep across the dark windows of the neighbouring houses. *I'm seeing their dreams.*

Intertwined with these confections are a handful of darker dreams, as old or older than Leona's memory of his mother and equally laced with pain: of school rooms full of humiliation and sobbing children desperate to go home.

The residential schools. He knows the stories. Everyone up here does. *To receive even a glimpse of what they endured . . .* Dave stops in his tracks, trying to take it in, to give the memories the space they require. Xhen burns in his back, insistent. There's simply no time to match the dreams, happy or dark, with their owners or to begin to understand why he's seeing them. But he stands for another moment in the moonlight, trying to grasp this new glimmer of purpose. *I'll come back. When Annie's safe and everything's done, I'll come back, and I'll figure out why the ancestors have gifted me with this knowledge.*

He starts the truck and takes the back roads down to Sudbury.

Dave's always loved driving at night, especially up here. The bush presses in around the truck's cab, a companionable, peaceful force.

When he gets closer to the city and the two-lane road morphs into a four-lane suburban thoroughfare, snippets of broken conversation from the occasional wakeful mind press against his thoughts. As he drives deeper into Sudbury and more lighted windows line the street, the stray thoughts grow louder and more numerous until he can barely see the road.

Annie. Focus on Annie. She needs you.

To distract himself, Dave turns on CBC Radio 2 and sings along to the Tragically Hip at full blast, grateful when he merges onto the Trans-Canada Highway. It carries him away from the city and its restless people. The truck bears him through smaller communities full of more sleepers, but he casts their dreams free without examining them. They fall away, pebbles bouncing loose off the asphalt road of his mind.

Through it all, danger burns across his lower back. Dave's got a monstrous headache by the time he reaches Parry Sound. Leona's coffee is long gone, and he's yawning every five minutes, so he pulls off the highway at a truck stop for more.

It's there that Kalos finds him.

Chapter 9

Anna – Three to One

Toronto, ON: Tuesday, August 19

The SkyDome's gate disintegrates in a hail of glass shards and twisted metal. Old exercises flood Anna's mind as she drops to her knees and then forward into a prone position. Xhen coalesces around her hands and spreads over her, forming a screen to protect her body as the debris showers the sidewalk and road.

Without any comparable defense, the officers fall. As soon as the rain of wreckage stops, Anna lifts her chin to look. She gasps. There's blood everywhere. One of the men is yelling as he tries to get up; the other is motionless. *Shit!* Rising, she starts to go to them.

Draw the creatures away. Winning is the fastest way to help.

At the sound of Kalos's voice, a fresh adrenaline wave floods her body. Forcing herself up into a run, Anna lurches east toward the CN Tower. There's open parkland outside the train museum on the other side of the street. Blue light quivers around her body as she dashes over the concrete toward it.

With every step, her sense of urgency grows. *Move, move, move!*

Noiseless in flight, the creatures circle the stadium and the base of the CN Tower, flying far enough apart that she can't keep all three in view. Yet beneath their triplicate eyes, Anna's back burns. Recalling the garage and how xhen felt in the instant before she made the energy leap from her palm, she readies herself, knowing it's only a matter of time before they attack her again.

A moment later, the nearest elongates its sinuous body into a fluid dive. Anna raises her hand, her pace faltering as she tries to run and aim. Blue light puddles around her fingers. She blasts it up at the creature. Her shot misses its head but pierces its tail. *Gotcha!*

It roars in answer. From inside its mouth, that strange pale tentacle flares bright white. The air around Anna shivers. Behind her, the next gate in the SkyDome's curving wall explodes. In that instant, she catches something moving in her peripheral vision. Spinning away from the blast, she spots a second creature flying low across the parkland, straight for her unprotected back.

Startled enough to scream, Anna wraps herself in xhen. She drops in a sideways roll, barely evading the flying fragments and the second creature's snapping tentacles. Luckily, she's far enough from the stadium that the concussion wave is nowhere near as bad. She's on her feet again in seconds, searching for the third monster's attack.

They're so goddamn fast! But the last creature is still circling. *Studying me*, she realizes as the roaring monsters converge. *They're intelligent. And they're hunting me together*.

Anna runs farther east, away from the stadium. Something wet spatters her upturned face. Grimacing, she wipes away clear fluid. It has a thicker consistency than water and reeks of sulphur.

Just like the one in the garage. It must be like their blood. If so, I wounded that one more than I hoped. A second later, the creature with the gaping wound in its tail, clearly visible to her from the ground, drops back as though unable to keep pace with its companions. Twisting, it veers south toward Lake Ontario.

Unwilling to let it retreat, Anna pools and thickens her xhen into a long bolt. She aims and fires. This time, her shot pierces its head. Pleasure rushes through her as the creature curls up on itself like a potato bug. It plummets from the sky, vanishing behind more condos. A moment later, the ground shakes. *One down. Two to go.*

Her reprieve is momentary. The larger monster of the two remaining peels away from its partner. It drops toward her, purple tentacles flicking on the sides of its fearsome face as it closes the distance. *Come on,* she thinks, holding her ground as she stares it down, a plan unfurling in her mind. *I'll kill you, too.*

At the last instant, Anna drops to one knee as the monster rockets past her head, twisting to fire another bolt. She misses. The creature's grasping tentacle misses her shoulder by inches. She's too off balance to strike again. As she regroups, the second dives for her.

I'm too exposed here. RUN!

Anna sprints in a zigzagging pattern, cringing as a tentacle brushes the side of her head. Then the first emits more orange light and a bone-curdling screech. Anna searches for its target, ready to defend herself. *It can't be the stadium doors. They're too far away.* She glances up. Understanding freezes her belly. Looming above her is the gigantic TV billboard that advertises baseball games to traffic on the Gardiner Expressway. *They drove me toward it,* she thinks hollowly before the display explodes in a shower of sparks, glass, and metal.

Unable to reverse her direction, Anna wraps herself in xhen. The energy protects her skin, but the force of the sonic explosion knocks her down. She raises her arms in time to protect her head but hits the concrete hard, skidding several metres. Debris rains down on her barrier. For a long moment, she can't do anything but lie there, stunned.

Get up. Get up now or they'll kill you right here! Her left side aches fiercely as she rises, ears ringing, sight blurred, palms skinned raw. Above, the two wingless bodies undulate through the night sky. Their roars thunder across her city like grotesque laughter.

Dragons, she thinks, tracking them as she runs toward the parkland in front of the train museum, fighting to keep her balance and her xhen as fragments of her mother's bedtime stories seep through her mind. Whether grounded in the storytelling traditions of the East or the West, Chun-Mei had loved dragon stories. And with their large heads, thick crests, long snouts, scaled hides, sinuous bodies and whisker-like tentacles, there's a resemblance between these creatures and her mother's legends.

No, Anna decides. *Those hideous things don't deserve an elegant name. They're more like crested, flying worms. Skyworms.* Xhen pulses around her hands as if to confirm her thought.

As she watches, the skyworms thread the surrounding condo buildings, blowing out whole floors of windows with each pass. Then, with a brilliant burst of hot white light, they burrow inside and through separate towers. Furniture bursts through walls and over balconies, marking their passage along the buildings, accompanied by frequent flashes of orange and a silent, glittering cloud of falling glass. At this distance, Anna can't tell if any of the plummeting shapes are people.

It's a distraction, she tells herself, feeling sick. *I can't do anything to help them.*

She keeps moving. As she runs, her foot catches something heavy. Anna trips and falls forward, hands flying out to protect herself.

The object she lands on is sticky, but its flesh yields beneath the pressure of her palms. *Oh fuck, it's a person!* Instinctive horror makes her scrabble back onto her knees. *No*, Anna thinks a breath later, her stomach in free fall as she takes in the rigid, unmoving posture. *It's a body.*

It's a girl. She looks all of sixteen, but enough like Anna that they could be cousins. She's on her back, her black bangs in her eyes. Her long hair is spread across the concrete like a fallen banner. A look of pure rage is frozen on her symmetrical face. Blood has congealed around the half dozen puncture wounds in her unmoving chest, staining her red-and-black basketball shirt and matching pyjama bottoms. A smartphone, its screen smashed, lies just beyond the reach of her splayed fingers. But it's the hint of xhen clinging to her, green as apples and faint as smoke, that brings bile up Anna's throat for the second time.

You tried to fight them, too. She turns from the dead girl's face, swallowing her vomit. *If I'd gotten here faster, I could have helped you.*

Skyworm howls split the night. To the east, the two remaining monsters swoop back toward her. Reluctantly, Anna leaves the dead girl's side. She runs forward. Overhead, the skyworms separate as though guided by some signal she can't hear, peeling left and right to split her attention. Exposed in the open, there's nowhere for Anna to run. *What if they make me explode like that billboard? How do I stop them?*

They will try to consume you like the girl. Kill them now.

Anna knows that soundless voice better than her own name. She stops across from the CN Tower and plants her feet. Encased in an ocean of xhen and with the assurance of Kalos's presence in her thoughts, she feels solid, like a breakwater bracing against an incoming storm. It's exhilarating, this awareness of her surging power. Behind her scarf, Anna shocks herself by grinning as she shapes her xhen into a long, thick cable.

Not a cable. A leash. Take them down.

Turning, Anna targets the left skyworm as it closes in, mouth open, inner tentacle writhing. Three mad eyes—pale yellow to either side, the higher central eye split-pupiled and blazing purple—fixate on her, glittering with malice. Anna hesitates, panting as she awaits instruction. With them in the sky and her on the ground, the advantage is theirs. Her leash feels too insubstantial to shift her survival odds, but she must do something. And Kalos is silent. *I've got nothing to lose! Hit them!*

Hefting her leash in one hand, she propels it at her attacker. It misses, glancing off the skyworm's body. But the creature pulls up as the leash falls away, aborting its attack. Immediately, Anna whirls on her heel, looking for the second monster. Hope fountains in her chest as she gathers her leash for another throw. She tenses, trying to block out their unceasing screams and the gathering pain in her back. This time, she strikes faster and with greater precision, catching the skyworm's exposed neck right behind the rigid, platelike crest that separates its body from its head.

Roaring, the skyworm rushes around her, so fast it's nothing but an orange blur as light flares around its hurtling body. Concrete cracks around and beneath her feet. In her distraction, the leash slithers from the skyworm's neck like an unclasped necklace, freeing it to soar over her.

She gathers xhen as the creature banks sharply around the CN Tower's base. Hot orange light pulses from its scales. Like a sickly meteor, it rejoins its companion. They twist around another condo tower before hurtling back in her direction to start a fresh assault.

Target their mouths. Shell and cup.

Anna obeys, tearing across the grass and past the museum's outdoor collection of steam engines as though she's given up and wants to die. With every stride, she balls xhen in the small of her back. The dead girl's face flashes through her mind as the skyworms take the bait and fly lower, prepared to meet her head on. *No distractions. Focus.*

To her right, an antique train car explodes. Absorbed in crafting her weapon, Anna is slow to form a protective barrier. A piece of shrapnel strikes the back of her leg. She stumbles but ignores the sudden agony because they're closing, closing, and panic won't help her win. Instead, Anna waits until she can taste the sulphuric stink of their breath. Then she reaches behind her back and slams her glimmering ball of xhen down the leftmost skyworm's throat.

Its orange body liquefies like an exploding star, ripped apart by her xhen from the inside out. Chunks of its disintegrating carcass careen into the second creature. It also crashes to the sun-bleached grass in front of the brew pub beside the train museum, plowing a deep furrow in the earth as scales, muscle, and who knows what else envelop Anna in a stinking cloud. From somewhere very far away, she hears faint cheers. Exhilarated, she wipes guck from her face and darts forward for a better look at her remaining adversary.

On the ground, the skyworm is easily three times her height. Recalling the garage, she readies another leash, carefully visualizing her xhen snapping into place like one of those cloth-covered metal slap bracelets she and Jason played with as kids. She hurls the leash at the skyworm's neck. Something hums inside her as it locks into place. The pain in her back is still there, along with her other injuries, but it's countered by her intense pleasure at the skyworm's subjugation. The monster roars, twisting to squirm away. Anna can't help it: she laughs.

The skyworm screams defiance, making her ponytail bob in the current of its fetid breath. Its writhing body flares a brighter orange, the lone mouth tentacle turning white. Cracks appear in the earth beneath her feet as Anna tightens the leash, keeping it taut so the skyworm can't strike her with its thrashing tentacles, three on each side of its head. Another train engine explodes, too far away to damage her or it. *It's too distracted to aim*, she thinks as its ghastly eyes lock upon her face, blazing with inhuman fury. She quivers, fear spiking beneath her bravado. *Get this over with.*

She pulls the leash tighter to slam the monster's head against the broken earth. Yet the skyworm doesn't move. Anna tries again. And again. *I'm not strong enough!*

Oh fuck.

The nearest purple tentacle snaps toward her legs. Anna barely jumps over it. She tries to lengthen the leash, but the skyworm strikes forward. Another dark tentacle gropes for her. She dodges, not laughing now. Sweat drips down the back of her hoodie. She's concentrating so hard that she doesn't see the pale mouth tentacle come over the top of her shoulder until it gives her a foul kiss on her cheek.

Visions flood Anna's mind. She cries out as her brain tries to process the triplicate view from the skyworm's three eyes and its tidal wave of hunger—deep enough to drown her world. Closely coupled to that hunger is desire, a fierce desire to consume her. And in that moment, battered by its monstrous delight, the skyworm whispers a word through her mind that she thought was secret, a word she thought no one knew, not even Jason or Dave.

XENTHIAN.

Sickened to the roots of her soul, Anna stumbles back and rips herself free. As she reels, another purple tentacle lashes onto her leg, instantly subsuming her again in the skyworm's all-consuming hunger. Another tentacle finds her right arm. Anna's xhen falters. Her kidneys are on fire. She gasps for air, but that burns her chest.

Concentrate! A tingling wave of pins and needles spreads from the latched tentacle up and down her leg. The muscles in her thigh, calf, and knee begin to shake. Everything's going numb. Her hold on xhen vanishes.

As she scrambles to reclaim it, the skyworm's wicked face looms above her. A triple image flashes through her head. It's a human face, confusing when seen from three directions but familiar. *It's me*, she thinks at first, but the face is too young, the black hair too long. *The dead girl*, Anna thinks numbly, as the hunger sensation intensifies. *It killed her! And I'm next.*

Something—a tentacle?—strikes the backs of Anna's knees. The girl's image vanishes. Helpless, she drops to the grass, landing on something hard and ridged. She tries to twist, to grab it, but she can't move. Panic constricts her throat because the skyworm's jaws are widening, the pale tentacle inside descending for her face. Its roar is loud enough to break the world.

"Stay down!" a voice bellows.

Completely pinned, Anna almost laughs. "I am—" She gasps just before a close-range gunshot sounds. Someone wearing a black Kevlar vest and a blue short-sleeved shirt storms into her field of view, unloading a handgun into the skyworm's face at point-blank range. The skyworm strikes out with a tentacle. The officer ducks. As she does, her hat falls to the concrete, revealing her graying hair. *B. Edwards*, Anna thinks with dazed amazement.

But the skyworm doesn't flinch beneath the bullets striking its monstrous face. Only its roars change, ratcheting to a more piercing frequency. Orange light flares through its body as it shifts its tentacles to attack the officer. Anna feels the two pinning her to the ground loosen. She twists free. In a rush, feeling returns to her limbs, but not xhen. Anna grabs the long hunk of iron that was underneath her, perhaps from the destroyed train. One end is sharp and curved, like a pickaxe. *Distract it!*

Gripping the metal, Anna crawls forward on her hands and knees, but the writhing tentacles are blocking her way. Unable to get farther, she shifts tactics and whacks at them like vines in a jungle. The skyworm ignores her, its white tentacle pressed to Edwards's cheek, who is on her knees and moaning in a high, long howl. The creature's scales glow with scalding light, so bright that it sears Anna's eyes. *It's going to kill her!* She strikes blindly, so desperate to help that it takes her precious seconds to realize her metal weapon is useless.

"Stop! STOP IT!" she shouts, both at the skyworm and herself. Anna's forehead prickles and her kidneys burn. Dropping the metal to grasp her returning xhen, she lunges forward. She shapes the energy into a long length as thick as her discarded iron bar. Gripping its base, she lunges for the skyworm's slit-pupiled third eye. It pops like a rotten grape. The creature recoils, snarling.

Jubilation surges through Anna's entire body. She shifts to a two-handed grip so she can swing and smashes the skyworm's face. It reels. Anna sharpens her weapon into an axe-like shape, forming jagged edges to better cleave scale and tentacle. She aims for its gaping maw of teeth. The skyworm's midsection and tail twist and thrash as it tries to find an angle to strike her. Frantic to maintain her advantage, Anna moves faster. After her paralysis, hitting her enemy fills her with manic, satisfying glee. "Die! Die! DIE!" she spits as pale fluid oozes from the skyworm's scales. Each blow spatters her skin with clear, stinging ichor.

By the time she's reduced the head to an oozing, mangled pulp, her hands are numb, and she reeks of sulphur. Anna staggers back from her kill. Exhaustion falls over her in a wave. Xhen flickers weakly around her palms, losing form. Her head aches badly and her side burns, but she doesn't release the energy.

Instead, Anna drops to her knees, using xhen to push and cut through the inert, severed tentacles still wrapped around B. Edwards. *There's so much blood.* It takes several minutes for her to clear enough of the skyworm's carcass to find the woman's grey face and the police vest punctured by no fewer than four tentacles. *She's dead, just like the girl.*

But the officer's stony eyes flicker open. They find her, filled with an eerie gleam that Anna last saw in her mother's eyes in the minutes before Chun-Mei died. "Anna," Edwards breathes. Like they're old friends meeting over coffee.

She rocks back on her heels. "I didn't tell you my name."

Those unearthly eyes stare past Anna's shoulder. "He did."

Hardly daring to hope, she turns.

To her regular sight, the pavement is empty. Yet her mind's eye, filled with xhen, sees his familiar presence. Every hair on Anna's body jumps to attention. *You're deluded!* she remembers Jason shouting years ago. *Everything you think you know about him is a lie! He's not real!*

Anna stares at the tall dark-haired man, dressed in the same elegant, unadorned black clothing she remembers. *Kalos.* To her shock, the face she recalls as being immeasurably old is perhaps a mere decade older than her own, though the aura of age seeping from her teacher remains ancient. Her hands ball themselves into fists as tears prick her eyes. *Where have you been?* she wants to scream. *Why the hell did you leave us?*

Edwards coughs. Reluctantly, Anna tears her gaze from Kalos and back to the dying woman. "Why?" she demands as the first of her tears fall.

"Listen to me, Anna Lin." Sirens wail in the night. In the

distance, people are starting to gather. Anna makes another xhen barrier to shield Edwards and herself from their intrusive eyes. "I chose this death when I saw your light in the sky." The officer's voice is quiet and her face peaceful. "He told me what you are, what was needed. You've given me a purpose." She chuckles, the sound startlingly girlish. "I've been looking for that a long time."

Anna takes her reaching hand, slick with blood.

"My life for yours. I don't regret it."

Xhen flares around their interlocked fingers, quick as a match flame. Pain, not hers, washes over Anna in a flood. She gasps. Edwards sighs, her relief palpable. Her breath is growing shallow, her words hard to hear. "You'll need more help, all three of you, to survive what's coming. He says you mustn't refuse. To let us shield you."

"To die for me," Anna says. The years she spent raging at Kalos and longing for xhen to return take on a sudden, dark heaviness. "For us. That's what you mean."

Edwards squeezes her hand. "I would stay . . . help you. Give George my love. But that was . . ." Her eyes shift to the dead skyworm. "Glorious." The hand in Anna's goes slack. She stares into the officer's sightless eyes, unaware of the tears slipping down her cheeks.

Go home, child. Rest.

Her anger stirs at the sound of Kalos's unmistakable voice, as beautiful as she remembers. "But what are they?" she demands. "Why have they come? What do they want?"

Death and power. Your Kalxhan comes to shelter you.

"My what?" Anna tries to shake off her mounting confusion. *Focus.* "But that girl I found. Was she—"

Kalos is gone.

Still on her knees, Anna stares at Edwards, utterly spent. *It's not supposed to be this way,* she thinks. *No one else is supposed to know what we can do, let alone die for it.*

"Anna!"

She blinks. The voice sounds like Malcolm, but it can't be. *Am I hallucinating? Jason says auditory hallucinations are more common than visual ones.* She's pretty sure he discussed it at dinner with their father when he was home once with Margo, but she can't remember what they decided. Without the pulse of combat, she's uncomfortably aware of her injuries. Her side hurts. Her palms ache. Her bleeding leg is fire. A tear rolls down her face. *I need to go home.*

"Anna!" It is Malcolm, storming through her barrier like it doesn't exist, wearing a police vest thrown over his rumpled undershirt and sweatpants. Relief slams through her exhausted body as he takes her into his arms. "Oh, thank God." He says more in Ukrainian that she doesn't understand, clutching the back of her head with one strong hand.

This is real, she thinks. *It's all real.* Releasing xhen, Anna sags against him, sobbing in earnest. For herself and B. Edwards, whose first name she doesn't know.

Without another word, Malcolm stands. He's only three inches taller than she is, but he lifts her as easily as he would one of their children. Too exhausted to wonder at that, Anna turns her face into his chest, thankful beyond words for his presence. She hides her eyes from the first responders and spectators starting to crowd in, waiting for someone to ask questions she can't answer without sounding insane, or accuse her of murdering Edwards and the girl, or summoning the skyworms, or a thousand other idiocies.

But no one stops them. No one says a word. When Anna lifts her head, all she sees are stunned faces giving them a wide berth.

Malcolm carries her to a car she doesn't recognize and helps her stretch across a plaid blanket that covers the leather back seat. She's asleep before her head hits the cushion.

Part Two

Questions

Chapter 10

Malcolm – Epicentre

Toronto, ON: Tuesday, August 19

Malcolm Nazarenko pulls his next-door neighbour's borrowed Cadillac into her Junction driveway and turns off the ignition. *Anna's alive. We're home. Now what?*

When he'd awoken earlier that night, he had been bewildered to find himself on the playroom couch, clammy as a fever patient. Motionless, Malcolm had listened to the house as he forced down the fear clawing at his throat. *Nightmare? Mine? One of the kids?* But no telltale cry came from upstairs. His own mind was astonishingly blank.

Anna, came his next thought. Reflexively, he'd sat up, feeling in the darkness. When he touched nothing but cool cushions, Malcolm bolted upright, alert in every fiber. *Where is she?*

Gone, whispered the knot in his gut. Shivering, Malcolm rushed upstairs. By the time he'd determined that Anna wasn't in the house, his teeth were chattering hard enough to rattle his jaw. His head was pounding in time to his pulse. *Something's wrong,* his bones muttered. *Find her.*

This is nuts, he thought, fumbling for the ibuprofen in the cupboard over the stove. *It's just a cold. Erin probably picked it up at daycare.* He shook two pills into his palm and grabbed a water glass. *I need rest.* He popped the pills into his mouth, swallowing them dry. *But Anna should be home by now.* His eye fell on his phone, lying on the kitchen counter. He had a text from her, sent at 11:09 p.m.:

Dinner ran late. On my way.

No other messages. Malcolm stood in the kitchen, mulling over his wife's unusual digital silence. *She's worn down with her parents' house, but this is odd. When did it shift? She started acting weird last night after chasing off those raccoons—*

"The garage!" He dashed for the back door. Outside, he'd tasted the tang of sulphur on his tongue a second before smelling rotten eggs. *Gas leak?* he wondered. *The closest line is halfway down the block.* His unease had quadrupled as he burst into the garage and pulled the light bulb string dangling from the ceiling, his eyes sweeping the space like searchlights.

No Anna.

Around him, the garage had been eerily still. The smell of sulphur, which he had dismissed earlier in the day, was so overwhelming it made him gag. Every hair on his body screamed with its wrongness as another gut-churning shiver swept over his damp limbs. *Where the hell is she?*

A half second later, he spotted the SUV's flat tire. *When did that happen?* From there, his eyes hopped to a pair of out-of-place plyers, an assortment of rearranged toys, and a plastic bin awkwardly pushed into place. Dragging it out and popping the lid was the work of seconds.

"Christ!" Malcolm had staggered back from the stinking, fearsome thing inside. *Anna hid it,* he thought, half wild with fear. *She must have. But what is it? Did it hurt her? Are there more?*

The last question brought a scorching awareness to his mind, accompanied by a massive, thrumming pull. It lurched through Malcolm's belly from his solar plexus all the way to his kidneys, physically spinning him to face southeast. *She's that way*, he thought with sobering certainty, his body quivering like a magnet drawn by a massive lodestone. *Go. Now!*

The next thing Malcolm knew, he was standing on Nancy Coleman's doorstep, trembling as he begged their neighbour to stay with his sleeping children while he borrowed her car. Mercifully, she hadn't asked questions, although her sharp eyes promised a thorough follow-up. He hadn't cared. In his rush to open the Cadillac's door, Malcolm had dropped her keys three times. He drove down Keele Street with manic speed, wishing he'd grabbed his emergency siren along with the police vest he'd somehow managed to throw over his clothes.

High Park's shadowy forest was a blur as he drove to Lakeshore, the urgent command sounding in his blood like the tick of a clock. He found himself praying for Anna's safety, making bargain after bargain with God. *Protect her and I'll get the kids to church every Sunday morning instead of sleeping in. Keep her safe and I'll be patient, even when they're going nuts. Bring her back to me and I will never tease her about her obsession with tidiness ever again.*

Sitting now in Nancy's car, the only other thing he remembers about that drive is . . . odd. The memory lingers, stranger in its way than the creature Anna killed. Malcolm's consciousness continues to shy away from it, just as his eyes had when he first glimpsed her by the SkyDome.

Anna had been wielding a shining blue light as she attacked a gigantic horror of a thing. *Impossible*. But when he blinked hard and looked again, she was still there. Fighting it.

Kinetic energy had surged through Malcolm's body, suppressing his awe. *Protect her!* it commanded. And he ran, closing the space between them faster than he thought it was possible for him to move.

By the time he'd reached Anna's side, the monster was dead, and she was kneeling over a police officer's body. Woman. Late fifties. Short greying red hair like faded ribbons around her blood-spattered face. Her badge identified her as B. Edwards of 51st division. Malcolm didn't know her.

Without thinking, he'd picked Anna up and fled . . . *a crime scene? A terrorist attack? Some sort of monster invasion?* He'd spotted at least two hulking corpses, both an order of magnitude larger than the creature in their garage. Whatever the hell had happened, whatever Anna had done, he'd bet his badge there were more victims. And he'd made no effort to help.

Safe now in Nancy's car, Malcolm takes a deliberate breath. *You fled with her*, a quiet voice observes. *There will be consequences. The chief will have no choice.* Throughout his career, Malcolm's done his best to keep the friendship between the Lins and the Montcalms on the down low, but it's widely known that his wife grew up with Dave, the chief's only son. *He can't risk being partial. It'll hinge on how fast photos surface.*

At first, leaving with Anna, he had feared they'd be mobbed. He can't recall anyone taking their picture; the crowd had seemed too stunned. Yet he's done enough street work to know that in the smartphone era, it's a flimsy hope. *When photos emerge, you'd better have a story.*

Anna stirs in the back seat, jolting his tired brain from its ruminations. *Slow down*, he tells himself. *There's no need to panic.* Malcolm coughs and belatedly realizes just how bad the car smells. *She's soaked in its fluid. Blood? Whatever. Nancy's going to be furious.*

He gets out. The night air is cool and fresh against his skin. He wishes Nancy wasn't waiting for them in the house, but there'd been no way around involving her. Resigned, he opens the back door. Anna's on her side, the soggy blanket bunched between her and the seat's buttery leather. Her mouth is slightly open, her face slack. She looks so much like their children that he smiles. *Did she really kill those things?* Standing over her, he hardly believes it.

A dog barks down the street. Wary of prying eyes, Malcolm clicks the remote lock on Nancy's car key and slips it into his pocket. Bracing himself for back pain, he reaches into the car and gathers his wife in his arms. Anna sighs as he pulls her and the disgusting blanket to his chest. He gets a good grip, hefts her, stands, and knocks the car door shut with his hip. Some remnant of adrenaline bears them to the house. *I'll pay for this tomorrow*.

The front door opens as he comes up the steps. Nancy's curious face peers at him through the storm door's screen, studying every detail. He beckons with his chin. Nancy steps onto their porch in her frumpy housecoat, adjusting her red glasses as she holds the door open for them.

"Good Lord!" she whispers, nose automatically wrinkling from the smell as he carries Anna inside. "She's a sight! Were you downtown? I watched TV while you were gone. It's like a war zone down there. You should have taken her straight to St. Joe's Hospital, Malcolm," Nancy huffs, gesturing to Anna's leg. "She's bled right through Rex's blanket."

"If the stain won't come out, I'll replace it," Malcolm promises, puffing as he heads for the stairs. "Please, would you go up ahead and open our bathroom door?"

Nancy's brown eyes narrow. She makes a disgruntled noise. Malcolm stiffens his shoulders. *Don't start, please*. Something in his face seems to change Nancy's mind. His neighbour sweeps past him, her head tilted at a stubborn angle.

In the en suite bathroom, Nancy opens the shower door as Malcolm gently sets Anna on its floor. He moves her into a sitting position, stretching her legs out and propping her slumping head up against the corner. Together, he and Nancy work the blanket free.

Anna's yoga pants have crusted to her wound. It takes Nancy a while to pick away the black cloth. Beneath, her leg oozes blood around a small piece of metal. "You better hope it hasn't cut muscle or a vein," Nancy mutters and continues a stream of complaints about the stupidity of conducting field medicine in the twenty-first century.

"It doesn't look deep," she says, getting their first-aid kit out from under the sink. She expertly cleans and dresses the injury.

"The children were fine," Nancy tells him as they finish. She stands with effort, holding on to the vanity's ceramic top for balance. "Not a peep."

Malcolm nods and deflates against the bathroom wall like a three-day-old balloon, hoping his neighbour will take the hint and go.

"She may have other injuries," Nancy continues, her voice full of professional authority as she picks up the sopping blanket and folds it into a messy square. Clear liquid immediately begins to drip from the blanket's tasseled fringes, intensifying the bathroom's reek.

"Her clothes are ruined. You'll have an easier time cutting them off." She gives him a sidelong look. "Why was Anna downtown, Malcolm? Except for her work on her parents' house, she's been an absolute homebody since Chun-Mei died."

God, I wish I knew. "She had a client meeting. Scissors are a great idea, but I'm okay from here," Malcolm says, forcing himself to his feet. "I'll walk you to the door."

Nancy's lips twist. "I can help."

"We're good, thank you," Malcolm says with genuine kindness, putting a firm hand on Nancy's shoulder. "You must be exhausted, too. It's so late." He firmly escorts their neighbour downstairs. "We're so grateful for your help," he says. "Here's your key. I'm sorry about the mess. You'll want to get the car's interior cleaned for sure. Please keep your receipt. I'd be happy to reimburse you."

"I—"

"Thanks again, Nancy. You were such a lifesaver. Good night now." He closes the front door on her indignant glare and locks it.

Upstairs with the scissors, Malcolm gingerly cuts Anna free of her clothes. Her whole left side is scraped and bruising. Her palms are skinned. She doesn't stir while he washes her clean with the detachable showerhead, taking care to keep her leg dressing out of the water.

When she's in fresh pyjamas, Malcolm tucks Anna into bed. As he lies down beside her, a wave of vertigo crashes over him. The pillow swims beneath his head. The alarm clock on his nightstand reads 3:09 a.m. He closes his eyes. But his mind, no longer preoccupied with tasks, brims with questions. *Why didn't she tell me? What are those things? Where'd they come from?*

Malcolm rolls over. As his eyes adjust to the room's darkness, Anna's face comes into focus on the other pillow. He vividly remembers the first day they met. Early into his time with the force, he'd attended one of Chief Montcalm's community picnics. Anna, at loose ends after finishing her Classics degree at the University of Toronto, had been recruited by Sarita Montcalm, the chief's wife, to help organize the event. Malcolm had spotted Anna standing by the barbecue station, hip cocked, clipboard in hand, giving instructions to the volunteer cooks. Instantly, he was smitten. Still, it had taken him the better part of the day to find an excuse to talk to her.

He tries to fit both Annas together: the confident young woman who'd turned with a knowing smile and saw right through his dumb question about where to find more serviettes, and his level-headed wife of nine years who snuck out to kill monsters.

It makes no sense, he thinks, brushing a piece of damp hair from her face while a wounded feeling tightens his chest. *I know you better than anyone. What were you thinking*? The temptation to shake her awake and ask is overwhelming. Instead, Malcolm watches her eyeballs flicker behind her eyelids like fish darting in an aquarium.

A soft chime echoes in the bedroom, accompanied by the false dawn of his phone flaring with an incoming text. Malcolm reaches for the device. It's from Staff Sergeant Mitchell Waddington:

Folks, I regret to inform you that we lost Constable Marc Ernsting tonight. Wanted you to hear it from me first. Happened outside the SkyDome. I just left his house.

His family is gutted. I'm gutted. He was a damn good investigator.

We've had other officer and civilian fatalities and are actively

working to determine who's missing. Please confirm your receipt of this message.

Instantly, the thread explodes in a mix of confusion, sadness, and outrage. Malcolm flicks the phone's sound off and turns it face down on his nightstand as his eyes burn. He doesn't know Marc well. They were both at the academy, both married with kids. *He and his husband have girls,* Malcolm thinks. *Older than our kids. Jesus, his family. How will they cope?*

He tosses in the dark for another hour. Sleep doesn't come. At 5:45 a.m., he sits up and flips his phone over. A missed call notification jumps to his attention. It's from Chief Montcalm.

Anna's car, he thinks with a sudden rush of unease. *They found it downtown.* Malcolm forces himself to get a drink of water from the bathroom and scrub the grit from his eyes. *Easy. No one's worried about cars when people are missing or dead.* Closing the door, he calls back.

"Nazarenko, what time did you turn in last night?" Chief Montcalm demands without preamble.

"Around eleven." Malcolm clears his throat. "I heard about Ernsting," he says, hoping the chief will attribute his strain to shock. "What do you need—"

"The situation's evolving," the chief says in a tight voice. "I'm on site at the SkyDome, which seems to have been the epicentre of last night's attack. I've got Bob Cloar putting together a task force. I want you here by 0700."

Malcolm swallows. "Anna's sick, sir. I've got no one to watch—"

"Nazarenko, I've got over three hundred confirmed dead and a thousand reported missing," the chief says in his zero-nonsense voice. "I've got three officers down, carcasses in the streets straight out of a Hollywood horror movie, and the mayor on the horn with the prime minister and the premier formally requesting a state of emergency. No one's got tape of the monsters, but the media apparently have footage of someone who fought back and then disappeared without a trace."

The chief pauses to take a breath. Malcolm, realizing he's been holding his, angles his mouth away from the speaker and lets the air out in a controlled rush as the chief continues. "Call Sarita if you must. She'd never say no to your family. But I need my best here."

"Yes, sir." Malcolm hangs up. Thinking of his flat tire, he texts his partner for a ride, grateful that carpooling isn't unusual in their working relationship. *One less complication.*

As he comes out of the bathroom, Tim stumbles into their bedroom, knuckling his eyes.

"Come on, big guy." He sweeps his seven-year-old son into his arms before the boy can climb onto the bed beside his mother. To Malcolm's surprise, his back doesn't ache at all. "Let Mommy sleep."

Downstairs, Malcolm plunks Tim at the kitchen table with a bowl of Cheerios and a book, setting out extra food for Erin. After making coffee and gulping down the first scalding sip, he turns on the TV. The screen fills with crowd-control barricades and impromptu shelters. Before Malcom can absorb much, Tim comes into the playroom, book in hand. Hurriedly, Malcolm turns on Netflix.

"I've got to work," he tells his son. "Watch TV with your sister if you want. Mommy's upstairs in bed if you need her. She's not feeling well."

"Okay." Tim yawns. "Are you going to take me to summer camp?"

Damn. "I don't think there's any summer camp today, buddy. It's probably canceled."

Tim's skeptical expression is exactly like his uncle Jason's. "Why?"

Malcolm wracks his mind for the child-appropriate version of events. "There was a big accident last night. Some people got hurt and they need help, so I've got to go." He pulls his son close, running his hand through Tim's silky hair. "You've got the whole day to play with Erin. Mommy won't be going to Grandad's house today. And I'll be back as soon as I can."

Tim's gaze is already sliding past his face to the TV. "Okay."

Outside, a horn honks. Malcolm drops another kiss on his son's head and rushes upstairs to change. From what little he saw during his midnight jaunt, the attack site will be messy. He opts for slacks and a Toronto Police golf shirt instead of his usual suit. He buckles his plainclothes holster and clips on his badge. On his way outside, he slides on a Toronto Police windbreaker and grabs a travel mug full of coffee and his key to Anna's car.

"Crazy times, my man," his partner says as Malcolm gets into the car. Fortunately, Detective Constable Christopher Barry is the extrovert in their partnership. He easily fills the car with one-sided speculation for the whole ride before dropping Malcolm off. "I'll park and join you."

By daylight, it's worse than Malcolm feared. *This is a goddamn apocalypse*, he thinks. Ruined condo buildings dot the horizon. The summer air, already hot, tastes of sulphur and smells of decay. Inside the police line, the area swarms with first responders controlling foot traffic, triaging the injured, and setting up impromptu shelters for people who can't return to their cordoned-off homes. Instinctively, he heads to the place where he found Anna.

"Nazarenko!" a deep baritone bellows.

Malcolm spots Chief Henry Montcalm, a stocky man of sixty-five with greying hair and whiskey-coloured eyes, standing with Deputy Chief Bob Cloar and a group of officers almost exactly where he'd found Anna the previous night. The fallen officer's body is gone. A chalk outline marks the place where she fell. Behind the chief, crews in yellow hazmat suits are hastily assembling white tents around the two monster corpses. In the distance, Malcolm spots the peak of a third tent shining in the morning sunlight. *Another? How many did she kill?*

"Nazarenko?"

Malcolm jerks to attention. In his fog state, he's somehow followed the chief and the deputy several metres past Anna's battle site toward a white-shrouded body a little farther down the road. "Sorry. Didn't sleep much."

The chief places a meaty palm on Malcolm's shoulder, his firm grip steadying. "We need you sharp." Sighing, he steps back. "I've got a press conference in five. Cloar will brief you."

Cloar, a force veteran of an age with the chief, leads Malcolm toward the draped body. "Forensics did a back-of-the-napkin estimate. They think a third of our victims were killed by falling debris or collapsing structures. But they also think the creatures directly killed two-thirds of the deceased. They have the same puncture wounds on their torsos. But a few . . ." He pauses. "A few got special attention."

Cloar nods to two police officers standing next to a young man in a coroner's jacket. The closer officer swallows, visibly steeling herself. Her partner shifts, subtly angling his body to keep the corpse out of his line of sight as she folds back the cloth. Her face is stoic as she stands, gaze on the horizon. Only the coroner joins Malcolm and the deputy in observing the body.

It's a teenager. She has four puncture wounds in her basketball pyjamas, the blood dried to a crisping black. But it's her straight dark hair and brown eyes that freeze Malcolm's guts. *She could be Anna*, he thinks, grateful his stomach is empty. *She could have died, and I wouldn't have known until it was too late.*

"Her name was Marissa Chang," Cloar says as the officer respectfully covers the dead girl's face. "Witness reports say the creatures chased her down."

Malcolm tries to speak, but only a gasping sound comes out of his throat.

The deputy takes out his phone and flips to his photos. He hands the device to Malcolm, pointing to a condo building on the horizon. "I've got two more just like her outside that condo tower."

Malcolm stares at the photo, which shows a blond teenager with long, skinny arms in a pink Hello Kitty nightshirt lying on a patch of grass, her chest heavily punctured.

"Megan Kolpak." Malcolm's barely taken her in when the deputy reaches over and flips to another photo of a boy face down on a sidewalk, clad in green pyjama pants, the same puncture wounds visible in his back. "Asan Ghanei."

Malcolm stares at the wrenching image, remembering the texture of his son's hair between his fingers that morning. "God have mercy on them," he murmurs. "And their parents."

"All students at Oasis Alternative High," Cloar tells him. "Beyond that, we don't understand the connection. I've got people interviewing the families and canvassing the area for security footage. Our working theory, however, is this was a second attack. The first seems to have been stealthier. Remember the three South Asian kids who died out in the Beaches on Sunday night? Same injuries, same pattern of leaving the house in the dark."

Anna! Malcolm's mind screams, thinking of the grotesque thing hidden in the garage. *They came for Anna, too.*

"But that's not why the chief called you." Cloar moves away from the other officers. Struggling to stay impassive, Malcolm follows. "Witness reports say someone else fought back and"—he gestures at the white tents—"did that. We're looking for a woman dressed in black. Whoever she is, she has more answers than we do. Brenda Edwards fell assisting her, and someone with a police vest carried her from the scene." He looks Malcolm square in the eye; Malcolm's stomach turns in a squirming flip. "I'm leading the task force to find them. I want you on it."

No. No. This cannot be happening. Malcolm stares at the deputy's exhausted face while the world seems to lurch around him. *I'm going to get fired.* "Me?" he manages when it's clear Cloar expects an answer. "I'm not Homicide anymore, sir. Wouldn't they be more qualified?"

"Son, no one's qualified for this mess." The deputy leans in. "But the chief needs answers fast. The army's going to be called up. We need to know what happened before they get here." Cloar's hand falls on Malcolm's shoulder with the weight of a boulder. "I need lateral thinkers. The chief personally recommended you."

Malcolm swallows. "Yes, sir," he says. "Thank you, sir."

"I'll take you to see the kills," Cloar says. "We can't photograph or film them, even dead. The physics prof we hauled out of bed over at the university can't explain it. But seeing the corpses will help you see how dangerous our vigilante could be."

Dangerous? Malcolm follows him toward the tents. *Anna, what have you dragged us into?*

Chapter 11

Anna – Muffins

Toronto, ON: Tuesday, August 19

Anna opens her eyes. Her bedroom ceiling fan whirls gently overhead. Despite the room's warmth, there's a duvet tucked under her chin. *I'm home*, she thinks, surprised.

The pale curtains over the bedroom's bay window aren't fully drawn. Between the thick cracks, a familiar pattern of light and shadow splashes across the bed, walls, and ceiling, cast by the swaying evergreens outside. She's incredibly hungry, but the idea of getting up is also overwhelming. Instead, Anna drifts as she watches the dance of light, her sense of time spinning slow and long, like she's swallowed a couple of cannabis candies.

"Mommy?" Erin appears in the doorway. There's a reddish stain —jam?—down one side of her blue pyjama shirt. She turns bright, inquisitive eyes on her mother. "I'm hungry."

"Me, too. What time is it?" The clock reads 11:43 a.m. *I was supposed to meet Walter at ten!*

Anna sits upright, the words to ask Erin where her father is and why no one woke her on her tongue, when the night comes rushing back: the garage, the burning city, Jason, the skyworms, Edwards, the dead teenager, Kalos—everything. She stares at her five-year-old daughter, her mouth hanging open, unable to articulate the thousand thoughts cascading through her head. *I touched xhen. I killed skyworms. And they killed all those people. How many died?*

Erin meets her flummoxed gaze. "I want pancakes, Mommy," she says after a moment. "Can you make some? Please?"

"Yes," Anna manages, trying to compartmentalize her wild thoughts and slow the frantic beat of her heart. "Give me a hug."

Instantly, Erin flings herself onto the bed and scrambles over the duvet. Small hands wrap themselves around Anna's neck. Erin's knee thuds against her left side as she wiggles closer. Pain flares along Anna's torso. She grunts. "Sorry, Mommy." Erin starts to pull away.

"It's okay." Anna holds her daughter close and rests her chin on top of Erin's head, inhaling the familiar smell of baby shampoo, Cheerios, and milk. If she closes her eyes, she can remember how it felt to hold Erin as a baby, to feel that soft, trusting weight against her body. With her child in her arms, the battle is a distant nightmare.

Until the dead teenager's face pops back into Anna's mind. *I was too late.* She shudders. *Were you like me? Did Kalos train you, too? Are there more of you?*

Erin squirms. "Too tight!"

"Sorry." Anna lets go. Erin slides down to the floor. Anna starts to follow her, but when her calf flexes, a swift, stabbing pain claws up her leg. "Go ask Tim if he's hungry, too," she manages, struggling to keep the distress from her voice. "I'll be down in a sec."

"Okay." Erin scampers down the hall. A moment later, her feet pound their usual furious rhythm down the hardwood stairs. "Tiiiiiii-im," she calls. "Are you hungrrry?"

Anna flips the duvet back. There's a wide bandage wrapped around her right leg. The wounds on her hands and side are clean; her deeper scrapes are bandaged.

Malcolm, she thinks with gratitude and apprehension. *How do I explain what happened? Will he forgive me for leaving? How did he find me downtown?* She has no idea.

"Mommy!" Erin calls from downstairs. "Are you coming?"

"Yes, let me get changed!" Anna slides her legs off the bed. Tentatively, she stands. The stabbing pulses, and white haze lines the edges of her vision. It eases as she shifts her weight to the other leg. *I'll manage.*

In their en suite, she finds a sopping clump of torn fabric in the shower. The small room reeks; bandage wrappers litter the blue and white floor tiles. There's a tiny chunk of metal on the back of the toilet, which she guesses came out of her leg. It's smaller than she feared. She wrings water from what's left of her clothes and throws them in the garbage with the wrappers, tying the bag shut to contain the smell, leaving the metal fragment. *Proof for Jason when he comes.* She expects the thought of him to sting as much as her insides do as she carefully sits down on the toilet, but her awareness is factual. *Kalos can deal with him.*

Her stomach rumbles as she washes her face and dresses in jean shorts and a T-shirt, running a brush through her hair before stuffing her phone into her back pocket. Anna glances in the bedroom mirror, some part of her expecting a change. Something in the set of her eyes, perhaps, or the lines of her mouth. Some confirmation of what's happened. But it's just her face, eyes shadowed from her late night and pillow creases on her cheek. *The scar on my leg will have to do.* Sighing, she pops a couple painkillers and goes downstairs.

In the kitchen, a second wave of more intense hunger twists her belly. Anna rummages through the cupboards for something high in protein and finds a jar of almonds. She eats them in handfuls as she assembles the ingredients for pancakes. There's half a pot of cold coffee on the counter, too. She drinks its remnants as she cooks, not bothering to heat it in the microwave, and welcomes the ensuing buzz of caffeine.

Once the table is set and the children are eating, Anna devours three large banana pancakes with sliced strawberries and maple syrup. She chases that with yet more coffee, hot this time, which she swallows in four scalding gulps. She cradles her empty mug, which bears a hand-painted daisy that Tim gave her for Mother's Day, and watches the children eat, wishing she'd made more food. When they rush back to their blanket fort in the playroom, Anna shamelessly cleans the food from their plates.

How am I still hungry? She sits back in her chair, listening to the babble of their voices. The house seems too normal. She touches her leg dressing. Pain flashes through her body. *You didn't dream it*, the throb insists. *It happened.*

A moment later, her phone chimes with a text. It's from Walter Delal:

My apologies for canceling on such short notice, Anna.

Would Wednesday morning work for rescheduling the appointments? Please advise Cynthia if so.

He canceled on me? Anna thinks, utterly confused as she opens her email. To her relief, Walter did indeed send an email at seven a.m. to cancel their meeting. *That was lucky*, she thinks as she types three more emails to her building contacts, asking if Wednesday morning could work. Given everything that's changed, moving the appointments feels chancy. *Are those buildings even open? I've a few hours to figure it out. Whatever's going on, we still need money.*

She skims her other messages, acknowledging her father's text about working late at SickKids and Malcolm's request that she let him know when she's up. There's nothing from Dave, though her text to him has been read. Worse still, there's no message from Jason. *Typical.*

The doorbell rings. Anna puts down her phone and hobbles to answer it, expecting door-to-door fundraisers or a delivery. Instead, Nancy Coleman stands on her porch, bearing an actual wicker basket lined with an embroidered cloth and piled high with fresh, steaming muffins.

"Good morning," Nancy says in her too-cheery voice. She's dressed in a summery skirt and blouse, the kind Anna's mother saved for church or temple services. "I'm so glad to see you up and around." She peers at Anna over the red glasses perched on the end of her nose and lowers her voice to a conspiratorial volume. "How are you feeling, dear?"

"I'm well, thank you," Anna says automatically, unable to stop herself from eyeing the basket as her stomach growls again. "Muffins! That's so kind."

Nancy doesn't pass it to her.

What's she doing here? Their neighbour has always reminded her of the grandmothers who were fixtures along the porches when her family lived on Dovercourt Road: always watching, always judging, and, in Anna's mind, watching her, Jason, and Dave most closely. She knows the association's unfair, but Anna has instinctively kept Nancy at a distance. They exchange pleasantries about the weather. Nancy leaves cards and candy for the children in their mailbox at Christmas, Lunar New Year, St. Patrick's Day, Easter, and Halloween.

Chun-Mei, closer in age to Nancy, had more natural rapport with her. Anna often found them exchanging gardening tips over the fence when Chun-Mei babysat. *She's harmless,* her mother had said when Anna asked her to discourage the relationship. *Busybody aunties love to fuss. You have so little support here. Let Nancy help you now and again. It lets her feel important.*

Pinned by her neighbour's keen eyes, Anna doubts helpfulness has prompted this visit. The awkward silence stretches until Anna says, "How are you?"

"Never better," Nancy replies, smiling. "But I wasn't downtown last night." She gives Anna's bandaged leg a meaningful glance.

Anna tucks her injured leg behind the other one, wishing she'd worn jeans.

"Has the bleeding stopped?"

"Yes," Anna says. "Were you—?"

"Oh, I was here. Your Malcolm practically beat down my door at 12:45 in the morning." With a strange chuckle, Nancy launches into a detailed account.

Anna listens in stunned silence, her apprehension growing with every word. *Oh, baby*, she thinks in dismay. *Why her?*

" . . . reeks of sulphur," Nancy's saying. "You must have been pretty close to get that much fluid on you." Her eyes are sharp, like a bird of prey spotting movement in an open field. Anna blinks, playing for time. "To the creatures," Nancy adds. "What do they look like up close?"

"You know, I-I didn't get a good look," Anna manages.

Nancy, still smiling, gives a little shake of her head that says, *Try again, dear*. She puts a hand on Anna's arm. "I heard on the news the police are looking for a woman. Dressed in black." She pauses, letting her words sink in.

Anna considers shutting and bolting the front door.

"A man in a police vest carried her off." Her smile is as bright as a knife. "What a coincidence, eh?"

"Yeah," Anna swallows. "I—"

"Mommy!" Tim calls from behind her. Relieved, Anna half turns to see him coming up the hall clutching the family tablet, last year's Christmas gift from Dave. "I have something to show you. Hi, Mrs. Coleman. May I have a muffin, please?"

"Of course you may." Nancy holds the basket out. "What lovely manners you have, Tim."

Anna uses the opportunity to grab a muffin as well. It's carrot and smells heavenly. She tears the paper wrapper off the bottom and devours it in three bites. Nancy's eyes widen. "Mmmmm," Anna murmurs around the crumbs. "Thank you so much."

It's not a polite lie. In her ravenous state, Nancy's muffin is unquestionably the most delicious baked good she's ever eaten. On impulse, she gives her neighbour a hug and a quick peck on the cheek. The older woman flushes, momentarily disarmed, and Anna takes the basket. "I'm so sorry, I've got to go. Do you want your basket back? I can pop the muffins in another container."

"Oh, no, no," Nancy says. "Bring it back when you're finished. We'll have tea."

I don't think so. "Great," Anna says aloud, clinging to her smile. "See you later, Nancy." Tim tugs her hand as she locks the front door. "What is it, sweetheart?"

Her son leads her into the living room. "I saw the lady," he says quietly, pushing his mother into an armchair.

"What lady?" Anna asks as he climbs into her lap.

"The one Mrs. Coleman told you about. I didn't go looking," he says quickly. "There was a notification." He taps the CBC news icon. "I didn't show Erin, but . . . did something break the CN Tower?"

Anna suppresses a shiver. "No, honey," she says as calmly as she can. Some remnant of the rage that powered her through the previous night flickers in her gut as she stares into her son's earnest face. *How many other kids are worried this morning?* "The tower's just fine."

"Because the lady in black stopped them," he agrees, visibly pleased by the idea. His short, stubby fingers flick expertly at the screen. "She saved the tower. Watch."

Anna stares at a grainy version of herself surrounded in pulsing light that makes the camera flicker. Then a blurred mass of pixels swoops into the frame. She waits for the image to resolve, but it doesn't. *Like the photos I tried to take in the garage.*

Despite this shortcoming, the scale and speed of the combat hits her like a gut punch. She watches the fight play out until earth and grass spray across the ground outside the train museum, signaling the skyworms' crash down. Tim punches the air like they're watching a movie and the bad guys have just lost.

Anna scrambles to pause the feed, but before they get to the part where the skyworm knocked her down, the newscast pauses. Three photos of uniformed police officers appear superimposed over the pixelated footage. Anna reads their names, etching them into her heart: Constables Marc Ernsting and Robert Poutney, with Sergeant Brenda Edwards between them.

"Mommy? Did those police officers die?"

"Yes, honey," Anna manages around the thickness in her throat. *Brenda Edwards. Brenda Edwards died for me.* "They did." She holds her son tight, feeling tears prickle. "Listen, no one understands what's happening." *Least of all me.* "But you're safe. Nothing's going to hurt you."

Tim gives her an odd look. "I know." He clambers off her lap and runs back to Erin.

Anna watches him go, her stomach growling. She takes a second muffin from the basket. In her mind, she sees Edwards's awe-filled eyes, startling in their conviction. *You've given me purpose,* she'd said. *I'd been looking for a long time.* Anna wipes her own eyes.

Years ago, they'd speculated about what would happen if anyone learned about their connection to xhen. Jason said lab experiments. Dave said the smart money was on institutionalization. Anna assumed it wouldn't be dramatic: general ridicule and shunning. Sitting alone in her living room more than fifteen years after that conversation, she's ashamed they never imagined generosity or courage as a possible response.

Or petty scrutiny, she thinks, reaching for a third muffin. *Nancy's put it together, I know she has.* Taking a large bite, Anna glances out the window, half expecting to see a media scrum and a fleet of police cars on the front lawn with her neighbour at its centre. But their street is quiet.

She's halfway through the basket when the doorbell rings a second time. Anna jumps up from the chair, her belly finally full. *I guess Nancy changed her mind.*

Before she reaches the hall, Erin thunders toward the door and pushes past her. "I'll get it!"

"Wait!" Anna calls, trying to see if she can spot Nancy's grey hair on the other side of the glass while stepping around her daughter as fast as her sore leg allows. "Let me answer, Erin!"

She's too late. Squealing, Erin throws the door open. But the person waiting for them is not their nosy neighbour, nor an impromptu press conference.

Dave Montcalm grins as he scoops her younger child up in his large brown hands. He spins on his heel, making Erin shriek with delight as she whirls through the air. Anna slumps against the doorframe. “Thank God you’re here,” she says, equally delighted and relieved.

“Uncle Dave! Uncle Dave!” Tim cries, also pushing past her. “Did you bring us presents?”

Dave kneels down to appease the children, but it’s her eyes he finds above their heads. *Fucking crazy night, eh?* His deep voice is as clear as a bell in her mind. *Hell of a chase you led me on, Annie. You might have saved some of the fun. How d’you like this new trick?* One of his dark-brown eyes winks at her.

It’s too much. Dave’s still grinning like he’s discovered the funniest joke in the universe as Anna faints in the hallway.

Chapter 12

Dave – Sister

Toronto, ON: Tuesday, August 19

"Damn." Dave leans over the plastic bin to consider the dead skyworm. Crouching on his heels, he reaches out with a tentative hand to touch the dark-purple tentacles that dangle limply from its head. The hole Anna blasted through its face is the diameter of his forearm, the scaled flesh around it charred black. There's very little left of the creature's mouth save a few teeth, making it difficult to imagine the original shape or structure. He stares at its empty triple eyes and the pale tentacle severed from its ruined mouth, part of him unwilling to accept its reality. The smell, however, is grounding. "It's like something out of a movie."

"Careful." Beside him, Anna crunches through an apple and tosses the core into a garbage can. Immediately, she pulls a protein bar from her pocket. It's gone in two bites. Since waking, she's done nothing but eat and radiate embarrassment for fainting. "They sting."

"You're such a mom." He brushes the nearest tentacle. A crackling jolt, similar to the kind of shock he sometimes receives working on circuit boards, jumps up his arm. Dave hisses and pulls his hand back, shaking his fingers like he would to dispel pins and needles. "Numbing, like you said."

She tosses the wrapper in the garbage, too. "But you wouldn't take my word for it."

"Nope." He uses his other hand to poke more gingerly at the orange scales. Its head is crested, the veins beneath the platelike structure prominent like those of a leaf. The colour of the scales brightens along its underbelly, narrowing to a whipcord tail with serrated edges. Supple and cool to the touch, the scales make his skin tingle, but the effect isn't as pronounced as with the tentacles. "You said they can't be filmed?"

Anna nods.

"Wonder why. It must be some sort of distortion." *Hal would have theories*, he thinks out of habit. He touches the scales again to dismiss that thought, biting his lip against the mild jolt. "Makes me think of an electric eel."

"Show me an electric eel that does that." Anna gestures to the heap of long serrated metal fragments, beige on one side and dark grey on the other. She picks one up and hands it to Dave. "That's what's left of our propane tank. Thank God it was empty. You saw what it did to the SUV." Between them, they'd managed to change the flat and park it on the street. "And if you think that's messed up, wait till you see what the big ones did."

Yeah, you showed me, he thinks, and Anna startles. He smiles, trying not to overwhelm her. In the garage's dim light, the side of her face is scraped and bruised. He's always thought of this sister of his heart as striking rather than pretty. Even she jokes that Jason got the looks.

Despite her injuries, however, there's a purity to Anna this morning that makes his breath catch. She has her mother's straight inky hair and wide-spaced eyes, combined with her father's strong jaw. Intelligent and smart-mouthed, she'd scared the hell out of his friends at Waterloo. During the Rune years, his reception team lived in fear of her after a new hire mistakenly assumed Anna had come to make a delivery, not to have lunch with the company's co-founder and CEO.

He's often wondered if her temper or her overwhelming sense of justice drive her courage. *Probably both.* In one of his earliest memories, Anna's standing over him in the schoolyard, screaming defiance at some bigger kid with blood streaming from his nose. She'd heard the boy, half a metre taller than them both, calling Dave the usual names and sucker punched him square in the face. She'd been suspended for two days, but the boy never bothered Dave again. Neither did any of his friends. Studying Anna's profile, he has no trouble accepting that she single-handedly fought and killed three monsters.

Anna rolls her eyes. "You're making me blush, Dave." It's his turn to be startled. He hadn't realized he was broadcasting his thoughts. "I had help." She puts her hand on his shoulder for balance as she stands, keeping her weight off her injured leg.

Without warning, Dave's suddenly falling against hard concrete, blue energy a haze between him and the police officers crumpling fifty metres away, like paper dolls smashed by a willful child. Something screams above his head and blood thunders in his ears. In the next heartbeat, everything is eerily quiet and he's kneeling over a woman's pinched face, her police vest punctured by four purple tendrils the width of his bicep. Sorrow and regret surge in his throat, threatening to drown him.

She's as loud as Leona, Dave thinks, stepping away to physically withdraw from the tsunami of emotions tumbling through Anna's mind. Since nearing her house, he's had remarkably few other mental intrusions, even from her children. Her mesmerizing thoughts, thick as morning fog rolling off the lake, drown out all other noise. They're less immersive than his aunt's memories but have the same absorbing pattern of sound, smell, and sensation, particularly when she touches him. *Is that because we're practically family? Or because of xhen?*

"Those officers chose to help you, Anna," he says aloud. "So put that guilt down. There's nothing wrong with you."

It's happening again, Leona whispers in his memory, pushing away the last remnants of Anna's thoughts about the dead officers. *Why else would I let Chun-Mei arrange for the Montcalms to adopt you in Toronto after we lost Rose?*

How many times had Dave wrestled with that question as a child? Thousands upon thousands. He'd always known he was adopted: His parents had been open about it from the time he was small. But his uncertainty about where and how he fit in the world lingered, even after he'd started spending time with Leona. *Why didn't you adopt me?* he'd wondered. It was the one question he'd never been brave enough to ask.

And while Chun-Mei Lin has been a force in his life for as long as he can remember, he would never have guessed she played a role in his adoption. Dave opens his mouth to tell Anna, and then stops. He doesn't need telepathy to know his exhausted sister needs the stress of that conversation like a hole in her head. *I hardly know the story. I need to talk to Auntie Lee again.*

"It's creepy that you can do that." Anna scrounges in her pocket for yet another protein bar. "Kalos will have to teach me some tricks so you can't go rummaging around in my head."

"Sorry." Dave stands up and squeezes her shoulder. The monsters dive through the sky of her mind until he lets go, once more pushing her recollections away. Before they came out to the garage, he sat in her living room and heard—and felt and saw—her story twice from start to finish. "It's new for me, too. Kalos said I'll get better at controlling it."

"Where'd you see him?"

"Truck stop outside of Parry Sound." Dave stretches his stiff back, remembering his jolt of utter disbelief at seeing their teacher materialize out of the trees across from his parking spot. "He didn't say much. I'd already figured out shit was going down and you were involved. He said you were safe and to take my time driving. I said, 'Safe from what?' but he didn't answer. By the time he left, my back had stopped burning. I found a motel room, slept, and drove the rest of the way this morning."

"That's Kalos for you." Anna shivers and rubs her arms, even though it's not cold in the garage. "Cryptic as hell." Her expression darkens. "Have you heard from—"

"Jason?" This time, they both grin.

"Your parlour trick is delightful," Anna says, the faintest hint of jealousy in her voice.

"Yeah," Dave agrees, cheered to see her smiling more like the Anna he remembers from their teens. *She hasn't had many reasons to smile lately. I should have come down more often*, he thinks. He'd gone to Chun-Mei's funeral, of course, but the logistics around his workshop had sucked him back to Miinikaa soon after. "We would have gone nuts for this back in the day, huh?" They exchange a deeper smile, though there's sadness again in hers.

Of them all, Anna struggled the longest to adapt to life after Kalos. They'd known next to nothing about him, only that the village where he'd been born no longer existed in modern-day Turkey. His existence seemed entirely focused on teaching them to use xhen. When pressed, he'd refused to explain anything more.

The mystery had haunted Anna. Once, over beers at the Madison Pub, she'd told Dave that she'd chosen classical studies to increase her ability to hunt for answers. At one point, she'd considered graduate work overseas to expand her search. Then she'd met Malcolm and her focus had irrevocably shifted.

Dave nudges her side. "Do you remember all the silly shit we tried to make Kalos come back?"

"And Jay was so furious when none of it worked," Anna says, hanging on to her smile despite her twisting lips.

Dave nods. There'd been nights when the twins fought so bitterly over what had happened to them that Dave feared they'd never speak again. Weeks passed when they hadn't, leaving him caught between his two best friends, unable to choose a side. To Dave, the question was moot. All that mattered was that their training was over and it was time to move on.

"Yeah. Jay's a stubborn dude. I texted him this morning," Dave says. "Nothing yet. I'll call him from Mum and Dad's and get him on a plane the second Pearson Airport reopens." He flashes a wicked grin at her. "So long as Kalos doesn't get to him first."

Anna frowns. "Or the skyworms show up in Vancouver."

"Shit, I didn't think of that." He exhales noisily, annoyed to have missed the kind of strategic risk he used to pride himself on anticipating. "How likely do you think that is? Hard to play backup across four provinces."

They contemplate the skyworm's corpse for another long minute. Anna's wrapped in bone-deep sorrow, familiar as his old hoodie. At the centre of its crushing force are Jason and her mother. Dave slips his arm around her shoulder, acutely aware of the vast distance between them and the third corner of their triangle. He pulls Anna and her layers of pain to his side, accepting the deluge of emotion. *You know, Annie, I'm really fucking glad you didn't die last night.*

"Me, too." Skyworms loom in her mind, their three-eyed heads seething with menace alongside a teenage girl's frozen face. She presses her eyes into his shoulder, not bothering to put words to her feelings. They stand that way together in silent communion. Then she sniffs the red cotton of his sweatshirt. "You smell like cigarettes." She glares. "I thought you quit, Dave."

"Had one in the car." He scrubs a hand through his hair. Halina had introduced him to smokes as a serious pursuit. Back in the day, when it had been just them working all hours in a computer lab or a coffee shop, they'd gotten in the habit of taking smoke breaks. As Rune expanded, Halina quit smoking. Dave had doubled down. Now, he can't think about cigarettes without thinking of the knot in his chest that had never loosened once he'd met Charles Larkin, which makes him think of the heart attack, which makes him think of lying in his hospital bed suffering through nicotine withdrawal.

What would Hal think of xhen? he wonders, and pushes thoughts of his co-founder and Rune away. "I haven't lit up in three years. Spare me the sermon."

Anna's eyebrows narrow. "If you get back on that train, I'll sic both Dr. Lins on you."

"Your dad's scarier." He stretches again, taking a step away. "So. Skyworms are that big, huh?"

A line furrows her brow. "Don't change the subject."

It needs changing. But now that the moment's arrived, he feels a different kind of sickness. *What if I can't summon xhen?*

"You will," Anna says, exuding confidence. She'd been the same the weekend she'd driven to Waterloo for a visit, and he'd asked her if he and Halina should incorporate Rune. In the garage, he quivers with anticipation as she limps across the room and closes her eyes.

A familiar burning prickle washes over Dave's forehead from the bridge of his nose to his hairline, lighting his kidneys up in an echo of the soft blue light that seeps from his sister's skin. Dave gapes as Anna's eyes open, every hair on his body standing at attention. *Wow.* He can't do anything but stare, feeling the last of his disbelief spiral away as her xhen coalesces into a long slim line. She deftly throws the pulsing cord at him, like a hunter angling for a slippery fish. It coils around his arm. Her grin widens.

Against his skin, Anna's xhen feels cold and . . . fuzzy. Dave twists to try and break her leash. She holds him fast. "Damn, Annie. I mean, I was ready but not at all ready, you know?"

He starts to laugh when she releases him, the same way he used to when they smoked weed in her parents' garage during the terrible spring and summer after Kalos vanished. He'd let himself mourn what they'd lost, taking long walks with Jason at night or playing video games in his basement with Anna. When he'd moved to Waterloo that fall, he had put xhen away with the rest of his childhood.

"I feel it," he manages, hearing the thickness in his throat as he holds a hand to his navel. "It's right here, ready to break me open, too."

"Well, come on, Dave," Anna says, and he doesn't know if it's her memory or his, but they're eleven or twelve, working up the nerve to jump off the ten-metre diving tower at the Summerville pool out in the Beaches. "Do it."

Dave closes his eyes. At first, he does nothing but breathe, waiting for his pulse to slow. When he can't bear the nervous waves washing against the inside of his stomach for a second longer, he lets his mind's eye seek the centre buried in his solar plexus, which is also a doorway to the universe. A burning sensation prickles up his back, chased by a delight so raw that the centre of his bottom lip cracks beneath the force of his grin. Flickering light dances across his eyelids, bright as the last rays of sunset. When Dave opens his eyes, his body is bathed in deep crimson xhen. It flickers in the dimness, forming a living flame that wreathes his body as it undulates. He raises one hand, admiring the way the energy flows across and between his fingers without burning.

On the other side of the garage, Anna laughs. Her eyes dance in the dark, reflecting his fire.

It's so crazy wonderful. A tear slides down his cheek. He wipes it away, half expecting it to sizzle. *Shit, Annie. I forgot it was like this.* He meets her shining gaze, his chest heavy and light all at once. *I never let myself believe that xhen would come back.*

"You and me both," she says as the giddy truth beneath her words washes over him. He knows then, that for all her outward nostalgia and reluctance, she had also believed xhen was gone forever. Anna smiles, her grief momentarily forgotten, as energy pulses between them in a shared, joyous current. "Jason has to come home. Will you help me convince him?"

Dave nods. *I drove over four hundred kilometres to be here, Annie. I'm all in.*

Behind them, the garage's side door opens. Dave spins to block the entrant's view of the skyworm's corpse. Anna turns, too. But the person entering isn't one of her kids or the nosy neighbour she mentioned, but Malcolm, wearing khakis and a wrinkled golf shirt, carrying a metric ton of worry in the set of his shoulders.

"Goddamn," he says, wide eyes leaping from Anna to Dave and back. He chuckles, the sound echoing the awkwardness of his posture. Something flashes over his face, but the emotion is gone before Dave can parse it. He's always found Anna's self-contained husband difficult to read. "Should have guessed you were part of this, Dave," Malcolm says. He looks at his wife. "Jason, too?"

"Not yet," Anna says, releasing xhen to embrace Malcolm. "I'm glad you're back." But the stiffness doesn't leave his stance as he takes in the xhen flames still dancing up and down Dave's arms. Faced with such naked curiosity, Dave can't help himself. He holds his palms up, letting xhen arc between them like he's a street busker. Malcolm smiles, finally relaxing, and Dave releases the energy. For a fleeting moment, they're three old friends standing in a garage.

"Good to see you, man," Dave says before the atmosphere gets too weird. He likes Malcolm, always has, but they're friendly, not close. He concentrates as they shake hands, curious if Malcolm's thoughts are different from Anna's or Leona's. To his surprise, the police officer's mind is completely closed to him. As they shake hands, Dave gets nothing beyond the briefest flash of crowds, tents, rubble, and people in yellow hazmat suits.

Strange. He returns his attention to Anna. His surprise deepens when he realizes there isn't a drop of pain or worry leaking from her as she stands with one arm around Malcolm's waist. *What changed? Why?*

"I was afraid you were one of the kids," Anna's saying.

"They're playing LEGO." Malcolm paces over to the creature. "The three things you killed downtown were so big." He looks at Anna. "You got lucky both nights. You know that, right?"

Tension thrums between them, but Dave catches no corresponding thoughts in their minds. "Don't touch it," he cautions as Malcolm drifts a little closer to the corpse. "The scales sting."

"They stink, too. Let's box this up before someone realizes where the smell's coming from." He fits the lid back in place and glances at Dave. "I saw your dad. He says the federal government's going to declare a state of emergency."

Years of being grilled in board meetings keeps Dave's expression neutral. "It's a logical step," he says. "Dad will hate the loss of control, of course."

"Yeah," says Malcolm, turning to his wife. "He expects the army will take command of the situation in Toronto soon. You should both talk to Chief Montcalm before they arrive."

"No," Anna says. "Not until we understand what's going on." She catches Dave's eyes, and this time he hears her thought, clear as a bell. *And don't you dare agree with him, Dave Montcalm.*

"Anna, there are hundreds of people dead," Malcolm insists. "Officers died, kids died—"

"I saw her," Anna says shortly. "The dead teen."

"There were two more," Malcolm tells her. "Another girl and a boy, all the same age. They went to high school together. And three more kids, all boys, out in the Beaches on Sunday night."

Dave shivers, sickened, as he locks gazes again with Anna. He doesn't have to touch her mind to know what she's thinking. *Groups of three. Just like us.*

Malcolm's not finished. "You're the reason the attack ended. If you understand why these things have come here, if you have a single scrap of useful information about how to protect people, you need to come forward." His gaze swings to Dave. "Today."

Dave starts to bristle at the imperative. *It's challenging for people used to giving orders to know when to take them,* his leadership coach used to say when he was going through a particularly fractious period with his board of directors. *Knowing when to listen and when to stand your ground is what makes a successful CEO.*

He takes a deep breath, feeling his way into the other man's point of view. *Malcolm's like Dad. They're chain-of-command people. Anna's inadvertently pushed him out of his comfort zone. Of course he wants to get back in his lane.*

Before he can offer any perspective, his sister's hands curl themselves into fists. *And if I've got an anti-authoritarian streak, Anna's is a mile wide.* Dave takes a step toward Malcolm, shifting their focus to him. "A lot has changed," he says. "We don't fully understand all of it yet." He looks at Anna for confirmation. She nods. "Back when we were learning, none of this was tangible. Annie couldn't make leashes. I couldn't do this." He holds up his hands, letting the fire arc again. "Or hear thoughts."

Malcolm does a double take. "You what?"

"Don't worry, man," Dave laughs. "You're, like, the one person I can't hear."

Malcolm doesn't look reassured.

"But we shouldn't kid ourselves, either. Something big has shifted. The skyworms will be back." He looks at Anna, who nods, crossing her arms.

"Skyworms," Malcolm repeats, tasting the word and grimacing.

Dave nods. "The big question in my mind is whether we get Jason here in time."

"If he agrees to come," Anna grumbles.

"Hey, let's assume the positive," Dave counters. "We've got new information."

"Dave," Malcolm says, his voice strained. "Would you give us a moment? Please?"

Unease crackles between them, dangerous as a downed power line. *They haven't had any time to talk*, Dave realizes. "Sure thing," he says, squeezing Anna's shoulder. "Why don't I check on the kids?" He slips out through the garage door and closes it behind him.

In their backyard, Dave looks down at his hands. Xhen flickers in his mind's eye, and he lets a thin trickle dance across his knuckles. *Here again after all this time*, he thinks, humbled and amused. His hospital days after Rune had been rife with navel gazing: about who he'd been, who he should be, and which of his possible new selves would bring the most benefit to his community. Never once had xhen been part of any of his tentative answers.

Smiling, Dave releases the energy. *Leona would say Creator sure has a wonderful sense of humour. Let's hope that will inspire me to motivate a stubborn doctor.*

Pulling his phone out, he walks into the house and dials.

Chapter 13

Jason – Kalos

Vancouver, BC: Tuesday, August 19

Jason's bare toes grip the diving tower's pebbled edge. Ten metres down, Anna and Dave bob midair in an empty Olympic-size swimming pool, their arms and legs moving as though they're treading invisible water.

"Jump!" Anna orders, her voice echoing and thin. "Hurry!"

"There's no water," Jason shouts back.

Dave smacks the empty air with his hand, producing a faint splash. "Come on!"

Jump, a voice says in his ear. ***Jump or they die***.

Jason blinks. The pool is full of liquid, but it's red, not blue. Anna's glaring up at him, her face stained crimson. And there are things circling beneath her and Dave in the bloody pool—impossibly massive things with crested heads—and as he leans forward to look, vertigo seizes him, and he's falling and . . .

. . . Margo's shaking him awake. "Jason. Jason, wake up. You're dreaming." She leans over him, one hand lightly shaking his chest. Her brown eyes are wide with concern. "Are you all right?"

He tilts his head on the pillow to look up at her, frowning.

She shrugs slightly, as though embarrassed for him. "You were screaming."

"I was?" His throat's dry. Jason reaches for the glass of water he always keeps on his nightstand. The clear plastic cup is red, and he recalls Anna's crimson face. *He spoke to me in the garage. I heard his voice.* Jason freezes, his fingers halting in midair.

Margo takes the cup and waits until he's sitting up to pass it to him. "Yeah," she says. "'Stop touching my head! Stop touching my head!' You shouted that over and over." She grins like she does when someone's made an awkward joke at a dinner party, inviting him to shape the gaffe into something amusing. But his stomach's a block of ice, and the glass feels like a stone.

Kalos.

Years ago, there had been a period of perhaps six months when Jason would have given his right arm to hear that distinctive non-voice whisper in his thoughts. *Anna probably still would.* But that time is long gone.

"You're so pale," Margo tells him, touching a hand to his cheek. "Are you sick?"

"Maybe." His aching head feels muffled, like it does when he's coming down with a sinus cold. *Maybe I'm going crazy.*

"Poor doctor," Margo chides, sliding her hand down his stubbled cheek until she's cupping his chin. "I'll take my chances." Smiling, she lifts his mouth into her orbit. Her lips taste of coffee and sugar, as they always do in the morning, but he can't kiss her back.

Anna. Dave. They swim through his thoughts, stirring alarm. *Stop it,* he tells himself. *It was just a dream.*

Margo draws back as though aware he's not fully in the moment, but her expression is playful. Normally, she's keyed up and tense in the run-up to previews for a show. *Last night's dress rehearsal must have been spectacular.* "You really aren't well," she observes with concern.

"I'm fine."

"Liar. You're all sweaty. You should go back to sleep." Margo points toward the clock. "You've barely had three hours. And I have my cast meeting at eleven. Take advantage of the quiet."

"Too late." He swings his legs over the side of the bed, massaging his forehead. The pressure sends needlelike arcs of pain across his temples. *Something attacked me in the garage.* He drinks water, aware he'll get a migraine if he doesn't heed Margo's advice. But if he sleeps, he might dream again. "I'm up."

"Mmm. So I see." Margo slides her hands over him, putting truth to her observation, and then she's climbing into his lap and kissing him again. "You've got another shift tomorrow," she says in a teasing voice, her teeth gently nipping at his ear lobe. "You need to be on your game."

Jason pulls her close. She's reassuringly solid against his bare arms and chest. As he holds her, he feels the strain inside him ease. *This is real.* She's wearing one of his white dress shirts knotted over a black tank top and skirt. He kisses Margo's neck and the hollow of her ear as he slides a hand up her leg. "I'm always on my game."

"Not on three hours!" She laughs. "Let's get you sleepy."

Jason smiles into her neck, turned on despite his poor sleep. "You're going to be late."

"Director's prerogative," she murmurs around his tongue.

Desire jolts through him. Her hands rake his hair; his unbutton her shirt. In the space of a heartbeat, they're naked beneath the sheet and Margo commands his attention. In her arms, everything else falls away.

She comes. Jason's orgasm hovers teasingly close before the image of the pool and the creatures surfaces again. *I heard his voice.* His erection collapses. They persist for a few more minutes before agreeing to let the moment go. Margo grants him a last spectacular kiss and then climbs out of bed.

When she's dressed, she bends to pick up her purse, catching his eye as she smiles. *I'm the luckiest man in the world.* Jason smiles back at her, tempted to pull her back into bed and kiss her again. "Have a good cast meeting."

"Oh, I will," she says. "Everyone was so jealous of my flowers yesterday. And you gave me the most fantastic brainwave."

Folding his arms behind his head on the pillow, Jason gestures for her to continue.

"Ivy and I are going to send a basket of chocolates, flowers, and four tickets to every sorority on UBC's campus. It's a play for and about women. If they like it, we'll have word of mouth jumpstarted like that." She snaps her fingers, the picture of confidence.

Jason grins at her, enraptured.

"You better be here with more inspiration when I get home. Rested!" Blowing a kiss, she turns to leave in a swirl of her orchid perfume. But at the bedroom door, she pauses to look back. "Oh, your sister texted me. Twice. And your friend. Dave? You should call them."

Alarm fires through every synapse in Jason's head, banishing his good mood in an instant. *Great*, he thinks as Margo's heels click to the front door. A glance at his phone confirms his unease as he flicks on the device's sound: seventeen texts and two missed calls from Dave, a missed call from his father, and one text from Anna:

Call me today.

God, she never gives up. It's the aspect of Anna's personality that he finds most infuriating.

As unease balloons inside him, Jason leaves the bedroom with his phone in hand. In the living room, the TV is off. Margo rarely uses the flat screen for anything but Netflix. She hates social media. *The news is so depressing!* she's always saying to their friends. *They want you to be afraid of everything. Why make space for that negativity in your life?*

I bet she hasn't heard about Toronto, Jason thinks as he picks up the remote. He jumps to CBC and half listens to the commentators gamely trying to parse the same pixelated images he saw the previous night. Then one says, "We're going to footage captured from security cameras at the base of the CN Tower. Police are looking for this woman—"

Jason doesn't hear a word after that because it's his sister on the screen, pulsing with light. *Anna, what have you done?* She's hooded, but Jason would know her anywhere. The bottom of his stomach drops out of his body as he watches his twin charge across a field of grass, shining with what can only be xhen, toward two strange, pixelated blurs. *Was she telling the truth?*

Jason.

Refusing to look, Jason walks into the kitchen and pours a cup of coffee from the half-empty Bodum sitting on the counter. But when he turns to the refrigerator for cream, his eyes see empty air, but his mind sees Kalos beside the stainless-steel appliance. His old teacher's serene expression is the same, his symmetrical face framed by a neat salt-and-pepper beard and moustache. Perhaps two inches shorter than Jason, Kalos's dark eyes hold the same cool distance he remembers in a face Margo would describe as dignified rather than handsome.

Jason sets down his mug, hatred leaping in his chest. "No," he says. "No. You're not real."

Kalos inclines his head. ***Child.***

"You left us!" Jason shouts, partly shocked by his fury. "I have a life now! Whatever you've come back for, whatever you want, the answer is no. I want no part of you."

Kalos's expression doesn't flicker. As a teacher, he was stingy with praise and insistent on perfection in their endless drills. Jason had once believed Kalos was human, yet he seemed so deeply attuned to xhen that he'd theorized their teacher had forgotten informal human gestures like smiles. There was the ritual of instruction between them, and little else. And yet, Jason had once loved him more than anyone.

Your training was complete.

"You told us to go back to our lives." The bitterness is as fresh as the night Kalos vanished in the glow of an alley streetlight, never to return. He remembers how furious he'd been to hear those words. How deeply they'd cut after everything he'd endured under Kalos's guidance. He can't count the nights that he, Anna, and Dave went out, separately or together, to get so stoned they couldn't stand. It had been like they were making up for lost time. It was then that his doubts about what exactly had happened to them crept in.

And you did. But the world has need of you, Jason. You and your triad.

"That mess in Toronto has nothing to do with us." In the corner of his eye, his sister sprints across the living room TV, her every step unraveling his words.

It was the site of their first attack. Anna killed four skyworms there. Yet the veil between worlds is thinning. They will come again.

"That's a lie."

I do not lie, Xenthian.

"Xenthian?"

For the first time, something soft relaxes the stern lines of Kalos's face. ***So you are, xhen-wielder. As was I, once.***

Memories come back in a hot rush: that night behind the Montcalm house with Dave, the way an opening in the fabric of the world seemed just beyond his reach, the crushing pressure as he tried to grasp that edge and push and push and push—and then nothing but dust beneath his bare knees and the stale taste of sweat on his lips. "I haven't touched xhen in years."

Yet it touches you. And skyworms have come to harvest our xhen, as they have come before. Two thousand years ago, they attacked this world. Xenthians rallied to resist in the Levant, across North Africa, in Southern Asia, and across Southern China. A shadow passes over his face. ***That war claimed many brave souls.***

Jason grips the counter as he hears himself laugh as though from a great distance. "Are you going to tell me that's when you fought them? Do you expect me to believe in all your children's stories again?"

Not then. Skyworms have attacked us twice. My sisters and I allied with the Mesopotamians to fight. We fell within sight of Babylon's walls.

Cold shivers through Jason's body. *If that's true, Kalos is at least 3,000 years old.* Shaking his head, he begins to pace. "No," he says. "That doesn't make sense. You would have told us years ago." He turns to sneer. "You would have said anything to make us trust you."

Xenthians are always trained in case the skyworms return. But you do not shoulder pointless worry for a war that may never come. That burden is mine.

The sneer dies on Jason's lips. Before he can check his curiosity, a question rushes out. "How many times have you trained people like us?"

Child, says Kalos, and his infinite gentleness draws Jason's gaze to his calm face. ***More times than there are hairs on your head. Go to your family. Your triad must be whole before the skyworms return.***

And then Kalos is gone.

Jason stares into his cooling coffee. *This is how people break. Believing self-serving nonsense tangled in half-truths.*

His phone rings. Jason automatically picks it up, hoping it's Margo calling to say her cast meeting is canceled. *Margo's my family.* But she would text, not call, and the lock screen shows a photo of Jason drinking beer with Dave in his parents' backyard. Jason clicks the TV off and answers on the third ring. *Here it comes.* "Hey, Dave."

"Have you booked a flight east?" Dave asks without preamble.

Jason closes his eyes. "She got to you, too?"

"No, jackass. My sudden telepathy and the dead monster in Anna's garage got to me."

The phone slides out of Jason's suddenly damp hand before he can catch it, tumbling to the kitchen's marble tiles. He bends to pick it up and curses. Despite the protective case, a single crack runs down the middle of the display. "What are you talking about?"

"Your TV broken?" Dave asks. "Turn it on. I'll wait."

"You mean that blur of pixels? I don't know what kind of hysteria's sweeping Toronto, but—"

"Oh, you've seen the footage. Well, that woman is our Annie, Jay. She killed four of those things. Serpents, dragons, flying worms, I don't know what they are, but they're scaled, orange, and massive. Three cops died trying to help her. And we've both spoken to Kalos."

Jason reels. Abruptly, he's in that alley again with xhen so close he can taste it, the air like a heavy door that he could shove open if only he had a key.

"You probably do have a key," Dave says, startling him a second time. "It's so different compared to when we were learning, you won't believe it. My xhen is literal fire, man." The wonder in his voice shivers up Jason's spine. "Look, Annie fought them. And she won."

"That's impossible."

"Wrong, Jayo," Dave says, his voice gentler. "Look, I get it. Failure's easy to internalize when you're the leader. And you *were* our leader. I wanted you to succeed that night in the alley more than I've ever wanted anything."

Jason blinks. After they went inside, he and Dave never talked about what happened.

"But don't you see? It wasn't for nothing."

There's a long pause on the phone line as treacherous longing unfurls itself inside Jason's chest. *It would be so easy to believe them.*

"It is easy. Come home. We need you. And Kalos—"

"Kalos." His name is as bitter as any medicine on Jason's tongue.

"You've seen him, too."

"No."

"Liar," Dave says with equal quickness. "He told me this is only the beginning. So come clean to Margo"—Jason winces—"do what you have to do, and get your ass on a plane to Hamilton or Kitchener or Buffalo or wherever the fuck they'll let you land."

"I can't leave." Jason's heart begins to pound as he paces, trying to fortify himself against Dave's forceful personality. It was formidable when they were teenagers and Dave was trying to convince him to go to a new club or listen to a new band. Now, after a decade of wooing investors to give him millions, bending others to his will is like breathing. "My life is here."

"You can," Dave insists. "Tell the hospital that Annie was injured in the attack. It's true. You should see the shrapnel Malcolm pulled out of her leg."

Jason stops pacing. "Malcolm knows?"

"Yeah," Dave answers. There's a second pause. "I don't get what's happening with them. This territory is new for all of us." He sighs. "We'll figure all the rules out when you get here."

Jason shakes his head. "I've got responsibilities to my patients and my colleagues, Dave. And to Margo. They didn't sign up for this madness, and neither did I."

"Yeah, I know." Dave sighs. "It's important or I wouldn't ask. But, Jay, it's like the end of the world here. If you don't come, I don't know what'll happen. And I don't want to find out."

"Don't push me!" Jason snaps. It takes considerable effort for him to speak at a normal volume. "I'll do what I can."

"You better, man. Or we're probably dead."

The line clicks off as the red pool from Jason's dream resurfaces in his mind. He stares at his cracked phone. *He's as crazy as she is. None of this makes any sense.*

What if you're wrong? another part of him counters, the part that always sounds suspiciously like his mother. *You're gambling your skepticism against their lives. Can you live with being wrong? You owe it to them to be sure. You owe it to me.*

With a migraine blossoming across his skull, Jason opens his web browser. *I'll fly out for a few days and settle them down. I'll be back in time for next week's shifts and Margo's opening night.* Reluctantly, he starts to search for a flight.

Chapter 14

Anna – Promise

Toronto, ON: Tuesday, August 19

Anna blinks bright spots away from her vision as Dave exits the garage in a brilliant flash of sunlight. The lone bulb hanging from the ceiling casts harsh shadows over Malcolm's face, every line of which is taut with expectation. Seconds tick past as they stare at each other, unspeaking. The back of Anna's head begins to prickle. *You lied to him,* whispers a small voice. *In his place, you'd be furious.* Resigned, she clears her throat. "I'm sure you have questions."

"You think?" His mouth makes a poor imitation of his usual one-sided grin. "Can't you tell?"

"I'm not Dave," she says. "I can't read your mind."

"But I feel *you,*" Malcolm insists. "Can't you feel me? Isn't that how this works?"

Anna frowns. "What do you mean?"

Malcolm makes a strangled sound. "I thought you knew!" His forehead wrinkles above the bridge of his nose. "You've turned me into some kind of Anna magnet."

Completely baffled, she gestures for him to continue.

"It started last night. I felt it again this morning. And Jesus . . ." He shakes his head. "It's an apocalypse down there. The news doesn't do it justice. Ruined buildings. All the dead, and those goddamn *things*." Malcolm shudders. "I watched the forensics team go at one." He points at the closed bin. "The corpse was a hundred times worse than that. And when I thought about you killing it, BAM!" He claps his hands, startling her. "There you were, pulling at me. I knew where you were. I could have pointed in your direction. I probably did." He shrugs, helpless. "I feel your sadness, your relief, everything. You need to explain."

Anna inhales a deep breath of sulphur and cedar as she reaches for words. There's nothing from her past to draw upon. "I don't know what to tell you."

Malcolm steps closer, his face implacable. "It's related to what you went through with Jason and Dave, isn't it? I never pushed you to talk about any of that, but after last night, you've got to tell me. We both could have died. Our kids could be orphans today. You know that, right?" He waits for her to nod. "So," he says, "talk. You owe me."

"I owe you?" Part of her could kiss him for giving her an excuse to let loose with every choked emotion she's held back this morning. The other part could slap him. "Malcolm, I didn't ask for anything to happen. I don't get it either. Neither does Dave."

"You know a lot more than me," Malcolm says. "I'll prove it." He pulls two outdoor chair cushions from their hooks on the garage wall and throws them on the floor. Anna grunts as she sits down beside him, her injured leg protesting. "I was in Nancy's car, halfway down to Lakeshore," he begins. "All of a sudden, there was this . . . this man in the passenger seat."

The hairs on Anna's arms rise.

"I could see him from the corner of my eye, but not when I turned my head. Like I wasn't seeing him with my eyes." He glances at her as though expecting contradiction. "I was so startled that I almost crashed the car."

Anna keeps her face neutral. "What did he look like?"

"Old," Malcolm says without pause. "Like really old, though not in an obvious way." He lowers his voice. "I mean, his hair wasn't completely grey, and his face wasn't super wrinkled. But he gave off this . . . feeling. That's what made me think he was old."

Oh God, what do I say? She pauses, half expecting Dave to weigh in with his new gift, but he doesn't. *How do I explain Kalos without sounding crazy?*

Malcolm takes her hand. Despite their mutual annoyance, his touch is reassuring.

Anna shifts closer, tucking a piece of hair behind her ear as she gathers her courage. "He calls himself Kalos," she says. "Did he talk to you?"

"Yeah," Malcolm says. "He said you needed me. That the panic I felt was . . . your need. That I had to get to your side as quickly as possible. I'd already figured that much out."

Anna squeezes his warm hand. Touching Malcolm abruptly brings back the feeling of Brenda's blood-covered hand in hers. She shivers but doesn't let go. "What else? Tell me everything."

Malcolm scrubs his free hand through his wavy hair. "He said others would come, and that I would decide who should help. I told him that didn't make any sense. Then he said something really strange." He swallows. "He said I'm 'bonded' to you. 'Kalxhan to Xenthian.' That it was already done." Malcolm blinks, his gaze expectant. "What's a Xenthian?"

"Me." The fear in Anna's belly flexes, shifting to dread. "The skyworm called me that."

Her husband's jaw drops. "They talk?"

"Only when its tentacles were touching me, and only that word."

Malcolm throws up his hands, clearly exasperated.

"I've always known that word, but I thought it was something I made up to explain me to myself. Because God knows Kalos isn't the best at explain—" Anna breaks off, replaying the previous night. *Your Kalxhan comes to shelter you*, Kalos had told her as she knelt over Brenda Edwards's body. "We had sex Sunday night," she begins slowly. "Remember?"

"Yeah." Malcolm's sudden grin is incandescent, dissipating a little of the tension in the garage. The insistent prickle in the back of Anna's head shifts to a gentler fizzing, like bubbles bursting above a glass of soda. "I felt so close to you."

She smiles back. "Like we were one person."

He nods, still grinning. The feeling grows stronger.

"Shit," she says, letting go of his hand. "Don't you see? That's when it happened!"

Malcolm tilts his head, his expression baffled.

"We were having sex when everything changed."

***Yes*.**

As one, they turn to the corner of the garage where the shattered propane tank once stood. Kalos is there, implacable as ever. Malcolm gasps, instinctively tightening his hold on Anna's hand.

Xhen changed as the skyworms entered this plane of existence, as did your connection. When Malcolm Nazarenko spoke the vow, he became your Kalxhan.

"But what is a Kalxhan?" Malcolm asks.

An old title for the brightest of our beloved protectors, Kalos answers as his expression softens to something almost sad. ***Given to those who support Xenthians by leading the tarkan bonded to their service. Through you, her xhen will grow and amplify as others join this triad.***

"Tarkan means *shield* in Maltese," Anna muses aloud. "Brenda said—" Her voice cracks. She clears her throat. "She said Dave, Jason, and I had to let others be our shields." She gives Kalos a hard look. "Can we undo it?"

***All are needed to defeat the skyworms. No worthy tarkan may be refused*.**

So that's a no. "And Malcolm's . . . the first of these shields? These tarkan? He decides who gets to work with me?" Anna says. "Is that what you mean?"

Tarkan must freely swear the oath. It is always their choice whether to serve. But they do so at the Kalxhan's pleasure and the Xenthian's pain.

"W-what?" Anna splutters. "What pain?"

Malcolm's still frowning. "What are the skyworms?" he asks. "What do they want?"

To harvest human xhen. They are sentient, as you have seen, and hunt for both pleasure and plunder. Kalos meets their stunned gazes with bottomless calm before turning to Anna. ***Tarkan will rally to protect your triad, child. You must not refuse them. Without Xenthians to battle the skyworms and tarkan to assist you, this world will fall.***

"And those kids," Malcolm says. The back of Anna's skull starts to spark with a different, crackling sensation. Brighter, and far more furious, the flare mirrors the anguish in Malcolm's voice. She grips his hand as sorrow closes her own throat. "Were they Xenthians, too?"

They would have been, had I time to properly conduct their training, Kalos says in his non-voice, turning to Anna. ***Xhen changed before I could intervene. They took the energy up to defend themselves, as you did, child. Harbir and Ali Persaud could not hear me. Vic Desai fled. Speaking to Megan Kolpak broke her mind. Asan Ghanei would not let me into his body to teach. Marissa Chang fought me as hard as she did the skyworms. Despite their shared promise—and it was considerable—they were overcome. I mourn their loss as you do.***

Anna sees nothing but Marissa's unnaturally still face. There's a harsh, ragged sound in the garage. Belatedly, she realizes it's her breathing. "So? You should have saved them!"

They were untrained, Kalos answers. ***Without time to prepare, they could not accept my help.***

"What about our children?" Malcolm asks. "Are they in danger, too?"

They are too young for xhen. They carry her family's potential, but skyworms will take no special interest in them yet. The last word makes them both flinch. Kalos stands completely still, a gesture Anna long ago learned to read as his equivalent of a shrug. ***Defeat our enemy, and you have no cause to fear for your family***.

"Like hell," Malcolm mutters.

Despair serves the skyworms as deeply as fear or complacency, Malcolm Nazarenko. Your world is waking to this danger, but this triad is among the strongest I have ever trained.

Pride seeps through Anna's chest, warm as sunshine. *He's manipulating you,* she cautions herself. But she can't help it. Kalos's praise is intoxicating after so many years of silence.

Beside her, Malcolm laughs. "This is insane."

Fear of insanity is the crutch of your age, child. Many Xenthians living in this time have discounted and rejected their power, Kalos says. ***Even now, xhen transforms your body. In time, your strength and agility will be undeniable to all who see you in the field***.

Anna blinks as her teacher bows to her husband.

You are the first to swear the tarkan oath in this cycle. Soon, the world will turn its panicked eyes to you. Trust in Anna Lin's xhen and the strength of her triad. Serve boldly, and you need not fear.

For the first time, wonder breaks across Malcolm's face. He stares at Kalos from beneath his long bangs. "You're asking a lot," he says and blinks, turning his head. "Hey! Where'd he go?"

Anna shrugs. "You get used to it."

Malcolm gives her a considering look. He stands, helping her up as well. In the next instant, his hands are against her back and knees, carefully avoiding her injuries. Then Anna's in the air above his head, her face distressingly close to the garage's wooden beams.

"Hey!" she squawks. "Put me down!"

Instead, Malcolm extends his arms. Anna twists her neck to avoid bumping her head. She squirms, but Malcolm doesn't let her down or drop her as he lowers and extends his arms, bench-pressing her entire body. When he does set her down five repetitions later, Anna eyes him. "You might have said."

"Last night, I carried you so easily," Malcolm says, his voice caught between awe and disbelief as he looks at his hands. "I didn't wake up sore. And I was faster than I should have been, too. It seemed crazy, but after what your ghost pal just said about the world ending . . ."

He sits down on the cushion, his wide eyes riveted to the bin containing the skyworm's corpse. The same crackling prickle spreads across the back of Anna's head, but it's a bonfire now, fierce, insistent and brimming with determination. Instinctively, she reaches for it the way she would for xhen, but this energy is different. *And tied to Malcolm*, she realizes as he turns his intense gaze back to her. *Is this what he meant about being able to feel me?*

"There's a lot here," he says after a while. "And it's bigger than us. I'm not going to pretend that I understand my role in all of it. But if I'm going to adapt, we have to be honest with each other." His steady eyes never leave her face. "I'm pissed off that you lied to me, that you put yourself in danger, and that you talked to Dave about everything first."

Her internal bonfire pops, showering her brain with sparks. She shivers.

"You can't do that if we're going to work together. Everyone needs backup. Promise me that next time, you'll ask."

"I promise." She takes his hands as Marissa's face fills her mind again. "But I also won't wait. Those kids downtown might have lived if I'd gotten there faster. If I say we have to go, we go."

"Fine." The pressure in her head flows away like ocean water from a broken wave sliding back down the sand. He half smiles. "Why didn't you just tell me when I got up and came outside?"

"Habit." Anna shrugs. "Xhen was between Jason, Dave, and me." She sighs. "Not that calling Jay did me much good."

Malcolm raises an eyebrow. Anna briefs him on her second phone call to her brother, her dinner with Walter, her rush downtown, and the fight. "If Brenda hadn't come after me . . ." Grief constricts Anna's throat, but she forces the mangled words out. "I would have died. I know that."

Even as she says the words, she feels herself retreating from their immensity. *If I truly accept it, I'll never fight a skyworm again. And they're coming back.* As she looks at Malcolm, the gentler, comforting feeling returns to her head. "Brenda swore to help me, just like you. Her gun didn't hurt the skyworm, but she distracted it. She was so brave, and she—" Anna breaks off, unable to continue.

"Come here." Malcolm opens his arms.

Anna presses her face against his chest. As he enfolds her, she feels safe for the first time all morning.

"I didn't know Edwards," he tells her, stroking her hair as she composes herself. "I got a lot of sad, angry texts from people who did. I knew Ernsting well. I'd met Poutney a few times. They're already missed, all of them."

"I'm so sorry," she whispers again. "I would have saved them if I could."

"I know." Malcolm takes her hand again. "And if you hadn't gone, it would have been worse." She notices that several nails are broken, the burgundy polish scratched. "But we have to come forward, Anna."

As she stiffens, Malcolm runs his thumb over each of her nails in turn and tells her about Chief Montcalm's new task force. She closes her eyes, listening to the familiar rumble of his voice through his chest, which makes his mild Ukrainian accent more noticeable. "The longer we wait, the greater the odds that I lose my job."

Ahh, she thinks. *That's why you want us to talk to the chief so badly. I should have guessed.* She sits up to wipe her puffy eyes. "I want a better grasp of what the new rules are with xhen before we do anything drastic. Let's give it a few days."

"I don't think we can," Malcolm says. "Nancy's car smelled awful by the time I got back. The backyard reeks. Sooner or later, she'll realize why."

"She's already putting it together," Anna concedes, and tells him about the muffins and her outrageous hunger. The crackling prickle returns to her skull as she tells him about Nancy. "I wouldn't put it past her to turn us in," she finishes. "I've rescheduled my appointments with Walter Delal for tomorrow morning. If I'm going to close this deal, I need to work fast before there's another attack, while I'm still under the radar. We need the money."

Malcolm doesn't nod, but there's hesitation on his face, and the crackling in her skull isn't half as intense.

I'm right, you know I am. "Want to hear something sad? I went to bed Sunday excited that I'd be working this week for the first time since Mom died."

Until xhen returned, her conscience whispers. *Then you couldn't get down there fast enough, could you?*

Ignoring that thought, Anna looks beseechingly at Malcolm. "My appointments are all near the police station," she says. "Can we wait until after lunch? Please?"

Malcolm exhales. "Okay. If you promise to talk to Chief Montcalm right after."

"Deal," Anna says, feeling a rush of satisfaction.

"Anna," Malcolm says quietly, his eyes huge. "You're glowing."

She looks down. Faint blue light edges her hands and arms. Embarrassed, she releases xhen and shoves her hands into the pockets of her shorts.

"Don't," he says, reaching forward to tug at her arm. "Show me."

Watching his face for signs of alarm, Anna lets her xhen rise through her skin. "It's so different. I couldn't hold it in my hands before." They both consider the energy bubbling from her scraped palms. "It wasn't like this." *But if it had been, I would have loved it.*

Glorious, Brenda Edwards had said. Remembering how it felt to flood her body with xhen and kill the skyworms, Anna can't disagree.

"Dave's xhen is red. Do the colours mean something?" Malcolm asks as he touches her hand, gently running his fingertips across her palm and through her xhen. "Does it run in families?"

"I'm not sure," she says. "When we were kids, I thought the colours reflected our personalities, but it manifests differently for Dave than for me. Maybe everyone with red xhen has flames. I don't know."

Malcolm nods.

"As for families," she continues, "we aren't related to Dave. The kids out in the Beaches might have been family, but the rest of them probably weren't." She shrugs. "Maybe it's like any skill. Some talents run in families, but they don't have to."

Malcom puts his hands in hers. The glow in her head intensifies, but his touch doesn't disrupt her concentration. If anything, it helps her to draw more xhen until it's his turn to shiver. "We're in this together, Anna," he says. "We'll figure it out, no matter how weird it gets."

Exhaling, Anna releases xhen and hugs Malcolm, praying that he's right.

Chapter 15

Dave – Homecoming

Toronto, ON: Tuesday, August 19

It's late when Dave leaves Anna's house in the Junction to drive across town to Dovercourt Park where his parents still live. Their two-story red-brick house with the big oak tree in the front yard isn't located in the kind of swishy Toronto neighbourhood favoured by other senior brass on the police force. Unlike the Lins, who moved to a bigger house with a larger garden in North York after the twins left for university, his parents stayed where they were.

Dave had assumed their decision was financial. After his Rune exit, he'd offered to buy them a bigger place uptown. His mum had refused. "This is where you grew up," she said with great incredulity when he raised the subject. "You were a toddler here, and a boy. The neighbours are friendly. Why would I want a big house over those comforts, David?"

On some level, he understands. The feeling of the city pushes in as Dave drives down the familiar streets lined with semi-detached houses, their narrow porches and front-yard vegetable gardens encased with white iron railings that reflect the neighbourhood's historic Portuguese influence.

Toronto's his home, but now that he's lived up north with a daily view of the lake and sky, the loss of vista is crushing in some ephemeral way. It's partly why he's never bought property in Toronto, other than a storage locker. He still has the condo down the highway in Waterloo, bought during his early Rune years, which he rents out. When he's in the city, he stays with his parents or with Anna and Malcolm.

Mum would never forgive me if I bought my own place. She barely forgave me for moving away for school.

Light shines through the living room curtains and from his parents' bedroom window as he pulls the truck up against the curb and gets out. *Mum's still up. Dad's probably downtown.* For years, his dad has kept a camp bed in his office for emergencies, much to his mum's disgust. *It'll be easier to talk to her alone. Probably.*

Dave climbs the porch stairs. The top step squeaks loudly, as it always does. He has to duck to avoid an extremely ornate lantern, new since his last visit and complete with three fat red candles. Now that he's so rarely home, his mum keeps forgetting to allow extra headroom when bitten by a fresh wave of design fever.

As a kid, having a French-Canadian dad and an Indian mum with skin as brown as his generally seemed to confuse other people. Most of the time, they assumed he was mixed race, rarely realizing that he was both adopted and First Nations. But as he kept growing—six foot four to his mum's five feet and his dad's five foot eight—Dave's height began to give him away, making him feel conspicuous when he was with his parents outside their home. So many people stared or asked rude questions, although he got better at deflecting their interest as he got older. It strikes him now as oddly great training for the time when Rune's success became public knowledge, and his wealth became the defining thing that rude strangers were most curious about.

Dave pauses before the dark wooden door, fingering his keys.

How many times did I stand here as a teenager with xhen buzzing in my head? He'd always struggled to let go of its intoxicating force and had nearly given the game away in front of his dad more than once. Talking to his parents about it was unthinkable then. *It's better if they hear it from me now. And Dad will be easier to deal with if Mum's already on my side.*

Dave rings the doorbell. With perfect clarity, he hears his mum's thoughts as she sets down her journal and pen to get up, wondering who would call at so late an hour.

"David!" Sarita Montcalm squeals as she unlocks the security chain and opens the door. She flings her arms around him at shoulder height. She's far too short to reach his neck. "What a surprise!"

"Hey, Mum." Hugging her tightly, he stoops to drop a kiss atop the whitening braids looped and pinned at the back of her head. When he was a kid, her hair was as dark as Leona's. The white started sprouting in his teens and now covers most of her head. "There's more snow in your hair every time I come home."

"That is your fault," she says, self-consciously adjusting a bobby pin. She steps away, smiling. *I used to worry about you and drugs*, she thinks. *Now, I worry about you and heart attacks.*

Shit. Dave tries to push her thoughts out of his head, but Sarita's mental voice is almost as piercing as Anna's.

He is the last person I expected, his mum thinks, not seeming to have heard his inadvertent reply. *Did something happen with his workshop?* She casts him an appraising eye as they head for the kitchen. *He looks tired. Gaunt. I must call Leona. She must feed him more.*

Dave resists the impulse to respond to her internal monologue. Instead, he takes his seat at the oak table and stretches out his legs, more than happy to delay their inevitable conversation. Sarita bustles from the counter to the kitchen island to the refrigerator and back again. Her outward chatter washes over him, as soothing as the chai she prepares. The thick frilly red-and-gold cushions on the kitchen chairs are new, but the trace smells of cardamom, jasmine, and ginger are familiar, though different from the scents in Leona's kitchen. Superficially, all his aunt and his mum have in common besides him is their love of bright colours and delicious food.

But the feeling of welcome is just as powerful. While Sarita talks, Dave feels the tension he accumulated at Anna's house slide away. After Charles Larkin irrevocably changed Rune's culture, he'd started coming home more frequently, aware on some level that he needed to put his stressful life on pause and unsure how to do so.

Why is he home? his mum wonders as she hands him a mug, keeping up a continual stream of chatter about the new roof going on the Lins' old house across the street, her thoughts as swift as a spring wind. *He has no bag. Perhaps he left it in his truck. But he did not call.*

The CN Tower, ringed in smoke, flashes through her thoughts, a lightning image there and gone. It's enough to puncture Dave's feelings of normalcy. *He has probably come to check on Henry. Darling boy to worry about his father.*

"I'm not here because of Dad, Mum," Dave says with an apologetic smile.

Sarita cocks her head, too startled by his interruption to question it, so he rushes on before he loses his nerve.

"I came home because of the skyworm attacks."

"The what?" Sarita freezes like a rabbit sensing a stalking wolf, her chair half pulled out from the table. "What are you talking about?"

Dave swallows. *Well, come on, Dave,* Anna says in his memory. *Do it.* He clears his throat again. "It's Anna, Mum."

Frowning, Sarita stares at him, but her hands are starting to tremble.

Dave tries a third time. "You've been watching the news, right? The woman in the video, the woman fighting back, that's Anna Lin. I've come home to help her."

Sarita continues to stare without comprehension. Rising slowly, Dave goes to her. He takes one delicate ring-covered hand in his larger one. Slowly, carefully, he allows xhen to spark inside him.

Prickling rushes out from the small of his back and along his arms as tiny flames kindle in his other palm, reflecting in the too-wide whites of her eyes. "I've come home to fight the skyworms, Mum. With Anna and Jason, whenever he gets here."

Sarita gives a shriek that reminds him of bathroom spiders discovered on summer mornings and staggers into him. Dave scrambles to support her. Just before she collapses into his arms, Dave receives a sharp memory from his mum's thoughts.

It's summertime. Sarita's outside in a garden—probably Mrs. Lin's rose garden at their Dovercourt house, but his mum is looking at her friend's face so Dave can't tell. Everything else is out of focus. They're young, perhaps in their early forties, but hardly much older than he and Anna are now. Mrs. Lin is holding a wineglass and swirling the red liquid beneath her nose; the conspiratorial smile she shoots Sarita above its rim is mischievous.

"Don't worry about David, Sarita," his mum's best friend says, her lively dark eyes full of secrets. "He's exceptional and exactly where he needs to be. You watch: one day, he and my twins will do great things."

The memory vanishes as Sarita slumps against him, leaving him inundated with a mix of bafflement, curiosity, and dread. Dave leans against the kitchen island, cradling his mum as the memory washes over him. *She knew*, he thinks, utterly stunned for the second time in twenty-four hours. *Auntie Lee was right. Mrs. Lin knew the whole time. Why didn't she say anything?*

He wants nothing more than to take out his phone and call Leona, but his mum groans softly. Dave shifts his grip to carry her to the couch. He sets Sarita down among the lacy cushions as gently as he can. The air-conditioned den is chilly, so Dave grabs a quilted blanket off the back of her rocking chair and wraps it around Sarita. His mum's face is motionless and pale, which reminds him of visiting Mrs. Lin in the hospital during the final wretched weeks of her illness.

Mum's startled, not sick, Dave tells himself sternly, but his grief for the woman who was like an aunt to him still knots his throat. *Oh, Chun-Mei. What I'd give to talk with you tonight.*

Sighing, Dave sits down on the other end of the couch. As his mother breathes, the den's soft lamplight catches on the fine gold threads around the collar of her emerald housecoat, a gift from Mrs. Lin after their family trip to China so long ago. *She'll be fine,* he tells himself.

A muscle flexes in his chest. Rubbing his scar, Dave leans back against the cushions. *What's the most productive thing you can do right now?* How often had he and Halina asked each other that question during their eight years in business? Too many times to count.

Dave pulls out his cell. As if summoned by his thought, there's a text from his co-founder:

What's it going to take to get this paperwork done?

Stalling changes nothing but our reputation.

Rune's not a shop that breaks client deadlines.

You saw to that.

Snorting at the perfect mix of guilt and command, Dave deletes her text. *Your paperwork is the least of my worries, Hal,* he thinks as he calls his aunt's phone. Voicemail. He tries again, dialing her house this time. No answer. *Come on, Auntie Lee, pick up. What good is being a telepath if you don't answer my calls?* But she doesn't pick up, so he leaves a message asking her to call him immediately. Next, he sends a text to Ryan to ask if he's seen Leona.

Feeling unsettled, Dave opens Facebook. Over three hundred notifications pop up, most from international friends and business contacts demanding to know if he's okay. There's no concerned message from Halina. *Surprise.* He scans his feed: Toronto is losing its collective mind. He ignores the wilder conspiracy theories about the attack. He posts a quick "I'm safe, thanks for all the kind thoughts" note before logging off.

People are going to find out. Hal will know. And Charles. And everyone at Rune. The realization shouldn't feel like a bolt from the blue, but it does. *I've got to give Dad something. He'll want specifics. I should have asked Kalos exactly when the next attack will come.* Dave sighs. *Kalos is even better than me at ignoring other people's demands.*

His email pings. Dave's heart leaps, hoping it's Leona. Instead, he finds Jason's flight itinerary.

"Yes!" Dave cries, pumping his fist. "Finally, some good news!" Beside him, Sarita stirs. He pats her feet through the blanket as he skims the rest of the email, on which both he and Anna are copied. Jason's asking to be picked up on Wednesday afternoon at Hamilton International Airport, a mere hour down the highway from Toronto.

Riding that victory, Dave picks up the TV remote. *Showing Mum what Anna did may make it easier for her to accept.* The channel's already set to CBC. He sits through a cycle of talking heads before they return to the SkyDome footage. As he watches, something fast, pixelated, and incomprehensible to his eye rockets into the frame. *Skyworm.* Heat climbs Dave's back. *It looks like a camera glitch, not a monster.* Xhen curls around his fingers, pooling in his palms to clasp his hands like a lover.

"Is that Anna?" his mother asks in a weak voice.

Dave turns to Sarita as she struggles up against the couch's pillows, doll-like in her robe. "Yes," he tells her as she reaches for his hand. Letting go of xhen, Dave takes her cold fingers in his as they study the TV.

On screen, Anna's xhen arcs into the sky to strike at the skyworms. In answer, elation blooms in Dave's body. "That's xhen," he cries, pointing. "The energy we summon." He demonstrates. His mum blanches. "Sorry," he says, releasing it.

Sarita's mind whispers something in Hindi.

"What?" Dave can't tear his eyes from the TV. *Why can't we film them?* He's tempted to text Halina. *She'd have a theory by morning.* He rubs the back of his itchy neck. It felt the same way when he glimpsed a gap in the market during customer meetings. He'd rush back to the office on fire with his new insight, not caring that he couldn't yet see all its permutations. In the early days, he and Halina had pulled dozens of all-nighters after meetings like that, conceptualizing new features for their products. Or new products altogether. As he studies the news footage, Dave feels that same sense of expansive possibility for the first time in three years. *This is a hell of a problem to solve.*

"David, how can you be so sure that these monsters are real? That picture does not look like anything. This is all so crazy."

"This part of my life has been crazy for a long time, Mum. I just didn't tell you when I was younger."

She sniffles.

Dave glances over. Sarita's face is streaked with tears. He gently thumbs them away. "Aw, don't worry about me."

"I will cry," his mum insists, pushing away his hand. She scrubs her palms against her eyes. "And I will worry. I am your mother, and it is very upsetting, everything that you have told me." She retakes his hand, her grip tight. "Can someone else fight these things, these sky monsters, David? Why must it be you?"

"Because, Mum." Dave's smile is there before he can stop it. "They're coming back." He gestures at the screen. "And we'll need everyone we've got to stop them."

She sniffs again and gives him a hard look. "Does your father know?"

"Not yet."

"Then you had better tell him."

"I will. Just in my own time, okay?"

"He is not answering my texts," Sarita says, leaning back against her cushions to give her son a reproachful look. "I will not tell him if you wish it." She sighs. "What would I even say?"

The blue-white light of the TV flickers over their faces as they sit in silence, watching Anna Lin defend their city.

Interlude: Frenzy

The moons rise and set before the veil begins to pulse with our hunting party's return. After the first three victorious scouts crouch low and lift their mouth tentacles, the dazzling power they bear makes our scales even more lustrous. We cast a shimmering rainbow across the cliffs and the ocean waves. Again, the swarm flexes against our coils, keening their delight. This time, we are generous.

We spread our maw wide to extend our mouth tentacle between our jaws and spray the swarm with the barest mist of our new skal. Snapping and biting, they wrestle to catch the drops, no matter how minute. Not one falls upon the sand. Absorbed into their scales, it will quicken their speed and sharpen their attacks upon both greyfish and enemy scouts from other nests.

Our frenzy lasts long into the night until the cliffs echo with our celebration. Yet, when dawn comes, the three remaining scouts have not returned. As we watch in stunned surprise, the veil's pulse slows and then ceases, signaling the end of this crossing.

More loss, observe our mother-sisters. ***You cannot afford such sacrifices***.

Scouts are feckless, we insist, refusing to show concern, lest we alarm the jubilant swarm. ***They fell to discord among themselves***.

We shall search the nest memory, whispers the eldest of our mother-sisters, her withered voice as soft as wind through sea grass. ***This skal tastes familiar***.

Search as you wish, we reply. ***But this power shall not escape our grasp***.

Never, our mother-sisters agree, echoing our irritation. ***Send the black hatchling from the last clutch to lead the hunt. If the stars are bountiful, when they succeed, you shall have the skal you require to arm your hunters and breed a new clutch.***

Annoyance curls our tentacles. Our nest has not boasted sufficient skal to produce a clutch in several seasons. ***The veil puncture is too small for any but scouts to cross.***

The hatching is a runt, insist our mother-sisters. ***It has grown to its full size but remains narrow enough to pass through the veil. Send it to bring focus to this hunt.***

We call the hatchling forward to inspect it alongside nine more scouts. It is indeed the smallest black we have ever hatched. Some defect of its egg formation has left its body unnaturally narrow and short. It stretches not a third the length or width of its dark brethren, who boast the longest tails of our swarm. Shunned for these deficiencies, it bears old scars of acid and flame. Yet it swells with purpose as it raises its head to return our regard.

Bear the scouts to battle, we command it. ***Return in might***.

Part Three

Queen's Park

Chapter 16

Malcolm – Partner

Toronto, ON: Wednesday, August 20

Malcolm sprints along Lavender Creek Trail north of their Junction neighbourhood. *I'm not tired,* he thinks, exulting in the feeling of complete effortlessness. *This is so goddamn weird.* His jogging route through the area's interconnected parks varies between ten and twenty kilometres. The rapidly approaching street means he has less than a kilometre left. The trail is empty, and the sun is only a glimmer through the trees. Eager to brush the edges of his new abilities, Malcolm pushes his speed.

Is this how Olympians feel? he wonders as he streaks down the path before slowing to a stop as the trail meets the newly opened Stockyards Shopping Centre. He's sweating, sure, but not a lot. And he's not short of breath. His muscles feel fresh and his body light. *I could turn around and sprint it again.* Despite his concerns for Anna, their family, and his job, which drove him out of bed at 4:30 a.m., Malcolm grins. *As benefits go, this is pretty great.*

Keeping a less conspicuous pace, he jogs home. After Dave left and the kids went to bed, he'd spent the evening testing his strength in the basement, trying to drive images of Marissa Chang and the other dead teens from his mind. He'd loaded his modular dumbbells with increasingly heavy weights. Each time, he'd been certain that the next set would mark his limit. Yet he'd easily done deadlifts and bicep curls. He'd been tempted to go outside and see if he could lift the back of a car. He might have tried if Nancy Coleman hadn't been skulking around her yard, a long-suffering agent from the gas company in tow. Malcolm had gone inside, surprised to discover his hunger rivaled Anna's. *We're going to spend a fortune on groceries.*

He jaywalks across St. Clair Avenue West, careful not to slip on the gleaming streetcar tracks still shiny with dew. The neighbourhood's early-morning emptiness reverberates against the eerie feeling growing inside him. *Why is this happening to us? Why have those creatures come now?*

Yesterday, keeping a stoic face in the presence of his colleagues had left him more exhausted than this run. *They're bound to know more by the time the task force assembles*, he thinks. *If only Edwards had lived. We could have figured things out together.* Malcolm lets out a sigh as he turns onto their street, feeling another wave of sadness. *Kalos said there will be others. How am I supposed to know who they are? Do I find them? Do they find us?*

Disconcerted, he unlocks the front door. As he comes into the kitchen, Malcolm immediately spots Erin and Tim on the other side of the playroom's French doors. Erin is sitting outside the fully extended walls of their toy castle, surrounded by a horde of Duplo farm animals, dinosaurs, unicorns and pegasi. Tim kneels inside, carefully placing action figures in defensive positions along the parapet. Malcolm tears a paper towel to wipe his face and pours a glass of water, listening. An only child, he finds their ability to play in relative harmony a great source of joy. He nudges the door open.

"No, Erin," Tim's saying. "The animals aren't the bad guys anymore." He makes the action figure of Jasper Rigg—yet another gift from Dave—walk the nearest rampart and point an arm over the wall. "'We're fighting flying snakes now, team!'"

Malcolm nearly chokes on his water as Tim twists a model boa constrictor through the air over the castle. Dropping the snake, Tim takes the action figure up again and pushes a button on its back. The knight's orange-and-black fist punches the snake's mouth. "'The Valoi Knights win!'" he intones. He gives his sister a superior look. "Just like the lady in black."

"She's not a Knight," Erin says with the scorn of a true fan. "You made her up."

"She's new," Tim says loftily. "I saw her on the news."

A lump rises in Malcolm's throat. *Jesus*, he thinks. *When do we tell them what's going on?* Do *we tell them?*

Anna enters the kitchen, still limping and dressed in khakis and a short-sleeved white blouse, her straight black hair pulled into a ponytail. "Mommy and Daddy have to work this morning, sweethearts," Anna calls to their children, oblivious to both his dilemma and the nuances of their game. She holds out two backpacks. If he concentrates, he can feel the ache of the injury dragging on her consciousness like poor aerodynamics on a badly designed car. "Pack up the toys you want for today. Camp is still closed, so Daddy's taking you to Auntie Sarita's house."

"She tells the best stories!" Erin crows, taking her backpack. "Even better than yours, Mommy."

Watching Anna as she cajoles Tim into packing up his things instead of continuing the game, Malcolm tries to reconcile this picture of domesticity with the creatures Anna slew. *It's not going to make sense for a while,* he decides as Tim debates which toys from the castle game to take. *Incomplete information always creates uncertainty. Stop expecting the fog to lift.*

As if aware of his thoughts, Anna glances up. "You going to have a shower?"

"Yeah," he answers. "I'll be quick. Chris texted to say he's working from home, so I don't have to pick him up."

"Good. The kids ate. I'm taking the subway to MaRS Discovery District to meet Walter at 8:15." Seeing his frown, Anna pokes his chest with a finger. "Stop your worrying right there. Dave's going to meet me at Ossington Station. We'll meet you around 11:30, maybe noon at the latest."

"All right," Malcolm says, spreading his arms to offer her a sweaty hug. Squealing about her clean clothes, Anna accepts the briefest kiss and then ducks under his arm. He looks back at her as he heads to the stairs. She seems happy, her injury notwithstanding, as she helps Tim to pack up the toys. *She'll be fine*, he tells himself. *She can handle it.*

He hurries through his shower, not pausing to enjoy the heat against his back. When he comes downstairs in his office clothes, badge and gun on his plainclothes holster and his police vest tucked under one arm, Anna is indeed gone. Her absence chafes at his mind, throbbing like a scrape. Ignoring the itch to go after her is an act of will. "Let's go, kids."

Traffic is comparatively light as he drives to the Montcalms' house. Despite his best efforts, his background awareness of Anna continues to nag at his thoughts. Sarita is waiting for them at the screen door, dressed in designer sweats in a deep, cheerful pink, her wrists covered in jeweled bangles and her braids whiter than the last time Malcolm saw her.

"Welcome, dear ones, welcome," she says, stooping to hug Erin and Tim. "You are in luck," she tells them. "Since you were here last, I found some of David's old toys in the basement. They are waiting for you in the den. Go and introduce yourselves."

Grinning, the children drop their bags, kick off their sandals, and run into the house without so much as a look at Malcolm. "Thank you for taking them," he says, picking up the backpacks.

"It's a pleasure," Sarita says, plucking the bags from his hands and tucking them away under a bench. "They are the closest I will come to grandchildren until David stops his stubbornness and finds a sweet, kind woman to marry." She smiles, showing the dimple in her right cheek. "He will be a wonderful father. Just like you."

"Mmm," Malcolm says, feeling the tips of his ears flush pink. "Well, I should—"

"Will you stay for chai?" Sarita asks.

Malcolm shakes his head, inching toward the door. "I have to get downtown."

"Of course," Sarita says. She takes a paper bag from the bench and presses it into his hands. Malcolm starts to thank her, wondering if she knows about their strange bursts of hunger. Sarita waves off his words with an elegant hand. "No thanks are necessary, my dear." She pats his wrist, regarding him with knowing eyes. "Having a partner in public life is an uneasy thing."

"Public life?" Malcolm echoes, his brow creasing.

"Inevitably," Sarita says. "With time, she will understand how much she is asking of you. How much they are asking of all of us."

As she holds his gaze, Malcolm sees that the skin around her eyes is puffy and red beneath her makeup. *She's as freaked out as I am*, he thinks, and steps forward to offer a hug that Sarita accepts.

As they step apart, she says, "For now, I wish you to know that however she seems, Anna needs your love and support more than ever. Never lose sight of your most important role: as her partner and advocate for your children."

Kalos said that, too, Malcolm reflects in the car once he's made his goodbyes and hugged the children one more time. *To focus on helping Anna with all these mysterious others.* He opens the bag, which smells heavenly, and takes a generous bite of omelet, deliciously seasoned and rolled in a chapati. *Does that mean two people? Fifty? A thousand?* He shakes his head, trying to picture it. *Is she really going to do this? Am I? It couldn't have come at a worse time.*

While they've kept the house running somewhat smoothly for the kids' sake, his mother-in-law's death created a deep rupture in their lives. *Anna's done nothing all summer but obsess over that house and cry. I should have insisted she go to grief counselling.* He eats the last of the omelet and wipes his fingers on the napkin thoughtfully tucked in the bag, wishing there was more. *But therapy doesn't work if it's forced.*

He'd gone himself after his mother, Sofia, had died of a stroke eight days after his police academy graduation. Losing his only living relative had caught him completely off guard and sent him into a profound depression. His father, Anton, fifteen years her elder, had died of influenza in Ukraine when he was three, before they immigrated to Canada. Malcolm, who'd been called Maksim then, hardly remembers him.

After assessing her options, Sofia sold their farm in Poltava. Malcolm went to live with his paternal grandfather, Maksim Nazarenko Sr., while Sofia flew to Canada to start the immigration process. At first, they'd shared little beyond a name, but his grandfather had become his world. They lived together in that tiny house for three years. Telephone calls to his mother had been expensive and infrequent. Malcolm had consoled himself with letters, occasional packages from Toronto, and taking walks in the forest with his grandfather to look for mushrooms.

In 1986, his mother's long-awaited summons finally came. The two Maksims flew to Canada a few months after his sixth birthday. To his lasting sorrow, his mother anglicized his first name and failed to convince the elder Maksim to stay. He'd returned to Ukraine when Malcolm started school. They had two in-person visits after that: once when Maksim came to Canada for the summer when Malcolm was eight and again when he and his mother flew to Poltava for a month when Malcolm was thirteen.

His grandfather's unflappable aura and nail-biting stories about the war had made quite an impression. Malcolm flew home wishing his mother hadn't decided to change his name. When Maksim died the following August at the ripe age of ninety-four, Malcolm asked her to change it back. His mother said the paperwork was too onerous. *You're Canadian now. Having a name like other boys will help you.*

For her part, Sofia had kept working, taking endless shifts in a jeans factory to put him through school. He misses her laugh, her sense of style, and especially her cooking, particularly during the holidays. His deepest regret is that she never met Anna or his children, but he knows she would be pleased with his successes. *I have a good job. We have a great place to live. The kids go to a good school. She laid the foundation for all of that. I wasn't looking for more.*

And yet, Maksim, he imagines his grandfather's voice saying, *more has found you.*

He expects to meet barricades on the drive into Toronto Police Headquarters, located at Bay and College. There aren't any until he gets to University Avenue, where the traffic increases. So does the foot traffic. The day's turning sunny and warm, the sky is clear, but smoke from the previous night lingers, making the back of his throat itch. The same heavy feeling from his morning run returns as he counts the people on the sidewalks, walking briskly or waiting for streetcars and buses. *How much of the city is still open?* he wonders. *The chief can't believe it's a one-off thing, not with two attacks on separate nights.*

Inside headquarters, the scene is even more chaotic. People clutching photos line the corridors. *The missing,* Malcolm thinks. Four lines snake back from the desk in the atrium, down the hall, and out of sight.

"Officer?" asks a woman's voice. Turning, Malcolm locks eyes with a short Asian woman in an immaculate cream business suit. He guesses she's about Anna's age. "Do you know where I'd find a washroom?"

"Down the hall," he says automatically, thinking of Sarita as he notes this woman's red-rimmed eyes and worn face. "Third door on your left. It's well signed."

Nodding, she looks back at the next person in line, a Black man in jeans and a short-sleeve golf shirt. He's older than them both, his hair flecked with grey, and holding a handful of printed photographs. "Thanks for holding my spot," the woman says. "I'll be right back."

"We got nothing but time," the man tells her, and turns to Malcolm as she pushes off through the tightly packed crowd. "How long do you think the wait is from here?"

Malcolm shrugs. "I just arrived, so I'm not sure. You're filing reports for missing persons?"

"Yeah," the man answers. "Her dad's missing. So are my neighbours." He points at the pictures. "They're in their nineties. She's got a walker. Whatever happened to them, there's no way they made a run for it."

"I'm so sorry for your loss," Malcolm says, thinking of the immensity of those alien carcasses and what Cloar said the creatures had done inside the condo towers before Anna brought them down. Anger flickers in his gut. He meets the other man's eyes, aware of the people around them leaning in to listen. "We'll do our best to get you answers."

The man gives him a considering look. "Is it true? Was it some kind of alien?"

"Nazarenko!" a voice bellows. On his left, he spots Deputy Chief Cloar leaning out of a conference room, beckoning to him.

Saved, he thinks. "Excuse me," he says aloud to the man, who shrugs, clearly prepared to ride out the long wait. Malcolm makes his way across the atrium and into the conference room.

Inside, the room is packed. "Get some coffee," Cloar says, steering him toward a carafe, a stack of paper cups, and a box of protein bars at the back of the room. Malcolm follows on his heels as the deputy refills his cup and mutters in an undertone, "Interesting developments overnight. The feds aren't buying our reports. None of the photos or video came out right." He gives Malcolm the smirk of a man who has seen it all yet finds himself plumbing fresh depths of bureaucratic incompetence. "They're classifying the attacks as 'domestic terrorism.'" Cloar guffaws as he dumps two creams and two sugars into the cup. "Which makes our girl in black the number one person of interest." Lifting his coffee, he eyes Malcolm. "And our only lead."

"Shit," Malcolm says weakly as Cloar moves through the crowd to take his place at the table. *She'll be here in less than three hours*, he tells himself. *Cloar and Chief Montcalm will understand why you had to wait.*

Smoothing his face, he stuffs a few protein bars into his pockets, just in case his unusual hunger returns. He pours his own coffee and settles in to listen.

Chapter 17

Jason – Departure

Vancouver, BC: Wednesday, August 20

Jason puts his carry-on bag on the floor of the Miata's passenger seat. He barely has time to climb in and pull the door shut before Margo throws the car into reverse and backs out of their narrow parking space. He fumbles for his seat belt as she swerves around the rows of parked cars, gunning for the garage's exit. "You trying to send me back to St. Paul's?" He means to sound teasing, but his voice brims with asperity. "Slow down!"

"You want to make the flight you're late for?" Margo slings back, swerving around a station wagon full of yawning teenagers. Jason grabs for the holy shit handle above his window as she maneuvers them onto Davie Street. "You have to be checked in by five a.m., so don't criticize."

I set that alarm, I know I did, he thinks as they slow for a stoplight. But his phone didn't chime at 3:30 a.m. "Sorry," he says. "We wouldn't have overslept if I'd set my alarm."

Margo turns an appraising eye on him. But instead of saying whatever's on her mind, she grabs an elastic band from her wrist and wrestles her hair into a knot. The light changes. Expertly, she shifts up to third gear. "Traffic never used to be so bad this early," she grumbles.

Jason's lived in Vancouver all his adult life, and he can't remember the traffic ever being good. *Which is why I set early alarms. Stupid. I must have forgotten when I went to bed.* "I walk so much I don't notice, I guess."

"You walk. I cab," Margo says as she drives across Granville Street Bridge. Her hand darts to the console. Pop music blares from the car's speakers.

"True," Jason says, releasing the handle to turn the radio volume down to a tolerable level. He wonders what he's forgotten. *What do you pack to join your sister's imaginary war?* He shakes his head, letting the urban sprawl pass in a blur. Despite the confusing news reports, Dave's astounding ability, and Kalos's appearance, none of this—the suitcase at his feet, the electronic boarding pass on his phone, or the emails he sent to his boss pleading another family crisis and requesting time away—feels real, except for his heart. It's pounding in his chest as though it's trying to beat its way out.

Deep breaths, comes his mother's voice, as it always does when he's on his way to the airport. *Think about something pleasant.*

Jason turns to his wife. Margo's expression is disdainful as she navigates the early rush-hour traffic. A few pieces of dark hair dangle loose from her impromptu knot. Chun-Mei's ruby catches the reflected headlights of a passing car. She's commandeered another of his dress shirts, black this time over a bright blue camisole and jeans.

She frowns at the Camry ahead of them. "You're staring," she says without turning her head. Her smile is laser quick, and Jason knows he's forgiven for their mad rush out the door. "Take a picture."

So he does. Three of them. "I'm going to miss your play."

"Just previews," she says. "We're working out some details. It'll be polished by the time you're back for opening night." She grins. "I can't wait for you to see it!" Margo changes lanes but keeps glancing at him, clearly waiting for him to say something.

Am I going to be back? His ticket is one way.

They drive in silence for another few minutes. Then Margo says, "You know, Jason, you don't have to go home if you don't want to."

"It's booked." He tries to chuckle, but Kalos's face looms in his mind. *Breathe.*

"That's not what I mean," Margo says. "You set your alarm last night. I saw you do it. And you turned it off this morning—twice."

"What?" His palms start to sweat. "Why didn't you wake me up?"

"I only half heard the first one. The second time, I was awake. But I didn't think you wanted to be." Margo flicks a practiced eye over to him. When they were first dating, her ability to distill insight from body language struck him as magical. Back then, Vancouver still had an NBA team. A couple of times a season, he'd buy a pair of tickets. Margo would sit beside him, lazily watch the Grizzlies play for ten minutes, and tell him as much, if not more, about the team's interpersonal dynamics as any sports column he might read the following day. "I don't think you want to fly to Toronto." She slows for yet another red light and turns her head to hold his gaze. "At all."

Jason looks away from her frank assessment, folding his arms over his chest. "Well, I'm going."

"But why?" Margo puts a hand on his arm, her voice gentle. "You seem almost nervous. And I don't just mean the usual stuff about the flight."

"I'm not nervous," he scoffs as his belly rolls over.

"Uh-huh." The light changes. "And the traffic's great."

Margo pulls her hand back to take the gear shift. Jason puts his hand on top of hers, rubbing his thumb across her knuckles. Her skin is so smooth and warm. *I want you to come,* he thinks, but that would mean telling her everything.

Your triad must be united before the skyworms return, Kalos had said. He shudders.

"Whatever it is that you're dreading, you don't have to do it," Margo says.

Jason flinches, recalling Dave's eerie ability to follow his thoughts.

She puts her hand on his leg, commanding his attention. "Do you hear me? You have permission to stay here. Anna will get over it."

Jason looks down at his tennis shoes planted on either side of his carry-on. One is scuffed. He bends to buff the dust off with his palm. His sister and his wife aren't hostile, but he wouldn't exactly call them friendly either. When together, Anna inevitably sits stone-faced through Margo's stories about her theatre company while Margo rolls her eyes at Anna's efforts to get Jason to reminisce. *Clinging to the past signals an impoverished spirit,* Margo told him once. *It's how people console themselves when they can't—or won't—grow.*

"Anna is why I'm worried," he says aloud. From the corner of his eye, he sees Margo glance sharply at him. The Camry ahead of their Miata is suddenly way too close. "Watch the road!"

Margo downshifts to put a more comfortable distance between the two cars, but her attention continues to alternate between him and the traffic. "You can't say something like that and stop." She brakes for another red light. "What's going on, Jason?"

Outside their car, people stream across the intersection, hauling briefcases and backpacks. In his chest, his past and present feel like parallel streets designed to never intersect. *There's still time,* his conscience whispers. *Tell her.*

The light changes. Margo doesn't move. Behind them, a car horn blows. Swearing under her breath, Margo rockets the car forward. The sudden motion thrusts Jason back in his seat. His heart lurches as they comet through the traffic. Reflexively, Jason runs his hands against the grain of the khaki pants he always wears when traveling. The motion soothes him, but no words come. *I'm not that person anymore. I haven't been for years.* His heart races faster. *Just start somewhere. Anywhere.* "Anna was injured. Monday night, during that incident in Toronto."

"What!" Margo's incredulous face whips to the right. Her dark eyes fix on him. "What the hell was she doing downtown so late?"

"Great question," Jason says as the Camry's bumper looms too close again. "I don't know." It's not a lie. He's watched the disturbing online footage again and again, trying to make sense of the pixelated noise in the images as he replays his memory of their conversation. He can't make sense of her choice to seek out more trouble or how it must have felt to stand there. He's tried to imagine doing the same and failed. "She hurt her leg."

Margo's stunned silence is more damning than a thousand expletives from anyone else.

"She's okay, but . . ."

Tell her, insists that quiet part of him. *Tell her what Dave said: that Anna fought strange monsters. Now is your chance.*

Jason's throat tightens. His heart pounds. Minutes tick past. Sweat beads his forehead, his neck, and the small of his back. He turns up the air-conditioning. Margo turns off the radio. In sour silence, they speed past gentrified stores and low-rise apartments, which give way to the more lushly landscaped suburbs. Before he knows it, Margo's taking the ramp for Vancouver International Airport. Rapidly, their car closes in on the terminal.

She slows down, signaling as she pulls into the drop-off lane. "Why didn't you say anything about Anna until now?" Her voice is light. When they were first married, he would have been fooled into thinking her genuinely curious, not deeply affronted and rapidly shifting to cold fury.

"You know Anna," Jason shrugs. "She's always been a bit reckless."

"I don't know, actually." Margo inches the car up to the curb and flashes him another blinding grin. But there's pain in the corners of her mouth. As a child, he often saw the same dismay on the faces of kids who wanted to be friends. Inevitably, they found themselves on the outside of his twin bond with Anna. Long before xhen, Dave was the only one who seemed unthreatened by their closeness. Breaking that pattern was part of the reason Jason applied to universities with medical schools in British Columbia, Nova Scotia, and Québec.

Jason touches a hand to his wife's cheek. "You aren't the problem, Margo."

She pulls away. "So why didn't you tell me?"

Jason pulls his hand back to his lap. His clammy fingertips and palms leave faint water stains on his khakis. *Classic panic symptoms.* Yet his medical understanding of what's happening to his body does nothing to lessen its impact. "What time is your rehearsal?"

She frowns. "Don't change the subject."

Around them, people get out of their cars, pop trunks to retrieve their luggage, and embrace for one last hug and kiss. *I should go. I should tell her the truth.* Jason sits rooted to his seat, unable to make the two roads of his life merge. His memories of xhen sit lodged inside his chest, crushing any word he might summon to explain his complicated relationship with Anna and why she's asked him to come home. *Margo will think I'm crazy.* I *think I'm crazy.*

"Hey," Margo whispers. The anger's gone from her face as she touches his hands, wiping them with a tissue hastily retrieved from the box in the car's centre console. "Tell me, Jason. Whatever it is that's got you so freaked out, I'm listening."

A security guard standing on the curb blows his whistle, beckoning for them to leave the drop-off area. "I love you," he blurts. "When I get back, we'll go to dinner. Okay? No friends. Just you and me, anywhere you like. And we'll talk."

Margo frowns. A car beeps behind them, eager to take their spot. *Please,* Jason thinks. *Don't make me do this now.*

After a moment, Margo nods. "Kiss me."

And he does, until the security guard taps on their window. He holds a pad of parking tickets up in warning.

Regret follows Jason into the terminal like the smell of Margo's orchid perfume. *I should have told her. What if something happens and I can't get back for a while?* He shakes his head. *I'm starting to think like Anna. It'll be fine.*

With Pearson Airport still closed in Toronto and the news full of uncertainty, the terminal is emptier than Jason's ever seen it. There's no line at the check-in counter for domestic flights, but there's a small queue at the security gate. *I guess I'll make my flight after all.*

Snippets of Cantonese surround him as Jason joins the line. After concentrating for a moment on the conversations, he decides there's an international flight leaving for Hong Kong. A glance at the departures board confirms his guess, but he feels no sense of satisfaction.

You're embarrassing yourself, his mother used to say whenever he tried to puzzle his way through a sign or menu during their Chinatown lunches when he was an undergrad. *I wasted so much money on those Saturday classes. I should send you the bill.* He'd taken a few language courses as electives at the University of British Columbia, but neither he nor Anna learned to speak Cantonese to Chun-Mei's satisfaction.

What would Mom think of this mess? Jason wonders, tugging his carry-on behind him. *She'd want me to go home for Anna, no question. Would she want me to tell Margo?* He considers his parents' relationship—in which his father contentedly departed for the sanctity of his research lab and learned only the details that his mother chose to share about the twins' day-to-day life at home—and sighs.

Ahead of him, a woman with a large-brimmed floppy hat and designer sunglasses turns to adjust a tag on her equally expensive luggage. She meets his eyes. Something in Jason's face seems to give her pause because she smiles brightly and reaches out to pat his arm. "Don't worry, honey," she tells him in Cantonese. "The flight will be fine. You going home, too?"

"Yes," Jason answers with his terrible accent, wishing his mother would be at the airport to greet him with a smile as warm as this stranger's. "Guess I am."

Chapter 18

Anna – Discovery

Toronto, ON: Wednesday, August 20

Anna gets onto the eastbound subway car at Keele Station. She slept terribly. Her injured leg is killing her, but she forces determination into her step. *This morning, I'm going to find Walter Delal a new office*, she tells herself as she eases her way onto a seat. Yesterday, between making lunch for the kids and talking to Dave and Malcolm, she'd managed to rebook all three office tours. *He's going to love one of those spaces. I'm going to close my first deal in a year.*

The affirmation feels hollow in the alarmingly empty subway car. Normally, by the time rush-hour trains reach her stop, they're jam-packed with commuters, parents schlepping kids to day camp, and teens working summer jobs. *Six people? That's it?*

There's a *Metro* newspaper folded on the seat beside her. Anna picks it up, skimming headlines. The centre spread is an aerial collage of the 400-series highways around Toronto, absolutely blocked with cars. *Everyone with a cottage or vacation home is leaving the city.* The streets closest to the SkyDome are still closed.

Crews are continuing to assess the surrounding buildings while identifying the bodies being unearthed in the rubble, she reads. *Chief of Police Henry Montcalm refused to speculate on whether the attack was a one-off occurrence or a serious threat.*

Anna bites her lower lip. *Smart man not to take a public bet like that.*

"He's pretty decent at politics," Dave agrees, taking the seat beside hers. "Lots of practice."

Anna blinks. Outside the train's windows, Ossington Station is disappearing in a blur of crimson and gray tiles. "Where'd you come from? Weren't we supposed to meet on the platform?"

"Would you believe me if I said you're an extremely loud thinker?" he asks and laughs when she smacks his arm. "How are you? How's Malcolm?"

"Fine," she says and then frowns. "Pretty tense, actually."

"Mmm," Dave says, one eyebrow raised. "Based on early data, I'd say getting called up to save the world seems to do that to a person." He extends an arm, considering its lean muscle. Tall enough to play pro basketball, Dave moves with an easy grace that Anna's always envied. "Do you think this whole tarkan thing is going to make Malcolm super jacked? Maybe I should become one, too. How does it work? I drop to my knees and pledge my undying—"

Anna shushes him, her eyes flicking around the car. "Don't talk so loud."

No one's listening, Annie, says Dave, his eyes shining with mirth as his voice fills her head like she's wearing invisible earphones. *I'd know.* He jerks his chin at the empty seats and says aloud, "People aren't going downtown unless they have to. If they can, they'll work from home."

Anna rubs her neck, thinking of the bills. "I wouldn't go either if we didn't need the money."

Gentleness sweeps over Dave's face. "If things are tight, I can—"

"No."

After his wild success with Rune, it seemed to Anna that she and

Malcolm were the only friends from Dave's Toronto circle who hadn't found excuses to ask him for handouts or donations to their pet causes. He'd still showered their kids with presents and taken their families on a perfect vacation to St. Lucia while Chun-Mei was healthy enough to travel.

"I'm finding Walter a space for his venture firm today. We'll be fine."

"Sure," Dave says, wearing the half grin that means he thinks she's being ridiculous. He turns his head, surveying the car. "Did you check Facebook? The clubs were packed last night!"

"The people I know are too busy changing diapers to go clubbing," Anna says, "even if the world's ending." She smiles, feeling herself surrendering to Dave's ever-present need to cheer her up. "Don't you find this whole thing weird? Xhen used to be our biggest secret. Telling Malcolm was so strange. I can't imagine talking to my dad about it. How did Sarita take it?"

"Not well," Dave answers. "She was crying in the kitchen this morning. Keeps saying she 'did not raise me to die in a monster war.'" He shrugs. "We're lucky Dad's at work. There's no way she would have kept it quiet." He exhales, his fingers twitching as though he wants a cigarette.

Anna eyes his hand, remembering all the times that Dave's dad nearly caught them neck-deep in mischief. "How do you think he'll take it?"

"I'll get bluster for the first half hour," Dave says, and shrugs. "Has to be done. Ping me after you're finished with Walter. We'll find Malcolm, and Dad and I can talk while you two give your statements or whatever. Then we'll go pick up Jay."

"Assuming the police let us go." Anna rolls her shoulders to release the tension gathering there. "It was good of Sarita to take the kids for us today. Thanks for that."

"Oh, you owe me big time." Her brother in all but blood gives her a wicked smile. "Mum's going to get on my ass about grandchildren again."

Anna snickers. Movement draws her eye as another passenger enters clutching a *Toronto Sun* newspaper. Her amusement dies. On its cover is a grainy photo of her in front of the SkyDome. **WHO IS SHE?** the headline screams. Anna swallows. When she left the house that morning, Nancy Coleman had peered out at her through her living room window. It's starting to feel like there's a giant I KILLED THE MONSTERS: ASK ME HOW! sign floating over her head.

Dave follows her gaze. "That could be anyone," he murmurs. "No one's going to know it's you."

I hope you're right. She glances at Dave, but he's silent. Since her garage conversation with Malcolm, Dave doesn't seem to hear the thoughts she wishes to keep private. Her internal weathervane with Malcolm is equally silent, perhaps because of the physical distance between them, or perhaps because he's distracted with work. Either way, she misses his presence.

Anna lets Dave help her up as they change trains at St. George Station. The absence of riders is even more obvious on Line 1, which normally funnels suburban commuters into Toronto by the thousands. *Relax,* Anna tells herself. *I'm going to show Walter the spaces, get him excited, and close the deal. I've done this hundreds of times. Take a cue from Dave. Be cool.*

They ride two stops to Queen's Park and surface into the early-morning humidity. Immediately, Anna spots Walter Delal talking on his phone as he paces the wide sidewalk outside the MaRS Discovery District, the city's biggest entrepreneurship hub.

"Good morning," he calls, ending his conversation to stride toward them. He's dressed in a spotless linen suit. His matching silver cuff links and tie pin, adorned with enameled tiger heads, glitter in the sunlight against the deep blue of his shirt and the brilliant yellow of his tie. He sweeps his thick mane of silver-streaked hair back from his forehead before he wraps Dave in a back-slapping hug. "You're looking well, Dave. I hear you owe Halina Mendes some paperwork."

"Oh yeah?" Dave says, smiling, but there's a flinty light in his eyes. "You two still talk often?"

"No, not very often," Walter says easily. He turns to Anna and takes her hand, covering it with both of his. "And how are you, my dear?" He frowns. "You're limping. What happened?"

"Oh, I had a little accident in my garage. No big deal." Faced with his immaculate attire, Anna feels distinctly sweaty in her damp blouse and creased khakis. "Were you able to get to your sister's home the other night?"

"Barely," Walter says, turning to look south down University Avenue. Following his gaze, she spots crowd-control barricades in the distance blocking the street. "An awful night, I'm afraid."

A memory surges, and for a moment, she's standing over the skyworm, swinging her xhen axe at its head. Dave puts a hand on her shoulder, but it doesn't help. *Breathe,* Anna tells herself. *Just breathe. Close the deal, talk to the police, and get Jason. We'll be ready when they come.*

Walter sighs and turns to her, smiling. "We can't let fear govern us, can we?"

"No," Anna says, aware of Dave's presence yet unsure how to draw him into the conversation. *Focus on the client.* "Do you still want office space in this area?"

"Wiser men than I have argued that the key to business is keeping your head when everyone else is losing theirs," Walter answers. "And we must move. We're bursting at the seams."

"I need to walk," Dave says. "You two have fun. Good to see you, Walt." He catches Anna's eye as the men shake hands. *Text if you need me. I don't know how close I have to be to hear you.*

"All right," Anna says as Dave heads toward the intersection and the University of Toronto campus on the northwest side. She forces a smile as she turns to Walter. "Just us."

Walter sighs. "I shouldn't have mentioned Halina."

"He'll get over it," Anna says, checking her notebook as she steers Walter toward the building. "I have three office spaces to show you on University Avenue, but I think MaRS is the best fit."

"And the Ontario government's across the street." Walter's smile turns bemused. He gestures to the Legislative Assembly of Ontario building on the other side of College Street. "Didn't Dave tell you? I'm raising another venture fund. I want the province to co-invest."

Anna's smile falters. It's the sort of detail she prides herself on knowing about her clients. *I'm here. That's a win.* "See and be seen," she agrees, trying to shake off her unease. "Let's find the facility manager, shall we?"

Inside, the building's four-story lobby is deathly quiet. Glass ceilings and steel catwalks vault overhead, mixing the city's craze for internationalist architecture with the original brick walls of the old Toronto General Hospital building. Anna scans the long atrium, which runs at varying heights for the entire block, and can't spot a single person. The contrast to her previous visits—when hearing Dave speak or attending networking events—is so stark that her skin crawls.

The world has changed, whispers a small voice inside her. *I can't pretend otherwise.*

Three hours is all I need, she tells herself, focusing on Walter as they find the manager and head for the elevators. They tour half a dozen available suites in the west tower, discussing how each space might be customized to meet Walter's needs. As they walk, Anna finds herself glancing at the wide expanse of sky outside the tower's floor-to-ceiling windows. As if on cue, her kidneys twinge. *Muscle tension. Ignore it.*

For their last stop, the facility manager brings them to a suite on the fourth floor. "I think you'll like how they've used the space," she says as they enter a stadium-sized boardroom. Plaques bearing an assortment of corporate logos line its walls like animal heads in a hunting den.

"Start-up incubator," Walter murmurs with appreciation. He straightens his already-straight spine, eyes glowing as though pleased by how his own portfolio of companies compares to this one. "Yes, this is exactly the kind of space I need."

"I knew you'd say that," Anna lies. *If he loves it, maybe we can skip the other locations*. The manager leads Walter along corridors of white-on-white cubicles punctuated with lime green. Anna's leg continues to ache, but she follows, feeling giddy. *I can close this deal right now*.

Movement flutters in the corner of her eye. Immediately, her back begins to burn. Anna's eyes fly to the window. Kalos is there, beyond the glass wall. He beckons to her.

Not now! she shouts, as duty, old and new, pulls her head in two directions like the opposing poles of a magnet. *Another twenty minutes and I'll have it!* But her teacher's face is implacable.

"Excuse me a moment," she murmurs to Walter. Instead of answering the siren call of xhen, Anna enters the cubical nearest the southwest corner window. She yanks the sunshade up.

Outside, Kalos waits on a large, flat, rail-less balcony. ***They come***. Past him, University Avenue's row of hospitals and the CN Tower shimmer in the rising August heat.***Join me here***.

"I can't," Anna whispers. Giddy and sickened, she reaches for her phone. "They'll see!" *Dave. Malcolm. I have to text them!*

Your secrecy is at its end, child. Be inside that building when the skyworms attack and everyone with you is dead.

"Can I help you?" asks an unfamiliar voice.

Fumbling with her phone, Anna glances over her shoulder. She locks eyes with an irritated-looking blonde woman in a white blazer, blue T-shirt, and dark jeans. "Just a sec." Anna opens her messaging app. "I need to send a text." *Dave, Dave, Dave.*

"From my office?" The blonde lifts an eyebrow and steps closer, using her considerable height to loom over Anna as her smile thins.

Anna taps wildly at her keyboard. None of the words on the screen make any sense. *Fucking autocorrect. Dave!*

What? What's happening?

Anna's so shocked to hear his voice that she drops her phone. *They're coming!* She scrambles under the desk to retrieve her device, wincing at the pain in her leg as she scurries out of the blonde's proximity. *MaRS building. Kalos is here. I'll be on one of the lower roofs. Southwest corner. Tell Malcolm.*

You got it.

Don't be so excited, she admonishes. *This is serious, Dave!*

Perfectly serious. His gleeful smile is plain in his mental voice. *It's my city, too, Anna. You don't get to be the only one who smashes monsters.*

Walter's looking at her strangely as she climbs to her feet, phone in hand. "Are you all right, Anna?" he asks. "You seem . . . distressed."

"Hold this for me." Anna shoves her phone into her purse and pushes the bag into his hands. "You need to get everyone out of the building."

His wide brown eyes blink. "Pardon me?"

"The skyworms are attacking the city—all the towers, probably all of University Avenue. Get everyone out. Call 9-1-1."

"Skyworms?" Walter echoes. "You mean those . . . Anna, you're not making any sense." He tries to give back her purse. "Shall I fetch you a glass of water?"

"Listen!" Anna drops her voice to a hiss, pulling Walter closer. The blonde regards them with curiosity. "The creatures that attacked the city are called skyworms. I killed three at the SkyDome. They will attack again in a matter of minutes. Get moving. *Now.*"

"Anna . . ." Walter begins. "I think you need to lie down—"

"No arguments," Anna snaps. "You're wasting time." She pushes past the blonde, casting about for a heavy object, and settles with satisfaction on the woman's office chair. It's heavier than she expects, so she jerks it toward the large expanse of windows.

"Hey!" the woman protests. Bracing herself against the pain in her leg, Anna hefts the chair and slams it against the glass. It rebounds with a crash, doing no damage.

"What the hell, lady!" The blonde rushes her, pulling the chair away. Heads rise above the low cubical walls. Walter and the facility manager continue to stand there, doing nothing, as the blonde shoves her chair back under her desk. The woman rounds on Anna, fury blazing in her blue eyes, and raises her voice. "Someone call security before this woman destroys our office!"

Anna's eyes flick between the confused faces. *Useless!* She spots a fire alarm over Walter's shoulder and pulls the switch, imploring him one last time. "You're in charge, Walter. Get them out!" She raises her voice over the blaring alarm, meeting the blonde's eyes. "Everyone out!"

Now, child.

"I know!" Anna grasps xhen. Waves of energy rise through her skin and her white blouse, their ocean blue startling under the fluorescent lights.

Walter drops her purse.

A terrible roar shakes the building, lighting Anna's spine with a now-familiar ache. Glass implodes along the tower's south and west walls. Anna casts xhen in a wide, shallow arc, protecting as many people as she can. Despite her frantic efforts, screams fill the air. She doesn't turn to see if Walter is hit. She can't. *Fuck, fuck, fuck. Hurry, Dave!*

Fortunately, the window she tried to break has shattered. Anna awkwardly climbs over the jagged remnants onto the balcony to join Kalos. "Where is it?"

Circling north. Three more come from the south. The veil is thinnest over water. A pause. ***More have crossed. Perhaps six. You must be swift.***

"Ten? How the hell do I kill ten skyworms?"

Carefully. He extends a hand. ***Come***.

Anna swallows hard, knowing exactly what he intends. "Do it."

Kalos's spectral fingers close on hers. Cold rushes up her arm and spreads down her back, numbing her body's fear response. Anna shuts her eyes. Her solar plexus lurches. Adrenaline surges in a feverish burst as every cell in her body bends to Kalos's will. Her nerves shriek like fingernails on a blackboard, only the slate is her skin. Then she's riding in the back of her head, watching through her eyes as Kalos takes control of her body. All of her senses are muffled, including her awareness of her sore leg. Anna chafes against the control, her eagerness to reclaim her flesh strong. But doing so would also prevent her from learning Kalos's lesson.

He works her xhen into a shape she's never seen—a wide, sharp crescent with deadly points about a foot long. He bends the energy in a new, shining twist that caps off both ends. ***They last half an hour***, he explains, crafting a second more slowly so that she can follow. ***You may apply the technique to other shapes, but never ride a skyworm without crescent knives.***

WHAT? She'd run if she could. *I'm terrible with heights, Kalos.*

Trust your xhen. Finishing the second knife, he knots more xhen into a ball. He holds it before her eyes, letting Anna study its shape. ***This ball is woven of interlocking xhen filaments. When opened, the pieces will find their way to worthy tarkan and request their service. If they choose to answer its call, they must then swear the oath to cement their tie to you. Make and drop such balls every time you fight. Teach your brothers to do the same***.

Okay, she thinks. *How do I open it?*

In answer, Anna watches her arm toss it over the ledge, seemingly of its own volition. Kalos's control of the ball flexes. It bursts apart, splattering bits of blue light like confetti blasted from an invisible cannon. She's overwhelmed with the impulse to follow the drifting filaments. But under his control, she can't do anything but watch as he makes her hands tuck the knives into the waistband of her khakis. *Thank God I wore pants today.*

Another roar rocks the balcony ledge. Kalos turns her head. Two orange creatures rise to circle the CN Tower's observation deck. As they watch, the skyworms loop north toward her position. Below, car horns blow. Traces of her blue confetti drift along the congested street, almost too small to see. People stream out of office buildings and emerge from their cars to run. It's chaos.

Kalos turns her as the third orange skyworm circles Queen's Park. *That one blew out the windows.*

Yes. He crouches her body low, making her hands coil xhen in a long cable. The skyworms roar, surging through the air. Anna, eager to fight, strains to tense and can't. ***Patience.***

On her left, glass and brick explode from the nearest hospital tower. Kalos ignores the noise; the rubble falls short of her position. The skyworms close, their roars shaking Anna's spine. More glass, brick, and metal rain down on them from the office floors directly above, bouncing off her teacher's conjured barrier as he keeps the path clear between her and the building's edge. Anna wants to run, to do something, anything—yet Kalos holds her steady until all three skyworms are practically on top of them. Then he launches her leash at the nearest skyworm, snaring the scales of its neck behind its tall, ridged crest. It howls, bucking.

"Anna!" Malcolm shouts from somewhere behind her, his presence crashing into her awareness. She fights to turn. Kalos jerks her forward. She runs across the balcony.

And jumps.

NO! Panic—both hers and Malcolm's—floods her mind beneath the fist of Kalos's control. Like some wingless bird, Anna hangs in the air for a sickening, weightless second. Gravity seizes her. As she starts to plummet, Kalos hauls xhen into her body with sufficient force to turn what should be a suicidal plunge into a reverse rappelling move. Straining to follow, Anna hurtles toward the dodging skyworm, knowing her life depends on this lesson.

Kalos flings her arm and leg over the skyworm's back, clinging there as he expertly lashes her to its scales. The skyworm thrashes, its outrage reverberating through her with the same pulsing buzz she's felt standing too close to large speakers at rock concerts. Then vertigo seizes Anna as street and sky whirl in a dizzying blur. She strives for calm, but her crushing need for corporeal control overruns her consciousness. Her heart should be pounding, her mouth dry, her palms wet, and her blood an oceanic roar in her ears.

ANNA. She'd flinch if she could. Kalos so rarely uses their names. ***Observe***.

Kalos inches her up the skyworm's neck toward its large platelike crest as the creature flies over the street. He treats its dodging with the indifference of someone striding up the aisle of a moving subway train. Ahead, the skyworm's crest is thicker than she expects, creating a pocket that shields her from the reach of its tentacles and much of the wind. Swiftly, Kalos strikes one of his conjured knives into the meaty flesh at the base of the plate, cutting a deep slash.

Howling to shatter every window within five hundred metres, the skyworm pulls up and carries them into the blue. Kalos digs Anna's free hand through its flesh. Her fingers wrap around three thick cords that he pulls free. Sulphureous gas clogs their shared eyes and nose as ichor coats her bare hands. Kalos separates the middle cord from the others. Severing it, he tucks her knife away as the skyworm's agonized howl echoes over Toronto and the very end of its tail goes slack.

Suddenly, Anna has a stomach-lurching view of the emergency helipad at SickKids Hospital rising to meet them. *Oh shit!*

It wants you panicked. Kalos tightly wraps her left hand around the leftmost cord. He pulls hard. The roaring skyworm exits its dive and banks right. He takes the rightmost cord in her right hand and pulls. The skyworm veers left. ***Drive it to David.***

What? I don't understand! Below her thighs, the skyworm quivers. Anna braces for it to buck.

Instead, the skyworm does a barrel roll. Her stomach somersaults as her mind screams danger because it's Anna riding a half-controlled upside-down skyworm hundreds of metres above the nearest rooftop with nothing to protect her but her wits and her xhen.

Kalos is gone.

Chapter 19

Malcolm – Precinct

Toronto, ON: Wednesday, August 20

Malcolm shifts in his chair, nursing his third cup of coffee. He's only half listening to Constables Krista Johansen and Raymond Leong present their assessment of the security footage confiscated from the SkyDome and the area's adjacent businesses.

He sips the tepid liquid, willing the minutes to tick past the way he used to in elementary school. Johansen's hands tremble as she speaks. Leong keeps fidgeting with the laser pointer. They're twenty minutes over time. Malcolm clearly remembers his nerves the first time he presented to such a senior group, but he's got no patience today.

Come on, he thinks as Johansen continues to read her presentation word by bloody word. *Get to the point.*

He can't fault their analysis. They've determined where he and Anna parked, when they arrived and departed the scene, and the makes and models of both cars. They've also got a partial plate for Nancy's Lincoln. Other constables are cross-referencing the car data against records requested from the telecom companies. They've gathered all cellular traffic records from the cell towers nearest the SkyDome between 23:00 on August 18 and 04:00 on August 19.

The data builds on the eyewitness reports that other task force members have compiled. Thousands of calls have already come in to the dedicated tip line set up the previous afternoon. Targeted efforts to canvass the condo towers still standing are in progress. *At this pace, we'll be identified before the end of the day. Not that it matters.*

Malcolm taps the coffee cup as his focus shifts from the presenters to the conference room's clock. *Anna and Dave will be here in less than an hour. Then we'll all turn ourselves in.* Anna had bristled when he described their plan that way, insisting that she'd done nothing wrong. *But I have. This is a waste of time and taxpayer money.* He surveys the ring of intent faces, mentally tallying the hourly salary burn. *How many of them will be furious?* He can't begin to guess.

His eyes move to the glitchy crime scene photos tacked to the evidence board. They've been supplemented with artists' compositions, sketched after direct study of the monsters' corpses and eyewitness accounts of the creatures in motion. Looking at them, Malcolm lets himself appreciate the impossibility of what the skyworms truly represent. *How would I feel if I hadn't seen them with my own eyes? If I didn't know about Anna, Dave, and Kalos? Having actual humans to track down is better than feeling powerless.*

He considers the two composite sketches, ringed with grainy cellphone photos, at the top of the evidence board. The one of Anna in her mask is terrible, which Malcolm finds reassuring. His own isn't half bad. When he first spotted it after sitting down, he felt so conspicuous he nearly got up and walked out. But no one's made the connection.

Of course not, Maksim, says his grandfather's confident voice in his memory. Maksim Sr. had delighted in secrets. A gifted woodworker, he'd built Malcolm a set of beautiful wooden boxes with hidden spring-loaded compartments for storing his boyhood treasures. He'd spent hours exploring each box's mechanisms, an experience in methodical process that helped, in some ways, to prepare him for police work. *If you remember nothing else, remember this,* his grandfather had said as they searched the forest surrounding his tiny house for mushrooms that final summer. *The safest place to hide is always in plain sight.*

Malcolm tucks the memory away. *11:35. Where are they?* His knowledge of the skyworms feels dammed up inside him, his own secret door straining to spring open. He studies his team, feeling like an interloper. *Is this how Anna felt for years? How did she stand it?*

Thoughts of Anna seem to activate their connection. Malcolm's awareness of his wife leaps from its latent corner to the forefront of his mind, shining like a beacon. As her emotions stream through him, Malcolm struggles to stay in his chair. *She's excited,* he thinks, amazed by his certainty, although he doesn't know why. His new spatial sense tells him Anna is due west and what feels like no more than a kilometre away. *Which means she's still at MaRS. With luck, Delal is in a signing mood and they'll be here soon.*

Across the conference table, Malcolm notices Deputy Chief Cloar glaring at him. He freezes before realizing that he's tapping his wedding ring against his empty cup. He mouths a sorry to the head of the task force. Leaning back, he folds his arms and tries to look attentive.

". . . and as you'll see on the board," Leong's saying, gesturing across the room, "We have—"

But Malcolm never learns what Leong wants them to see. Through the conference room's glass walls, he spots Nancy Coleman standing in the atrium directly outside the room. She's dressed in a navy suit and a cream blouse like she's come for a job interview. She leans over the desk set up to handle missing persons' inquiries, grilling the constables on duty. *I'll bet she didn't wait in line.* As Malcolm watches, everyone at the desk turns toward the glass wall. Nancy meets his eyes. She points straight at him, her mouth moving in triumph as though they're starring in a reality TV show, and she's orchestrated a massive gotcha.

Instead of dread or fear, relief crashes through Malcolm as the people behind Nancy crane their necks. *Cloar will have an APB out in minutes. I don't have to pretend anymore.*

Suddenly, his gut starts to churn, not with nerves, but with danger. *They're coming for Anna*, his bones whisper, just as they had when he woke on the couch Monday night. *Get to her!*

"Sit down, Nazarenko," Cloar drawls with easy authority, and Malcolm realizes with a jolt that he's standing, the empty cup clutched in his hand. He puts it down on the table. "We're all eager to hit the pavement, but you can hear Johansen and Leong out with the rest of us."

A wry chuckle echoes in the room. Both presenting officers flush at the deputy's mild rebuke.

Malcolm doesn't sit down. He can't possibly, not with panic flushing down his spine, demanding that he get to Anna. In the atrium, Nancy is storming past the worry-stricken constables, coming at him like a heat-seeking missile. Sweat beads on Malcolm's brow and the small of his back. *She doesn't matter. Get to Anna.*

Gamely, Malcolm tries for calm. "Excuse me." He bolts for the door, not concealing his new speed. Shock ripples around the conference table. He doesn't care, not with Anna pulling at his mind like a spaceship straining to punch through the atmosphere, commanding him to follow her into orbit.

In the doorway, Malcolm collides with Nancy. She stumbles back. "Oh no you don't!" his neighbour crows, righting herself with the indignation of a medieval queen about to order a peasant's execution. She points at the terrible sketch. "That's Anna Lin!" she announces to the stunned room. "His wife fought the monsters!" She rounds on Malcolm. "And you ruined my car's beautiful upholstery bringing her home!" Nancy dangles the Lincoln key from her finger as though it's the crucial piece of evidence that will put him away for life. "I found a dead creature in your garage," she seethes. "You're in this up to your neck!"

Pandemonium.

Sweat drenches Malcolm's shirt as Nancy, Deputy Cloar, Johansen, Leong, and all the rest push in around him, demanding explanations he has no time to give. In the chaos, his phone pings. Malcolm glances down. A text from Dave flashes across the lock screen:

skyworms at MaRS, southwest corner

she's on the lower roof

The information falls like a filter over his mind, discarding everything his body deems irrelevant. Malcolm immediately pushes toward the door, using his new strength to muscle his colleagues out of the way.

"Nazarenko, stop!" Cloar shouts over the din. "That's an order!"

The instinct pulling him to Anna's side wrestles with thirteen years of duty. There's no contest. "With respect, Deputy, I can't," Malcolm says. He turns again to go.

"Be reasonable," Cloar insists. "I want to help, but if you leave now, you aren't police anymore."

His next thought is instantaneous. *No. We're something new.*

Without another word, Malcolm takes his badge and gun from his holster, pushing them into the nearest set of hands. Johansen blanches as her fingers tighten around the once-treasured markers of his professional identity. "They're attacking Hospital Row and the Discovery District. Evacuate the downtown core."

Uproar ferments behind Malcolm as he bolts from the room, shoving past Nancy Coleman and her open mouth. In the atrium, people and civilians crowd the space, drawn by the commotion. Malcolm vaults onto the nearest desk. He leaps from it to a chair to another chair as easily as he once jumped across the stones in the forest streams near his grandfather's house. He lands beside the line of civilians, ignoring their gasps and hardly feeling the impact in his knees. Pumping his legs like pistons, he runs out of the building and onto College Street. He turns west.

Summer air trembles as a creature—the first living skyworm he has seen—flashes overhead in a speeding orange blur. *Holy Mary, Mother of God. It's huge.* Distantly, Malcolm hears breaking glass and screaming. *Anna*, his pulse insists, the beacon trumpeting its message straight to his heart. *Get to Anna. And never leave her side again.*

His dash to MaRS is as much of a blur as his midnight ride downtown. Instead of Kalos, he's trailed by a few people from the station. Whether they've followed out of curiosity or to arrest him, Malcolm neither knows nor cares. In the distance, sirens also wail as police cars and emergency vehicles mobilize. Their sounds drop away with the other runners, outpaced by his tremendous speed. Some part of him thrills with how rapidly he closes on the entrepreneurship hub's entrance, instinctively following the tug of Anna's xhen. He spots bits of it floating through the sky like pieces of confetti and hopes that doesn't signal bad news.

Malcolm launches himself through the lobby, ignoring the damage to the building's ceiling and the rubble on the floor. Like an Olympic hurdler, he dashes up the west tower's staircases to the fourth floor. The main corridor is deserted. Following his inner compass, he tries the doors to the most likely suite. *Locked!* But they fly open a moment later as a group of wounded people push into the hall, herded by an elegant South Asian man in a tan linen suit with a bleeding face.

"Take the stairs," Malcolm orders, diverting them from the elevators. "Head east toward the other side of town, past police headquarters." He's not in uniform, but the sound of command must remain in his voice because the bloodied man and his flock obey without question. Malcolm slips past them, heading for the office's southwest corner.

Anna's outside on the balcony, just like Dave promised, shining like a jewel. "Anna!" Relief floods Malcolm's limbs as he races toward his wife, climbing over debris, broken glass, and overturned furniture.

And then, to his sheer horror, she leaps off the side of the building, plummeting toward University Avenue. "No!"

To his amazement, she somehow flies up, not down, landing like a fly on the back of one of the creatures. Frozen, Malcolm watches her vanish into the sky. And while Dave's gift strikes him as inherently wrong, in that moment, he would give anything to touch Anna's thoughts.

"My God," says an awed female voice behind him. "How did she do that?"

Spinning, Malcolm sees two incredulous faces: an Asian woman, accompanied by a Black man. On their foreheads, drops of xhen glimmer like sapphires. They seem familiar, but he can't place them. School friends? Parents of his kids' friends? Malcolm flips through the facial Rolodex in his head. "We spoke in the atrium at police headquarters," he blurts, positive their foreheads weren't glowing then. "Why did you follow me?"

"You seem like you've got answers," the man says. "I'm Carl Mason. This is Nina Reyes."

"What's happening?" Nina asks. "Who is she?"

Before Malcolm can answer, two more sets of feet thunder down the hall. He freezes, leery of interference from Deputy Cloar or one of the senior officers, but it's Johansen and Leong.

"Cloar said to stay with you," Leong blurts, but Johansen nudges him to silence.

Malcolm stares at the newcomers, wondering if they know their foreheads are also marked with Anna's xhen. Like Carl and Nina, their faces are expectant, their attention utterly focused on him. *The world will soon turn its panicked eyes to you for guidance,* Kalos had told him. *Tarkan will rally to protect your triad.*

Behind them, a skyworm roars. *Anna's on its back,* he thinks, stomach churning. *But if she can bring it down, maybe we can help her kill it.*

"Let's get to the street," Malcolm says. "I'll explain what I can."

Chapter 20

Dave – Campus

Toronto, ON: Wednesday, August 20

Dave crosses the University of Toronto's St. George campus, completely blind to both the foot traffic around him and the beautifully clear summer morning. *Walt was my connection*! he fumes as he walks. *I'm the reason Hal met him! I'm the reason he invested in Rune! How dare she use him to get to me!*

Since their Monday call, Dave's received a nonstop barrage of texts and emails, some from Halina, some from Charles Larkin, and still more from Beakhead Capital's legal team. He flips through his phone as he walks, deleting message threads and email chains. *I'm not signing.*

A car horn blares. *Look at this fucking idiot!* bellows an unfamiliar mental voice.

Dave looks up as a taxi skids to a stop, inches from his legs. He's standing in the middle of the intersection of Harbord and St. George streets, outside Robarts Library. Adrenaline reflexively floods his chest, making his heart tighten. The driver rolls down his window, shouting epithets into the humid air. *How'd I get all the way up here?* Dave wonders as more horns join the cacophony.

The driver, now red in the face, revs his engine. "Sorry!" Dave calls, holding up his hands in appeasement as he backs out of the intersection. Glaring, the man's mind continues to hurl insults as he guns the car and speeds off along Harbord Street.

Dave catches more invective from the minds of other drivers as more cars stream past him, their anger lapping against the shore of his carelessness. In the next layer below their rage, the city hums with tension and anxiety. *Everyone's freaked out by the skyworms, even if they don't yet understand what they are.* Shaken, he puts his phone away and walks back along the tree-lined street, passing the university's hodgepodge blend of Edwardian, Brutalist, and modernist buildings. He focuses on his breath, taking it into his body and releasing it. *One thing's for sure: I need to build better mental filters to block out everyone else's stress.*

Craving a peaceful atmosphere, he cuts through the courtyard behind Wilson Hall Residence, where Anna lived during her first year. The oak trees standing between the residence and University College are gnarled and massive, their leaves brilliant green in the light. It's the best of U of T's green spaces in Dave's opinion, and reminds him of his years in Waterloo. When the weather was good, he often went outside to read for his electives, drink coffee, and chill.

Until Rune started and I threw that habit away along with everything else about my life that was halfway reasonable, Dave thinks as he drops onto a shaded bench. After the hospital, Leona had encouraged him to spend more time outdoors. She'd also reintroduced him to walking and breathing meditations. Once he was discharged, she'd taken him to visit sweat lodges, where he'd received the idea to start the pilot program for the coding camp.

Wonder what she'd make of this? Stretching his legs out onto the path of interlocking bricks, Dave dials his aunt's cell. After twenty-four hours of frustrated attempts, he's unsurprised to get her voicemail. Again. He hangs up, his mind whirling with possibilities. *Did her knee give out? Is she physically unable to answer?* He pictures Leona lying helpless on the bathroom floor or at the bottom of her stairs. It makes more sense than her dodging his calls.

Worrying isn't productive, he reminds himself. He texts Ryan again, asking if he's seen Leona, and then opens his group chat with the coding camp's teaching assistants:

Hey, sorry I had to bail this week. Hope class is going well. I can't reach Leona. It's urgent. Is she there?

Haven't seen her since yesterday morning when she told us you'd be away, Ian texts back a few seconds later.

Oh, Dave types. **Could one of you pls swing by her house?**

We'll go at lunch, Emma writes. **Hope everything's okay**.

Dave sends a thumbs-up emoji and puts away his phone. *That's something.* Between his mum's anxiety, Anna's stress, his concerns about Halina and Rune, and the city's background burble of fear, it's already been one hell of a morning. *And it's what? Ten a.m.?*

If you need space, be present and take it. Leona had said that to him during one of her hospital visits, and it's become one of his go-to reminders to slow down.

Dave closes his eyes. He breathes in and out, but his mind is like a monkey, picking up thought after thought instead of letting them drift through his head. *Would I be better at relaxing if I'd grown up in Auntie Lee's house? Or with Rose as my mom?* He snorts, tallying the causes to which his aunt donates her time. Working with other Indigenous leaders to push the Canadian government to correct the unjust financial terms for the bands covered under the Robinson Huron Treaty, including Miinikaa First Nation, is her most pressing project. But she's involved in countless other community initiatives. *Probably not.*

Dave stubbornly keeps at his meditation practice. Behind his closed eyes, the sunlight streaming through the trees makes shifting patterns against his eyelids. Then he lights a cigarette and takes a deep drag. Summers with Leona gave him a taste of his birth culture but were a far cry from growing up with full access to their reserve, elders, and traditional knowledge. In the beginning, he hadn't fit in very well. Preoccupied with his Toronto life, he'd been resentful about going north during the summer. And if he's being honest, he was too much of a snob to invest time in forming genuine friendships. During the Kalos years, he had stopped going altogether.

Since his illness, Leona has helped him forge new connections with the families living on the reserve and with elders within and outside their band. Through her land rights advocacy work, he's met dozens of other adults like him, Indigenous people adopted by white families. Most of the people he's met were placed through the deceivingly named Sixties Scoop, an insidious government program designed to disrupt their culture by breaking families apart, which had extended well into the 1990s. Until Monday night, he'd assumed that his own adoption had been arranged through the program, too. Knowing now that Chun-Mei Lin had been the one to change his fate is, and always will be, staggering. At the same time, it doesn't change his appreciation for how lucky he was to grow up with positive relationships with his adopted parents, his aunt, and his community, or his growing awareness of how much of his heritage he'll never fully access no matter how hard he tries.

And then there are the residential school survivors, he thinks, recalling the dreams he touched as he was leaving Miinikaa. Those images are still so vivid in his mind, and part of what he wants to talk about with Leona. *What can I possibly do to help them?*

Auntie Lee will have ideas, he tells himself. He takes another drag. *Until I can talk to her, I need to figure out how to tell Anna and Jason. I won't be able to delay that after Jason gets here. If Leona knows about Kalos, she must be a Xenthian, too. But why didn't she or Chun-Mei tell us? It doesn't make sense.*

Dave watches the tobacco smoke curl up into the trees as he broods. The occasional dog walker strides past, but it's blessedly quiet. When he finishes that cigarette, he lights another, allowing his family, the reserve, Halina, Rune, and the coding camp to mingle in his thoughts. The skyworms are there, too, swooping around and between everything else, but they feel abstract, like something he's studied.

Is Mum right? Am I enlisting in a monster war today? Sitting on the bench in the sun, the idea should feel impossible, yet he feels the coming shift like an itch in his lower back. He hasn't felt this way in a long time, not since the night before he and Halina closed their ten-million-dollar Series A financing. They'd been in Toronto to meet with Walter and the other investors, and Halina had insisted that they have dinner at the CN Tower's restaurant. Just the two of them.

"That's super cheesy," he had told her. "It's for tourists."

"Indulge me," she'd said.

They drank a bottle of champagne and laughed themselves silly as the restaurant turned slow revolutions across Toronto's darkening skyline. But the longer they sat, the deeper Dave's sadness grew. Getting the funding they needed to grow their company was the culmination of his dearest dream, and an irrevocable milestone. By the time they stepped into the elevator, he'd felt the long descent back to the city like the end of everything.

When will you come here again? he asks himself on the bench, just as he had done while looking into the elevator glass that night. *Who will you be when you do?*

Fucking autocorrect, Anna's foghorn thought blares through his mind. He drops the cigarette. *Dave!*

He jumps to his feet, stamping out the ember as his heart pounds. *What? What's happening?*

They're coming, she gasps, sending him a distorted image of office cubicles and some white woman's furious face. Dave frowns. *MaRS building,* she tells him. *Kalos is here. I'll be on one of the lower roofs. Southwest corner. Tell Malcolm.*

Some wordless part of him snarls in readiness. *You got it.*

Don't be so excited, she scolds. *This is serious, Dave.*

Perfectly serious. A grin that Halina Mendes would recognize from dozens of board meetings spreads over Dave's face. He starts to run. MaRS is a twelve-minute walk from his bench. He can sprint it in six. *It's my city, too, Anna. You don't get to be the only one who smashes monsters.*

She breaks contact. Trying to reach Malcolm's fortress of a mind feels futile, so Dave texts him.

skyworms at MaRS, southwest corner

she's on the lower roof

Dave tucks the phone back into his pocket just as the first unearthly roar echoes over the campus. Hundreds of minds scream. Dave tries to shut them out as pain flares in his back from his kidneys to his nape. He sprints across the ring road that encases U of T's circular lawn toward the walkway between the Medical Sciences and McMurrich buildings. His sneakers slip on the grass, still slick with morning dew.

As he rights himself, an orange skyworm shoots across the cloudless sky, not directly overhead but closer to Queen's Park. *Look at that,* he marvels as it flies over the buildings. Its body is double the size he expects. Its orange scales range in colour from a dark, burnt orange along its back to a brighter, almost sun-kissed shade along its belly. Three dark-purple tentacles undulate on either side of its predatory face, matching the dark gums of its jaws and the third eye in the centre of its forehead.

Some primal part of his brain yells for him to turn and run. Instead, Dave concentrates. Xhen flares down his arms in thick spirals. Wrapped in its light, the roaring feels manageable. *Anna. Get to Anna.*

Above, the skyworm banks in a fluid, sinuous curve. *It's coming back, Annie!* Dave might as well scream the warning for all the good it does. He receives no answering brush from her thoughts. The ring of Gothic buildings on this part of the campus has never seemed so vast. He's not even halfway across. *I shouldn't have walked so far. Malcolm!* he shouts, knowing it's equally unlikely that the police officer will hear him. *Malcolm, Anna needs you! They're coming! Help her!*

No response. His feet drum a frantic two-step into the earth.

Fast-er. Fast-er. Fast-er. More roars rumble like thunderstorms across Toronto. They carry some bass undercurrent that makes his head hurt through the insulating glow of xhen.

Movement catches his eye. Dave glances up to see the orange skyworm flash overhead again, its body coiled in a tight curve. This time, something blue and shining moves along its back. Dave stops dead, his mouth falling slack as his kidneys burn with fresh intensity.

Anna!! What are you doing?! The skyworm wheels south, carrying her away. Dave starts to run again, stumbling over the ground as he studies the sky. *Kalos must be with her*, he tells himself as he watches her inch toward the skyworm's neck crest like a tiny lumberjack scaling a writhing orange cedar hundreds of metres above the ground. *Even she's not that crazy.*

In seconds, campus buildings block them from his sight. But two more skyworms rocket into view, both the same pulsing orange. Roaring, they chase after Anna and the third skyworm.

Like hell. Dave stops again on the lawn, panting as his xhen flares. Following his call with Jason and her talk with Malcolm, he and Anna had spent the previous afternoon discussing strategies and practicing tactics within the limited confines of her garage. But everything they worked out is theory for him, not knowledge. *Time for the mother of all launches.*

Packing flame into a tight sphere, Dave hurls xhen into the air. His missile flies higher and faster than he expects, passing harmlessly between the skyworms. Their giant heads turn toward him. Six unholy eyes crawl over his body. His urge to run intensifies as their roars change, sharpening in pitch as they undulate and pivot in midair toward him.

In the middle of the front campus lawn, there's nowhere to hide. Dave holds his ground as they dive, xhen raging around and through his body as he creates two more burning globes, these the size of beach balls. Hefting first one and then the other, he flings them at his attackers.

The closest skyworm sinuously rises up and over his first ball, blocking the second creature's line of sight. They easily evade his missiles, but Dave grins as an idea ignites in his mind.

He forms and aims two more missiles at the first skyworm, releasing them in a bigger spread that forces it to veer wide to successfully dodge his attack. And then he launches a third set.

As anticipated, the first skyworm's movements block the second creature's view. As the first adjusts its course and the second comes back into Dave's line of sight, the third set of fireballs, hidden in the blind spot created by the first's evasive maneuvers, slam into the second skyworm, catching it in the face and side.

GOTCHA! Pleasure shivers up Dave's back. Howling, the second monster careens to the right, circling wide over the campus road as it struggles for altitude. Dave whoops, giddy with success at scoring some damage. *There's more where that came from!*

Yet the first skyworm is undeterred. Dave pelts it with smaller fireballs in a blistering pattern, trying to slow it down. Half of them land, but the skyworm's speed seems to increase as it roars. Its orange scales take on a strange incandescence as though kindling xhen of its own. As the skyworm's triplicate gaze bores into him, its jaws open and a seventh tentacle, so pale an orange as to be almost white, emerges.

Dave glances left and right. There's nothing that the skyworm can use against him with its sonic voice weapon. He readies another fireball and pauses, registering a tremor in the ground beneath his feet. Just as he realizes how badly he's misjudged his enemy's intent, two things happen: the grass lawn explodes upward as if he's stepped on a land mine and something heavy crashes into his left shoulder, violently propelling him away from the explosion's epicentre.

Dave gets his hands up in time to stop his chin from skidding across the grass, but he still hits the ground with a thump that momentarily knocks the breath from his body. Ears ringing, he tries to sit up. Something heavy is pinning him down. On instinct, he draws more xhen, fearing the weight is somehow connected to the skyworms. The heavy thing pulls away. Before he can rise, cold water splashes against his head and back.

"Agh!" Dave cries, rolling over. The skyworms circle over the west end of campus, their heads turned toward him. He thinks they're too far away to attack, so he wipes the water dripping from his sodden hair. As he looks up, he meets a pair of wide brown eyes in a narrow face beneath hair a slightly brighter shade of red than his xhen.

"You're on fire," the girl shouts, pointing at the flames coating his arms and hands. Freckles and acne spatter her pale face. Dave doubts she's a day over twenty-one. She lifts an empty U of T water bottle and brandishes it at him, visibly outraged. "I soaked you! How are you still on fire?"

"Get out of here." Dave's head pounds. Moving hurts, but he has no choice. *The skyworms will be back any second.* Vertigo tilts the lawn as he sits up and brushes dirt from his clothes. "Run!"

"Is that what they are? Skyworms? I figured you had some kind of weapon, but you don't, do—"

You heard me? Dave blinks.

"From Robarts Library," she says, like it's the most normal thing in the world. "You almost got hit by a car. Who are Anna and Malcolm? How do you do that?" She gestures at the flames.

Another roar shakes the ground as the skyworms close from the east and west. "They'll pin us between them. We need to get to Anna."

"I can run if you can." The girl extends a hand.

As he clasps her palm so she can yank him up, xhen flares around them. Her eyes widen, and her face goes utterly still. "My life for yours, Xenthian." The words seem to startle her . . . no, they *do* startle her, as much as they do him. Dave's certain because the city's background hum of mental terror has gone silent and there's a knot of emotion flickering in the back of his mind. It's her, this girl. *Woman,* he corrects himself. *My Kalxhan?*

She gives him a strange look, shoving her water bottle into her bag. "I'm Jenna," she says as they resume his sprint toward Medical Sciences.

Their feet pound the grass as they run. The campus is eerily quiet. The sirens have died away. The ring road is empty. And then the skyworms roar.

Without xhen, Dave expects Jenna to scream or run in the other direction. Instead, she sprints up the steps of the Medical Sciences building, heading for the glass doors. *No!* he calls. *I can't fight in there.*

"Here," she counters. The concrete-walled walkway between the Brutalist buildings is full of boxy, concrete sculptures. There's an overhang on the left-hand side near a set of doors.

"Hide underneath. Blast them as they go by."

It'll work once.

She raises a coppery eyebrow. "How many shots do you need?"

Dave glares. Jenna laughs, her excitement brightening the back of his head. "Got a weapon for me?"

No, he says curtly, resenting the distraction. *Get to a basement. Pretend there's a tornado coming. Hide in a doorway or under something solid.*

"Nope," she says firmly. "You've got a weapon that works against them. If you die, we're sunk." She grimaces as she points into the sky past his head. "Here they come."

Orange scales flash as the nearer skyworm swoops low over the buildings, its fire-damaged patch of scales clearly visible. Dave waits until it's practically on top of them. Then he forms and slings the biggest ball of flame he can imagine into the sky.

The creature falters, dropping several metres, but still manages to turn its head and roar. Its mouth tentacle shoots out as its scales glow brighter than a sunset. Then the concrete explodes above their heads.

Dave counters with xhen, forming a wide barrier as Anna demonstrated the previous day. It blocks the debris but not the concussion wave, which drops him to his knees. As he falters, Jenna seizes him by the wrist and hauls him up. Stumbling after her, he concentrates on maintaining the barrier around them as the skyworms dive.

"Stairs!" Jenna shouts. Somehow, Dave makes it down the concrete steps and across more grass toward University Avenue without breaking his ankles. As they run, he alternates between xhen barriers and fireballs as the skyworms give chase, grateful to delegate route-picking.

They'll use anything large and metal against us, he cautions. *We need open space.*

As if to prove his point, a sizeable tree and a manhole cover explode on the skyworms' next pass. Dave blocks most of the debris, but a long, skinny piece of wood slips past the edge of his barrier and slices his thigh as it shoots past. He grunts. Immediately, Jenna pulls his arm across her shoulders and hustles him onward.

Ahead, University Avenue's southbound lanes are empty except for an abandoned orange taxi in the middle of the road. The teal-green driver's door and the rear passenger doors stand open. A woman's purse has fallen into the street, its contents spread under the taxi's wheels.

"Curb!" Jenna shouts in his ear. Dave winces as he limps beside her in a shuffling stumble. Warmth trickles down from his leg as they reach the trees ringing Queen's Park.

"Don't stop," he pants.

"There's another skyworm coming up University," Jenna reports, peering up through the branches. "It's black." She gives him a curious look. "What do they do?"

"Fuck if I know." Dave pokes his head out in time to see the creature soar overhead. *Holy shit!* It's double, no, quadruple the length of the orange skyworms. *Like a skinny hockey rink took flight*, he thinks as its passage temporarily blocks out the sun, throwing the parkland into shadow. He can't tell whether Anna is on its back, but the orange skyworms are changing course to pursue it, giving them a momentary reprieve.

With Jenna steadying him, Dave scuttles out from the trees onto the legislature's lawn for a clearer view of the sky. He concentrates on the nearest orange skyworm, which sports the telltale dark patches of previously damaged scales. Xhen leaps into his palms. Dave's other arm is still across Jenna's shoulders, which seems to change the amount of xhen he can use. Fire fills him from the soles of his feet to the roots of his hair, doubling what he could previously hold.

Instead of a ball, he forms the energy into a molten stream. It streaks up from his hand, taking the skyworm broadside. Clear fluid sprays in an arc from its ruptured scales. Roaring, the monster pinwheels to the ground, wreathed in Dave's brighter flames as clear fluid gushes from its massive wound. It crashes into University Avenue right on top of the abandoned taxi.

The impact of its falling body knocks them both down. From his knees, Dave drills a second blast through its head to finish it off. He sits back on the asphalt, panting.

Instantly, Jenna's on her feet, laughing triumphantly as she reaches down to help Dave up a second time. "That was awesome!" she crows. Her hand throbs in his, her whole being racing with joy. She tilts her head at him, grinning. "What's your name?"

Chapter 21

Anna – Rodeo

Toronto, ON: Wednesday, August 20

Hands shaking, ponytail whipping in her face, Anna clings to the orange skyworm's back as it struggles for freedom, bucking and twisting beneath her legs. Shutting her eyes doesn't mitigate the sickening plunges, which are a million times worse than airplane turbulence. *To think I wanted xhen back.*

Directly above her is a deep notch in the skyworm's ridged crest. Grimly, Anna pulls xhen into her body and rises to her knees to peer through the gap. She carefully braces her legs, still leashed within Kalos's impromptu harness. Holding xhen makes the nausea, shakiness, and disorientation tolerable, provided she doesn't look down. Experimentally, she pulls on the skyworm's rightmost neck cord. It lurches left in a banking, downward turn toward the city. Startled by the direct effect, she loosens her grip.

The skyworm throws its head back, evidently trying to crush her between its crest and back. She falls into a seated position as it plunges ten metres. The small amount of slack in her harness slams her head forward. She barely gets her arms up in time to shield her face. *I can do this*, she thinks. *I've got to.*

Again, she rises and redoubles her grip on the cords, continuously tugging at them to keep the skyworm focused on what she's doing. Turning it away from Lake Ontario and back toward University Avenue is like playing a scarier version of the monster fights in Tim's video games.

Thinking of her son is a mistake. Her yearning to be on the ground, far away from danger, with Tim in her arms, is so intense that she nearly loses xhen. *Focus, Anna! Kalos left you here because he believes you can win!*

Eyes watering in the wind, Anna squints. Ahead, two more orange skyworms circle Queen's Park, swooping at something on the ground. A second later, she spots a massive ball of crimson fire racing into the sky. It collides with the nearest skyworm. *Dave!*

Anna grins, hauling on the cords to force her mount in that direction. It drops lower between the buildings, flying fast toward the park as she forms the haziest of plans. It bucks again. Her grip slips. The skyworm twists against a nearby office tower, scraping its sides along the street-facing wall like a horse trying to dislodge a rider with a low-hanging branch.

"Shit!" Frantically letting slack into her harness, Anna scrambles around the skyworm's neck, yanking her left leg up and out of the way. It's a struggle to keep her bonds loose enough for movement yet tight enough for safety.

Don't look down. Do not *look down.* Her ankle clips a window ledge with a painful whap—*Sprained? Broken?*—and there's a scary moment where she fears the leash is unraveling around her thighs, but it doesn't. Thrilled not to fall to her death, Anna reaches for the neck cords. A fresh wave of fear rolls through her belly as she immediately grasps the skyworm's strategy. *I can't steer from here. Oh hell!*

All three skyworms roar. Every window in Anna's field of view shatters. Changing direction, her reluctant mount shoots back into the sky, its body shifting left and right as it gains altitude. When they're well above the tallest roof, it levels off to swing south. Anna clings to it, furiously thinking as she tries not to vomit, fall off, or lose xhen. In the distance, she spots a massive black thing approaching the city over Lake Ontario. Six familiar orange shapes cling to its sides. *Kalos was right: there's ten of them. And the black one is huge.*

Her orange skyworm roars, angling to join its pack. *Get to its neck cord.* Anna releases her harness long enough to grab the first of Kalos's blades, which she gingerly holds between her teeth like a pirate. The blade feels amorphous in her mouth, its consistency something like cotton-batten crossed with the mild reverberation from a malfunctioning electronic. The buzz echoes along her jaw, sending more pain through her head. Ignoring it, Anna climbs.

The skyworm does two quick nauseating loops, slowing her advance. She clings to its back with muscles and xhen, searching for the rest of the pack. Something dark pulses on her left, recalling the black lights that were trendy in night clubs during her university years. Anna blinks as the flash dissipates. Then she gasps. The ridiculously large black skyworm now blocks her view of the city below. *What the hell? How'd it get so close so fast?* Roaring, the six other skyworms push off its back—and head straight for her.

Anna redoubles her efforts to get to the gash Kalos cut in the skyworm's neck, moving as fast as she dares. The nearest skyworm closes. As its jaws open, she spots a slender tentacle inside emitting waves of sound so thick she can almost see them streaming from its mouth.

Her skyworm mount rolls again, turning her directly into the oncoming attack. But that also gives Anna the last bit of momentum she needs. She reaches up with her left arm to grasp its neck cords. Her fingers close on them just as the sonic attack crashes into her. She screams, dropping her knife as pain engulfs her arm and back, blasting her leash apart instead of her flesh.

No, no, no! In an eye blink, Anna's dangling from the first skyworm's back, nothing holding her aloft but the sticky, wet cords wrapped around her left hand.

She feels her grip slide as agony—she can't accept it as hers—wracks her arm from shoulder to wrist. "Kalos! Help me!"

No answer comes.

Pull up! She tries to lift her wounded arm. Fails. The skyworms roar, diving around her in disorienting patterns. *Oh fuck, oh fuck, I'm going to fall!* A tentacle strikes her hip. As it latches on through her khakis, Anna again glimpses the world through the skyworm's triple eyes. Her grip slips, as does the skyworm's tentacle. *NO!* Her belly lurches as she tumbles head over heels through the air, falling too fast to scream.

In the next instant, she collides with something surprisingly squishy with the force of a belly flop from a ten-metre diving tower. It's wide. And black. Dazed, Anna spits blood and part of a tooth, frantically reaching for xhen. She forms a harness to lash herself to the black skyworm and—

—loses all sensation. Pain vanishes from her mouth, arm, back, and ankle, along with sight, sound, and smell. *Am I dead?* Her existence is TV-static nothingness. Even the skyworm is gone. But xhen remains, prickling through her mind, assuring her that she lives. Anna holds her breath, centering herself—

—as she emerges from the non-place, still clinging to the black skyworm's back.

To her shock, the skyworm pack is several kilometres south of their position, closer to the lake. *How the hell did it . . . Is that how they travel? Teleportation?* The black skyworm roars, its sound plaintive rather than scary as it loops over Queen's Park. Its flight is surprisingly smooth compared to Anna's rough ride on the smaller orange beast. *It must be too big for acrobatics.*

Behind them, the pack answers the black skyworm's call, their bodies flattening into sleek, arrow-like shapes as they streak toward Anna and her new ride. *It wanted to escape*, she realizes, hearing outrage in their roars. *And they're pissed that I went with it.*

Anna grins. She flexes her right arm. It still aches, as do her ankle and shrapnel-injured calf, but she's left the worst of the pain behind.

Lucky, she decides, leaning into her remaining discomfort and adding it to her body's baseline. *I had two kids without drugs. I can do this, too.*

Gripping her last xhen knife, Anna lengthens the harness holding her against the skyworm's back, turning it into more of a safety line. *Go!* She crawls forward as fast as she can toward its crested head, dragging the tip of her blade through the black scales as she goes. In seconds, her nose burns with the rotten-egg smell of skyworm blood. Clear ichor soaks her pants. She shivers in the wind as the creature howls. The sound reverberates through her hands and legs, making her ears ring. Answering roars come from below. Anna peeks over the edge of the skyworm's body. Two orange skyworms are rising to greet the black one—at least until a stream of fire engulfs the nearest monster, bringing it down.

Dave! She can't spot him on the ground. *Get to its crest.* Anna scrambles forward. Its back seems to stretch forever. As she nears the crest, she passes a fin-like ridge of scales so pale a violet that they're almost white. *Did they evolve from the sea?*

An orange skyworm streaks over her head, tentacles striking. She flattens to her belly and keeps crawling, abandoning all thoughts of skyworm evolution. Its huge crest is almost in reach, but the deafening roars tell her the main pack is closing in. *Don't stop. Don't look back.*

One last lurching rush brings her to the crest. It ripples in the sunlight, shining indigo, deep violet, and midnight black. And it's so massive she can't see a thing around it. Something thuds against the skyworm's belly, each impact reverberating through her knees. *Dave's fireballs.* Anna plunges her knife into the base of the crest plate, slicing through its purplish scales as she searches for the cords. *Where the hell are they?*

Agitated sparks flash in her head. *Malcolm.* Anna automatically turns in his direction and spots an incoming orange skyworm, glowing like the sun. *Not again!* Digging faster, she seizes two of the cords. *Which are these?* There's no time. She slices one and yanks the other.

The black skyworm's body shudders. It veers left, lifting her out of the path of the incoming sonic attack. Unbalanced by the movement, Anna falls heavily to her side. She rights herself, sticking her precious knife back into her pants as the skyworm howls and—

—they're enveloped by TV static. In the empty calm, Anna's next move reveals itself as though she's playing chess with Jason and he's three moves from checkmate. Readying her courage, she—

—reemerges with the black skyworm. They're two hundred metres above Queen's Park. As anticipated, the rest of the pack has closed in on them. And there's an orange skyworm even closer than Anna dared to hope. *I can do this, provided my leg holds up.*

Before she can overanalyze this fresh act of lunacy, Anna forms a new leash. It strikes the orange skyworm, snaring its neck as she releases her harness and her hold on the black.

ANNA!! Dave screams. *DON'T!!!*

No choice! she shouts to him as she sprints the half dozen steps across the black skyworm's massive back and jumps.

As she falls, Anna wills her xhen to do what it did for Kalos. She flexes the newly formed muscle memory connecting her brain to xhen. Sighting the leashed orange skyworm, she makes the creature the point to which she falls. With a lurch, the leash retracts, dragging her up. Wind rushes past her face, pulling tears from her eyes and blurring her vision. It confuses her depth perception so badly that she doesn't see the skyworm coming until she slams, face first, against its orange side.

Air rushes from her lungs. Her arms flail, but she throws them wide around the skyworm's flexing body. She forms xhen into loose coils, lashing her body to its scales. Gasping, Anna gets her feet under her and shuffle-crawls the two metres from her landing point to the skyworm's crest.

Then Kalos's knife is in her hand as she cuts open the skyworm's scales and digs through its tissue. Compared to the black one, its cords are easy to find. Anna grasps the left and wrenches it up, pulling as hard as she can. The skyworm cants to the right, its head pushed up by the speed of their fall.

Because they are falling—straight into a fireball.

Anna braces for the impact, crouching as low as she can behind its crest. Dave's flames pass around her, scorching her skin. She grunts but doesn't let go.

The skyworm isn't so lucky. It convulses, twisting head over tail in a nauseating roll. Anna slices both remaining cords. The flesh beneath her goes completely limp, like she's severed its spinal cord. *I guess I did . . .* Unable to dodge, its head is engulfed by another fireball as it pitches down toward the bronzed roof of Ontario legislature. Blackened tentacles flap around her like spent sparklers against the summer sky. Below, the sun-blasted grass rises to embrace them.

Time to get off the ride. Hurriedly, Anna retracts her leash and loops it around her waist. She fires one blast of xhen through the skyworm's head to be sure it's dead. Then she crouches on the balls of her feet, holding the loose end of the leash in one hand. *Jump!*

Her leash flies ahead of her to clasp the top of the Queen's Park flagpole just like a skyworm neck. Swinging, Anna circles toward the ground, arms and legs flailing as she tries to control her descent. Somewhere in the distance, there's a sickening metallic crunch. Twisting, she sees the skyworm crash into an abandoned tour bus outside the legislature's entrance. Wind whips Anna's jubilant laughter away.

Her glee is short-lived. The landing rushes up, and she's swinging way too fast. Anna tries to roll like an acrobat but her momentum's wild, throwing off her timing. Her already banged-up foot jams awkwardly into the grass. The snap is audible.

"FUUUUUUCK!" Her fist strikes the ground in a vain effort to transfer her pain to the inoffensive grass. *It's not fair! I've never broken a bone in my life.* She screams again, more in frustration than agony, trying to get up on her elbows to search the sky. *They'll regroup. I've only got moments.* Agony shoots up her leg. Anna grimaces, trying to stand anyway.

"Child." It's Dave at her side, dripping with sweat. His pupils are so wide that Anna can barely see the rich brown of his irises, his expression eerily impassive. *Kalos,* she realizes.

"Where the hell were you twenty minutes ago?" Anna demands. "Are you trying to get me killed?"

Her teacher doesn't answer, his gaze fixed upon her head. Above, the black skyworm is visibly struggling to join its surviving orange brethren.

Anna tries to stand. "We need cover."

Kalos-Dave pushes down on her shoulders. "Be still."

Panting, Anna swallows another scream of frustration. Pale pink flames, not Dave's usual red, flare around her brother's hands as they touch her. Calm wraps Anna like a blanket. For the first time since jumping off the roof at MaRS, she feels safe. "What're you doing?"

"Embrace xhen." Coming from Dave's lips, her teacher's voice sounds as weird as she remembers, like it did years ago when it was his turn to host Kalos for an embodied lesson.

Her mind is like boiled spaghetti, which reminds Anna that she's ravenous, but she obeys. Kalos-Dave's xhen slides under hers, lifting it like blue flotsam on the crest of a pink wave. Together, they send the wave of xhen toward the dead skyworm in the bus, enveloping the corpse. Kalos-Dave forms their xhen into long fingers, each wrapping around the threads of shining orange energy to pick them free as Anna wraps the loose strands together.

The assembled orange-pink mass glows around Kalos-Dave's head, luminous as a sunset. They put one hand on her broken ankle and the second on Dave's bleeding thigh. "Taking xhen from a healthy skyworm will kill you," Kalos warns as freezing heat courses through Anna's leg from the tips of her toes to her knee. "They must be dead or dying."

Sweat breaks out across her forehead. She shivers uncontrollably as Kalos heals her injuries, shifting partway through to address her shoulder, the wound in her calf, and even her missing tooth. Only her lightly singed face, caught in the edges of Dave's fireball, doesn't seem to heal.

Her teeth continue to chatter as Kalos works. When she lifts her head, Dave's lips are blue. Hers feel like ice cubes compared to the too-hot skin of her cheeks.

"They will sense Jason's approach," Kalos tells them. "Get to him first."

As though on cue, a pulsing dark flash cuts through the sky. As the black skyworm vanishes, a fresh pit of fear opens in Anna's stomach. *We'll never make it.*

Chapter 22

Jason – Flight

Vancouver, BC / Toronto, ON: Wednesday, August 20

Jason's first twinge of unease comes after he clears airport security. *I must have slept funny last night*, he thinks, picking up his carry-on. Long hours at St. Paul's have made him no stranger to back pain. Without Margo, he can't access the more comfortable frequent traveler lounge, so he makes his way to the gate where he stretches and rubs the muscles in his right lower back before taking a seat.

It's no use. He can't get comfortable. He stands instead. By the time he lines up at the gate to board, the left side of his back aches, too.

Jason puts his carry-on down and does a few last-minute stretches. *It wasn't bothering me when my shift ended yesterday morning or when I woke up today. What could have messed it up?* He looks down at the beautiful leather weekender bag that he uses for short trips, his final birthday gift from his mother. *It's not that heavy.*

On board, he checks his seat assignment and sighs. He's got the middle seat in a group of five, right in the centre of the plane. *That's what I get for booking a last-minute flight to Hamilton when Pearson Airport's closed.* Jason stores his carry-on in the overhead bin, ramming it against someone's backpack to make it fit. He drops into the faux leather chair and lets his head fall back against the headrest.

He takes deep breath after deep breath as he and all his medical school classmates were taught years ago in an emotional intelligence elective. Taking his time, he thinks deliberately of each muscle group, clenches each one tightly and then releases.

It doesn't help. Jason's never liked planes. *Anna's not wild on them either.* He's not sure why they bother her. His own fear is grounded less in the sensation of turbulence and more in the utter loss of control. When their parents took them to China on a family vacation the summer after they finished high school, both twins flew medicated. Neither of them slept. He has vivid memories of holding Anna's hand during the worst of the turbulence over the Pacific, wondering if she longed for the reassurance of xhen as deeply as he did. Kalos had been gone a mere four months then, but they'd already agreed to stop talking about him.

Or, more accurately, he'd made Anna agree to stop bringing him up.

Relax, he tells himself, as the plane taxis back from the gate. *It's fine. You're fine.*

Yet, as the airplane climbs into the sky toward Toronto, Jason's back begins to prickle. At first, he experiences tiny flickers of heat. When the in-flight map displays the plane clearing the Rocky Mountains west of Calgary, the sensation blossoms into a dull, familiar ache on either side of his back, deep in his kidneys. Jason inhales sharply, his nose filling with the scent of sixteen-year-old dust. *Xhen.*

No. It's muscle pain. He retrieves two liquid gel painkillers from his carry-on bag and swallows them without water. He leans back in his seat, closing his eyes. *It's in your head. Let the drugs take care of it. Sleep.*

Another hour passes as he fidgets, then two. Jason's tired enough to know just how badly he needs rest. Every time he gets close to nodding off, his back seizes with a fresh spasm. *It's psychosomatic,* he tells himself. *You're stressed about flying. Your brain's interpreting it as back pain. You've observed this kind of thing a thousand times in the ER. Stop reinforcing it.*

"Ladies and gentlemen, this is your captain speaking," says a deep baritone voice as the route map freezes on Jason's in-flight entertainment monitor. "We're about twenty-five minutes outside of Hamilton . . ."

"Thank God," Jason breathes, trying to knuckle his back without elbowing the people beside him. The woman on his left offers a sympathetic smile.

". . . begin our descent. Weather in Hamilton today is sunny with clear skies and a ground temperature of—"

The airplane's loudspeaker clicks off. Jason grunts as a fresh wave of heat pierces his kidneys, like something's trying to burn a hole through his spine from the inside out. Around him, the passengers exchange baffled looks, waiting for the pilot to continue.

Without warning, the plane banks hard to the right, making a sweeping turn. Several people cry out. Two of the flight attendants, who had been moving through the aisle to collect trash, clutch at nearby seats to stop themselves from falling. A warning ping sounds as the emergency seatbelt sign flashes on, seconds too late to be useful.

"Attention, passengers! This is your captain." The man's voice shakes on the last word. "We will be making an emergency landing at Pearson Airport. The flight attendants are trained for this situation. Please remain calm and follow their instructions."

Alarm spreads like wildfire through the cabin as the flight attendants scramble to get seated, clinging to their veneer of calm with fixed, too-wide smiles. Fresh sweat breaks out on Jason's forehead, accompanied by another bone-crushing spasm.

"Look!" a woman screams on the cabin's left side, several rows ahead of his seat.

Straightening his back, Jason cranes his head high enough to see that she's pointing out the window.

"There!"

More people begin to panic. Adrenaline surges like a freight train through Jason's chest, just like it used to when Kalos took them out to hunt. His breath is short and fast as his stomach churns. *No, no, no,* he thinks, unable to deny the burning in his back for what it is and equally unable to recall how to summon xhen. *I can't fail again, not here in the sky!*

There's a shuddering lurch. The plane's wing dips to the right. Jason catches a flash of something dark against the windows. The screaming takes on a new intensity.

"The wing!" someone cries in a ragged voice. "There's a monster on the fucking wing!"

Another flash of movement draws his eyes to the porthole window on the plane's left side. Turning in his seat, Jason stares into a non-human eye: split-pupiled orange with an inner ring of startling purple against black scales. It fills the window, radiating malice.

The eye vanishes. Jason glimpses large violet tentacles before a roar shakes his seat. The burn in his back is now scorching, climbing his spine to strike across his head, accompanied by ear-splitting pain. Someone nearby has lost control of their bladder. *I'm going to die in this seat,* Jason thinks as his nostrils fill with the smell of urine. *We're all going to die.*

The light in the airplane's cabin darkens as though a shadow has been thrown over his vision. It's so quickly there and gone that Jason's mind cannot process it. An instant later, there's a hole a metre wide in the cabin ceiling five rows ahead.

The airplane depressurizes. Panels fall open. Breathing masks tumble loose. Jason grabs for his mask out of reflex, pulling it to his face and filling his lungs with oxygen. Ahead of him, a seat row breaks free from its moorings and slams up toward the gash in the plane's ceiling. Only the massive tentacle pushing into the cabin through the hole stops the passengers, strapped to their chairs, from being sucked out into the sky.

Jason gulps air, feeling time slow exactly as it used to when he was in the operating room during his residency and the surgery was going well and it felt like he had all the time in the world. He rides the bubble of calm, prepared to face death with perfect clarity as the tentacle-like appendage strikes blindly through the cabin. Each flail brings it inexorably closer to him.

The airplane tilts toward the ground, momentarily halting the monster's advance. Wind howls too loudly for Jason to hear screams. Overhead bins spring open. Suitcases and bags bounce free, some landing on people's heads. Others are struck by the monster's grasping tentacle. It makes no difference. After all of Jason's doubts, all of his denials, he knows exactly whom the monster has come to claim.

As it roars a second time, Margo's beautiful face fills his mind. There's no way he can reach for his phone in time to say goodbye. *I should have told you everything. Forgive me.*

Her face vanishes, replaced by Anna's. Pinned to his seat, unable to summon xhen, Jason suddenly hates his sister more than he has ever hated anyone in his entire life. *They came for you and now they're coming for me and I'm going to die and it's all your fault.* He starts to close his eyes, but the movement of a faint shadow on his right forestalls him.

Turning his head, he stares into Kalos's serene face. ***There is no time. Take my hand, child.***

Jason reaches for his teacher.

Chapter 23

Dave – Battleground

Toronto, ON: Wednesday, August 20

Dave staggers as Kalos rushes out of his body like air from an inflatable toy. *You'd think I'd be ready after so many times.* Jenna is immediately at his side, supporting him as he dazedly regains control of his fully healed legs. Inhabiting his own flesh after an embodied lesson always leaves Dave hyperconscious of his meat-bound existence. His bones feel astonishingly heavy, as though banded in steel. Not for the first time, he wonders how Kalos exists without a body. *Is he ever tempted to stay inside one of us? What would happen if he did?*

"Are you okay?" Jenna demands as she slides an arm across his back. Reassured by her fully human presence, Dave leans against her. "You looked super weird for a minute there."

Tell you later, he thinks, too weary to speak. *If we live.*

Jenna's face blanches in tandem with the emotion cluster at the back of his skull. Dave mentally kicks himself. In business, he'd learned to keep his circle of confidence small. Each time he and Halina strayed from that practice, they paid for it in people.

Jenna rolls her eyes. "If I can accept your voice in my head, you can trust me. I'm Hal now. Whoever she is."

Co-founder of my old company, Dave says, and grins. *She'd like you. Or hate you. Maybe both.*

Jenna grins back, but her smile fades as she looks past him into the sky. Instantly, her bright place in his head darkens.

Dave follows her gaze. The remaining orange skyworms are circling over the city.

"They won't stay up there forever," Jenna says. "We need cover."

No, we need to see them coming, Dave insists.

"So that they can hit us on all sides at once?" Jenna gestures at the lawn. "Uh-uh. We killed one and Anna killed one. The injured black one may come back. That leaves seven of them and two of you. Hiding's your only advantage unless you can pull them out of the air." She points to the half circle of maples edging the road on either side of the legislature. "They won't see us under the trees. We can move under the canopy, pop out, and hit them when they're not expecting it. Like Dave and I did back at that overhang." She jerks a thumb over her shoulder at U of T's campus. "We need to disappear while they're regrouping."

At this distance, Dave feels more than sees seven sets of triplicate eyes crawling over his skin. His back prickles. *They really are sentient.*

"And as capable of teamwork as we are," Anna agrees from the grass. Dave looks down. His sister's hair is a windblown mess. Skyworm ichor stains her clothes. But her rage has evaporated with Kalos's healing, leaving a rocklike determination. "Malcolm's on his way. We need to kill the rest of the pack and get to Jason before that black one does."

Dave stretches out a hand to help Anna up, instinctively bracing himself for a torrent of mental impressions. "What possessed you to ride that thing, Annie?"

"Kalos, of course," Anna says.

Jenna cocks her head, her curiosity flaring in Dave's mind as

Anna grasps his hand and forearm to haul herself up. When they touch, Anna's ride aboard the skyworm ricochets through Dave's head like bad steady-cam footage. Her fall from the orange one almost makes him vomit as he grasps exactly how close she came to death.

"The black one can teleport," she explains to Jenna. "It took me through some weird non-place that numbed the pain from my shoulder."

Anna flexes her arm as Dave experiences the sensationless void by proxy. He shivers.

"Don't worry," she continues, testing her ankle joint for range of motion. "I'm sure as hell not doing that again. But you heard Kalos. Jason's in danger. We're outnumbered." She swallows hard, and Dave glimpses the fear swimming beneath her bravado. "He's in denial about xhen. They'll eat him alive."

Brushing off her grimy clothes, Anna looks past Dave to Jenna, an appraising light in her eyes. "This your Kalxhan?"

Dave nods, noting Jenna's confusion at the term. Another thing to explain later.

"Good," Anna says. "Her plan's solid. Let's go."

With that, Anna runs for the trees. Glowing with pride from every pore, Jenna tugs Dave after her with far more force than he expects. And then she freezes, her wariness knotting the back of Dave's head again. This time, she's not looking at the sky. "Cops," she says softly.

Dave follows her gaze, alarmed until he spots the small group running toward them. Malcolm's got a substantial lead on two uniformed officers and a pair of civilians, all of them red-faced as they puff along behind him.

"That's our backup," Anna corrects. She points at Malcolm. "The one in front is my husband."

Jenna relaxes, but Dave doesn't. Behind the runners, the top half of the MaRS west tower is . . . gone. His eye continues down University Avenue, spotting more damage to the Toronto Hydro building and the nearest hospitals, too. *How'd they cause that much carnage so fast?*

Malcolm's arrival cuts his assessment short. While his mind remains completely silent, Dave sees distress and relief in every line of his face as he folds Anna into a crushing hug. "You jumped," he says raggedly. "What the hell were you thinking? Are you all right?" He pulls back to look at her at arm's length. "What happened to your face? You look sunburnt."

"Long story," Anna says, her knifelike focus wavering as she hugs him back, visibly relieved by his presence. Behind them, the four trailing runners come to a panting halt.

"Cover, Dave," Jenna insists in a tone that brooks no argument. "Now."

Get under the trees, Dave orders. The mental command feels different even as he issues it, turning every head to face him, even Malcolm's. *Some sort of broadcast mode*, he decides as he feels the newcomers' minds startle like park pigeons, echoing the surprise and confusion etched on their faces. But they follow Jenna, glancing sidelong at Dave through wide eyes.

Overhead, the skyworms roar. Dave glances up, expecting an attack. But as he looks, the creatures split off toward something else. A minute later, the unfamiliar scream of a jet engine echoes across Toronto.

Oh shit. Five fighter jets pass in tight formation, immediately summoning Dave's childhood memories of the annual summer airshow at the Exhibition. Aghast, he turns to keep the planes in view. "The skyworms will rip them to pieces."

"Nothing we can do," Anna says without pause. Her stomach rumbles audibly, which makes Dave realize he's hungry, too.

To his surprise, Malcolm pulls a handful of protein bars out of his pockets and shoves them into Anna's hands and his.

"My xhen's got a range of maybe two hundred metres," she continues, inhaling the first bar. "I can't hit them easily from the ground."

"We have to try," Malcolm says quietly. "Can't you catch another one and ride it up there?"

"Too risky," Jenna counters. "We need to regroup. They'll be back once they're finished with the planes."

The police officers, Malcolm included, look askance at her.

"Jenna Kovi," she says, offering Malcolm a hand to shake. "I'm doing a master's in military history at U of T."

"You *were* doing a master's in military history," Anna murmurs.

"Constable Krista Johansen," says one of the uniformed officers. No older than twenty-five, she's staring at Anna like the sun shines from her eyes. Belatedly, Dave spots a bright blue dot glowing beneath the brim of her hat, right in the centre of her forehead.

Kalos helped me make a xhen confetti bomb, Anna says, touching Dave's arm to share her memory of that lesson. He watches carefully, noting their teacher's dexterous movements. *I think it marked them to join us as tarkan. Called them up? Something like that.*

"Something," Dave agrees. The newcomers, startled, exchange more glances. Dave gets the same feeling he used to have during brainstorming sessions when there were too many people in the board room and the discussion lacked focus.

"I'm Dave Montcalm," he says. "This is Anna Lin." There's another flurry of looks and several minds recall the TV footage. "You've met her husband, Malcolm Nazarenko. And this is Jenna Kovi. I'm sure you have more questions. We don't have time." It's an understatement: The pounding urgency he felt upon waking at his aunt's house Monday night is back. He glances at Anna, who looks equally worried. "We need to kill these skyworms and get to Hamilton Airport."

Krista nudges the second officer, who's also dark haired, his skin covered in acne. "Raymond Leong," he says, hardly seeming to breathe as he looks at Anna.

They can't be more than a couple years out of the academy, Dave thinks.

"You were in the video with Brenda Edwards," Raymond

manages, awe radiating from his mind. "Who are you? How come you can fight these things? Malcolm says bullets don't do shit to them."

"He also said there's no time," says the Black man in civilian clothes. "I'm Carl. This is Nina." They're both at least a decade older than the police officers, but their eyes on Anna are no less keen. "What do you need?"

In answer, xhen spreads between Anna's fingers. She quickly draws her hands apart, forming a long blue length between them. Everyone except Dave gasps as the light thickens, sharpening into a knife shape. Wordlessly, she offers it to Malcolm as Jenna and Nina study it with hungry eyes. Malcolm gingerly takes the knife as though it's a balloon that might pop if handled roughly.

"What is that?" Nina breathes.

Despite the furious air battle raging over their heads, Anna's smile is one hundred percent Cheshire Cat. "Xhen." She extends the next knife to Nina, who takes it and, after a deep breath, sinks to her knees in the grass. Blue light encircles both women in a shared halo as Nina utters the same vow Dave heard Jenna speak barely an hour before. The dot on Nina's forehead vanishes, along with her presence from Dave's mind. He nods, guessing that Anna now has a second pocket of tarkan emotion nestled in the back of her head.

A skyworm roars, the sound deep and unmistakable. A loud explosion echoes across the park. Jenna darts out to look. Dave follows her in time to see two fighter jets spiral out of control. One blows apart in midair, the wreckage disappearing into the buildings farther south. The second crashes end over end down University Avenue, shaking the ground as roars thunder in Dave's ears. Overhead, the skyworms resume their circling above Queen's Park.

"It's suicide," Anna mutters, glancing up as she finishes accepting the oaths of her new tarkan.

"Which is why I wanted you to come forward," Malcolm says, each word laden with reproach. "What were they supposed to do? No one except you understands skyworm capabilities."

We can argue about do-overs later, Dave tells the group, stuffing the last of his protein bar into his mouth. He meets Malcolm's glare, for once grateful that the other man's mind is closed to him, as he clumsily forms a xhen knife for Jenna. *Stick to Jenna's plan. We need to bring them close and hit them hard enough that they can't get off the ground.*

"You mean kill them." For all her tactical caution, Jenna's eagerness to fight strains against Dave's mind like a Doberman itching to be off leash. "I count seven of the orange in the air."

"They move fast," Anna cautions her new recruits as she hands the last knife to Carl. The oath process has clouded their minds to Dave, just like Malcolm's and Nina's, and further dimmed his awareness of Anna, too. "And they hunt together. Watch your backs."

All things considered, they do okay for the first few minutes. Leading the way with Dave, Jenna keeps the group moving beneath the trees. Malcolm and Anna cover the rear, keeping the new tarkan sandwiched in the middle. As the skyworms dive, searching, Dave slings fireballs and Anna hurls leashes, which miss more than they hit.

It's torturous to wait for the creatures to fly low enough for interception, but Dave finds Jenna's presence steadying. In addition to expanding his ability to draw xhen, she's far more patient, cautioning him to wait for clear shots. Her delight when his missiles strike home is euphoric, warming him like a mouthful of great scotch on a cold evening.

The skyworms close for another pass.

"Duck!" Jenna shouts.

Dave flattens himself in the grass. One of Anna's leashes whips over his head, grasping the nearest skyworm's neck. Its scales flare orange as it roars, obliterating the nearby flagpole and a sizeable swath of grass. Chunks of metal and dirt fly in all directions. Dave's hastily formed barrier neutralizes the brunt of the debris. Grunting, he switches back to fireballs, dripping sweat as he pelts the skyworm.

Anna strains to keep the creature grounded. Malcolm has both arms wrapped around her waist to stop the skyworm from jerking her forward, his heels digging twin trenches through the grass as it struggles for freedom.

It's panicking! Dave broadcasts to every mind. *Don't let it escape!*

Anna's four new tarkan rush the creature, stabbing with their bright knives. Malcolm hangs back under the canopy with Anna. Her xhen ripples like gas flame around their bodies as he continues to brace her against the skyworm's increasingly desperate struggle.

"Aim for its eyes!" someone shouts.

"The belly!"

The skyworm snaps a tentacle toward Dave, and Jenna slashes it off with her red blade. The purple thing drops, twitching, to the grass. Hot, fresh sulphur fills Dave's nose with its now-familiar burn. The skyworm howls. None of the tarkan flinch. It's on their ground now. Jenna thrums with a painful thirst for victory. Thinking of his mum's fears, Dave takes no risks. He launches another barrage of fireballs, taking care to avoid Anna's circling tarkan while focusing on its head. In moments, they've reduced the skyworm to a blackened ruin.

Anna's ragtag group cheers, echoing the primal triumph burning in Jenna. "One down and six more orange to go, plus the black one," she tells Dave.

He's panting too hard to do more than nod, but he wearily pumps a fist before looking up. The remaining orange skyworms are circling at a lower altitude.

What are they doing? Dave wonders. Behind him, xhen glows around Anna's body as she strips bright orange energy from the dead skyworm's corpse, funneling it into her tarkan and healing their minor injuries.

Before they can find cover, a police siren wails in the quiet. Then everything happens at once.

On the far side of Queen's Park, two SWAT vehicles screech to a stop. A dozen officers in riot gear spill out, carrying heavy-duty assault weapons.

Krista and Raymond exchange a horrified glance before running toward their colleagues, incoherently shouting at the top of their lungs.

Jenna's dread thickens to tar in the back of Dave's head. *Stop!* he orders. *Stay together!*

Too stricken to listen, Krista and Raymond put on an extra burst of their new preternatural speed as they run toward their vulnerable comrades.

Skyworm roars rattle Dave's head as two creatures, swift as vipers, strike the police vehicles from alternate sides.

The vans explode beneath their sonic attacks.

Uniformed bodies drop like dominoes.

A third skyworm lands in the carnage, its dark tentacles hungrily lashing at the survivors. Orange light bathes the street in an unholy dawn. The sound of a shared scream rises from half a dozen throats.

It's feeding on them! Anna shrieks. The thought slams into Dave's mind as images of Brenda Edwards and Anna's own capture at the SkyDome smash into his head despite the muffling presence of her tarkan. Blue bolts fly from her raised palm as she screams, "Kill it!"

Trying to block out Anna's panic, Dave sends a pair of fireballs at the creature. He misses. One of her bolts strikes a tentacle, blasting it in half. The skyworm only twitches. Then Raymond and Krista are upon it, their knives flashing as they strike tentacles, its flank, whatever they can reach. Anna and Malcom are halfway to them with Nina and Carl. At a loss, Dave starts to follow.

"*Behind you*!" Jenna screams with her voice and her mind.

Dave spins on his heel.

Above him, more skyworms drop from the heavens, closing on their scattered party as neatly as he might fold the ends of a box. The last hangs back, observing.

It's a trap, he thinks hollowly. *And we fell for it.*

Beneath his feet, the ground explodes.

Chapter 24

Jason – Pearson

Toronto, ON: Wednesday, August 20

Pain rips through Jason's back and across his temples as Kalos's consciousness boards his body. Kalos shoves Jason's awareness to the back of his mind as easily as Jason crammed his carry-on into the plane's overhead compartment. Xhen crackles around him. It's midnight black, shot through with the deep purple of African violets, just like he remembers. Yet with Kalos present, it's also ribboned with bone-white energy.

Adrenaline pumps through Jason's heart as xhen coats his body. Then he senses it again, that edge in the fabric of the world. *No!* He rears back, skittish as a balking horse. *I failed!*

Kalos holds him steady as he manipulates the forming break in reality. Pressure builds, a vise squeezing Jason's temples—

—and stops, relaxing like an expertly loosened muscle as xhen flashes around Jason in a wide purple-black-white ring, tearing a hole that his mind can't fully grasp. Air blasts his face with skin-peeling force; the sensation of free fall shifts his stomach before a second flash blinds him. Then there's a jarring thud as his seat lands on something hard.

The neatly severed ends of Jason's oxygen mask drop into his lap. He blinks, unable to comprehend that he's back on solid ground. To his left and right, the people seated beside him continue shrieking before breaking off in stunned surprise. In the next second, they're out of their seats and running in all directions.

Pearson, he thinks in shock as he looks at the massive stretch of tarmac lined with weedy, sun-bleached grass. In the distance, the CN Tower looks like a child's toy. *I landed at Pearson Airport after all.*

Jason tries to pull the useless oxygen mask off his face, but it's like he's got sleep paralysis. He can't move his hands. Instead, Kalos turns his head to the sky.

Perhaps 15,000 feet above him, the damaged airplane plummets toward the ground in a nose-down, pin-wheeling spiral, the black creature twisted like a massive vine around its wings and fuselage. *Anna killed three of those monsters?* He can't comprehend it.

Do not be daunted by their size. Observe, Kalos says, just as he did when Jason was seventeen and their time was infinite. His teacher seems equally indifferent to the panic pounding through his automatic nervous system and the plummeting aircraft. ***You carry black-veined xhen. With it, you may open portals anywhere in this world.***

Prickling races up Jason's back as the pressure in his head mounts again. Xhen fills his body. He wonders if his mind will break like a circuit loaded with too much electricity. As his forehead burns in answer, triangular shapes cover the space around him in a delicate 3D latticework, gleaming with potential in every direction he can see.

These are portal seams. With them, your triad gains both movement and a powerful weapon.

What weapon? Jason asks, dazed.

With fierce concentration, Kalos splits his xhen into dozens of minute threads, recalling their exercises from long ago. Wielding them like slender needles above the tarmac in front of Jason, his teacher knits the corners of first one seamed triangle and then another, rapidly stitching them together until they form a solid ring. With dozens more xhen needles, Kalos forms a second ring high overhead, below the falling plane.

Something inside Jason's mind twists, but his arms and hands remain inert. Above and around them, xhen flashes purple-black-white as the rings fold together and some sort of portal flares open, cleaving a long, deep gouge along the creature's back. The monster howls as a strip of its flesh drops through the other end of the opening at Jason's feet. Overhead, the creature hastily peels away from the airplane. A dark pulse flashes in the sky as it vanishes.

How did you do that? Jason demands.

With care, Kalos says, keeping Jason's gaze locked on the aircraft. ***Catching objects with a portal is a difficult yet necessary skill. Grasp and link the seam edges to build one side of the portal ahead of the object. Place its other side where you wish the object to travel.***

Xhen fires across Jason's forehead as Kalos, with the same mind-bending speed, connects two more sets of disparate seam edges—the first quite a distance below the airplane and the second about two hundred metres from where they stand. He bends thousands of xhen threads with the precision of an origami master until the two rings are each the size of a hockey rink.

Fold the edges inward, and the space between the rings shall collapse and open. Kalos twists the shining purple-black-white rings inside themselves. Jason's head clicks with the firm pleasure of matched puzzle pieces as the back of each ring vanishes in a flash. ***The portal will slow thrown or falling objects as they cross its threshold***.

The airplane vanishes through the skyward portal and drops a mere six metres to the tarmac, landing on its side with far less force and speed than it should. Even so, one wing crumples under the impact as the weight of the plane's main cabin pushes it into the concrete. Metal screams as the aircraft shifts until its other wing slants straight up in the air as though pointing a warning. Smoke curls from the rear of the airplane, thick and black.

Fire! Jason fights to stand, but his body may as well be set in concrete. Under Kalos's control, his consciousness remains firmly tucked inside his own head, like a toddler waiting in a quiet corner for a timeout to end. *I'm a doctor! I've got to help them—*

You help by never leaving a skyworm free to hunt.

Skyworm? Is that what they're called?

In this age, yes. Kalos finally removes Jason's oxygen mask and seatbelt. He stands to study their surroundings. The black skyworm is nowhere to be seen. ***Surgical training taught you to think in three dimensions. We shall apply that knowledge now.***

Xhen masses around Jason's body like a thundercloud. Seam edges leap into his mind's eye, standing in sharp relief against the perfect blue of the summer sky. Again, he tastes dust in the back of his throat as Kalos orients him to the shifting pattern.

Group the seams into clusters of six, Kalos says, demonstrating as he threads and twists the triangles into hexagons. ***Link these to make wider seams more rapidly***.

As Jason watches, the hexagons multiply into connected rings that widen or narrow at Kalos's will. Before he can ask another question, a burning rush floods his kidneys. The skyworm appears above them, so colossal that it blocks the sun. Jason tastes sulphuric rot at the back of his throat as the half dozen orange tentacles around its mouth lurch for him. *Holy shit!*

His body disobeys his instinct to run as Kalos links two fresh hexagonal rings—one a millimetre before his nose and the other at the end of a runway, perhaps a kilometre away. Jason feels pressure and release as Kalos folds the space between the two points. The air inside the portal is distorted, shimmering in the sun like a mirage as Kalos widens its matched rings to human size. He neatly jumps Jason's body across the divide and snaps it shut.

Before Jason can fully process what's happened, the skyworm summons its own black portal. With a dark pulse, it follows them, roaring as it comes. *They can travel through space, too?*

The black ones can, Kalos confirms as they leap to another point on Pearson's runways. ***This one is small for its kind. Your triad wounded it. Note the burn marks on its scales, the sheen of ichor on its back, its erratic movement.***

Jason's eyes involuntarily focus on two duller points on the skyworm's hide. Their matte finish stands out against the skyworm's otherwise shining scales like a bad patch of paint on a sports car.

Your sister cut one of three nerves behind its neck crest. Had she severed them all, the skyworm would have been immobilized.

Cool disappointment, not his own, floods Jason's body for an instant. Before Jason can ask more about Anna, Kalos continues.

It came seeking your xhen to heal its injuries. If it returns to its brethren bearing extra energy, more of its swarm will cross here and hunt.

Instead of opening another portal, the skyworm slithers across the airfield toward them, its attention fixed upon them as though weighing its options. Kalos takes Jason through a third portal, keeping enough space between Jason and the monster to give him time to take in its blunt snout, writhing tentacles, and gaping maw beneath three thirsting eyes.

On the ground, it moves like a cobra. It's noticeably slower and does appear to be favouring its right side, lacking all its airborne grace. It lurches from side to side with an erratic, head-bobbing list that reminds Jason of the midnight regulars in St. Paul's Emergency Department. Yet it also manages to cover the distance alarmingly fast, malevolent intelligence obvious in its purposeful approach and burning eyes. His false comparison to the harmless people Jason treated in the ER vanishes.

It's come to kill me.

It has come to harvest, Kalos corrects. ***Do not let its tentacles touch your skin. You need not fear its portals as maiming weapons—***

What?

—for it will want your body whole to paralyze you and drain your xhen. Stay clear of its traps until you find a Kalxhan and recruit tarkan to guard your back.

Kalxhan? Tarkan? Jason doesn't know whether to laugh or cry, although both reactions feel appropriate. It hardly matters. With Kalos's calm voice in his head and his teacher's firm guidance, everything is both surreal and astoundingly familiar. *So what do I . . .?*

Open a portal around its tail. Slice your way up its body. The practice will serve you well. Then take its head.

Abruptly, Kalos withdraws.

Jason reels as he regains control over his body. Blood rushes to his head as though he's stood too quickly, but xhen is there to steady him, purple-black with the white undercurrent gone. It feels like part of him still sits inert with his disbelief in the airplane seat, but another, half-forgotten part grasps for this new strength. It crackles through him, as familiar as the smooth, worn grooves in the handrail at the top of the stairs in his parents' old house. Taking hold of that current is just as euphoric as it once was to swing over the bannister's railing and free-fall the ten steps to the carpeted hallway below.

Torn between fear and exhilaration, Jason keeps the tantalizing rush at a remove, as wary of its allure as he was of his sister's outlandish claims. *Haste and brashness are a deadly combination*, one of the veteran nurses used to bark at all the new residents, and that warning has stayed with him. Margo's skeptical eyes also flicker in his thoughts. He forgets her and everything but the skyworm as seam edges flicker across his vision, turning the world into a pulsing honeycomb.

He forms threads to grasp the triangles and twist them into hexagons as xhen masses in his gut, in his hands, in his temples. The pressure is crushing. Grunting, Jason connects one set of hexagons into a ring fifty metres away and tries to form a second ring around the skyworm's tail.

Nothing happens—no light, no flash, nothing. The pressure in his skull continues, unrelenting. Stars bloom white before his eyes. *Kalos! What am I doing wrong?* Wildly, Jason scans the landscape for his teacher. No reassuring voice comes.

I'm alone. Great.

Roaring, the skyworm lunges forward. Jason spins on his heel and runs, scanning the shifting honeycomb of seam edges for an answer. Tentacles slap the tarmac as the monster slithers closer. Then there's a cracking black flash, and the skyworm looms over him, reeking so strongly of sulphur that Jason's eyes water. He blinks to clear his involuntary tears as he skids to a halt, fearful of losing xhen. Hastily, he collapses the now useless ring he'd built around the skyworm's tail and reforms it around the monster's new position. But he doesn't understand how to link them. *Think. Kalos said three dimensions. Fold the edges in on its centre.*

The skyworm strikes with terrifying speed. Jason barely evades the blow. Again, he tries to force the two rings to twist together. The pressure doubles in his skull, momentarily tunneling his vision into a blackened cone. Crying out, he stops pushing, disgusted with himself.

You've spent years denying that you can touch xhen, some part of him laughs. *Did you really think a two-minute lesson was going to save you?*

The skyworm roars. Its mouth opens to reveal a slender tentacle, pale as a maggot. It strikes for Jason's shoulder with wicked speed. Clear spittle from its maw flecks his face, making his skin itch.

Flinching, Jason ducks, slightly loosening his deathlike hold on xhen. Focused on evading the tentacle, he almost misses the moment when the hexagon rings fold in and reach for each other like twin babies in a bassinet. Without him trying to jam them together, Jason feels their gentle, clicking twist. His vision flashes purple-black as the portal slices through the skyworm's thick tail with the precision of a razor blade, as easily as he might chop a carrot. The pale violet tail fins, wide and sharp as blades, twitch as a scaled mass of flesh drops to the runway.

Howling, the creature lurches, spraying him with ichor as it shifts its weight. With a crack like thunder, the maimed stump of its tail snaps up and forward, flicking sideways over the rest of its coiled body toward Jason. He drops to his knees, instinctively picking a spot three hundred metres distant. He's faster to thread the seam edges and build the rings, this time holding them with greater delicacy in his mind's eye. Without any distracting pressure, he feels the shifting twist as they compress and bend the space, opening a narrow portal too small for the skyworm to cross. Jason scrabbles through the hole, closing it behind him.

On the portal's other side, the thin branches of a small bush sway in the wind. Rows of lights blink white-red-white-red, marking the end of the runway for nonexistent planes. Getting to his feet, Jason forms one hexagonal ring. Despite the instinct screaming at him to attack, he draws a deep breath as he waits to build his next portal's other side. Before he can exhale, black light pulses. The skyworm materializes, tentacles striking toward him.

Got you! Jason thinks as he builds the portal's other half farther up the skyworm's body and folds the two sides together.

The portal snaps open and shut. A large hunk of black flesh falls into the shrubbery a few metres away, stinking and useless. The skyworm roars.

The fight becomes a flashing ballet of cat and mouse across the airport's runways. Xhen-fired muscle memory, unused for a decade and a half, scorches fresh pathways through Jason's mind. It's almost fun. Sometime after his surgical experiment reaches a midpoint on the skyworm's back, the creature retreats. It opens a portal to launch itself into the sky like a hang glider jumping from a cliff. Clear fluid rains down on the tarmac as it struggles to stay airborne.

I have to kill it! Jason forms and clicks portal rings together as quickly as he can mentally conceptualize them. Glistening purple-black apertures slice up the skyworm's body with such speed that to his naked eye, the monster appears to spontaneously split apart in midair. Panting, Jason opens a final portal to cleave its head in two.

Massive chunks of flesh fall around Jason as he drops to his knees beside a runway, sweating rivers and gasping like he's run a marathon. He forms one last portal above his head, using it to divert the crashing pieces of skyworm away from him. The humid air is thick with the stink of rotten eggs. Despite the awful smell, his stomach grumbles. Revolted by the thought of eating, Jason ignores the pang to focus on his breathing. With the skyworm silenced, the airfield is eerily quiet. There's nothing to hear besides his breath rasping in his throat and the blood pounding in his ears.

I'm alive. And xhen . . . He lifts a hand, studying the shifting purple-black energy. No longer a metaphysical force sensed and not seen, it encircles his fingers and hums in his blood, begging for use. Jason scrubs a hand through his hair, pulling on the sweaty strands to ground himself. *I killed a skyworm.* After dedicating years of his life to saving lives, he's shocked by his own brutality. *But I did it.*

Sirens wail in the distance. Jason turns his head. Several kilometres distant, emergency vehicles cluster around the still-burning airplane. There's no sign of Kalos. With the skyworm defeated, he should go to the crash site. To ignore his physician's oath feels deeply wrong. But offering his services will mean answering questions. *What if more of them show up?*

Seeing no choice, Jason rises. Half a dozen muscles wail in protest. *I'd give anything for a hot bath.* He pictures himself in the condo's jacuzzi tub and Margo's disgust at his filthy appearance. He can't reconcile the thought of her with the pieces of slaughtered nightmare flung across the ground.

Then he imagines her watching this fight on television, the way he saw Anna at the SkyDome. *Would she recognize me? I should have told her. Where will she be now? Winding down rehearsal? I could call.*

Before he can fumble in his pockets for his phone, xhen pulses around him. The air crackles with unseen pressure as two hexagonal rings spring into possible formation. Jason stretches a hand into the air, feeling the energy dance around his fingers. He can see only one side of the nascent portal with his eyes. Yet, in his mind, he feels its terminus forming on the roof of his condominium in Vancouver. If he connects them, the portal will open. He'll be home. *I could tell Margo I missed the flight. Talk to her. Explain everything.*

Jason stands in frozen contemplation, part of him playing out that impossible conversation while a deeper part marvels at his ability. *This is what I almost touched that day in the alley. I was so close, and I didn't know it.*

And you threw it all away, his conscience whispers with his mother's voice. *And Anna with it.*

Xhen licks his spine as though answering Jason's thought of his twin. *Think in three dimensions.* As possibilities shift, the rooftop in Vancouver fades from his consciousness. Instead, a new portal destination tugs his awareness south, toward the University of Toronto's campus and Queen's Park.

Jason glances down into one of the dead skyworm's empty eyes. *Kalos said Anna wounded it. Would it have come alone?* Thinking of his sister recalls his wretchedness on the airplane. He remembers picturing Anna standing over him in the aisle, gloating at his failure. *Do you believe me now?*

She'll never forgive me, he thinks. *Not if we live to be a hundred.*

But you won, says the part of him that speaks with his mother's voice. *And she needs you.*

Another wailing siren pierces his consciousness—there's a police car driving in his direction.

Grasp and link the seam edges where you are, Jason thinks, squaring his back as he relaxes his hold on xhen. *Fold them against the edges where you wish to be.*

Purple-black light flashes one last time along Pearson Airport's runways as he opens a portal to fresh chaos.

Chapter 25

Anna – Tarkan

Toronto, ON: Wednesday, August 20

Anna's rage swells as the skyworm pounces on the SWAT team, its tentacles striking at their chests and faces. *It's feeding!* she shrieks to Dave, drowning in memories of losing her xhen to identical tentacles that filled her with helplessness as the skyworm drank her power. *Kill it!*

Her fury echoes in her new tarkan, amplifying their bloodlust. As Anna tears across the legislature's lawn toward the downed officers, all pretense of strategy gone, five golden pockets blaze furiously in her mind. Only Malcolm's presence—the largest and brightest in her skull—crackles with wariness, but she can't hold back. *We've got seconds before it kills them.*

Her breath rasps in her throat. Lactic acid burns in her thighs. New to their xhen-powered speed, Nina and Carl still easily outpace her, drawing their knives as they race to join Raymond and Krista, who have closed in on the creature. Anna snarls as their blades slice into the skyworm, spraying ichor in thick arcs. She raises a hand and fires a covering volley.

Before she shoots again, Malcolm's presence spikes in a firework burst at the base of her skull, simultaneous with Dave's shout of warning. The ground beneath her feet rumbles as skyworms thunder overhead. Anna stumbles as a sonic wave rips the grass apart, vaulting her into open air for the second time in an hour.

Anna twists, trying and failing to spot the ground and get her feet beneath her. Disoriented, she back slams into the earth. Sparks fly across her vision as dirt clods and stones pelt her stunned body. Ears ringing, she gasps for breath, trying to sit up. Yet breathing is harder than it should be. Her vertigo is monstrous. She can't do anything but lie there while xhen drifts like a raincloud beyond her reach. *Get up. NOW!*

A skyworm shudders to the earth beside her. Orange light scalds Anna's eyes as the creature's power washes over her in a drenching wave. She rolls, scrambling to her elbows. *No, no, NO!*

Viper-swift, its tentacles strike her wrist, her knee, her ankle. Alien triumph blossoms in her head mixed with an even deeper sense of surprise. ***XENTHIAN***!

NO! Anna clutches for xhen, but her ocean has turned to dawn mist. It seeps from her fingers and arms, flowing into the skyworm's body. The orange light intensifies, burning like a second sun. She screams, shutting her eyes to block out her agony and the skyworm's presence in her mind. Effortlessly, the creature shoves an image sequence into her head. She sees a fighter jet blowing apart in midair. Through the skyworm's eyes, she watches them catch the parachuting pilot. Clustering to feast, they radiate a rancid sunset that lasts a mere second. Then they pull the pilot apart, limbs from trunk, and let what remains of the broken body fall.

Sickened, Anna tries to recoil and feels only the skyworm's answering delight. She's aware that somewhere, Dave is calling to her, but his words are meaningless, like bubbles sliding down a bathtub drain. Two of the five golden lights in her head are dimming, but she can't help them. Her entire world is the skyworm's delight as it siphons her xhen—

—until contact breaks. Gasping, Anna opens her eyes. Malcolm's standing over her, brandishing his blue knife. Someone else slips strong hands under her shoulders, hauling her away. *Xhen. Reach for xhen.* She might as well carry seawater with her bare hands.

While Anna fumbles for her power, Carl darts past her to cover Malcolm's flank.

Duck! Dave shouts.

In unison, both men drop. A fireball whistles over their heads and slams into the skyworm's head. It reels, its scales blackened on the left side of its head. Jenna sprints up its back. Her arms rise in a two-handed strike as she slams her knife down behind the skyworm's neck crest. Its head lolls, dropping to the ground as clear ichor spills down its sides. Malcolm and Carl close in then, blue knives flashing as they hew tentacles and drive their blades through its eyes to finish it off. Three distinct rivers of satisfaction flow through Anna's head. The stink of sulphur fills her nose as the skyworm dies, and the minds of her three tarkan are so bright with pleasure they nearly block out the two fading presences.

Five skyworms to go, Dave broadcasts. *Keep watching the sky for the black one.*

Something's wrong, Anna thinks, dazed. Her head throbs in time to the flickering, dying sparks in her head. *What am I missing?*

Someone shakes her shoulder. Anna turns to find Nina crouching behind her, her pink lips forming words that Anna's ringing ears cannot hear. Her new tarkan points across the lawn, the cream cloth of her suit torn and stained. Blinking, Anna rubs dirt from her eyes, trying to focus. Her back hurts. Everything's happening fast.

Where are Krista and Raymond? And then, with slow horror, she grasps what Nina's showing her: three of the remaining skyworms crouched among the ruined SWAT vehicles, feeding on her tarkan, while the other two circle overhead.

Rage hot as the noon-day sun slices through Anna's mental fog. *They're mine! Not yours, MINE!* Xhen surges through her body as though sprung from a floodgate, prickling along every nerve. With Nina's hand on her shoulder, she draws deeply on its tide until her entire being thrums with furious current.

Her first blast takes the nearest skyworm in the back of the head. It's a lucky shot, shearing off half its face. As a fireball from Dave finishes it off, Anna turns her attention to the second creature. Her next blast sends only a single tentacle sliding off its face with a wet smush, but it's enough to make the monster abandon the human cradled in its parasitic embrace—*Krista?*—and launch itself into the air.

Anna fires another bolt. Her aim's off. This time, she misses. The skyworm roars. She strikes next with a leash, trying to snare it, but xhen is slow to bend to her will. It takes her three tries to grasp the skyworm's neck, precious seconds her tarkan don't have. *I can't be tired. Not. Now.*

But we are. Weariness layers Dave's voice. *And Jason needs us. Finish that one off. The other one's still feeding. Jenna and I will keep the two in the sky off your backs.*

On cue, more hands touch her shoulders—Malcolm and Carl. Knees trembling, Anna uses their bodies as the ballast against which to draw yet more xhen. Their strength steadies her enough to haul the approaching leashed skyworm from the air. It careens toward the ground, the back half of its body whipping from side to side like the tail of a kite in a high wind as it tries to slow the plunge.

But Anna's hold is relentless. The skyworm roars, igniting a fresh wave of pain in her back. The ground trembles. *Not again!* Thrusting a xhen barrier between her tarkan and the earth, Anna fires another bolt into the skyworm's side. Instantly, the tremor subsides.

"Get it on the ground! We'll kill it!" Malcolm cries. His voice, so close to her damaged ears, sounds muffled as though heard down a long tunnel.

Anna nods, aware of the skyworms circling overhead, kept at bay only by Dave's covering fire. The lone feeding skyworm is still crouched over its victims, seemingly oblivious to everything but its feast.

Abruptly, one of the golden lights in Anna's head flickers and goes out. Sorrow breaks in her chest. Her concentration falters.

"Focus," Malcolm shouts, his grip tightening on her shoulder. Nina and Carl hold on to her, too, the brightness of their contact balancing the dark pit cast by her two dead or dying tarkan. Anna clenches her teeth, fighting to hold on to xhen.

Erratic bolts arc from her raised palm as she tries to draw the skyworm down with her leash. She misses far more than she hits, but the effort agitates the creature. It opens its mouth so wide that she feels its howl reverberate through her bones. A vengeful smile curves Anna's lips as she abruptly reforms her leash into a massive bolt. *Wrong move, stupid.* And she fires, straight down the skyworm's gaping mouth.

Its body explodes in a shower of orange scales. Anna twists away, closing her mouth and eyes as skyworm guts soak her and everyone around her from head to foot. Extracting the creature's fading xhen from its stinking remains takes only seconds; she bathes in the hot orange light, swiftly restoring her hearing before pouring the rest into her tarkan.

Malcolm, Nina, and Carl pulse with health and determination, but the skyworm's xhen does little to boost the one remaining and rapidly dimming light. She funnels her stolen power to that spark, struggling to do so at a distance. As she releases the last scrap, hot fluid loosens and drips from her nose. Anna swipes the blood away with the back of her hand, clinging to her rage.

Anna, Dave interrupts. Instinctively, she turns west and spots the red glow of Jenna's knife under the trees on the other side of the park. *Jenna thinks they're prolonging the feeding to make you angry. If you attack, the two in the sky will hit us again. But one of your tarkan—*

I know. Regret reaches for her, a rogue wave eager to drag her beneath its powerful undertow, but she can't surrender. Not yet.

Stone-faced, Anna fires a fresh flurry of bolts at the feeding skyworm, but the protective hands of her tarkan warn her against venturing any closer.

"Three o'clock!" Malcolm shouts, a heartbeat before Dave's *Behind you!*

Twisting her neck so sharply the muscle wrenches, Anna whirls to see the two airborne skyworms as they dive at her party from opposite directions. Their scales are scored by fire. Blackened tentacles ring their howling mouths, but the ground still trembles at their approach. Anna hesitates for only a second, torn between a certain defense and firing a barrage straight into their roaring maws.

Keep everyone safe, she decides and forms a barrier to protect her trio of tarkan from flying dirt and reaching tentacles.

Outside her circle of enforced calm, earth fountains in wide sprays, uncovering an interlocking system of pipes, likely laid for lawn maintenance, that crisscrosses the legislature's park. Some instinct sends Nina and Carl peeling through her protective sea wall in opposite directions across the exposed metal latticework. As the skyworms soar overhead, they stab in eerie unison at the skyworms' exposed orange bellies. Nina scores a hit. As the skyworm shudders, slowing for the barest second, Anna leashes it, smashing its body down onto the pipes.

Water sprays everywhere, momentarily blinding her. Yet the metal doesn't pierce the skyworm's scales. Fortunately, Dave has joined them. He pelts the skyworm with basketball-sized fireballs. Carl is already scrabbling up the creature's back, stabbing behind its crest as Nina attacks its eyes. Ichor oozes from dozens of its wounds. Nina blinds the skyworm as Carl rips out its neck cords. The skyworm's mouth opens in feeble protest. Before it can roar, Anna shoves a ball of xhen down its throat.

The tarkan jump clear as Anna spins her back to the explosion of scales. She searches the air for their other attacker but spots nothing.

It pulled up and retreated, Dave tells her, stripping xhen from her kill. Only after Anna has spotted the retreating orange shape, its scales heavily pockmarked by Dave's fire, does she do the same, wishing skyworm xhen would assuage her exhaustion and hunger. *We'll watch your backs in case it or the black one returns*, he tells her. *Hurry, Annie. She's almost gone.*

Again, Nina and Carl sprint ahead of Anna, knives at the ready. The last feeding skyworm lifts its head. Grass and concrete rise in a ruptured wave as its sonic attack ripples toward her tarkan. This time, however, Anna and Dave are prepared. At his command, they form interlinked red-and-blue barriers as seamlessly as they once worked together in training, diverting the shock wave's effects. Anna's tarkan do not slow their head-long sprint, leaping over the torn ground.

"Get ready," Malcolm warns, hanging back to accommodate Anna's slower speed. She rolls her shoulders, bracing herself.

Somewhere in the distance, the retreating skyworm roars. The creature feeding on the ground takes to the air in an orange flurry, its tail knocking Carl's feet out from under him as it twists in a steep, curving ascent toward the open sky. Anna hastily fires a bolt. The skyworm dodges. Her next shot falls short. So does Dave's fireball. Panting, neither of them makes a second attempt.

They may circle back for another pass. Dave meets Anna's eyes across the lawn. *We'll watch your back. Go to her.*

Anna runs after Malcolm and her other tarkan, feeling her battle rage slipping away with every step until she's trudging across the war zone that used to be University Avenue.

She reaches Raymond first. Holes of varying sizes puncture his police uniform, crusted with congealed blood. His hazel eyes are open, guileless as those of a child. Knowing he would be dead and seeing his slack face are two different things. Anna gasps as the depths of her failure slam through her in a humiliating wave. *It was a trap*, she thinks. *What would Kalos say? We took the bait like fools.*

"Anna!" Malcolm's kneeling over the second body. Carl and Nina are with him, standing guard as they watch the second skyworm flee toward its companion. Both turn as Anna approaches, each touching her shoulder in mute sympathy, although their eyes never stop watching the sky.

To Anna's shock, Krista is awake. Her eyes fly to Anna's face as she kneels across from Malcolm. *Just like Brenda. I let it happen again.* Anna reaches for the young officer's hand, pouring all the skyworm xhen she carries into the other woman's body. One side of Krista's bloodstained mouth twitches like she's trying to smile. Anna stops some of the blood leaking from the holes she can see, but Krista's covered in punctures.

It took its time. Blood soaks the pavement beneath and around her body, the metallic scent stronger than the reek of sulphur. With xhen, Anna can feel all the deeper ruptures. And she hasn't got enough to repair them all. The deliberate cruelty of the injuries rattles her, as the skyworm no doubt intended.

Dave! Before she asks, he offers his stolen skyworm xhen, sending it to her in a red wave as Kalos did. Anna eagerly accepts, wishing she had a fraction of Jason's medical skill to put it to the most effective use. Despite her care, it's gone in seconds.

It's not enough! Anna cries. *More, please!*

Annie. Dave's voice is infinitely gentle. *Look at her.*

Wishing for a fresh pack of skyworms to face, Anna looks down. Again, Krista's eyes find hers. The fingers clasped in Anna's hand flex ever so slightly. "Mistake," she breathes. "Sor . . ."

"Don't be. We won." Remembering Brenda's death, Anna opens herself to her tarkan as peace mixed with satisfaction surges through their joined hands. There's pain, too—terrible pain—that Anna takes into her body as if trying to drain a firehose dry. The tension in Krista's face seeps away. Anna's stomach chooses that moment to growl. Ignoring it, she reaches for xhen, scourging the skyworms' corpses for a last flicker. She might as well reach for the moon.

She turns back to Krista, failure brimming in her eyes. "We killed them," Anna tells her. "And we saved a lot of people." Her world is Krista's brown eyes, each breath that rasps in her ruined throat. "I'm going to find your family, yours and Raymond's. They will know what you did here. I'm so grateful for your help, Krista. We all are."

Satisfaction crests around the spark in her head that is Krista. Then it flickers, fades, and is gone. Nothing remains but a burned, blackened place, a shattered crater in Anna's consciousness that matches the hollow left by Raymond and the pit that is Brenda Edwards.

Sadness clogs her throat like water rushing to fill a well. Anna sits back on her heels, too numb to cry. Malcolm comes to her side, wordlessly wrapping an arm around her shoulders. Comfort radiates from him. She also feels Nina's and Carl's hands on her arms. She leans into them, trying to take their light into herself, but the contrast makes the three holes loom more noticeably. They blaze with nothingness, tiny points of oblivion seared into her soul.

She waits for the recriminations, but only satisfaction seeps from her tarkan like a three-pronged river delta. *We won,* she thinks as her stomach rumbles again. *They're pleased despite the cost.*

As if in direct mockery of that thought, the fleeing skyworm roars.

Anna leaps to her feet, pushing free of her tarkan. It's too far away for a leash, so she forms bolt after bolt of shining blue, flinging them after the retreating skyworm as though, if she's fast enough, she might undo the last frantic twenty minutes.

"Anna," Malcolm's saying.

She pretends not to hear. *I should have healed Krista first. I could have saved her.*

"Anna, stop, for God's sake, and look!"

Before her eyes, blackish-purple xhen swallows the orange skyworm's body, shredding it to pieces.

Fear lurches through Anna as she spins around, searching the sky. *The black one's back,* she thinks numbly, reaching for xhen even as she staggers. *I'm so fucking tired.*

A hand—Malcolm's, it must be Malcolm—closes on her skull, the fingertips flexing to physically turn her head to the left.

Anna gasps as a tall dark-haired man in filthy clothes steps through a ring of xhen above the lawn of Queen's Park. His handsome face is bloodied and soot-smeared above the purple-black xhen wrapped around his body, but oh so familiar.

A relieved sob escapes Anna's throat as tears spill down her face. "Jason!"

Interlude: Fury

The moons set three times before the veil's pulse renews its frantic beat, signaling the return of our hunting party. Again, the swarm lines the ocean shore, crawling over our tentacles in their eagerness to sight the victors. We flex our scales to remind them of their place as we turn our own gaze skyward, ready to give welcome.

But when the hole widens, the cliff wind bears not the delicious scent of alien skal, but the death stench of our fallen.

Unthinkable, we roar, shaken by so much loss.

Around us, the swarm reels, equally alarmed by this shift in fortune. Our tail lashes, silencing them as we study the pulsing veil. At last, a lone scout pushes through the hole, its orange scales no longer jewel bright against the heavens. Scored and blackened, it plummets to the ocean.

We dive beneath the waves and chase its plunging body through the dark. When it is secure in our tentacles, we lift it back to the surface and place it in the centre of the nest. Bloodlust flows through the swarm like a tide, demanding satisfaction. Our body coils around the injured scout, holding their wrath at bay as we study it.

Its scales heave with imminent death. We pry open its mouth, extract its tentacle, and touch it to our own. Swiftly, we harvest its meager portion of alien skal. Yet in its mind, we also find images of ungainly two-legged beasts wielding skal that burns as strongly as our own.

Ground dwellers, we hiss. ***Insignificant***.

Swarm killers, the scout whispers as it shudders and falls still.

For the first time in our memory, true fear spirals through the swarm.

Overhead, the pulsing veil slows and ceases to move. The remaining hunters are truly lost, including the black-scaled runt. Fury grips us so tightly that we hear nothing but the pounding of the waves against the sand, echoing the wrath simmering through us. We gather the scout's body, wrapping its tentacles around its scales before offering it to the swarm. In silence, they consume its flesh.

Resistance, our mother-sisters hiss when the honour feast is done. ***Xenthians***.

Myth, we scoff to quell our rising panic. ***Nest tales told to make hatchlings obey***.

Fool, says our eldest mother-sister, releasing a wave of memories. ***They are an ancient foe, feared and desired by queens of old for their potent skal. With it, those queens of nests long past conquered all our lands, but at terrible cost.***

We shift our scales as our mother-sister shares memories stolen from the nest minds of our long-dead enemies. We see ancient hunting parties traveling the Xenthian home world: a vast, wide place, its lands lush and green.

Xenthians are the only skal-bearers with the power to seal the veil and end our hunts. It is a thought to shiver scales. ***The queens of old hated these beings***, our mother-sister continues. ***Their fear leaked into the nest minds of all the swarms they conquered, including ours. We stored this knowledge against future need.***

The wind shifts, and again our nose slits fill with the stench of death. Rage twists our guts. How dare these ground-crawlers threaten our swarm?

Before we can issue commands, our mother-sisters speak again. ***Thrice you have hunted on that shore***, they observe. ***The aliens breed as plains herds. Where you attack matters not. Strike elsewhere and breed fear of our might. Move the veil's exit and select another of their nests for destruction.***

We shall not abandon our hunt.

Never, they agree. ***Yet the aliens are primed to our coming. Reclaim our advantage.***

The stars wheel above us, remote and imperious. So must we be to these vermin. No prey is worthy of our direct vengeance, not even Xenthians.

We divide our hoarded power, keeping the largest portion of skal to succor our growing hatchlings as they coalesce inside their shells. We wield the smaller fraction of our strength against the veil, until the entrance hole is wide enough for more of the swarm to cross.

Join the hunt, we command. ***Kill the Xenthians***.

Part Four

Family

Chapter 26

Dave – Reunion

Toronto, ON: Wednesday, August 20

As the last remaining skyworm's body breaks apart with the violence of an orange splattering against an invisible wall, a deeply familiar presence strikes like a lightning bolt through Dave's mind.

Jason!

Jubilant, he turns as his chosen brother steps through a hole in a swirling cloud of xhen. On the other side of the strange purple-black aperture, Dave glimpses an air traffic control tower and a swatch of tarmac. The hole swirls shut behind Jason, burning away the last of Dave's worries about his continued absence. Jason's state of mind, however, is another matter.

Shock, anger, shame, and a razor-sharp sense of alertness radiate from the topmost layer of his mind. Underneath that is a faint sliver of awe at traveling so great a distance in such a way. His filthy white dress shirt and khakis cling to his lean body. Grime streaks the long bones of his handsome face. His black hair, longer than Dave's, is plastered to his head. Dave rapidly sifts through Jason's unfiltered mental broadcast, each fragmented image as strong as Anna's were in her garage.

After forty-eight hours of intensive practice, it takes Dave only seconds to sift Jason's memories into a cohesive picture. Despite the day's considerable losses, he grins as his brother's triumph over the black skyworm unspools in his head, shot through with midnight-purple xhen. *This stubborn jackass,* he thinks fondly, remembering the alley behind his parents' house. *He's got teleportation after all.*

"The last orange one escaped toward the lake, but it was wounded," Jenna announces, coming up on Dave's shoulder. "It made sure to keep low and out of sight. Do you think it'll come back with reinforcements?" When he shrugs, she nudges his side, gesturing at Jason. "Who's that?"

Dave gives her a chagrined smile as thirty years of backstory catch on his tongue. "Anna's twin brother, Jason," he manages after a moment. "He's like a brother to me, too."

It's not much of an explanation, but Jenna nods, her emotion cluster tired but content. "Cool. How many more of you are there?"

"Unclear," he says. "There's always been the three of us. Anna thinks the six teenagers who died in the attacks on Sunday and Monday night were all like us, too, but untrained. There may be more." Her curiosity flutters in his head like butterfly wings, but she's so weary. They both are. Dave squeezes her arm. "Let's worry about that later."

Jenna's dirt-smeared smile is wry. *If we live that long.*

He smiles back, pleased to hear her answer mind-to-mind. *Having someone who can teleport will transform our strategy. I don't think Jason's got anyone like you to help him yet, so let's help him get a head start in thinking through the ways we can use the mobility upgrade he brings.*

Intrigue flickers in Jenna's mind as it begins to churn with possibilities. *Sure.* She hands him her xhen knife.

Dave reabsorbs the energy, pleased by how easily he and Jenna have found a groove. *I can trust her*, he decides. *Thank you, Creator, for sending me a strategist as strong as Hal.*

"Jay!" Anna shouts, shaking Dave from his reflective thoughts. She staggers toward her twin, eyes luminous in her exhausted face.

They're dressed the same, Dave realizes as he starts toward them, two figures in grimy khaki and white. On any other day, it would be funny. Their mother loved to tell the story of Jason's refusal to wear matching outfits when the twins were in junior kindergarten.

"Do you believe me now?" Anna demands as she hugs Jason. "I told you I wasn't bullshitting."

"Yeah, well." Jason steps out of the hug and crosses his arms. "Rub it in later."

Here we go. Dave sighs, lengthening his pace toward them.

Anna pulls away from Jason, visibly stung. "I didn't mean it that way." She gestures at the surrounding mayhem, her joy at his appearance fading. "We knew there had to be more behind what happened to us."

Anger and shame crackle from his mind as Jason bristles at Anna's words. "I didn't," he says curtly. "And neither did you."

Anna flinches and then sags, her bone-deep exhaustion matching Dave's own.

Stop it, guys. Dave eyes them both as he steps past Anna to hug her twin. *Welcome home, man.*

Jason freezes for a split second in stunned surprise before he hugs Dave back. As he pulls away, the ghost of a smile touches his lips. "You really can do that." His eyes brighten with a flash of the true wonder that Dave remembers from their teens. Then he frowns. "You stink, Dave."

"Take a shower in skyworm guts and see how you smell," Malcolm says as he joins the group, still holding his blue xhen knife. "Glad you finally made it to the party, Doc."

"Malcolm." Jason shakes his brother-in-law's hand without

seeming to see him. His eyes are focused on the gleaming weapon. Then he looks at Nina and Carl standing behind Anna and Malcolm, matching knives in hand. Anna flicks her fingers. As the blades vanish, she turns to silently look at her brother with an open challenge in her eyes.

Ohhhh, Annie, Dave thinks as Jason's expression hardens by another minute degree. *You're not helping your cause here.*

Ignoring her, Jason focuses on Malcolm. "Anna brought you into this mess, too?"

"Yeah." Malcolm looks from twin to twin, equally accustomed to being a spectator to their arguments. He gestures at the other side of Queen's Park. "We need to get out of here."

Everyone turns. Police and emergency vehicles are arriving in force, jamming University Avenue's uncharacteristically empty northbound lanes. As they watch, a small fleet of Humvees painted military green and black pull in on the southbound side.

Dad won't be far behind, Dave thinks.

"I'm staying," Anna says, sorrow clouding her face as she stares across the grass at her fallen tarkan. Malcolm automatically puts an arm around her. Nina lifts a hand as though tempted to do the same, and then stops. She and Carl glance at the police cars, and then at each other, their wariness palpable. "I have to explain what happened," Anna continues, oblivious to their discomfort.

"No," Malcolm says. "You need food and rest." She starts to protest. Malcolm takes his hand from Anna's elbow. Without his support, she staggers. Anna glares, as irate at being confronted with the limits of her endurance as any of the young coders Dave once led. "You're leaving."

"I'll stay," Dave says. "Dad and I are overdue."

Anna nods. "Tell him I'll meet with their families. Once everyone is over the shock."

Before he can agree to pass the message, there's a tug on his arm. "We'll stay," Jenna corrects.

"Fine." Dave looks at Malcolm. "What about you?"

Malcolm shakes his head. "Anna and the team are my priority." His dark eyes flick to the bodies still scattered in the road. "It pains me to say it, but we lost Raymond and Krista because they didn't accept their new roles fast enough. I should have explained it better to them." He swallows hard before looking at Dave. "The chief will know by now that I've resigned. I'd appreciate anything you can do to help him understand."

"Will do," Dave says, trying to hide his surprise. Malcolm's commitment to policing has always struck him as iron clad. "Where will we find you?"

"Our house," Anna says, studying her husband's face.

She didn't know either, Dave realizes.

"Mom and Dad's place," Jason counters.

Malcolm nods. "That's better." He turns to his wife, grimacing. "Nancy Coleman outed us a few minutes before I left the station. Our house will be a circus."

"She really went there, huh?" Anna murmurs, shaking her head. "We need a car, then. Or, I guess, a van."

Jason shakes his head. Xhen flashes around his dirty clothes, wrapping him in a purple-black cloak. Eyes closed, he makes another opening about half a foot higher than he is tall and as wide as three people. Through the hole's crackling edges, cherry trees sway beneath the summer sun in Chun-Mei Lin's rose garden in North York, a suburb of Toronto some twenty kilometres away. The image is hazy, as though seen under heavy glass, but there's no mistaking the location. More fascinating to Dave is the array of images seeping from Jason's mind: rings of hexagons layering his xhen and the surrounding landscape.

Like code, Dave thinks in wonder. *Ordering the world.*

Cries of alarm from the official response interrupt his contemplation as soldiers emerge from the Humvees, guns drawn. Their minds bristle with fury. *Time to go!* Dave broadcasts.

Nina jumps through the portal. "All clear," she calls back.

Anna hesitates.

"Go," Dave urges her. "I've got this."

His chosen sister takes one last look at her dead, oozing regret, before allowing Malcolm and Carl to escort her through the portal. Jason follows. The opening closes, its residue fading to a grid of faintly hexagonal shapes before it completely vanishes.

"Follow my lead," Dave tells Jenna and drops to his knees. He laces his fingers behind his head. The soldiers are closing fast, helmet visors drawn over their faces. Rage froths in their minds. Tasting it, Dave guesses exactly how little the truth will matter in the next few seconds. *Could I command them to stop? Would speaking to them mind-to-mind make this worse or better?*

"What?" Jenna says, breaking his concentration as she kneels at his side. "Why? We saved—"

"All they know is that police and military have died violently, and we were involved," Dave says. He takes her hand to rapidly share a memory. He's fifteen years old, listening to Henry Montcalm instruct him in how not to resist an arrest.

You don't talk back, his dad had said. *Or glare. Or move too fast. Don't ever reach into your pockets. Make yourself small.* He remembers how he'd reacted, full of the same indignation as Jenna.

Your size alone will intimidate most people, his dad continues in the memory. *Intimidated police make bad decisions, Davy. They won't see the good person you are. They won't see me and our family, or your Auntie Lee and the fine people you come from. They'll see a big Native guy, and they'll project every bias they don't know they carry onto you.* His dad's younger face burns in his mind's eye, anguished. *I won't insult you: It's not fair. But until things change, you've got to survive in the city we have. Do you understand, Davy? If you run into trouble, you have to help them see you until I get there.*

What if they can't, Dad? he'd asked, spreading hands already so much bigger than his dad's in a wide, beseeching arc. *What if I scare them too much?*

And for the first time in his life, Dave had watched his dad cry.

He blinks away the memory as Jenna, tears in her eyes, puts one hand behind her head. She grips his forearm with the other, radiating strength and reassurance. *I'm with you.*

"I'm Dave Montcalm," Dave announces in a carrying voice. "My father is Henry Montcalm, Chief of the Toronto—"

But he doesn't get to finish. The soldiers surround them, shouting, and the first blow lands on his back.

Chapter 27

Jason – The Doctors Lin

Toronto, ON: Wednesday, August 20

My hands are shaking, Jason thinks as he boils water for tea in his parents' kitchen. The battle is three hours behind them now, but his heart still pounds in his chest. *I need to relax.*

Nothing around him is calming. Everything about the house where only his father now lives is both the same and utterly different. His mother's battered stainless-steel kettle and the tin box filled with matcha tea are on the counter, but he finds himself searching for vanished spoons and disappeared mugs, all replaced by Styrofoam and plastic. Likewise, he remembers the ladder-back oak chairs around the matching circular table, but their worn red cushions are gone, along with the dog-eared print of London Bridge that he once picked out at IKEA with his mother. In its blank place is a large sticky note with Anna's handwriting scrawled across it: PATCH HOLES & PAINT.

It's overwhelming, being here. No wonder she called so often. But it's not the chaos of a half-finished home staging that he finds truly unsettling. There's a deeper wrongness that, in his dazed state, takes him a long time to place. The answer doesn't come until he opens a cupboard to find his mother's pots, pans, and wok gone.

No one's cooked in this kitchen for months. No one's eaten pork dumplings with pickled cabbage or green onion potato pancakes or stewed chicken with mushrooms. She'll never cook dim sum here again.

The knot in Jason's chest tightens. He hadn't felt this distraught the last time he stood here, right after Chun-Mei's funeral, when the house was packed with their family and friends. *You didn't fight for your life that day, either,* his inner doctor answers. *This is shock.*

Abruptly, Jason aches for the open expanse of St. Paul's rooftop. *Was that two nights ago? Three? How did I get here?* He closes the cupboard door and stares at his bare feet on the grey-tiled floor while he breathes in and out, in and out. *How did I go from saving life to taking it?*

There's no regret in him for killing the skyworms. Far from it. Despite his long shower, a faint wisp of their stench seems to cling to his skin, as out of place in his world of antiseptic and latex gloves as the stale smell of takeout is in his mother's kitchen. He half expects Chun-Mei to come around the corner and scold him for making a mess.

That's exactly what should happen. He pictures her bursting into the room in one of her tidying hurricanes, imagines her diamond rings flashing on her elegant hands as she cajoles them into doing whatever she wants. *She'd put a stop to this madness.*

The kettle whistles, breaking his rumination. Jason brews tea and pours it into four Styrofoam cups. He carries them to his brother-in-law and the two strangers sitting at the table, all dressed like him in clean hospital scrubs scrounged from his father's abundant supply. Deep in conversation, they don't look up as he sets the tea down.

". . . caught in an undertow once," the woman, Nina Reyes, is saying. His father's clothes are as baggy on her short frame as her ruined cream suit was perfectly fitted. "I was swimming with my wife. It was our last trip back to the Philippines as a couple, right before our divorce. The ocean drew me out. I couldn't swim back. I was terrified. I wasted a lot of energy calling for help. And then I realized if I swam along with the current, parallel, like you're supposed to, I might live." Memory shines in her eyes as she looks up at the ceiling toward the guest bedroom where Anna is sleeping. "I thought of that today when I swore to her."

"It's bizarre," Carl Mason agrees, gesturing to the half dozen lengths of scrap metal on the table, scrounged from Erik Lin's worktable in the garage. Bent and folded into impossible shapes, the metal is scattered between empty boxes of granola and protein bars, a dozen apple cores, a half dozen banana peels, a box of crackers, and empty jars of peanuts and trail mix. Jason and Anna ate the lion's share before she all but collapsed at the table and Malcolm led her upstairs.

I need to sleep, too, and soon, Jason thinks as Carl experimentally bends another length of metal. "None of us should be this strong."

Jason says nothing. These tarkan and their freakish strength defy everything he understands about the human body. They make little sense to him, nor does their willingness to voluntarily join Anna's cause. Listening to their conversation over the last hour, all hope Jason secretly harboured of slipping away has vanished. *They expect the skyworms to come back. Which means Anna and Dave believe it, too.*

"Xhen, the energy they use, has brought us together." Malcolm glances at Jason as though asking for confirmation.

Don't look at me, Jason thinks. When he doesn't respond, his brother-in-law shrugs, refocusing on Nina and Carl. "You decided to follow me out of the police station because you thought I could help you find your loved ones."

They nod.

"I promise that we'll follow up on that as soon as we can. But I've been thinking about our sprint down College Street to the MaRS building." He looks each of them in the eye. "Did you see anything odd?"

"Oh," Nina exclaims, brushing a strand of chin-length brown hair back behind her ear. "You mean that little scrap of blue light." Amazement floods her face. "I thought I'd dreamed it."

"It looked like a soap bubble," Carl adds. "It popped when I touched it. I felt cold."

Nina nods in agreement.

"I didn't think about anything after that," Carl continues slowly. "I knew I wanted to follow you. The why of it didn't matter in the moment, but it felt crucial that I go."

"I didn't think about my dad either," Nina admits. "Running after you felt like running for my life." Her laugh sounds nervous. "I guess it was. And then later when those things were attacking us . . . I just knew what to do." She looks at Carl, who nods. "It was weird."

"I don't understand all the mechanics yet," Malcolm says, casting another inquiring eye at Jason, who shrugs. "I do know that our strength and speed will be critical to fighting the skyworms. And in return for our courage, xhen is changing us."

"Turning us superhuman," Nina says, smiling. "I mean, it beats the hell out of family law."

"And she'll grieve for us," Carl says softly, "If we punch it like those two kids did today."

"Or Brenda Edwards on Monday night." Regret shadows Malcolm's face like a day-old beard.

I shouldn't be listening, Jason thinks, lowering his chin to study his feet again. *It's private.* But he stays where he is, curious and repelled.

"Anna felt her die, too," Malcolm continues.

"No wonder she's so tired," Nina murmurs. All three of them look up at that same point on the ceiling. "Is the feeling . . . I mean, is feeling her feelings . . ." Nina trails off, her hand reaching for words none of them have.

"Part of the bargain, I think." If Malcolm finds it weird to discuss his wife's emotions with strangers, he doesn't show it. "It's new to us, too. Isn't that right, Doc?"

Their expectant faces turn to Jason. He almost laughs at the idea of himself as an expert in xhen. "Yes," he says, keeping his expression neutral for the sake of their dignity and his. "All of these aspects to xhen are new."

"What is xhen?" Carl pushes.

Spiritual energy, Jason thinks, remembering Kalos's lessons. *The energy of life that gives humans agency*. He takes a sip of tea, gauging their pragmatic faces, and wishes that Dave were here to field such questions. *Philosophy has never been my strong suit.*

"I don't understand xhen," he says. "I don't think anyone living does." Malcolm's lip twitches. *Does he know about Kalos?* Jason wonders. "The root word is Greek and means strange force." He shrugs. "It's energy, as you've seen. My sister, Dave, and I learned to touch it when we were young, but it was different then. More like something sensed than seen. Either way, it was gone for a long time." He flexes his hands, knowing seam edges will line the kitchen if he scratches the itch that crawls along his back, even now. "It returned to me today."

In as few words as possible, he tells them about the airplane, leaving Kalos out of the story. When he's done, Jason waits for the questions, the disbelief. Anna's new followers just nod.

"Thank you," Carl says, raising his cup in salute. Jason's not sure if he means for the tea, Jason's actions on the airplane, or the confession. "I've never killed anything bigger than a spider," he continues. "And I haven't thrown a punch since grade school. I manage an IT department for one of the big five banks. It's not adrenaline-heavy work."

He gives Nina and Malcolm a cock-eyed grin. "I did go skydiving once. Today was by far more intense." His grin deepens, his whole face lit with the incredulous disbelief that Jason's seen many times on the faces of family members learning their loved one survived a car accident with only bumps and scrapes. "Is it supposed to feel great?"

"I think so," Malcolm says, smiling back. "My changes began on Sunday night when Anna was battling one of those things in our garage. They progressed when she went to the SkyDome on Monday. It's even more intense today."

"Good," Nina says. "We'll need to be ready when they come back."

"If they come back," Jason mutters.

Malcolm meets his eyes. "Anna believes they will." He picks up the nearest iron pipe and bends it into an even tighter spiral so the packed coils touch. His muscles barely flex. "You can't dismiss her anymore, Doc." He puts down the piece of metal with a clatter. "That's done."

Anna's tarkan look from Jason to Malcolm before exchanging a wordless glance. "You got a landline?" Carl asks as he stands. "Battery's dead on my cell and I need to call my wife." He smiles at Nina, who suddenly looks pained. "Evelyn's never going to believe this."

No, she probably won't. Jason turns to get the handset from its place on the wall, but it's missing. "Anna might have left it lying around somewhere," he says, wanting an excuse to escape from Malcolm's stare.

Carl jumps up, waving him off. "I'll find it."

Awkward silence settles over the kitchen. Jason's hand automatically reaches for his phone, which miraculously survived both his flight and the battle. *I should call Margo.* Guilt tugs at him, inexorable as gravity. Between fleeing the scene and getting everyone fed, he hasn't had a moment. *Or I didn't want one.* He breathes deeply, steeling himself, and looks again at the screen informing him that he has seventeen missed calls and forty text messages, all from his wife.

Text me when you land, Margo had written minutes after dropping him off at the airport, followed by:

Where are you??

Are you safe?!

The airline won't tell me anything. Ivy says there was a plane crash at Pearson. Please tell me you're okay. Jason, I'm so scared.

Reading the messages, each more frantic than the last, makes

Jason's heart race. *What do I tell her? "Sorry, baby, monsters tried to eat my airplane, but I'm all good now?"*

I'm at my Dad's, he'd written back when they arrived at the house. **Perfectly safe. The plane had to land at Pearson. Don't worry. I'll call you later. I love you.**

Call me now! she'd told him. And then she called four times.

But he hasn't called her back. *She'll want me to come home. I owe her a conversation, but it'll be easier in person.* He steels himself, but before he can dial her number, a text arrives from Ivy.

Is this your sister????

Below the words, there's a link to a news story. *Oh no. No, no, no.* Dread blossoms as Jason clicks it. The CBC video starts to stream, the audio echoing in the kitchen as the screen shows police cars surrounding Anna and Malcolm's modest brick house in the Junction. The news crawl on the bottom declares: TORONTO RESIDENT ANNA LIN, 34, NAMED PERSON OF INTEREST IN DOWNTOWN ATTACKS.

"Oh shit," Jason whispers.

"It was bound to leak," Malcolm says, sounding resigned as he peers at the video over Jason's shoulder. "Is your mom's car still in the garage? The kids shouldn't learn about her on TV—"

"I'll get them," Jason says. "It'll be faster. You should be here for Anna anyway."

Malcolm hesitates, searching Jason's face. "Are you sure?"

"Yeah," he says. "It'll be—"

"Who are you?" a loud, familiar voice demands in the front hall, sounding more confused than angry. "Why are you wearing my scrubs?"

Jason shoves his cell phone back into his pocket as he dashes past Malcolm and out of the kitchen. In the front hall, Carl and Dr. Erik Lin stand in tableaux, staring at each other.

Jason's father turns to him, incredulity written all over his face. "Who is this man, Jason?" he asks, the Irish lilt in his voice made stronger by his irritation. "What are you doing home?"

"Hey, Dad." Jason puts a hand on Carl's shoulder to pause whatever he's about to say. "This is Carl. He's with me." He leans closer and whispers, "I'll deal with him." He claps Carl on the shoulder as the other man hastily makes an exit. "Anna's upstairs having a nap. Malcolm's in the kitchen with their, uh, . . . their other friend, Nina."

His father, dressed in wrinkled hospital scrubs, absentmindedly drops his battered leather briefcase on a bench in the hallway. It hits and rolls onto the floor with a heavy thud, but he doesn't seem to notice. "Have you seen the news? It's a warzone downtown. They evacuated all nonessential personnel from SickKids. The traffic getting home was brutal." He blinks at Jason. "Why are you here? You should be in Vancouver."

"I sent my itinerary to you." Jason picks up the bag and puts it back on the bench. He steers his father to the left, into the house's formal sitting room. "I flew home this morning."

"But the airport's closed," Erik says with his usual logic. "Why would you come? There's no reason for you to be here."

Great, here we go, he thinks. "I'm here to help Anna, Dad. Please, sit down. You've been at the hospital since Monday night. You must be exhausted."

"I slept in the break room," his father says, waving off Jason's attempts to steer him into an armchair. "Anna has selling the house well in hand. Who's covering your shifts?"

"Don't worry about it, Dad," Jason says, feeling his exhaustion ratchet up another notch.

"I don't understand why you're here," Erik insists, studying him through pale blue eyes that always reminded Jason of marbles as a child. He runs a hand through his full shock of hair, which has visibly faded in the weeks since Jason last saw him, going from its natural ginger to a papery grey. "I know Anna took a lot on her plate caring for your mother. That's why I let her organize the sale. I'm paying her a twenty percent commission." He cocks his head. "I didn't know her situation was dire enough for you to come home. She should have told me."

Were you here to be asked? Jason thinks but doesn't say.

After Chun-Mei died, dozens of family friends rallied to his father's side with kind words and casseroles, several of the widows among their circle obviously hoping to personally console the rail-thin doctor. Their father had wasted no time in retreating into his research. Jason has copies of the four papers Erik has finished and submitted for publication since his wife's death. Friends in Toronto's medical community send him regular updates about Erik's odd hours and the score of graduate students he's mentoring. While his department chair at the University of Toronto may be thrilled about the drastic upswing in Erik's research productivity, Jason has listened at length to Anna's concerns about Erik's decision to subsume his grief in his work.

"I'm not here because of the house," Jason begins. "Anna and I—"

"You were here for the funeral," Erik interrupts. "That was only two months ago." He cocks his head. "It's too soon for another visit."

"I know, Dad." When he and Anna were teenagers, their father's relentless pursuit of objective reality and his unwillingness to tolerate North American social conventions often put them in cringe-worthy scenarios. These days, his mannerisms don't rate much more than a shrug. Part of Jason wishes he'd inherited his father's indifference to social expectations, such as the stigma of changing the spelling of his name when he married. Another flash of pain tightens Jason's chest. *I'll never hear her tell that story at a dinner party again.* Aloud, he says. "It's about the—"

"You need me to go?" Malcolm asks from the doorway.

"Go?" Erik echoes. "Go where?"

Jason sighs. "We have to pick up Tim and Erin. They're with Sarita Montcalm."

"Sarita?" Erik says. "Why would they be with her?"

"Or I can go," Malcolm counters.

"Anna needs you here, Malcolm." Xhen crackles down Jason's back. "You should have sat down when you had the chance, Dad."

Seam edges line the living room, offering doorways to anywhere he wants. He pictures Sarita Montcalm's face and the backyard where he played so often as a child. Energy dances through his hospital scrubs, coating his skin. Malcolm tugs his father-in-law toward the living room's French doors. They both stare as Jason threads the seams and opens a portal to the Montcalms' backyard in Dovercourt Park. "I tried to tell you."

Erik is frozen, his mouth a silent "o" as he stares with naked shock at the opening in the world.

"Keep everyone out of the room," Jason tells Malcolm over his shoulder. "I'll reopen the portal in the same spot. I don't want you standing here when I do."

As the portal closes on his father's stunned face, Jason releases xhen. He crosses the backyard on long legs, stepping around the vintage toys that spill out of the Montcalms' shed. *I can't believe I did that.* His heartbeat's elevated; his fingers tremble. The whole moment feels anticlimactic. *No questions. No yelling. No denials.* Trying to expunge his nervous energy, Jason hops up the patio steps that he and Dave helped Henry Montcalm build one summer when they were home from university.

On the other side of the patio door, Sarita sits at the kitchen table with Jason's niece and nephew, all of them drinking from delicate china mugs that Anna would never trust to her children. *Chai mixed with a lot of extra milk,* Jason guesses, spotting the plate of cookies and remembering similar tea parties. *Some things never change.*

He taps the glass. All three turn, their faces startled. The children look overjoyed, but Sarita is pale as her eyes lock on Jason's like steel rivets. *She knows about the skyworms,* he thinks, registering her fear as she opens the door. *Dave must have told her.*

"Jason," says the woman who is more of an aunt to him than his father's rarely seen sisters. Sarita steps gracefully onto the patio to hug him as Tim and Erin, giggling with delight, wrap themselves around his legs. Her eyes, however, brim with wariness. "David said you were coming home. Is he—"

"Talking with the chief, I expect," Jason says. "Were you watching the news today?"

"Again?" she breathes, her voice catching. With a glance at Anna's children, she searches his face. "It happened again?"

"Yes, Mrs. Montcalm." He can't call her by her first name. Jason remembers doing so once at a Thanksgiving dinner when he was a teenager. His mother's public tongue-lashing lasted a good five minutes. "It did." In his mind, the black skyworm's split-pupiled eye fixes on him through the airplane window. "We, uh, we handled it."

Sarita touches his cheek. "Oh, my dear," she says, her brown eyes filled with pity. "I would not have chosen this for you."

Shivers course through his body.

"Uncle Jay!" Erin cries, pulling at his scrubs. He tears his gaze from Sarita as the child reaches up for him. "Did you bring us a present?"

"No, kiddo." Jason smiles, bending to lift her. Erin's hands wrap around his neck, refreshingly human. He holds out his other arm to Tim and pulls Anna's son to his side. They smell like chai, kid shampoo, and normalcy. With them held close, Jason feels the strain he's carried since Pearson begin to ease. "It's so good to see you."

"Where's Mom?" Tim isn't smiling as he pulls away. "She didn't say you were coming to visit."

"It was a surprise," Jason tells him. "She's with your dad at Grandad's house, so I came."

Tim frowns. "You don't drive."

"I can drive," Jason says, dodging his nephew's point. "I don't very often. Go get your things."

The children run off. Sarita follows them inside to help gather their books and toys. When they return, stuffed backpacks hoisted over their shoulders, Jason kisses Sarita on the cheek. Then he takes the children's hands and leads them down to the garden.

Tim glances back at the house. A scowl darkens his face, making him completely his mother's son. "Uncle Jay," he begins, as though reluctant to make Jason aware of his own stupidity, "the street is that way."

"We're not driving." Jason stops behind the shed, looking around. No one's puttering in any of the gardens, so he crouches down to kid height. "I'm taking you to Grandad's house. We need to go quickly, so I'm going to make a special door. We'll all go through it. It's important that you be quiet when it appears." He pauses to give them both a considering look. "Are you ready?"

Erin grins, her eyes dancing. Tim nods, clearly expecting grown-up bullshit. Smiling, Jason stands and reaches very carefully for xhen. He splits it into threads behind his back at first, not wanting to scare the children, and slowly allows them to seep around his body to cover him like a coat.

Tim gasps. Erin's eyes are like quarters. *Some part of this had to be fun,* Jason thinks, smiling, as he threads the seam edges into hexagons and rings, building one behind him and one on the other side of the city in his parents' living room. As he relaxes into the twist and the watery entrance opens, he spots Malcolm and his father on the other side.

Erik extends a hand to probe the crackling light. Jason gestures for him to move back. *Once a scientist, always a scientist.*

When they're clear, Jason turns to Tim. "You go first." With less fear than Jason expects, Tim approaches the portal, extending one hand through the opening. He looks back at Jason, who nods. On the other side, Erik takes his grandson's hand and pulls Tim into his arms.

"Uncle Jay?" Erin says, pulling at her lower lip. "I'm scared."

"You're perfectly safe. Let's cross together." Taking his niece's hand, Jason leads her to the portal, letting Erin step first. He follows the child, closing it behind them. Hunger twists his belly as he releases xhen. *How can I be hungry again?* he wonders. *I'm eating like a horse.*

"Dad," he begins, but whatever he's about to say about getting everyone a snack remains unsaid. His father kneels on the living room carpet with Anna's children in his arms, his face ghastly white as his mouth silently works above their dark heads. At the door, Malcolm spreads his hands, clearly as baffled as Jason.

"Dad?" Jason says again. *Did he get too close to the portal? Did I hurt him?* "Are you okay?"

"She was telling the truth," Erik manages in a monotone voice, his eyes wide and staring. "I didn't believe her." Jason's skin prickles as every hair on his body jumps to attention. "All those years, Jason, I thought your mother was lying."

Chapter 28

Leona – One More

Miinikaa First Nation, ON: Wednesday, August 20

The sun's setting when Leona LaRoque barrels up her driveway in her red F-150. She turns off the truck's ignition and rolls her ankles to stretch. The last thirty-six hours have been a frantic whirlwind. Her hip aches, as it always does when she's been on the road too much. She shifts on the leather seat, listening to the engine tick through its cooldown.

Mini catapults are built and hidden. Paperwork's updated and with the lawyer. I went to the clearing and ran through all the old exercises. What am I forgetting?

"Well, Rose," she says aloud. "This'd be a lot more fun if you were here."

Her memory of Rose in the car surfaces again. The vivid image, which David's telepathy has dredged up like a stone from its resting place, has stayed with her since Monday night. Rose's loss cannons through Leona's very bones, as it has periodically over the years.

Stop moping, Leona tells herself as she gets out of the truck, mindful of her aching joints. *If you're afraid, you could bring Ryan. He'd swear the tarkan oath. You know he would.*

The lights are on inside the house. *No*, she decides as she comes up the front walk. *We've been together longer than Rose was alive. I can't lose him, too.*

Ryan's dogs, Mustard and Relish, get up to greet her as she lets herself in and locks the door behind her. She peeks outside through the narrow panel of stained glass decorated with a hummingbird in flight. There's no sign of Kalos, though she half expects him to appear. Leona snorts. *Since when has Kalos ever done what you expected?*

"House smells good," she says aloud, putting her purse and keys down on a side table as the dogs wag their tails, sniffing the bits of mud still clinging to her boots from her preparatory prowl around the shores of Ramsey Lake. Tucking the boots away in the closet, Leona walks into the kitchen where her longtime boyfriend is cooking dinner. "Pasta?"

"Risotto," Ryan Charron says, keeping his eyes on the stove. "Extra veggies. How was town?"

Leona pads over in her sock feet, sliding her arms around his wide chest to press her cheek against his back. His grey cotton T-shirt is soft against her skin, but it's the steady heartbeat that tells her she's home. "Fine," she says, ignoring the sick feeling in her belly. Crested heads writhe through her mind, their triple eyes shining with menace. "I'm all set."

"Uh-huh," Ryan says, his disapproval thick. "Let's eat."

If you wanted a pushover, Leona thinks, taking a plate, *you should have dated someone else.*

The meal is delicious, like all of Ryan's cooking. Leona takes a long time to finish, savoring every bite. *It's not your last meal, no matter what Mei told you.*

On the other side of the table, Ryan puts down his fork and leans back in his chair. *He's aged well,* she decides, considering his salt-and-pepper hair. His skin is tanned from years of driving his boat on the lake. Five years her junior, he caused quite a scandal when he asked her out. Yet in all that time, they've never played games.

"All right," Leona says. "Say your piece."

He crosses his arms. "You need someone to watch your back."

"You helped me prepare," she says. "It'll be enough."

He lifts an eyebrow. "And what about Dave? Are we returning his calls? He's freaking out."

She sighs. "Don't worry about David. But someone does need to be here to answer his questions when he returns. Besides me, you're the only one with any answers."

Ryan laughs. "About what?" He spreads his hands. "I barely understood anything that went on at Camp Ashigan back then, and I sure as hell don't get it now. You told me yourself this plan of yours is practically suicide."

"Not exactly." Last June, the woman she'd once thought of as a second sister had called from her hospital deathbed to offer not a long-overdue apology but a final warning. *There's a last battle coming for you, Lee. You'll face skyworms alone before you're through.* Leona squares her shoulders. "You know where my journals are. They'll fill in the details."

Ryan pulls his chair around the table. He gently plucks Leona's fork out of her hand and tucks her fingers against his heart. Even after so long together, the intensity in his eyes makes her chest pound. "Then take me with you."

Ignoring the part of her that desperately wants to say yes, Leona shakes her head. "I won't risk you," she says. "Not again."

Under the kitchen light, Ryan's eyes flash. "My life for—"

Leona darts forward, cutting off the words of the vow with a kiss before he can finish them. They're rumpled when they pull away, smiling like teenagers.

"Have it your way," he says, but his tone is fond. He stacks the plates. "When do you go?"

"In the morning," she says, holding his eyes. "We have time."

They do the washing up and walk the dogs, talking about the

construction job he's working on with his nephew Wade. Leona's avoided the news channels all day, along with David's incessant messages. *Whatever mess he's gotten himself into with the Lin twins, getting out of it together will bond them,* she tells herself. *They need that strength more than my meddling.*

On the way home, they sit with the dogs by the lake. Moonlight from the waning crescent dances over the water. Leona feels the peace of the place sink into her bones, comforting and familiar. Part of her wishes she hadn't picked up Chun-Mei's call. *There's a task to do,* she reminds herself as they head home before the chill stiffens their joints. *You're the only one left.*

Unwilling to dwell on the day to come, Leona turns her attention to Ryan as they ready themselves for bed. Is it fair to deny him the power of a Kalxhan? He'd lose that bum knee and the ankle that gets stiff in the winter. On his side of the bathroom, Ryan says nothing as he brushes his teeth. *Nagging isn't his way. Never has been once he's said his piece,* Leona thinks. Reflecting on their life together, she's tempted to concede.

Selfish woman, Leona thinks as she and Ryan make love. Sleep comes easily to her on his chest.

Her alarm is set for six a.m., but her body wakes at five. Leona flicks the alarm switch off, not wishing to disturb her lover. Rising, she feeds the dogs and dresses in the clothes she left in the bathroom the night before. She skips the coffee, fearing the noise of the grinder. Instead, she grabs her keys and puts her sunglasses on top of her head. *They'll be hard to see against the glare of the water. Wretched things love to use the light to their advantage.*

She climbs into her truck, another gift from Dave. *Thoughtful boy. He'll be fine,* she decides as she stops at Tim Hortons to order a double double coffee and a raisin tea biscuit. The silence in the truck feels heavy as she gets back on the road. Leona aches for her triad sisters, both the beloved and the difficult. It's impossible that thirty-seven years have passed since they were foolhardy girls at Camp

Ashigan. *This trip should be a return to the old days. They should both be here.*

Leona takes the lake road toward Laurentian University and turns into the parking lot for the Vale Living with Lakes Centre. It's empty at this hour. She drives through and down a short service road to a smaller, less conspicuous parking lot. She finds a spot for the truck near the back, as close to the trees as she can get.

"Ryan will be back for you later," she tells the truck as she stashes her purse beneath her seat, pulls on her sunglasses, and locks the doors.

The lights are off inside the research centre. This part of Ramsey Lake, owned by the university, is underdeveloped relative to the residential neighbourhoods on the opposite shore. Normally, thoughts of land allocation and the choices of settlers would bring equally choice words to Leona's lips. Today, she's glad of the brush to hide her traps. She glances at the rising sun. *Plenty of time*, Leona decides as she takes the path past the building's edge, down to the shore.

Wind ruffles her greying hair as Leona walks toward the open rocky headland spotted with wind-stunted Scots pine. The giant rock she likes for a lookout point is there, steady as a sentinel against the placid water. Her hidden mini catapults surround it, primed and ready.

She stations herself against the rock to wait for her enemies. *Not long now.*

Chapter 29

Dave – The Chief

Toronto, ON: Thursday, August 21

Dave sits in an interrogation room in the bowels of Toronto Police Headquarters, sweating profusely. *Something's wrong with the air-conditioning. They probably do that on purpose.* His sore back aches. No one's read him his rights or tried to handcuff him, but he also hasn't had anything to eat or drink since waking. *Or a phone call. Or a bed. Or access to a lawyer. And I'm waiting here, not in Dad's office.*

On the plus side, Dave's still got his phone. The battery's low, but the lock screen informs him it's 7:34 a.m. Opening it, he starts a group thread with Anna, Malcolm, and Jason, texting them his status and location. He sends the same message to Leona and Ryan before checking his other threads. There's a long one from Halina, but for the first time in days, it's not about paperwork:

Dave, WTF is happening in Toronto?

Are you okay? I saw your Facebook post, but it's a couple days old.

This footage makes NO SENSE. Can you find me someone who's seen those giant blips IRL?

Like, are they really monsters? If so, they've got fantastic digital cloaking technology. The Beakhead guys are freaking out trying to figure out how it works.

I've put a team of junior analysts on the problem.

Could be BIG!

PLS CALL ME.

Dave smiles. *Same old Hal.* He resists the temptation to write back, although circumstances may force his hand if he needs to post a large bail against some bogus charge. Most of his cash is tied up in investments. *If I ask her for help, she'll make me sign those papers for sure.*

He puts his phone back in his pocket and runs a hand over his chest. Through his T-shirt, his fingers find nothing but smooth skin. *My scar's really gone,* he thinks again, amazed. *Does this mean my heart is completely healthy? Mum will be thrilled.*

He considers taking off his shirt to get a better look and decides against it. Someone—no, three someones—are studying him through the observation glass. He recognizes one mind from the soldiers who assaulted him at Queen's Park. The volcano inside him rumbles, but Dave turns his back on the window, ignoring them. He isn't short of distractions. His stomach is a hungry knot and his head is spinning. Behind that glass and in the rooms around them, too many minds are thinking too loudly, and most of them are angry. Images of civilian, police, and military dead thicken their collective thoughts, forming a haze of mourning.

One mind, locked in an identical room across the hall, is utterly furious. *You're going to shout your throat raw,* Dave tells Jenna. *They aren't listening to you. But from what I hear, it sounds like Dad will come to see me soon. Let's be patient.*

We've been here for sixteen fucking hours! she snarls. *If they don't feed you again, I'm going to rip the goddamn door off. You need to eat.*

You're probably strong enough to do that, Dave tells her, aware of

Malcolm's experiments in the garage the previous day. Instantly, Jenna's anger cools. *I don't want them to freak out. Help me keep the advantage of surprise for as long as we can, okay?*

Her frustration roils through his mind. *All right,* she tells him grudgingly. *Keep this channel open so I can listen in. And you've got twenty minutes. Then I'm coming for you.*

As though in answer to Jenna's silent deadline, the room's heavy door swings open to reveal the haggard face of Henry Montcalm, a greasy white paper bag and a two-litre bottle of water tucked under his arm. He pauses in the doorway to give his son his famous hairy eyeball. The second that skeptical stare bores into Dave's bones, it's like he's seventeen again, not a grown man and a multimillionaire. In the face of his dad's disapproval, he feels as sheepish as he did on the nights when Henry stayed up waiting for him to come home from his adventures with the Lins.

Dave stands up. Before he can say anything, Henry puts down the food and envelops him in a crushing hug. "Thank God you're safe." Relief, gratitude, and guilt pound into Dave's head as his dad slaps his back, hitting the bruises forming there.

Dave grunts.

Henry pats him more gingerly. "Sorry. Those soldiers shouldn't have hit you. I've made a formal complaint." Stocky of build and with the perpetually flushed nose of a man who enjoys a good glass of red wine more often that he should, Henry is short enough that Dave can tuck him under his chin. But as they pull apart, consternation darkens his dad's blotchy face. "What the hell is going on, Davy? How are you involved? Did you tell Nazarenko to resign?"

Of course not, Dave thinks, too tired and too hungry to stop himself from answering directly.

Henry freezes, his skin paling to an alarming shade of grey beneath the grizzled fuzz that stubbles his chin. "What did you say?" he rasps.

"Shit." Dave's sheepishness deepens. *I didn't mean to tell you about the telepathy this way. Sorry, Dad. Please don't have a heart attack. It's no fun, I promise you.*

Feeling his dad's heart thrum with panic like a startled bird, Dave guides him to a chair and opens the water bottle. "Rest for a minute, okay?" He sits down, too, his belly screaming for food. Dave rips open the paper bag. The welcome smell of chicken shawarma fills his nostrils. It's not a typical breakfast choice, but he's so hungry, he doesn't care. "Mum will kill me if you drop dead."

"Ha!" Henry barks, sipping the water. But he's still alarmingly pale.

They sit in silence while Dave eats and Henry drinks. On the other side of the observing glass, the watchers have swelled to ten, all of them equally curious and suspicious.

"Why am I in an interrogation room?" Dave catches his dad's gaze with his own version of the hairy eyeball. "Am I being arrested?

"No," says Henry. He radiates nervous tension. Some sort of report, accompanied by several outdoor images, flashes through his thoughts, but it's gone before Dave can parse it. "We . . . I needed to be sure you'd stick around long enough to answer questions. That's all."

"Uh-huh. That justifies keeping Jenna and me overnight? Or the beating I got from those military goons who brought us in?" Dave takes the bottle back and chugs half of it before wiping his mouth.

Henry flinches, his mind full of shame, but his acute physical distress has tapered off.

Stretching, Dave cracks his shoulder, and then his wrists and fingers. "Toronto PD's rolling with a real stellar bunch of guys. Guess the army's not up on its anti-racism training."

"We've lost so many people," Henry begins. "No one's slept much since Sunday. And to them, you're a vigilante, not my son." He looks down at his hands. "That doesn't excuse any of it, of course. I failed you, Davy." Emotion swirls between them as he meets Dave's eyes: the confusion and fear make sense, along with the exhaustion, but Dave's surprised by the depths of his dad's regret. "They all think

I'm biased." He scrubs a hand through his uncombed greying hair. "And I am. So please tell me what you've been up to since Sunday night." He shoots a meaningful glance at the mirror on the other side of the room. "Please."

"I was in Miinikaa on Sunday night with Auntie Lee and taught the coding workshop there all day on Monday," Dave says aloud. "I left her house sometime after midnight. Ryan was at his place, but she got up to see me off." He pulls out his wallet, flashing a receipt at his dad. "This is from the motel in Parry Sound where I stopped early Tuesday morning. Want it?"

"Yes." Henry pockets the paper and then visibly braces himself. "Tell me everything."

Oh, I'll do better than that, he smirks as he reaches across the table. It's a risk, but time is short. *This part of our conversation needs to be private,* he tells his dad. *Give me your hand.*

Henry swallows and cautiously extends his callused palm. Taking it, Dave gifts him with a selection of his memories, just as Anna did for him after the SkyDome. Henry grunts, his skin paling again.

When he's finished, Dave releases his dad before inhaling the last of his food. *Sorry. But you wanted to know, and that way is fastest.* His belly is still rumbling, but it's an improvement. Jenna's satisfaction pulses in his head, although no one's brought her anything. Dave turns to the glass. "My friend needs food and water before this conversation continues."

There's a scramble on the other side. *Thank you,* Jenna says a few moments later, her mind laced with gratitude and the same steely determination. *Five minutes, Dave.*

Across the table, Henry grinds his palms against his eye sockets. "Skyworms," he says at last, uncovering his face to stare at Dave through bleary, bloodshot eyes. "Xenthians." He reaches across the table for the water and takes a long swallow. "Which means the woman at the SkyDome really is our Miss Anna. And Nazarenko fled the scene with her and lied about it."

"A lie of omission, more like. Put yourself in his shoes, Dad. What would you have done?" Dave considers licking the shawarma wrapper. Instead, he contents himself with the last of the water before giving his dad a level look. "Malcolm's a natural liaison for you. Don't go hard on him."

"Jesus Christ, Davy." His dad grunts a second time. "Does your mum know?"

Dave nods and the hairy eyeball returns.

"*Did* she know?"

Dave shakes his head, tempted to speak of Chun-Mei Lin. But deference to her and to his aunt, coupled with Leona's lifelong wariness of police—even his adoptive father—keeps him silent. *Most suspicious people in the world*, he thinks, aware of the skepticism dancing in the minds of his unseen observers. Over twenty people now pack the tiny room on the other side of the glass.

Henry takes off his hat, finger-combing his sweaty hair. "My life would be simpler if you'd just been smoking pot as a kid like I thought. Do you know how many times I searched your room?"

"You're stalling, Dad."

Sighing, Henry takes his phone out of his pocket. He opens the photo gallery and slides it across the table. "I assume Nazarenko told you about these kids?"

Dave automatically leans forward and then draws back when he realizes he's looking at a crime scene photo. Henry flicks to a series of school portraits. *Marissa. Asan. Megan. Harbir. Ali. Vic.* Their names are engraved in his mind. *They were what, fifteen years old? Sixteen?* Cold with horror, he studies his dad.

In Henry's thoughts, adults enter a morgue to identify the dead children. Dave shudders as he flips back to the crime scene photos, trying to free himself from his dad's smothering sense of hopelessness. He taps the screen. "Skyworms did that. The two officers who died trying to help us at Queen's Park yesterday had the same injuries."

"Krista Johansen and Raymond Leong," his dad says heavily.

Behind the glass, anger flares bright and hot. "Why did they die?"

Because you sent them after Malcolm, Dave says, pushing his thoughts so they're heard by the watchers. He shifts in the chair to give them a clear view of his unmoving lips. *They chose to help us kill skyworms and died doing it,* he continues, part of him enjoying the shock rippling through the minds behind the glass. *No one feels their loss more keenly than we do.* The surprise in the observation room shifts to sorrow and then back to suspicion.

Dave stops the broadcast to focus on his dad. *Anna's offered to meet the families. If you feel that's appropriate.*

"That's something." With a finger, Henry closes the gruesome gallery. "And these kids? Is there anything you can tell me about why the creatures killed them?'"

Dave shrugs. "They were all outside when they died, right?"

Henry nods.

"All of them left their homes in the middle of the night."

"Yes," Henry says. "No one else heard anything—"

"But they did," Dave says. "Or sensed it. I'm not sure. But something in the darkness called them from their beds. Only they must not have had the same training that Anna and I do."

"Anna? Did she know them?"

"No, we had no idea they existed," Dave says. "But she also heard noises. She went outside and was attacked. If she hadn't killed that thing on Sunday night, you'd have photos of her, too."

"We found the corpse," Henry says. "That neighbour was more than happy to give us a tour. What a piece of work she is." He cocks his head, frowning at Dave. "Were you and Anna supposed to train these kids? Is it your fault they weren't ready?"

No, Dad! Dave thinks as his frustration boils over. Before he can stop it, xhen flickers around his hands.

Henry shoves his chair back, alarm blossoming in his mind.

Dave ignores him. *Haven't you been listening? We didn't know anything about them! We didn't know they existed!* The energy leaps with his frustration, hot around his fingers. Fear spikes behind the observing glass. Dave hastily smothers his xhen, but it's too late.

Jenna bursts through the door with fury in her eyes. "Dave's done nothing but save lives," she spits. "We're leaving. Right now."

"Who let you out?" Henry demands. He turns to the glass. "Get her back in that room!"

"I go where he goes," she says as four officers spill in from the hall. Jenna grins at them just as she did at the skyworms. The sheer ferocity in her face stops them dead. "Try me."

STOP IT, Dave bellows, breaking the standoff.

Every eye in the room turns to him, and he wonders if he really could have commanded those soldiers to cease the beating. *That's a dangerous thought,* he thinks in the most private pocket of his mind. Surrounded by police officers, it's clear that his dad spoke truly: Every mind in the room has presided over enough gruesome scenes in the last week to fill a lifetime. *And half of them blame us for it.*

He turns to Henry. "The creatures come here to feed and kill. Your guns and jets and all the other hardware appear to be useless against them. We don't know why. And . . ." He swallows as he turns to leave. "They'll be back."

"Davy." The soft gravity in the nickname stops him cold. "There's another attack happening now."

"What?" Xhen leaps around him as though he's doused in kerosene. Two officers draw their guns. Jenna hisses and jumps between them and Dave. He sees nothing but the pain in his dad's eyes. "Where?"

It takes Henry a long moment to answer. "Sudbury."

The bottom falls out of Dave's stomach. *Auntie Lee! Creator, shelter her!* The room seems to spin as he reaches for Jenna's hand just as she reaches for him. "Why didn't you tell me?"

His dad swallows. "I wanted . . ." He trails off, his hands rising as though to embrace his son again. "I had to keep you safe."

Dave waits for the familiar tight bands of constriction around his heart. Instead, his body feels expansive with the giddiness of profound dread. *Auntie Lee, what have you done? Is this why you wouldn't call me back?*

Jenna still has his arm. *Jason can take us*, she offers, shoving her own exhaustion down like bile as she pulls him toward the door. *Ask him. We can be there in minutes.*

"I don't know much," Henry says as the officers behind him shift in the hot room. "I can tell you that my counterparts called in the military from CFB North Bay, though I doubt that will have helped them any more than it did us." His voice sounds far away. "I have satellite images upstairs. They wanted my take on the similarities. I'll show you." He steps toward Dave.

"There's no time," Dave says. "Sorry, Dad." He puts a hand on Henry's shoulder as he lifts the crisp aerial images—photos and video —clean out of his head. The chief staggers. Dave slides an arm around his shoulders to support him.

Show me, Jenna demands.

That's Ramsey Lake in the middle of the city, Dave tells her, hurriedly sifting through the deluge of information rushing into him. *We were told the veil between their world and ours is thinnest over water*. Blackened holes pit the land around the lake. In some places, Henry used magnification to zoom in on the ripped wings of downed aircraft. Several tanks are also split apart like the propane canister in Anna's garage.

Someone resisted, Jenna observes a heartbeat later. *Right here, see?* Her mind's eye focuses on a point in the lake several hundred metres from shore. *Orange scales in the water means someone fought back*. She gives him a flat look. *Is your aunt like you?*

I think so, Dave says. *We'll start there*. He releases Henry, steadying him so he doesn't stagger. "I'll call you and Mum later."

"Chief," one of the officers behind Henry says, "you can't just let them waltz out of here."

"They're not under arrest," Henry says curtly before turning back to Dave. "Do what you can in Sudbury, but this situation will get bigger than police fast, Davy. Once the military gets fully involved, my ability to help will be limited."

"Keep my name out of the press for now, please. You can do that." His dad's distress burns in Dave's head, but he pushes it away as he lets Jenna haul him from the room.

Jason! he shouts, picturing his friend. *We need your help!*

Chapter 30

Anna – Twins

Toronto, ON: Thursday, August 21

The skyworm's tentacle jabs at Anna's stomach, twisting as it seeks purchase. She rolls, xhen shining around her fingers, and—

—wakes, panting and sweating, in a strange room. Her hands are balled around the bedsheets as though ready to wring a neck. *It was a dream. The skyworms are dead. You're safe.* Anna forces her fingers to unclench as she slowly recognizes her surroundings: the guest room in her parents' house. Her stomach growls. *You're just hungry. Again.*

By the pale golden light streaming through the east-facing window, Anna guesses it's morning. *Are the kids still with Sarita? Did they eat anything for dinner? I should text Walter and make sure he's all right, too,* she thinks, and then remembers that he has both her purse and her phone. *Shit. Okay. Time to get up.*

Yet Anna doesn't rise. A night's sleep has not healed the cost that victory burned into her head. Three pitted places throb inside her, although with less intensity than before she slept. *Malcolm was right. I wasn't up to speaking to anyone after that fight.*

She wraps her memories of Brenda, Raymond, and Krista with the gratitude they deserve and tucks them away to focus on three brighter clusters, one large and two noticeably smaller. *Did they grow while I rested?* she wonders. By their gentle fuzzing, she surmises that Malcolm, Nina, and Carl are close. *Two new tarkan,* she thinks. *What brought them to that battlefield? How many more will join us before this is over?*

Wary of that answer, Anna swings her legs out of bed. Her filthy clothes are gone, replaced by shorts and one of the threadbare T-shirts she keeps here to wear when working on the house. She rises slowly, but nothing hurts. *It's like the skyworms never injured me.*

Her eyes drift across the room, which also served as her mother's study. Unlike the rest of the house, it's not packed with cardboard boxes. There'd been so much to do that it had been easy to leave Chun-Mei's sanctuary intact. Most things are still where her mother last placed them. The antique chest of drawers faces the bed, beside an expensive office chair and a simple glass-topped desk. There, Chun-Mei indulged in her joint passions for photography and meticulously planning her gardens. Framed photos of her roses hang on the walls, though one spot is blank, marking the photo Jason took for his office.

Anna's eye is drawn to the lush green panorama taken from the top of the Great Wall of China. Erik had booked the family trip as a surprise for Chun-Mei the year of their twenty-fifth wedding anniversary, the same year Anna and Jason graduated from high school. *Our only visit there as a family,* she thinks, touching the photo's frame with a fingertip. After losing Kalos and xhen that winter, she'd been eager to find a new anchor.

They'd landed in Hong Kong and spent a few days exploring the island before traveling to Kaiping, the city in Guangdong Province where Chun-Mei's parents had lived. In preparation for their visit, Chun-Mei had exchanged letters and emails with cousins and family friends whom she, born in Vancouver after the Lins immigrated to Canada, hadn't seen in years.

Their relations had nevertheless graciously toured them through the city, pointing out changed or vanished landmarks. They saw the house where her Uncle Felix had been born, and a cemetery where several generations of their family rested. Anna had wished she could follow their relatives' conversations with her mother, which either flowed too quickly for her Cantonese or were conducted in their local dialect, Taishanese, which she couldn't understand. She had fond memories of the delicious food served at several large dinners held in their honour. Yet, as the visit stretched on, she felt increasingly disconnected.

That feeling intensified after they flew to Beijing for the second week of their trip. They'd seen the Great Wall and many other tourist sites, which had been impressive and beautiful. But standing in the crowds, conspicuous as a foreigner the moment she opened her mouth, Anna felt she could have been any Canadian tourist wandering through the stone ruins and modern cities. She'd been reminded at every turn—by her clothes, by her clumsy Cantonese, by the half-understood comments that her mother's relatives whispered when they thought she couldn't overhear—exactly how foreign she was.

After they flew home, Anna had stubbornly kept looking for something to help her understand who she was without xhen. She'd chased it through her undergraduate studies at the University of Toronto, convinced that if she knew more about Kalos or the languages and religions of Ancient Greece and Turkey, she would find the answers she craved. She'd worked hard at her studies and joined clubs for Asian students on campus. It had been fun and rewarding, but nothing had filled the gap left first by xhen and Kalos, and then by Jason.

Her father, pleased with her excellent grades, hadn't noticed. Chun-Mei had. Shortly after Anna's graduation with an Honours Bachelor of Arts in Classical Studies, she'd taken Anna for tea at the Windsor Arms Hotel. Anna, contemplating a master's degree or a PhD, had expected her mother to encourage her academic ambitions, like she'd encouraged Jason's pursuit of medicine. But that hadn't been on Chun-Mei's mind.

Dusty books won't satisfy you, her mother had said. *You should get a job. Make some money. Get serious about that police officer who's tied up our phone line every night for the past year. I want to be a grandmother before I die.*

They'd argued, of course. Anna vividly remembers storming out of the fancy tearoom, her vision practically black with rage. Unable to bear her mother's meddling, she'd still moved in with an elated Malcolm that fall. She'd downloaded applications to a dozen prestigious grad schools but had never gotten around to completing them. A friend from the Chinese Students and Scholars Association had suggested she take a realty course. One thing led to another.

Five years later, Anna had found herself married with a baby on the way and xhen a fading memory. *You were right about a lot, Mom. What I wouldn't give to talk to you about my problems now.*

Anna's stomach growls. As she turns to leave, she catches sight of the framed family photos clustered over the bed: her parents' wedding, her wedding to Malcolm, Jason's wedding to Margo, and baby pictures of Tim and Erin. There are school portraits of both twins, too, marking their graduations from high school and university, plus Jason's extra one from medical school. But Anna only has eyes for the enlarged snapshot in the center of the arrangement, taken during Christmas break six months before that trip to China.

In the picture, her parents sit on the sofa in the den of the Dovercourt house beside the Christmas tree. Anna and Jason are seated on the floor between the sofa and the coffee table. She's got an eyebrow raised, refusing to smile, while Jason smirks. Behind them, Dave sprawls across her parents' laps, his gangly legs hanging off the end of the sofa. He's got his head propped up on one bent arm, grinning at the camera like a madman. Her dad's eyes sparkle, his pale skin flushed a darker red than his cable knit sweater. Beside him, her hand tucked around her husband's arm, Chun-Mei has her head thrown back in laughter.

Anna touches a finger to her mother's face. *She had such a great laugh. God, we all look so young. And so happy, even if I was refusing to smile.* Anna studies the image, wishing she could reach into the frame and spare herself years of heartbreak. Kalos vanished mere weeks after that Christmas, ending their training and beginning her decade-long feud with Jason. *Depression*, Anna thinks, looking into her past self's bright eyes. *I was depressed for so long after that. I thought xhen was gone forever.*

There's a soft knock at the door. For a hair's breadth, Anna hopes it's her mother. Loss subsumes her again, fresh as a knife cut. She exhales. Steels herself. "Come in."

Jason enters wearing clean hospital scrubs. He's showered and shaved, but his dark eyes still have that haunted, hollow look. His handsome face isn't identical to Anna's, but looking at him is always like looking into a mirror: familiar and backwards.

He came home, she thinks, grateful for his firepower if not his presence. She takes a half step toward him, knowing she should offer the true welcome his return deserves. But his guarded expression stops her. She lets her hands fall to her sides. "Hey."

"Malcolm said you were up. Hungry?" When she nods, Jason offers her a granola bar. "It's the last one." He puts his hands in the pockets of the scrubs. "There's nothing much to eat downstairs. We're going to order something."

"Good idea." Her brother nods, his gaze drifting to the photographs over the bed. *When did we get so awkward?* Anna wonders, turning so that they stand side by side, contemplating their younger faces. "What time is it? Is Dave back? Did Malcolm get the kids last night?"

"After seven," Jason tells her, yawning. "Dave's still downtown waiting for his dad." His voice is even, but the way he continues to examine the pictures without looking at her pings a subconscious alarm bell. "The kids are here."

"Tell me now," Anna says, more sharply than she intends. "Whatever it is that you think will upset me." He swallows. "Is it the kids?" Another pang seizes her stomach, and her next words crack like a whip. "Did something happen to them?"

"No. Would you relax?" But he takes a deep breath.

Anna knuckles her hands, fighting the childish urge to beat the answer out of him as she frequently did when they were in grade school.

"Let me start at the beginning." He sounds like their father at his most pedantic.

Anna grits her teeth, forcing herself to be patient.

"You've been declared a person of interest in the attacks. There's a fleet of police cars and news trucks outside your house."

Anna blinks. "Already?"

"Malcolm wanted Tim and Erin with us after that," Jason continues.

Anna nods. Tension knots her hungry belly, itching for release.

"I picked them up. Don't worry," he adds. "I was discreet. No one saw anything. They were perfectly safe. And then Dad told us about—"

Her minds races ahead. *Discreet? Why would he think I'd be worried about . . .?* The phrase echoes in her ears, its meaning nearly lost until the answer breaks, wide as a gulf of storm-whipped water. "No one saw what?"

"Huh?" He frowns, flummoxed by her interruption. "Oh. The, uh, the portal."

Xhen springs into Anna's hands; her leash bathes the room in blue light. "You used xhen in front of my kids?!"

Jason backs toward the wall, purple-black shadows forming around his body. Instincts honed by old exercises and yesterday's strain kick in, and the air crackles with anger—hers and his. In the back of Anna's head, the pinpoint presences of her tarkan stir with alarm as she snaps a leash. Jason ducks. Blue energy streaks past his shoulder, knocking against the wall of pictures. Their shining faces bounce from their nails to fall with a smash. Her second leash pins Jason's arms to his sides. "What were you thinking?"

"You were asleep for twelve hours!" Jason shouts. Darkness intensifies in the room, snapping her leash. The force of the break shoves her into the opposite wall. Beneath her splayed fingers, drywall cracks. Air shimmers around her as Jason's xhen forms a cloud around his body. Geometric shapes appear and disappear in its murky depths. "What were we supposed to do? Waste time crossing the city? Get caught in some police blockade? It was fast. No one saw us. It's fine." *Except for you*, his expression says. *You and your endless drama*.

"How'd you explain it?" The fizzing in her head intensifies. Downstairs, she hears footsteps. *I should stop*. But yelling feels too good. "How did you explain xhen to my children, Jay?"

"I didn't." His voice would make ice cubes in a hot oven as his xhen flashes like an angry strobe light beneath her brighter blue. "I told them it was top secret and that you would tell them all about it when you woke up."

"Oh." Humiliation crests, rendering Anna's anger inert. "Thanks." She releases xhen, feeling impossibly small. Jason's face is impassive as his xhen vanishes. Anna heaves a sigh. "I'm sorry."

He shrugs. "You always are when you've had time to think."

Anger washes over her in a second hot wave. "You're so condescending—"

"Come off the high horse," he snaps. "You've had four days to absorb what's happened."

"You did, too! You just didn't want to believe me."

Jason's laugh is bitter. "One of those things ripped an airplane apart to get to me. I nearly died. I think some of the passengers did die. If Kalos hadn't been there, we'd all be—"

"Kalos?" Anna freezes. *Of course*, she thinks, mentally kicking herself. *How else did he learn how to make portals?* "A skyworm attacked your plane?"

"That's what I said."

"No wonder you looked so shitty at Queen's Park."

He shrugs.

Anna's regret deepens, flushing her cheeks. "Damn, Jay. I would have died of fright."

"No." Her brother's voice is unreadable. "That's the last thing you would have done."

Before she can ask him to explain, the bedroom door flies open. Malcolm takes in the jostled furniture, broken pictures, and cracked wall. He turns to Anna, his look of disgust perfectly matching the irritated fizz in her skull. "Whatever you're fighting about is over." He shoves a broom at her and tosses a dustpan to Jason. "There are two children downstairs who don't understand why they couldn't sleep at their own house last night, let alone why their mother's shouting at their uncle. Or why their grandfather's sitting at the kitchen table looking like their grandmother just died all over again."

Anna looks up sharply at the mention of her father.

Malcolm's hard eyes meet hers. "While you slept, I tried to explain this whole tarkan thing to Nina and Carl. They've got lots of questions." His angry gaze shifts to Jason. "You need to understand that they were ready to charge up here and kick your ass into next week after this little spat. So all this bullshit"—he waves a hand in their general direction—"stops now."

After a moment, the twins nod.

"Food will be here in ten," Malcolm says. "Clean this mess up and join us." The door closes.

"Now I know how Tim and Erin feel," Anna murmurs. She cocks her head at her brother. "What happened with Dad?"

Irritation washes over Jason's face. "That's what I was trying to tell you before you flew off the handle." He raises his hands in a mollifying gesture. "I wasn't trying to set you off."

Anna clamps down on her anger. "I'm listening."

Jason talks as they clean. This time, Anna doesn't interrupt. He tells her about the airplane attack, finishing with their father's revelation in the living room the previous night.

When he's finished, Anna sits on the bed. As her twin hangs a few of the photos back up, she props her elbows on her knees and lets her head fall into her open palms, her mind reeling. "Mom must have been Xenthian, too. It's the only explanation." The idea feels impossible even as she says it. *It'd be easier to believe she was a spy or had a second family somewhere.* "It doesn't make sense. Wouldn't we have known? We lived in the same house all through our training."

Her brother shrugs. "Maybe she was better at hiding xhen than we were at sensing it."

Anna frowns. "What did she tell Dad, exactly?"

"He's in shock. Nothing he said was all that coherent . . ."

Anna looks up as her brother's voice trails off. Jason's holding her high school graduation frame. "Anna," he says in a strained voice. "There's an envelope." He turns it over. "Look."

Anna's off the bed like a shot, clutching the ivory envelope with shaking hands. It's the size of a thank-you card. ANNA, it reads in her mother's beautiful penmanship. "Look at your photo," she says hoarsely. *You were her favourite.* "There must be one for you, too."

Carefully, he picks up his picture. JASON, reads the waiting envelope. He takes her place on the bed, opening Chun-Mei's letter with the care of a man defusing a bomb. Anna takes the office chair, swiveling her back to him to give them both privacy as she slides a finger under the envelope's flap. Instead of a card, she finds a folded piece of double-lined paper, crammed with her mother's elegant script. Cold prickles down her back as she reads.

Dear Anna,

You read this letter as the victor of the first skyworm attacks in their next invasion cycle. I salute your courage, Xenthian to Xenthian.

We moved to Ottawa when I was four, as you know. I was twelve when my mind opened to xhen. It was an unnerving experience that I dismissed at first. But I continued to have visions. At fourteen, I encountered Kalos and began training. I know now that my grandmother, Huilang, was also Xenthian, as were her mother, Jingfei, my great-great-uncle Jian, and great-great-grandmother Mei. Our strength flows from them. I have needed it in these last days of my illness and many years ago during the first months of your training. Watching you and Jason come into your power without interfering was the hardest challenge Kalos ever set for me.

I have never doubted that it was the right choice. Xenthians must be free to form triads. Our use of xhen, however, varies as widely as the colours of the energy we draw. Mine is the shade of a tangerine; my gift is foresight. From the beginning, I knew that while Kalos would train me for war, I would never fight one. The brunt of our family's duty falls to you, my twin children, and comes after my death. My life's purpose has been to prepare you and Jason to meet your future.

When I was fifteen, Kalos informed me that I must move from Ottawa to Montreal. With difficulty, I convinced my parents to let me live with Uncle Felix, who was finishing his degree at McGill University. I was a restless, uneasy child. My training prompted me to disobey my parents' rules without explanation. They were at a loss as to what else to do.

Felix, five years my senior, did not welcome my presence for obvious reasons, and our long-standing estrangement took root during those months. I do not have the space nor heart to detail it here. It is enough for you to know that I struggled greatly with loneliness in Montreal, which was more open to me in some ways and so very closed in others. You will find my diaries from those years with my papers.

Kalos's purpose in bringing me there was to meet Leona and Rose LaRoque at Expo '67. On sight, I knew them to be the triad sisters I had longed for all my life. As Jason and David have shown you, a triad bond is powerful and sacred. My years training with them while your father completed his residency program were among the happiest of my life.

After Rose died in 1980, my visions demanded that David be raised in Toronto. Contact with you and Jason was essential to your triad's formation. Leona could not leave Miinikaa First Nation and insisted that we should move north, but your father's research career made that an unfeasible choice for our family. My greatest fear was that David would be sent into foster care as so many Indigenous chil-

dren were, then and now. And so, I privately arranged for the Montcalms to adopt him and persuaded Leona to accept.

Leona understood my reasons, but our friendship was never the same. She blames me for taking David from her, and rightly so. That break, along with Rose's death, are the deepest regrets of my life. Leona and I have spoken periodically through the years and more often during my illness, but not with the openness of our youth. I ask you, Anna, to make amends in my name to the LaRoques and their kin. Be steadfast and clear-eyed in this pursuit.

As for your father, he could not accept all that I am. I did not dare to tell him what you and Jason are, nor what you will become. I do not fault him for this failure. Nor should you. As you and your brother have learned, xhen recedes between skyworm invasion cycles, maintaining enough tangibility on this plane only for the next cycle of Xenthians to be trained. Its presence otherwise remains too scant for it to be widely perceived.

My hope is that you and Jason will help your father to understand us. His love and dedication have, in every other way, made my life joyful. And by gifting you with my name so long ago, he has helped me to honour our ancestors. They, like me, would be proud to know that Lins will meet our enemy.

The skyworm onslaught will be relentless. Your triad will face them many times. I have not foreseen the war's end. Its paths are too clouded. I saw the creatures in the flesh only once under circumstances that will reveal themselves to you in time. They are fearsome, wickedly clever enemies. Guard yourself and those we love.

Many will join you in this struggle, Malcolm among them. Some who choose to follow your triad will surprise and even shock you. You must check your suspicions and uncertainties, Anna, and accept help where it is offered. I know that has never been easy for you. You are in every way my daughter.

Of all your allies, Jason remains the most essential. The rift between you has caused me great pain, then and now. I trust in you to do what must be done to mend this breach, and to be victorious.

All my love to you, Malcolm, Tim, and Erin.
Mom

It's dated April 11, 2014. *Days before she died,* Anna thinks, putting down the paper as the letters swim together. Her head is spinning. *She carried that her whole life, and she never breathed a word. Why didn't she tell us? Didn't she trust me?*

"Dave?" Jason suddenly stands, the sound and motion jarring in the silent room.

Anna spins to face the door. No one's there. "What is it?" she asks.

"We need to go!" Wild-eyed, Jason forms a portal. Through its hazy surface, Anna can just make out Dave and Jenna on the other side. "Get dressed and gather your people," Jason tells her as they step into the study. "The skyworms attacked Sudbury this morning."

Chapter 31

Dave – Auntie

Sudbury, ON: Thursday, August 21

The smell of smoke assaults Dave's nostrils as he leaps through the portal Jason opens to Sudbury. *Auntie Lee!* He strains his ears and mind, frantically listening for any indication of a human or skyworm presence. His gut churns as he runs along the narrow shoulder of the two-lane road that encircles Ramsey Lake.

Come on, Dave, he tells his leaden muscles. *Find another gear. She needs you.* Ahead, the road intersects with the main thoroughfare that would take him to Laurentian University. Beyond that T-junction, a tall tree canopy rises, marking the edge of the conservation area that borders the campus. *Auntie Lee! Where are you?*

Silence. The muscles in his shoulder blades lock in a familiar pattern as his back prickles with fear, not xhen. *Breathe,* he tells himself. *Panic won't serve you.*

On the lake's opposite side, Dave hears the cacophony of many panicked human minds. But in their immediate vicinity, the quiet is eerie. No cars. No birds. Wind shakes the brush between him and the edge of the lake, rustling the leaves. Water laps against the rocky shore. *We saw a dead skyworm in the lake. She's got to be here,* he tells himself. *And she's too stubborn to die.*

The others have joined him on the Sudbury side of the portal. Dave inhales as they gather around him, tasting smoke and sulphur. It lacks the pure tang of cooking fires in the bush. This smoke is thicker, its smell more industrial and layered with gasoline—the stink of skyworms, and a sicklier undercurrent of burnt flesh. The combination burns the back of Dave's throat.

"What's that smell?" Jenna asks, coughing as she joins him.

"Don't know," Dave lies.

"Human flesh," Jason says matter-of-factly, closing the portal behind Anna and her tarkan. A kaleidoscope of cauterized surgical wounds leaks from his thoughts as he looks around, his body tense as if expecting ambush at any moment. "Not a smell you forget."

His aunt's face, burned and blistered, darts like a minnow through Dave's mind. He pushes away his fear and concentrates on breathing through his mouth. "Dad didn't know whether the attack was still in progress," he tells the group as they walk toward a couple of empty cars parked on the roadside, although none of them are Leona's F-150. *Could she have borrowed Ryan's car?* "I don't hear anything, but be on your guard."

"I count twelve smoke plumes across the lake," Jenna says quietly, more to Malcolm on her other side than to Dave. Following their gazes, Dave spots the telltale flash of metal farther out on the lake. Pieces of metallic debris dance in the August sun, forming a macabre flotilla.

"Downed plane?" Dave guesses.

Malcolm climbs on top of a large boulder for a better look, shading his eyes. "Jet fighter," he confirms. He points farther up University Road toward the campus. "There's a piece of cockpit over there. I don't see any people."

Anna turns her head, sniffing the air. "Skyworms died nearby," she mutters. "Nothing else stinks like that. Someone must have fought back."

"But where?" Jason asks. He still looks jumpy as he surveys the empty sky. "I don't see fire trucks or ambulances."

"They'll be triaging the response." Malcolm points across the water at the smoke. "If that's a civilian-dense area, they'll focus there."

My dad's information was several hours old, but here's what he had, Dave says, broadcasting the satellite photos to the group. *It looks like the resistance was focused in this area. The sulphur smell would seem to confirm that. We'll spread out and search the shore of the lake. If we're right, that means other Xenthians are in play.* He takes a deep breath. Jenna steps a little closer to him, her mind bright with concern. Grateful for her silent support, Dave lets his aunt's strong face form in his thoughts. *My best guess is that my aunt Leona came in from the Miinikaa First Nation to fight the skyworms. If I'm right, we need to find her fast.*

The twins exchange a solemn glance, their thoughts filled with notepaper covered in Chun-Mei's handwriting. With Dave's gift, they'd needed mere seconds to share the stunning missives from their mother and hear his confirming details. Their collective shock is starting to wear off, but Dave still braces himself against fresh grief.

Instead, without anything being said, Nina drops into step beside Anna. Carl does the same on her other side. By the time Malcolm's climbed down from the rock to join them, his background awareness of her emotions has stopped.

Only Jason remains solitary, his sense of loss as palpable to Dave as a pulsing wound. Margo is also prominent in his mind, accompanied by regret so profound it makes Dave want to grind his teeth.

But Jason's face is outwardly impassive, and he seems unaware of Dave's scrutiny. "I'll check the hospitals." He gestures at the borrowed scrubs that he, Malcolm, and Anna's other tarkan are wearing. "I'll blend in there."

Dave nods with the others, relieved to have a good reason for

Jason to take his jittery presence off a potential battlefield. "If I find anything," he continues, "I'll call Malcolm's cell. Holler again if you need me, Dave." His portal flashes open and shut, faster than before. Dave sighs as his awareness of Jason's emotions recedes.

That man needs a Kalxhan, Jenna observes as they spread out, moving east away from the intersection toward a lakeside residential area. Dave glances at her, amused by the certainty in her mental voice. *And soon.*

He needs to talk to his wife, Dave says. *She deserves to hear what's happened from him.*

Jenna's eyes widen. *She doesn't know?!*

Not yet.

Jenna's eyebrows form disapproving red lines. *Will she join him like Malcolm's joined Anna?*

Never in a million years. A less pragmatic person would perhaps give Margo the benefit of the doubt, but Dave can't picture Jason's sophisticated wife combing through a smashed cityscape to hunt skyworms in spike heels and one of her quirky vintage blazers. What he can picture, all too easily, is his aunt quietly locking her house and driving to a fight to the death without asking anyone for help. *Especially me. Dad, why didn't you tell me sooner?*

"Hey," Jenna says. "We're going to find her."

Dave swallows, touching a hand to his missing scar. "She's the bedrock of my life," he explains. "When I was sick a few years ago, she was there in a way that not even my folks could be. Without her, I wouldn't know anything about my people." He pictures himself standing in the Miinikaa Community Centre, trying to explain how he let her die. His chest tightens.

Breathe, David, his aunt says in his memory as she sits at his hospital bedside. *Connect your body and your mind.* Holding on to her face like a talisman, Dave draws a shaky breath.

"Over here!" Carl shouts. This close to the lake, his voice easily carries through the quiet.

Dave and Jenna turn toward the sound. *Did you find her?* Dave demands.

Carl doesn't answer.

Adrenaline courses through him as they run back along the road. *Please let her be okay*, Dave prays as his feet pound the gravel, making his head throb. Ahead, Anna, Malcolm, and Nina are also running toward an office building near the lake. The four tarkan easily outpace Dave and Anna. *They're so fast. It's only been a day for everyone but Malcolm*, he thinks, part of him marveling a little despite his anxiety for Leona. *How fast will they get?*

He passes a roadside sign as he catches up to Anna. It reads: VALE LIVING WITH LAKES CENTRE. Turning into the driveway, they pelt through the parking lot. The back of his throat is dry, and the benefits of his shawarma have long since worn off. His stomach growls, but the intense smell of sulphur suppresses all thought of food as they run down a well-worn path leading toward the water.

The scene awaiting them where the path meets an open, rocky headland spotted with wind-stunted pines confirms Dave's worst fears. He takes hold of xhen, craving the assurance of its prickling burn. Two orange skyworm carcasses lie broken on the rock, their massive bodies blackened by fire. More torn pieces lie half submerged in the shallow water, their scales winking in the morning sun. The air is thick with the stink of their ichor and an underlying layer of rot. Around the carcasses, rupture attacks have scored deep furrows through the rock and trees. The damage converges on the highest outcropping, which is covered in dried blood.

No. You can't be dead. Wildly, Dave scans the area, searching for his aunt. Orange-red sunlight reflects in a dazzling pattern from the skyworms' scales, and from the threads of quartz in the black rocks. But there's no sign of Leona as Dave blinks against the brilliance. *Auntie Lee!* he shouts. *Call out if you can hear me!*

Jenna touches his arm, radiating sympathy, as Dave joins Malcolm in kneeling by the largest rock. Jenna, Anna, and Nina stand around them, warily watching the sky, while Carl slips into the trees, searching the ground.

"That's a lot of blood," Dave says, trying to keep his anxiety from his voice. "She's going to need help if it's hers." He glances at the skyworms, checking for a flicker of their strange xhen, but the creatures have been dead too long. Their carcasses are lifeless.

Malcolm nods. "Head wounds bleed a lot."

Dave glances at him and then at the ground. "How can you tell?"

Malcolm shrugs. "I'm guessing." He points to faint impressions in the dirt, tracing them with his finger. "Someone fell sideways here. See? Skull, shoulder, and hip. The blood's concentrated in this spot. I think there's a good chance it was a woman. The footprints around the rock are on the small side for a man. Shape of the sole's right. See how it's narrow across the ball and in the heel?" He looks up at Dave. "How tall is she?"

"Five foot six or so," Dave says. "I probably get my height from my birth father."

Malcolm nods, looking back at the dirt. Before he can say more, Carl emerges from the trees, carrying the remnants of something wooden. "Found this," he says, setting it down on the ground beside Dave. "There's four more just like it, all burned. I think they were catapults."

"That's one way to expand your firepower," Jenna murmurs. "Impressive."

"They took her!" calls a raspy voice.

Instantly, Dave's on his feet. Before he can take a step, the tarkan form a protective half circle around him and Anna as a figure emerges from the trees.

Don't think at him, Jenna cautions. *You'll scare him away.*

Dave touches her elbow in gratitude as he releases xhen. "Who?" he calls. "What happened?"

"Native lady," says the man. He's Black and at least twenty years older than Dave. He shuffles down the path toward them, favouring his left leg. Bald with a wide, paunchy dark face and a salt-and-pepper beard, he's wearing khakis and a fleece jacket with the research centre's logo stitched on the breast pocket. His clothes are stained with blood that doesn't seem to be his, but the palms of his dark-skinned hands are scrubbed clean as he spreads them to encompass the rocky, wooded area.

"She had fire like yours," he continues, nodding at Dave. "We saw them coming in low across the water. Big screaming devils." He shudders. Dave glimpses swift, lethal shapes in his mind interspersed with his aunt's face. "They blew out the windows. I had the others hide in the basement, but my knees are crap. We'd lost the elevators with the power, and taking the stairs hurt too much. I watched her fight those things." He holds Dave's gaze, his mind brimming with images of Leona on the rock, encircled by skyworms. "She saved our lives."

Auntie Lee. Numbness spreads through Dave's arms and legs as he looks back at the bloodstains. Before Jenna can steady him, he sits down hard on the packed earth. *I should have been here to help.*

Anna shoots Dave a concerned glance. "How many people are with you?" she asks.

The man glances back up the path, but no one else has emerged from the building. "Eight. All members of my research team." He nods at Dave. "Was that lady a relative of yours?"

"My aunt," he says weakly.

A smile cracks the old man's face. "Hell of a woman, your aunt. Most of the creatures were focused on the downtown area across the lake, but four came here, wreaking havoc. She collapsed as she killed the last of them."

The man spits at the nearest skyworm head. "When I was sure it was over, I called an ambulance. Came down here, tried to help her. She'd hit her head pretty hard. One of her legs was sliced up from the rock shrapnel. She wasn't conscious. We waited over an hour for help. Did what I could for the bleeding. Paramedics sent me back inside, told me to sit tight. Said it might not be safe. That was three hours ago."

Malcolm's cell phone rings. He picks it up and hits the speaker, already turning to Dave. "Whatcha got, Doc?"

"She's here at Health Sciences North," Jason tells them. "You better come."

* * *

The corridors of Health Sciences North's Emergency Department are so crammed with people and medical equipment that Dave's progress is frustratingly slow. Badly lit and painted the drabbest possible shade of industrial yellow, the hospital is clotted with pain and despair. He tries to ignore the background miasma as he beelines toward Jason's increasingly distinctive thoughts, his fear spurring him on as he barrels past nurses, orderlies, patients, and family members. Jason had insisted on opening the portal for Dave and Jenna at the very back of the emptiest parking lot. Avoiding panic made sense, but Dave begrudges every wasted second.

He spots the doctor's dark hair in the same moment that Jenna points. Despite his worries, Dave musters a smile. *We've been a team for what? Eighteen hours? Feels like ten years.*

Jason's leaning against a wall with his arms folded, his face expressionless. Dave looks down at the nearest bed, but it holds an elderly man on an oxygen tank, not Leona. "Where is she?"

"In there." Jason inclines his head toward a door across and a little farther down the hall. Belatedly, Dave notices a uniformed man dressed in army fatigues standing guard outside. "I caught a glimpse of her," Jason says, "But he won't let me in without hospital ID."

Dave's anger surges as the stresses of the last twenty-four hours—the battle at Queen's Park, Jason's and Anna's grief, the beating slowly purpling his back, his dad's delay, the gory scene at the lake, his agonizing fears for his aunt—tip him past some infinitesimal point. Dave tilts his neck to the left until the joint cracks. He grins at his brother before advancing on the door. *No sweat.*

The soldier tenses at the sight of him. "You stop right there," he orders. Indignation and machismo fill his mind. "This room is under—"

Dave kindles flame in his cupped palm, bright against his skin. The soldier breaks off, staring. "I killed three skyworms yesterday, friend," he says in a flat voice. "My aunt is in that room. She killed four. I'm her only family. I am going to see her. Right now."

The soldier pales until his already-pale skin looks like the fry bread batter that Leona used to make for Dave on Saturday mornings. Dave's much taller than the soldier, but there's a gun on the other man's belt. And he's reaching for it.

Try me, Dave whispers, the corner of his mouth edging into a sneer as the soldier quails at the sound of his mental voice. Beside him, Jenna subtly shifts to the balls of her feet, tense as a coiled spring. *Let's see who's faster.*

"Stop it!" Jason hisses, putting a firm hand on his shoulder.

Dave glares at him.

Jason shakes his head. "We've all seen enough trauma." *You included, Dave. Don't do this.*

Dave grimaces, aware how much he'd love to get a few licks in. But Jason's grip is implacable. Reluctantly, he releases xhen. "Stand aside," he orders the soldier through clenched teeth.

"Fuck you." The soldier's hand hasn't moved from his holster. Heads turn toward his raised voice. "I don't do shit for guys who send little old ladies to do their dirty work." The soldier's anger flares, laced with grief. "Where were you this morning, huh? Tell me. Where were you when fifteen of those things ripped my whole battalion and this city apart?"

Mirrored rage clenches a fist around Dave's heart, but the soldier's mind brims with dead friends. Seeing their faces fills Dave with the same hopelessness he felt from his dad upon seeing the photos of the Xenthian teens. He can't bring himself to seize xhen.

He's right, Dave thinks. *It's my fault Leona faced them alone.*

Before he can apologize, Jenna swiftly steps in front of him. Her thin hand shoots up, the knuckles whitening as she grabs the soldier by the collar. She thrusts him up and back against the door with an ease that should be limited to the special effects in a Valoi Knights movie. The soldier's thrashing boots thud against the hospital room's door.

"You think he doesn't know that?" Jenna snarls. "You think it's not eating him alive?"

The soldier gargles something incoherent, clutching at his throat with ineffectual hands.

"Enough," Jason mutters.

Dave's back itches as lightening crackles in the corridor, sending purple-black shadows crawling across the walls. A portal opens into Leona's hospital room.

Screams fill the hallway. As the bystanders stampede away from them, Jenna drops the soldier so fast his knees buckle. Dave automatically reaches out to steady him.

The soldier jerks his arm back as though burned. "Don't touch me," he spits. "You're as sick as those monsters."

"Skyworms," Jason corrects as he pushes Dave and Jenna through the portal.

It's the first time he's said the word aloud in Dave's hearing. He tastes discomfort in Jason's thoughts, though none of his trepidation shows. "I'm sorry about all of this. It's been a brutal week," Jason tells the soldier. "But we can stop it from getting worse if you'd give us a moment alone with her."

Inside the room, Dave only has eyes for Leona in her hospital bed. She doesn't stir as he blocks out all awareness of the soldier and the other agitated minds churning in the hallway. *Auntie Lee, I'm here! It's Dave!*

Her face is drawn, her skin ashen. Medical monitors beep and chirp in the room's relative silence. There's an IV in her arm. Her eyes are closed, her lips slightly parted. Yet she looks . . . not peaceful, but calm, as though her rest is a choice. Someone's shaved the side of her head to accommodate thick gauze bandages. It should make her look frail and vulnerable. Yet, looking at her, Dave can't apply those words.

He takes the hand without the IV line in his and gives it a gentle squeeze. *Auntie? Can you hear me?*

She sighs. Dave waits on tenterhooks as Jenna paces behind him, but Leona doesn't wake.

Movement draws his eyes. Jason picks up her chart from the plastic holder at the foot of the bed. "Guess there's one upside to antiquated hospital tech," he murmurs, flipping the papers. "Blunt force head trauma from a fall," he reads. "Cuts and bruises on her limbs, but nothing to worry about there. The big problem is the swelling in the MRI scan. They've induced her coma."

"Is that bad?" Dave asks.

"It's not good." Jason puts the chart back. "I'm not going to lie to you, because I can't. They won't know if she's got permanent damage until she wakes up."

"How long?" Dave asks.

Jason gives him a shrug identical to those Dave received from his doctors when he'd tried to set expectations for his own recovery. "They'll try waking her in a few days. We'll know more then."

Dave turns back to his aunt. *You fought them alone,* he thinks, trying to focus his thoughts so that Leona might hear them in the recesses of her coma. *That either makes you the bravest or the craziest person I know. Probably both.* He bends to kiss her hand and plants another on her forehead. *The researchers you protected are safe. Miigwech, Auntie. Rest now. Call for me when you wake. I'll be here.*

Chapter 32

Jason – Revelations

Toronto, ON / Vancouver, BC: Thursday, August 21

"The first time your mother tried to tell me, she'd just returned from a summer at Camp Ashigan, which borders Miinikaa First Nation," Erik Lin is saying as Jason drains the last of his matcha tea. He doesn't feel any more alert, but if he drinks coffee this late, he won't sleep.

Setting the cup down on the kitchen table amid the takeout containers from dinner, Jason crosses his arms. He glances at Anna across from him. *When was the last time the three of us were together?* After Chun-Mei died, there'd been the funeral to arrange and so many details to manage. *We never really had a moment.*

Erik's pale blue eyes are bloodshot, the skin around them puffy, as he continues. "I didn't understand why she wanted to work as a counsellor at a children's camp. She never seemed interested in other people's children. I was angry, so she tried to explain." He shakes his head. "I can admit now that I was deeply jealous of the time she spent with Leona and Rose LaRoque. After we married, I wanted her in Toronto, even if I spent eighty hours a week either at the hospital or in my lab." His smile is rueful. "But your mother was never one to put her plans on hold."

"She knew her own mind, for sure," Jason agrees, yawning. He stands to refresh his father's and sister's Styrofoam cups before pouring more tea for himself.

Anna catches his eye, offering a small smile for her filled cup. Since the fight upstairs and their sobering trip to Sudbury, she's been quiet. Talking with Erik after dinner had been her idea, especially with Nina and Carl at home with their families and Dave and Jenna sitting vigil at Leona's bedside in Sudbury. Malcolm quietly took the kids upstairs to give them space.

"She did," Erik agrees, his voice fond. "When we met at that dance, she plucked my shoe out of the pile and marched over to me like her destiny was written all over my face."

Jason and Anna exchange a glance. The story of their parents' meeting has been told and retold around this table so many times that it rivals the wooden surface for well-worn grooves.

"What did you think when she first told you about xhen?" Anna asks.

"I was unkind," Erik says, spreading his hands as though in apology for his younger self. "I defaulted to science's classic accusations for people with your mother's gifts: delusion, schizophrenia, the whole list." He catches Jason's eye, his smile bitter. "All of the labels that people in our profession would apply."

Jason flushes. Anna looks down at her lap, her lips twisting.

Erik sighs. "I presume that's why neither of you ever broached the subject with me."

When the twins lock eyes a second time, Anna's gaze brims with scorn.

Jason turns to Erik. "Yes," he says. "Would you have said anything, Dad, if you were us?"

"No," Erik says with a sigh. "I suppose not."

Maybe that's why Mom never broke Kalos's order to be silent,

Jason thinks. His hand automatically wanders to his wallet, which contains his mother's carefully folded letter:

Dear Jason,

You read these words upon returning to Toronto to join Anna and David in resisting the skyworms. I know how much this trip has and will cost you, my son, and I am sorry.

Once, I believed that watching you and Anna grow into your power would be the hardest challenge Kalos could ever set. But I did not know agony until I also watched you tear at each other after his departure. In this world, being a Xenthian has never been an easy burden. Between cycles, our gifts are not discernable to those who do not share them, and science, not mysticism, rules the West. The last skyworm attack occurred over two millennia ago. We are forgotten by the people whose lives it is our duty to defend.

Yet all your life, I have known that our family's burden shall fall heaviest upon you, my twin children, some months after my death. I have spent my days preparing you and Anna to meet your destiny.

I have no twin soul. I did not glimpse that kind of companionship until I met Leona and Rose LaRoque. On sight, I knew them for the sisters I had desired all my life. Even now, as I prepare to join Rose in death and still estranged from Leona, they hold deep places in my heart.

When Kalos ended your training, I hoped you and Anna would cling together as you once did in my womb. I understand now that this hope, like most held by mothers, was terribly naïve. Your sister is a warrior born. Like all of her kind, her spirit grows uneasy in peacetime. You are both more prone to pessimism and anxiety than I would wish. Whether that vulnerability is inherent to your nature, to my failings as your parent, or to the cost of living in this time, I do not know. I will not pretend that Anna has been easy to live with. She is headstrong and impulsive, but also intuitive. Believe this, Jason: it is you whom she will need most in the days ahead.

To David LaRoque Montcalm and his kin, we owe an immense debt.

My xhen gave me foresight and showed me that closeness to him was essential to your success. To ensure that prolonged contact, I arranged for the Montcalms to privately adopt him after Rose died. I convinced Leona to accept. As I approach my own end, it is the necessity of this act that weighs heaviest on my heart. I do not blame Leona for her anger, nor do I shirk the implications of my actions. The LaRoques, together with the Miinikaa First Nation, have supported Xenthians past and present in profound ways. Work with your sister and make amends for my choice.

I have written more to Anna of my visions, but I have not foreseen the war's end. What I can say is that war shall rearrange many aspects of your life, Jason. The roles you have played until now will fall away, and the courageous boy who led his sister and friend to train with Kalos in the dark shall return. It is he, tempered now with the wisdom and empathy earned in operating theaters and treatment rooms, who shall prevail. But I also caution you that some who love the face you have worn in peace may find this change in you hard to accept.

It is a pain I know well. Your father, for all his gifts, cannot accept all that I am. Xhen is too strange, too metaphysical for his scientific mind. I have not told him what you and Anna are, nor what you will become. I do not fault him for this failure, nor should you. My next foolish, motherly hope is that you and Anna will teach him what we are. Given time, he will dedicate himself to you as thoroughly as he once doted upon you as children. For all his gruffness, he is deeply loving, and determined when he sets his mind. Xhen holds many secrets, some of which will interest you both as physicians. Work with your father to unlock all that you can. Build a legacy of which we can be proud.

You have always been a dutiful son, Jason. Honour our ancestors and bring all that you are to bear in the war. Our family's survival hinges on your success. I believe in you.

All my love,

Mom

Anna leans in to rub his arm. "Mom wrote to us, Dad. She said she understood, and she never held it against you. She said you made her life happy in every other way."

Their father's eyes fill with tears. Anna gives him a hug, and Jason leans across the table to take Erik's other hand. "Thank you," their father mumbles, choking back a sob.

Anna rubs his back for a moment before rising from her chair. "I'm going to check on Malcolm and the kids," she says. "Might be a good time to call Margo, Jay."

"I'll handle it," he says.

Her eyes roll as she leaves the kitchen. Jason finds himself reaching for his phone anyway. Several new texts await him, all from Margo. His palms start to sweat as he scans them:

Ivy told me about Anna

Call me Jason, please

I'm so scared

Thanks to xhen, returning to Vancouver is a matter of when, not if. Yet he's no closer to knowing what to say to Margo than he was during their car ride to the airport. *Tomorrow morning*, he thinks. *I'll call her then.*

"Jason?" his father says quietly, wiping his eyes with a napkin. "Have you talked to Margo?"

"No," he says, and winces at his father's indrawn breath. "Look, I don't need—"

"Advice?" Erik finishes. "I beg to differ. Margo is a brilliant woman with many depths. She loves you very much, but secrets twist marriages. I might have saved my own a great deal of pain by listening to Mei the first time." His gaze softens. "Don't repeat my mistake, Jason. Go to Margo tonight. Tell her everything."

Ten minutes later, Jason's outside the door to his Vancouver condominium. He reaches for his keys before realizing they're still in the pocket of his ruined khaki pants four provinces away. Glancing from side to side, he confirms the hallway's empty. Purple-shot black light flashes in the corridor, and then he's standing in the condo's utility closet, which he knows will be empty.

He cracks the door open. Margo's perfume hits his nostrils, banishing all memory of jet fuel and charred skyworm corpses. In its presence, the battle feels as ephemeral as a dream. *I'm really here again. I'm home.* Like a sleepwalker, he enters the small bedroom that Margo uses as an office.

She's on the balcony talking on her cell, her hair pulled into a sleek ponytail at her neck, her feet bare, one of his white dress shirts rolled to her elbows over dark jeans. He watches her pace, her elegant fingers gesturing to make a point. *She hates sitting still. Just like Mom.*

Weary, Jason sinks into the overstuffed peacock blue armchair that Margo's had since her student apartment that she shared with Ivy. He leans back against the deep cushions, trying to gather his thoughts. *What do I say? How do I explain?* Before he comes up with a starting point, she spots him through the glass.

Her hand flies to her chest. Her mouth goes slack. She hangs up her call, and then she's before him, eyes wild as a spring storm. Standing, Jason spreads his arms to embrace her. Margo rushes toward him, relief written all over her face as she throws her arms around his neck. Before he can relax into the embrace, she pulls back, keeping him at bay with her fingertips pressed lightly against his chest. They stare at each other, neither moving, as tension crackles between them.

"I promised I'd take you to dinner," he blurts.

"The airports are closed," she says, speaking over him. "How did you get home?"

Jason slides his hands into his pockets. "It's complicated."

Rage and hurt strike like meteors across her face. "It's been twenty-four hours! You texted me once! No calls!!" She crosses her arms. "What the hell is going on? I've been beside myself. Ivy sent me links to all these news stories about Anna. They said she killed monsters in Toronto." Her grin is desperate, demanding that he share her amusement. When he doesn't, she shakes her head. "Jason, it doesn't make any sense."

"No," he says. "And talking about what's happening is very difficult for me." His throat is dry; he wishes he'd gone to the kitchen for a glass of water. "I should have talked to you sooner. But it's not a conversation we could have by phone. It had to be in person. That's why I'm here."

"What?" Margo pulls her office chair out from her desk. She spins it on its castors before dropping into the seat and crossing her long legs. Her eyes drill into him as she impatiently gestures for him to sit, too. "Come on, you're scaring me."

"Okay." Jason sits down. He leans forward, resting his elbows on his knees. But his hands, once the envy of his classmates for their steadiness, are trembling. *Coward.* He leans back, clasping his fingers to hide his weakness. "Anna was at the SkyDome the night of the attack, like I told you. But Ivy's also right. She's the woman in the video footage."

He waits for some sign of comprehension, but Margo's face is utterly blank. "She killed three monsters that night. And on Wednesday, she, Dave, and . . ." *Say it!* "She, Dave, and I fought them. They're called skyworms. They've come before, thousands of years ago. And when we were teenagers, we were trained to fight them. Only, we didn't know that. Until now." *Stop babbling.*

Margo says nothing for the longest minute of his life. Her lip twitches. Then she starts to laugh: first a chortle, then a delighted cackle, and finally a full, belly-rocking laugh. Jason watches as tears trickle down her cheeks for a solid minute. He gets up and hands her a tissue, which makes her laugh harder. Eventually, her manic laughter finally subsides. "Oh, wow," she manages. "You've got to have something better than that."

Jason waits until she's settled again. Then he lets xhen rise through his clothes.

Margo jumps out of her chair. "What is that?!"

"Xhen." He concentrates on the seam edges. Triangles twist

into hexagons, turning the familiar room into an uncanny space. Jason stands up as he opens a narrow portal, one side facing his chair and the other the doorway to the hall. Margo watches him step across, her eyes huge in her face, which is rapidly draining of colour.

He releases the energy. "It's the only weapon that works against the creatures. And it's how I came home today." Still, she says nothing. He tries for levity. "We could finish this conversation at Delphi. Remember our honeymoon? We had such a good time." Her face is a hollow mask. *I wish Dave were here. He'd know what to say.* "Or Bali. We wanted to go, remember? Well, we could. Right now. Anywhere you want."

Margo sinks back into her chair. "How do you do it?" she asks, voice shaking. "Mirrors? Projected video? I-I don't understand."

Jason thinks of Anna's second call to him on Sunday night, his smile bitter. "It's real, Mar."

She shakes her head as a tear runs down her cheek. "Stop it, Jason," she whispers. "You're acting crazy."

He goes to her, kneeling on the floor to take her hand. "It would probably be easier if I were crazy. But I'm not. And you promised to listen."

"Very well," she manages, sitting back and composing herself. "Tell me."

Jason does: about Anna's calls, Dave's texts, the airplane, Queen's Park, his mother's letters, all of it except for Kalos and the tarkan. When he's finished, Margo's face is impassive, her expressive body so very neutral that he has no idea what she's thinking. He suddenly has an inkling of how daunting it must be to audition for her and pities all those actors.

"None of this makes sense," she says softly, tenting her fingers. "I know there were casualties in Toronto. You say something attacked your plane. But interdimensional monsters?" The look she shoots him is almost wondering. "I feel like I don't know you."

Jason fights a shiver as they lock eyes.

"You said you trained to do this as a kid?" She waits for his nod. "How? Who taught you?"

Shit. He swallows hard as another door, this one containing secrets far deeper than the airport, opens in his mind. Old memories course through him. "He found us," Jason begins. "We call him Kalos."

Her gaze doesn't waver. "How'd you meet him?"

"The first time was in the alley behind the Montcalms' house," Jason begins. "It's not what you're thinking. He's—"

"Homeless? A drifter with mystical powers?" Margo rolls her eyes. "Give me a break."

"No." Sweat turns Jason's fingers clammy against his scrubs. He wishes he'd taken the time to find something better to wear to this meeting. *Not that it would have helped.* "It's not what you think," he says aloud.

Margo blinks.

Don't stop now. "He's . . . he's a spirit. He died fighting skyworms thousands of years ago, the last time they came." Jason tries to smile. "He doesn't talk much about himself." Her posture is rigid, her face frozen. "But he trained us to use xhen."

Her gaze is relentless as she lifts a perfectly plucked eyebrow. "Where? How?"

More memories flash from the pit in his head: of himself standing with Anna and Dave in a dozen shadowed alleyways, places he hasn't let himself remember in years. *She deserves the truth.* "The alleys behind our houses. Sometimes empty buildings. He'd disappear and have us track him down. We were forbidden to use artificial lights. When we found the right place, he'd ambush us in the dark."

Jason shudders. They'd spent so many nights crawling around abandoned buildings in industrial districts where he feared mugging almost as much as otherworldly threats. He'd never understood how his sister became a Realtor after that. "That's how we learned to work together while using xhen under duress."

As soon as the words are out of his mouth, he wants his secret back. Margo blinks, a mime performing a living statue routine. Jason waits for her scorn, for her disbelief, for anything. *I should have told you years ago.*

Margo lets out a heavy sigh. She rises to stand behind her desk, looking out at the balcony. "Why didn't you tell me?"

"I haven't thought about xhen or Kalos in years," he says. "It had nothing to do with us."

Her look is pitying. "Anna knew." The hurt in her voice staggers him. "And Dave. Not me."

"It wasn't important," he insists. "It didn't mean anything until Sunday night."

"Sure, this formative period that put you on standby for an apocalypse was completely irrelevant," she scoffs, tears glittering in her eyes. She visibly struggles to compose herself before she continues. "Everything is collapsing," she says in a tight voice. "All the theatres are shut down. No one's supposed to gather in crowds until they know if these strange attacks will spread. If they do, people will leave Vancouver like they're leaving Toronto. I'm going to lose thousands of dollars." Her voice shakes with the strain of holding back frustrated tears. "I haven't had to lay anyone off yet, but I can see it coming. All of our hard work is going to be for nothing."

One sob escapes her control. Again, Jason reaches for her, but Margo's outstretched arm keeps him at bay. "Luckily," she says in a more even voice, "Ivy and Lou bought a winery in the interior of British Columbia last year as an investment. It's outside Kelowna. They've invited us to join them there until this is all over." She looks him straight in the eye. "I'm sure the community could use another doctor with emergency room training. Go pack your things and let's go."

Jason blinks. "What?"

She takes his hands in hers. "Leave this bizarre episode behind in Ontario. Let Anna play the hero if that's what she wants. Start over with me. Tonight."

Jason's mouth feels like the surface of the moon as he pictures the battle on Pearson's tarmac playing out again among rows and rows of grapevines. "I can't," he manages. "I want to, Mar, I do, but they're . . . you have no idea. In person, the skyworms are like nothing I've seen. The glitchy video footage doesn't do them justice, not at all. One of them tore open the airplane's roof to get to me. If I leave, we won't be safe—"

Margo's face crumples. Releasing him, she grabs her purse and car keys from the desk and stalks toward the door.

"Wait!" Jason cries as he follows her, chest pounding with alarm. "Where are you going?"

"To Ivy's," she says. "I took my things to her place this morning. Her SUV's already packed." She grasps the door handle, eyes brittle. "I came back to pack a bag for you. Because when you said you were coming home to me, I believed you."

Jason gapes. "But I did! I just told you the truth! I told you everything!"

"How can I ever be sure?" Her voice is flat. "How can I trust you when it's clear you're not putting me and our relationship first?"

"Margo—"

"If you change your mind, you'll know where to find me."

The front door clicks shut behind her in a backdraft of orchid perfume.

* * *

Chun-Mei's rose garden is empty when Jason returns to Toronto. He sets his hastily packed suitcase and backpack down on the flagstones and drops into one of the brown wicker chairs, not caring that no one's set the cushions out. *What just happened? Is our marriage over?* He thinks of Margo having to contemplate laying off her cast and company, and of her heartbroken face. *I can't give up on her. She's my wife. The others will understand.*

He tilts his head back to study the clouded, moonless sky,

thinking of his mother's words: *Some who love the face you have worn in peace may find this change in you hard to accept.*

He sighs. *Did Mom know Margo would react this way? Did I screw it up? What else could I have done?*

"Jason," Anna calls from the patio door.

"Yeah," he manages, palming tears from his eyes. "Give me a sec."

The screen door squeaks as it starts to swing shut. "Can you, um, hurry? There's something you should see."

Composing himself, Jason goes inside. Anna, Malcolm, and Erik are huddled around the TV in the den with the lights off. He expects to see the footage of Anna at the SkyDome. Instead, it shows a hazy daytime view of a curving bridge spanning brilliant blue water. It has what looks like two triangular sails made out of white pillars and cables. He doesn't recognize it or the sprawling skyline behind it. There's no text on the screen other than LIVE in the upper corner.

"Where is this?" he asks.

Erik clears his throat. "Mumbai. It's early morning there. That's the Bandra–Worli Sea Link. They were building it when I was there in 2009 for a confer—"

"Shhh," Anna interrupts. "Look!"

A blur wheels over the bridge. A moment later, it's joined by four more jagged blips as an announcer's voice confirms the location. Then another five blips in the video footage. Then a dozen more. Heat climbs Jason's back as xhen crackles in his palms, itching for use.

"Skyworms," Malcolm breathes. "I count over twenty."

Near the top of the screen, a flicker of orange light partway down the bridge draws Jason's eye.

Before he can say anything, Anna exclaims, "Did you see that?" She points again. "The orange glow that looks like an exploding firework. That's xhen!"

Malcolm leans closer as if that will help him get a better view. "How many Xenthians? Do you think they've recruited tarkan, too?"

Anna shrugs, her eyes shining as she turns to Jason. "Don't you see? Mom, Leona, and those poor kids who died downtown aren't the only people like us. We're not alone."

Does that mean I can go home? Knowing the answer, Jason sits down on the sofa where he can see most of the screen. Part of him would prefer not to look, unnerved by the speed of the pixelated blurs. He thinks of Margo, driving into British Columbia's interior with only Ivy and Lou for protection. Longing grips him in a feverish wave. He wants to go to her right now, open a portal, and run straight into her arms. He wants to hug her and kiss her and never let her go.

You help by never leaving a skyworm free to hunt, Kalos says in his memory.

We are forgotten by the people whose lives it is our duty to defend, his mother had written.

Blue-white light from the TV flickers over Jason's face as he listens to his family dissect the battle, debating how many Xenthians are defending Mumbai against skyworms on the other side of the world.

I can't leave, he thinks as acceptance settles like a stone in his belly.

This is only the beginning.

Epilogue: Clutch

Day by day, we widen the tear in the veil.

Striking out against new shores across the Xenthian home world has proven advantageous. Again and again, our hunters return in triumph. Each time their heads reemerge from the veil between worlds, we open the nest like an eye to receive their bounty. Our scales swell, growing thick and lustrous until we gleam like a star.

Our larger, more fearsome hunters have proven more than a match for the Xenthians. Three times they have crossed the veil with our scouts. Many aliens have they vanquished, stealing into their strange, tall nests of metal and stone to drag them from their swarms and drink their power.

Of the six dozen we have sent, only ten have perished. No queen would decline such an exchange. We honour their sacrifice.

The captured skal quickens within us, strengthening our forming clutch. Already, we can feel their scales forming within the membrane-thin shells. Their third eyes have already opened to the nest mind and their battle cries, faint though powerful, have joined the swarm.

Your clutch comes with the dawn, whisper our mother-sisters. ***Make haste.***

We loop our scales around ourselves, prepared to give welcome. Our swarm, grown strong on the tidbits of power gifted to them, form ring upon concentric, joyous ring, ready to defend us. Within our scales, the eggs push through our twisting corridors to rest upon the sand. Our swarm's song of triumph ripples over the waves.

This time, we do not command them to silence. For our clutch is bountiful, and within its centre rests not one but two queen eggs, their shells pearlescent in the dawn light.

Soon, the queens of nearby swarms will learn that we have crossed the veil.

Soon, they shall know that we have hunted and feasted upon Xenthians, gilding our bodies with their strength.

And very soon, no enemy swarm or Xenthian shall stand against us.

END OF BOOK I

The Xenthians will return in

Chaos Armor
Book II of The Xenthian Cycle

Appendix

Acknowledgements

I wrote this book while living and working in Toronto. The city exists on land that is the traditional territory of many Indigenous nations, including the Mississaugas of the Credit, the Anishnabeg, the Chippewa, the Haudenosaunee, and the Wendat peoples. It is also home to many diverse First Nations, Inuit, and Métis peoples. Toronto is covered by Treaty 13, signed with the Mississaugas of the Credit, and the Williams Treaty, signed with multiple Mississaugas and Chippewa bands. To learn more about the land you live and work on, visit Whose.land.

The Truth and Reconciliation Commission of Canada (TRC) is doing crucial work to hold this country to account for its actions as a colonial state. The work of challenging systemic policies and beliefs that perpetuate racism and injustice against First Nations, Métis, and Inuit peoples benefits us all. If you haven't had the chance, read the TRC's summary report.

The Ojibwe People's Dictionary is a digital resource that I returned to throughout this project, particularly for its audio samples demonstrating proper pronunciations. Please see the Pronunciation Guide in the Appendix for specifics about individual words.

Ideation and Iteration

This story took shape while I worked at **MaRS Discovery District** and expanded during my years in Toronto's tech sector. During that time, many excellent colleagues went out of their way to encourage my passion project. While it's impossible to name all of you, please know that I treasured every conversation.

In December 2012, **Elle P.** and the TedxWaterlooWomen team said yes to my talk on superheroes, women, and work. I thought I was delivering a swan song to my dream of doing a PhD in science fiction. Turns out, it started a decade of follow-up work.

Before the pandemic, **Wattpad** and the **Toronto Transit Commission** (TTC) provided the most productive writing space I've ever known. Using Wattpad's app, I stood in the subway doors and wrote many chapters of this book during my commute. I've written about that experience on Medium. While I opted not to publish as I went, I'm proud to be a tiny part of this thriving international community. Thank you to **Dani Z.**, **Carmen H.**, **Brandon W.**, and **Tim J.** for their advice on navigating self-publishing.

For generously sharing their perspectives on growing up in Canada, my thanks to **Fanny S., Andrew E.**, **Alister E.**, **Marydean M.**, **Sabreena D.**, **Diana P. C.**, **Bella L.**, **Wesley L.**, **Quinton C. A.**, and **Rose C. A.**

Over the years, I received piles of feedback from my intrepid beta readers. Thank you to **Jerry, Mary**, **Stephen**, **Jim**, **Diana K.**, **Jennifer M.**, **Luke G.**, **Rose C. A.**, **Quinton C. A.**, **Brishen C. A.**, **Tanya D. Z.**, **Jen E.**, **Candice S.**, **Thamina J.**, **Stacey L.**, **Kayla M.**, **Wesley L.**, **Bella L.**, **Jenna S.**, **Tasha S.**, **Carla D.**, **Brad B.**, **Martina D., Jake F.**, and **Kirsten C.** Particular thanks go to **Jenny P. C.** who told me that my story would be best served by multiple books. Your support means the world.

More specifically, **Vince L.** walked me through the intellectual property landmines that can plague startup founding teams. **Jay P.**, **Mike B.**, **Hassan J.**, and **Luke G.** provided valuable perspective on what a plausible AI-linguistic start-up could have looked like in the early 2000s. **David L.** took a call from the Yukon to answer my questions about his experience as an officer with the Toronto Police

Service. **James E.** shared his experience working the night shift in the ICU, **Andrew C.** gave me insight into what goes on in an emergency room, and **Chris O.** and **Kirsten L.** offered their perspectives on patient care. Your willingness to field questions was a godsend. Thank you.

Last, when I decided to self-publish, I knew I needed one heck of an editor. I found one in **Julia McDowell**. Thank you for your patient partnership.

Crystal Watanabe of Pikko's House provided an excellent copyedit of the manuscript, greatly improving its quality and consistency. Crystal, it was a pleasure to work with you.

Lina Mockus delivered a Toronto-specific proofread at the end of my production process, ensuring I had all the nitty-gritty details right. Thank you, Lina, for your keen eye.

Indigenous Place Names

As observed in the Author's Note, Miinikaa First Nation is a fictitious community. I did not wish to use a real place name without direct permission. I discussed several options for how to situate the reserve with an Anishinaabe beta reader and with an Anishinaabe sensitivity reader. Ultimately, I opted to create a fictitious place.

The land surrounding Sudbury is acidic, which makes it ideal for blueberries to grow. I named the reserve using the Anishinaabemowin word miinikaa, which means "there are (many) blueberries."

In the world of the novel, Miinikaa First Nation would be part of the very real Robinson Huron Treaty, since the treaty includes the land around Sudbury. The Robinson Huron Treaty was signed in 1850 between the Government of Canada and the 21 First Nations living on the land it encompasses.

In 2012, these nations filed a claim to ask the Government of Canada and the Government of Ontario to increase the annuity paid to their members for the first time in over one hundred and fifty years. At the time of this writing, their case is still before the courts.

Learn more by visiting https://www.robinsonhurontreaty1850.com/.

On Diverse Stories

Writing about twenty-first-century Toronto means attempting to reflect the diversity of people, backgrounds, and perspectives that I encounter here, despite my individual limitations.

From the beginning, I embraced the importance of having sensitivity readers review my work for the inherent biases that I hold as a white woman and a settler. It's not for me to say whether my attempts to write inclusively are successful. I will say that I prefer by far to make the attempt—and listen, learn, and try again—than to write a version of Toronto that doesn't reflect the vibrant, varied, and wonderful people I have met here.

Throughout the project, I was fortunate to have access to many diverse perspectives via my beta readers. For example, when I wondered what Leona might have said to Dave during his convalescence (see Chapter 4), an Anishinaabe beta reader pointed me toward the Seven Grandfather teachings. We discussed how the story might allude to them without sharing an actual teaching, which I did not wish to do. If you'd like to learn more, Tanya Talaga's podcast Seven Truths is an accessible starting point.

After completing the structural edit for this book in 2020, I sought more formal feedback from two sensitivity readers, one for the Lin family's Chinese Canadian heritage and the other for the LaRoque family's Anishinaabe heritage. To respect their wishes, I've omitted their names. I'm thankful for their time and insight.

Any remaining shortcomings of this work are mine. You can find more about my approach to sensitivity reading in my website's Resources section: emwilliams.ca.

Building a Book Brand

Naming a novel is one of the more daunting tasks authors face when choosing to self-publish. I have named companies, products, and (not least of all) children, but finding my way through this process involved a lot of soul-searching. Thank you to **Amanda M.**, **Johnathan N.**, **Brad B.**, **Julia M.**, **Wesley L.**, and **Jerry** for your feedback and advice.

Helen He brought the skyworms to vivid life through her illustrations. Working from my descriptions, she immediately grasped their aura of menace. Helen, I was so excited when you suggested they should have a tentacle inside their mouths, too! Thank you!

I met **Wesley Lyn** in the trenches of Toronto tech. Beyond volunteering to act as a beta reader, Wes took on the series' cover designs and brand identity. His stunning work speaks for itself. Thank you, Wes! I'm so grateful for your friendship and expertise.

Richard Rudy has been building websites with me since we graduated from university. He built emwilliams.ca, too. You're the best, Rick.

Sim R. created the video trailers that launched this book to the world. Thank you so much for your wonderful work, Sim.

When it was time to test ebook layouts, **Tanya D. Z.** and **Mike Z.** patiently played with endless file formats until I got it right. Thank you both.

For marketing, positioning, and campaign advice, I am perpetually grateful to **Amanda M.**, **Brad B.**, **Will C.**, **Meredith A.**, **April D.**, **Sarah S.**, and the **GrowClass** Slack channel. You're brilliant.

A Journey, not a Destination

Across my writing life, I've been mentored by some exemplary people. For conversations great and small, thank you to **Jenny P. C.**,

Marian B., **Peter B.**, **Melissa N.**, **Jonathan N.**, **Fazila S.**, **Kay K.**, **Jenny H.**, **Sonnet L.**, **Valerie P.**, **Sever B.**, **Sabrina F.**, **Sana M. D.**, **Elaine S.**, **Sarah S.**, **Meredith A.**, **Lyssa N.**, **Mike B.**, **Bob R.**, **Nalo H.**, **Elizabeth A. H.**, **Connie W.**, and **Harry C.**

In 2005, I met **Diana K.**, **Hardy K.**, and the late **T. J. O'Neil** in a speculative fiction writing class via the University of Toronto's School of Continuing Studies. We formed a writing group that continued until 2012. It featured a lot of great work, good laughs, hard truths, and an abundance of cheese boards. Tim, we miss you still.

When this story came roaring at me, **Kay K.** offered encouragement, held space for my fears, and keep me focused. You're the best, K-Town.

In recent years, my writing sisters have held me accountable and kept me going. Thank you to **Diana K.**, **Jennifer M.**, and **Kirsten C.** for your unflagging love.

On my last pandemic mile, **Dayana Cadet** provided the coaching I needed to check my fears and commit to a launch plan. It was a pleasure to collaborate with you, Dayana.

Profound thanks also go to my advisors and extended family, past and present: I'm grateful for your love and insight. You're with me always.

My parents and brother remain my greatest champions. Mom, you truly are my superfan. All my love.

In my husband, **Jerry**, I have an in-house historian and a long-suffering beta reader who is always willing to diagram battle strategy, contemplate skyworm abilities, and push the limits of my thinking. Here's to the next round of one a.m. giggles. I love you.

This book is dedicated to our children: fine curators of memes, wrestling champions, TikTok enthusiasts, and my companions for our nightly reading sessions. Your unshakeable belief in and curiosity about my writing means everything to me. I can't wait to see which dreams you'll chase.

E. M. Williams
Toronto, ON
October 25, 2021

Character Index

In Toronto, Ontario

Anna Lin – a Realtor

Malcolm Nazarenko – Anna's husband and a detective constable in the Toronto Police Service's Financial Crimes Unit

Tim Nazarenko – Anna and Malcolm's son

Erin Nazarenko – Anna and Malcolm's daughter

Chun-Mei Lin – mother of Anna and Jason, Malcolm's mother-in-law, deceased

Dr. Erik (nee Lynn) Lin – father of Anna and Jason, Malcolm's father-in-law, and a clinician researcher at the Hospital for Sick Children (SickKids)

Henry Montcalm – adoptive father of Dave and chief of the Toronto Police Service

Sarita Montcalm – adoptive mother of Dave, retired from her nursing career

Walter Delal – a venture capitalist, early investor in Rune Software, and friend of Dave's

Bob Cloar – deputy chief of the Toronto Police Service

Brenda Edwards – sergeant with the Toronto Police Service

Krista Johansen – constable with the Toronto Police Service

Raymond Leong – constable with the Toronto Police Service

Christopher Barry – detective constable with the Toronto Police Service, Malcolm's partner

Nancy Coleman – Anna and Malcolm's neighbour

Nina Reyes – a family lawyer

Carl Mason – an IT manager in Toronto's banking sector

Jenna Kovi – a graduate student in the University of Toronto's History Department

Kalos – former Xenthian teacher to Anna, Jason, and Dave

In Vancouver, British Columbia

Dr. Jason Lin – Anna's twin brother and an emergency room physician

Margo (nee Cheung) Lin – Jason's wife and a theatre director

Ivy Wong – Margo's longtime best friend and business partner

Lou Wong – Ivy's husband

At Miinikaa First Nation

Dave LaRoque Montcalm – Anna's and Jason's best friend from childhood and the co-founder and former CEO of Rune Software

Leona LaRoque – Dave's aunt and a community organizer

Rose LaRoque – Dave's biological mother and Leona's sister, deceased

Ryan Charron – Leona's longtime boyfriend and owner of a construction company

Janessa Drake – a student in Dave's coding workshop

Emily – a teaching assistant in Dave's coding workshop

Ian – a teaching assistant in Dave's coding workshop

In Boston, USA

Halina "Hal" Mendes – Dave's former business partner and the co-founder and current chief technology officer of Rune Software

Charles Larkin – a venture capitalist, owner of Beakhead Capital and a major investor in Rune Software

Pronunciation Guide and Glossary

Anishinaabemowin Words

Dave, Leona, and Ryan speak Anishinaabemowin, the language of the Anishinaabe people, with varying degrees of fluency.

Rather than give loose phonetic pronunciations in English, I suggest you do what I did and visit the Ojibwe People's Dictionary at https://ojibwe.lib.umn.edu to look the words up. If you are reading a digital copy of this book, I've linked them for you. Many of the words have an orange volume icon that you can click to hear them pronounced by an individual speaker. The definitions listed here are cited from that source.

Anishinaabe – A person, a human (in contrast to a nonhuman being).

Anishinaabemowin – The language spoken by Anishinaabe people.

ashigan – A fish of the sunfish family (e.g., a rock bass).

miigwech – Thank you.

miinikaa – There are (many) blueberries.

piiche or **apichi** – A robin; the sensitivity reader with whom I worked shared the 'piiche' spelling of the word with me.

Invented Words

Naming things is hard. If fighting skyworms has been an underground global project for millennia, I wanted to find terms for my imagined worlds that were inclusive and suggested a blending of ideas and cultures in this effort over time.

Choosing the word "xhen" to name the energy that the characters use set the tone for many other decisions.

Words derived from Greek

kalos /CAL-os/ – in Greek, this word can mean good, noble, or handsome. It's also a masculine word. Kalos is a being motivated by his understanding of good and noble action, so it seemed perfect for him.

Xenthian /ZEN-thee-an / – technically, this word should have an "h" after the "x," but I prefer how it looks this way.

xhen /ZHEN/ – in Greek, xeno is the root word for strange or foreign. I thought strangeness was a good concept around which to ground the energy that the characters use. I added the "h" and dropped the "o" to make the word my own. It begins with the "zh" phonetic sound of "measure" or "usual."

Word derived from Finnish

valoi – in Finnish, "valo" is the word for light. I added the "i" to the end because I liked how The Valoi Knights looked and sounded.

Word derived from Gaelic

skal /sss-CAAL / – in Gaelic, the language of the Irish, scál or scaal can mean 1) a supernatural being or phantom, 2) a being or person, 3) a giant or a hero, and 4) also a burst, flash, or blast. I loved the idea of the skyworms being the supernatural hero giants in their own minds, so using skal as their word for the energy they use in bursts or flashes fit on a lot of levels. It also sounds a bit serpentine, which I liked. I changed the *C* to a *K* at my copyeditor's suggestion to help make the word more visually distinct.

Word derived from Maltese

tarkan /TAR-can/ – in Maltese, "tarka" is the word for shield. In my first drafts, I used "first shield" or "shields" to describe the brave people who opt to fight alongside Anna, Jason, and Dave. As I sat with the words over time and my thinking about the origins of xhen and Kalos became clearer, I wanted a word that was more unique to the story. Doing a word search on "shield in other languages" led me here.

Word derived from Turkish

Kalxhan /CAL-zh-aan/ – in Turkish, "kalkan" is the word for shield and the word "xhan" means dear or darling. I liked the idea of mixing these two words to make a hybrid: a beloved shield. The way it echoes the spelling of "xhen" also appealed to me.

Love This Book?

Three Ways You Can Help

Thank you so much for reading. If you enjoyed *Chaos Calling*, here's how to help it to find more readers:

1. **Recommend** *Chaos Calling* to three friends.

2. **Post an honest review** on Amazon, Storygraph, or GoodReads. Doing so tells the algorithms that run so much of our lives that this book is important. Every review you post—for any author—gives their books a better shot at finding a wider audience.

3. **Sign-up** for my newsletter to stay in the loop about what's happening with the rest of the series.

Your support means the world to me. 

About E. M. Williams

Born in Northern Ontario on Robinson Superior Treaty land, E. M. Williams has written all her life. *Chaos Calling* is her first published novel.

She earned a Bachelor of Arts in English Literature from the University of Waterloo and a Master of Arts in Literary Theory from the University of Guelph. She also completed a course in writing speculative fiction through the University of Toronto's School of Continuing Studies and is a former member of the Science Fiction Research Association.

In 2012, she gave a TedxTalk on women, superheroes, and power. Originally intended to put her past work in scholarship to a useful purpose, it inadvertently supercharged her writing.

E. M. Williams currently lives with her family in Toronto where she works in the technology sector.